I0769798

PRAISE FOR MELISSA GRACE

Meddling Under the Mistletoe

"With unforgettable characters, warmth, and humor, not to mention some adorable dogs, Melissa Grace tells a genuine and heartwarming story about love, family, and the holidays." —Bryn Donovan, author of *Her Knight at the Museum*

"Hilarious and heart-warming, Melissa Grace delivers the perfect 2000s-era romcom. The family is genuine, and filled with love, and I only wanted to live with them even longer. *Meddling Under the Mistletoe* is everything good about the holidays." —Julie Olivia, *USA Today* bestselling author

"Meddling Under the Mistletoe is an utterly perfect dash of Christmas cheer! It's witty, warm, with just the right mix of unexpected romance and emotional depth. The mother-daughter duo finding romance in the moth unexpected of places, with help from a few charming and mischievous pups will have you believing in holiday magic!" —Sarah Brown, Bound Booksellers in Franklin, TN

Marjorie & Me

"*Marjorie and Me* is a romance, but the most important relationship Kat finds is the one with a grumpy, 60+ Southern socialite ghost. I loved Kat's personal growth and not just the romantic love she finds, but the selfless love of the people who are truly family even if not genetically. I laughed, cried and, couldn't put it down." —Abby Jimenez, *New York Times* bestselling author

"*Marjorie & Me* is a warm, whimsical story of hope, love, loss, and healing, with a vibrant cast of lovable characters that leapt off the page (or out of the urn, as the case may be). A deliciously sweet confection of a story that I devoured in one sitting, and left me sighing happily in a puddle of my own tears." —Lauren Thoman, author of *I'll Stop the World*

"Funny, heartfelt, and full of unexpected magic, *Marjorie & Me* is the kind of story that makes you laugh out loud one moment and swallow a lump in your throat the next. Kat's journey is deeply relatable, but it's Marjorie—bold, brash, and hilariously opinionated—who steals every scene. I adored the dynamic between them and found myself genuinely moved by how this story explores identity, healing, and the people who love us into becoming ourselves." —Melissa R. Collings, award-winning author of *The False Flat*

Meddling
UNDER THE
Mistletoe

Meddling
UNDER THE
Mistletoe

MELISSA GRACE

AUTHOR'S NOTE

I wrote this book three years ago as a love letter to Diane Keaton and all of the quirky, charming, loving, magical mothers she played over the years. Whether she was meddling in Mandy Moore's love life or being the beloved matriarch of the Stone family that we visit each holiday season, Diane's characters were always a soft place to land for me. While unique and special in their own ways, each felt familiar, like a trusted friend. The vulnerability, impeccable wit, and heart she brought to every role were legendary.

In March of 2024, I shared a post Diane made about her book *Fashion First* and added to it that she had inspired the mother in this very story you are about to read. When she then shared that to her *own* page, I responded with many crying emojis and an excited "I adore you." She replied in all caps with "I ADORE YOU BACK!" It was a brief moment that I got to exist in her orbit, and I am forever grateful.

Diane passed away on October 11, 2025 at the age of 79. This book is dedicated to her and all who loved her.

"Memories are simply moments that refuse to be ordinary."
-Diane Keaton

1

———

LINDSEY

"Hey, I need you up front." My best friend and head vet tech, Kayla, looms in the doorway of my office, her face pinched with concern. She has a tiny wriggling puppy tucked under her arm like a football. It's ten after two the Thursday before Thanksgiving, and I just took a hurried bite of the sandwich I packed for lunch.

"Now?" I ask through a mouthful of ham and cheese.

She motions for me to follow her, and after one more bite, I do. "Your two fifteen is here, and he doesn't look so good."

"How old is he? What breed?" I ask, mentally preparing myself for whatever situation I'm about to encounter.

"If I had to guess, he's a senior citizen," Kayla says as we push through the door to the reception area. "And human."

"Huh?"

An older gentleman with gray hair and glasses is clutching his right side. To his left is a dark-haired guy with his back to me, his broad shoulders causing his flannel shirt to stretch within an inch of its life. His hand is on the older man's shoulder, as though he's trying to comfort him, and a black-and-white border collie stands at his side.

"This is Mr. Phillips," Kayla says, pointing to the gray-haired man. "He came in with his new puppy, June Bug" — she holds up the fluffy, wiggly pup the color of a toasted marshmallow— "and started feeling sick. I already called your next two clients and let them know you'll likely be running a little behind."

"It's Ron," Mr. Phillips manages, raising his head while Kayla uses her free hand to pick up the ringing phone.

I nod my thanks as I survey the scene.

"I suspect he has a ruptured appendix," the younger guy says to my sister Lucy, our resident dog groomer, who is standing off to the side with her phone to her ear. His tone is authoritative but kind, like this isn't his first rodeo. "He's having severe pain in his lower right quadrant, and he definitely has a fever."

Lucy repeats what he told her into the phone, presumably to a 911 dispatcher, before covering the receiver with her hand. "They're five minutes out."

I nod and shift my attention to the ailing gentleman in front of me. "Ron, I'm Dr. Haggerty," I introduce myself as I approach him and pull my stethoscope from my neck. "Mind if I have a listen?"

"This is quite embarrassing," Ron says. "I'm so sorry, hon."

I place a gentle hand on his back. Ron appears to be about the age my father was when he passed, and that fact alone heightens my concern.

"Don't be. I promise, we've seen it all here." I hold up my stethoscope and square my shoulders in a meek attempt at appearing more confident than I am. I don't often use my medical skills on humans. Though there was that one time when Kerry Winstead's water broke while I was at her farm doing a check on her pig, Steve. It took me half an hour to convince her she hadn't just peed her pants when she sneezed and was, in fact, in labor.

"May I?" I ask Ron.

He nods, sweat dripping from his brow. "Of course."

I place the drum against his chest and listen to the *thump, thump, thump* of Ron's heart. It's much faster than it should be.

"He's tachycardic," I say to Lucy, who relays my words into the phone.

"It's probably because of the pain he's in," says the dark-haired guy who's been directing Lucy. I see his face for the first time, and my own heart begins to beat out of rhythm. His dark hair is tousled as though he just ran his fingers through it, and he has the sweetest smile that causes the skin around his eyes to crinkle. "Sorry—I'm Oliver. Your two thirty. Well, Ace is." He gestures to the stoic dog at his side before placing a gentle hand on Ron's shoulder. "And Ron here is my neighbor."

"Good thing you two came together," I say.

Ron shakes his head. "We didn't, but I sure got lucky running into him. He knew exactly what was wrong."

"I'm a Firefighter EMT," Oliver explains as he grabs some tissues from the box on the desk and dabs at the perspiration on Ron's face. My heart squeezes at the gesture.

I blink, peering up at his strong jaw and the faint scar above his upper lip. My mind runs rampant with the possibilities of all the dangerous, brave things he might have done to get that scar. Falling while saving a baby from a burning building. Taking a plank to the face as he pulled a terrified family's golden retriever to safety before their home collapsed in a heap of fiery rubble. Or maybe he slipped on a ladder while rescuing someone from a third-floor balcony.

"The ambulance will be here any minute now," Lucy says as she joins us, snapping me back to reality.

Get it together, Lindsey. Seriously. You're a professional.

"I can't go to the hospital." The color in Ron's face surpasses white and goes straight to gray. "Who will take care of June Bug? I live alone. I don't have family here. She's only eleven weeks old."

"Don't worry," Oliver says. "We'll figure something ou—"

"I'll take her," I blurt without a second thought.

"Are you sure?" Ron winces, his breathing ragged. "I don't want to be a bother."

"You're not," I promise. "You focus on taking care of yourself. I'll handle the rest. Call us the second you're better, and we'll have June Bug ready to go home with you."

"I'll even give her a bath before you pick her up so she's all snuggly and fresh." Lucy smiles as June Bug whines and squirms in Kayla's arms.

"That's a hell of an offer, don't you think, Ron?" Oliver touches his shoulder and gives him a warm smile.

"We'll take good care of her," I say.

The sound of sirens in the distance grows louder as the ambulance pulls into our parking lot.

Ron gives a reluctant nod. "Let me pay you now, though, for the trouble."

"It's no trouble. We want to help," I say, and Lucy nods in agreement. "I'll give her a full exam today to make sure she's healthy, and we'll get her up-to-date on her shots. You just call us when you get settled, and we'll go from there, okay?"

Ron looks to where June Bug twirls like an angry tornado in Kayla's grasp. "I suppose if someone's going to watch your pup, there's no one better than the vet."

The front door chimes as the paramedics wheel in a stretcher.

"Rookie," one of them says when she sees Oliver. "What are you doing here? I thought you were off today?" She has on a City of Loving Fire Department shirt and her auburn hair is in a tight bun.

"You picked a good day too," the guy guiding the other end of the gurney says. "Chief tried a new recipe at lunch today. Another one of his Pinterest creations. There was some kind of questionable fish involved. If you're the only person on duty tomorrow, you'll know why."

Oliver wrinkles his nose before helping ease Ron onto the stretcher. "Ron, these are my colleagues, Helen Gibson and Gabe Martinez. They'll take good care of you."

"Yes, we will," Helen says.

I grab a business card from the holder on the front desk and quickly scrawl my cell number on it. "This has the clinic number, and I've written mine on here as well. You call us when you can."

"Thanks, Doc. Thanks for taking care of Junie for me. She can be a bit of a handful." As Ron places his hand on mine, I become acutely aware of Oliver's gaze lingering on me as he steps toward the reception desk.

"She's going to be just fine," I say, giving Ron's shoulder a reassuring squeeze. "Besides, animals are kind of my thing."

He gives me a weak smile as the paramedics begin asking questions about his symptoms and check his vitals. We give them room to do their workup, answering questions when asked. Moments later, I hold the door as they wheel him out.

"I'll see you soon, June Bug," he calls out as they roll him away.

"Poor guy." Lucy frowns as I shut the door behind him. She makes her way over to where Kayla stands with the puppy and leans down to allow June Bug to lick her nose.

"He's fortunate it happened while he was here, living alone and all," Oliver says, leaning against the counter.

"I'd say we were pretty lucky you were here too." I smile, stepping closer to him. "*Rookie.*"

His gaze drops to the floor as he waves off the compliment, knocking the business cards from their plastic holder in the process, sending them scattering across the floor.

Oliver's cheeks flame, and I have to bite back a grin.

"Sorry about that." He rakes his hands down his face as he kneels to pick up the pieces of cardstock.

"It's okay." I crouch to help him, but he lifts his head at the wrong moment, bonking me in the chin. "Ow."

"Oh God. I'm sorry. I swear, I'm usually a little more coordinated. If I wasn't, it'd be a bit of a job hazard."

"Really, it's fine." I rub my hand over my chin and join him on the floor. My fingers brush his as we reach for the same card, and a spark of electricity zips through me.

He raises his eyes to meet mine. "It was nice of you to take care of Ron's pup like that. Can I at least contribute to the cost of boarding her?"

I shake my head. The simple fact that he wants to help makes my insides turn to mush. "We're just doing what anyone would do. It's a small town. We take care of each other."

"I see that," he replies as we stand. He returns the

remaining cards to their home on the counter, pocketing the one on top. "I better hold onto one of these. Ace and I just moved here a couple months ago." The sweet drip of his southern drawl melts like hot fudge on a sundae. "That's why we're here. Need to get this old boy established with a good vet."

Ace stirs at Oliver's side as though balking at being called old.

"Well, my sister is the best vet around." Lucy beams.

"I don't doubt that one bit," Oliver says, not taking his eyes off me, and now I'm the one blushing.

I clasp my hands together. "Well, what do you say we get you in an exam room and check for ticks?"

Out of the corner of my eye, I catch Lucy's widening eyes, and the subtle shake of Kayla's head.

Oh my God. Did I just tell this man I wanted to check him for ticks?

Oliver grins. "Well, that's a bit unconventional, but if you insist."

I clear my throat. "I mean, we'll, uh, just be looking at Ace. Definitely not you."

Oliver's laugh comes easily. "He's a lot cuter than me, anyhow."

That's debatable.

"Come on back," I say, motioning for him to follow me. Ace might be the one I'm examining, but it couldn't hurt to steal a couple of glances at his dad.

"You're a healthy boy, Ace," I say, cupping the pooch's snout in my hands after wrapping up his exam. He gives me a happy lick, and I pull a treat from the pocket of my lab coat for him. I catch Oliver's eye across the exam table, and my chest fizzes as though I swallowed a mouthful of Pop Rocks. "I'll get your prescriptions, and we'll be all set. Any other questions for me?"

"So, how long have you lived in Loving?" Oliver asks casually, giving Ace a scratch on the head.

"I actually grew up here," I answer. "I've been a vet at the clinic for seven years."

"Did you buy out the place? I couldn't help but notice your last name happens to be on the sign out front."

I give him a wistful smile. "No, I didn't. My father was the original Dr. Haggerty. He passed five years ago, and I took over after that."

"Oh. I'm so sorry," he replies, his deep chestnut eyes softening.

"It's okay."

It's what I always say when a new patient brings up this topic, because what else *can* I say? How unfair it is that a man who was the picture of health died in his sleep of a widow-maker heart attack? Or how much I still need my father, even as an adult? Nothing about it feels okay, yet it just *is*.

My chest tightens. "He truly was the best."

"Well, for what it's worth, it looks like you've filled his shoes quite nicely," he says. "And since you're a born and raised Loving, Tennessee girl, maybe you can tell me what people do for fun here."

"Fun? What's this *fun* you speak of?" I joke. Though, to be fair, it isn't much of a joke. Fun isn't something I have a lot of these days.

He chuckles. "Come on. What do you do on the weekends?"

I shrug and tuck my hands into the pockets of my lab coat. "I think they host karaoke at Dos Margaritas on Saturday nights. My sister and her fiancée like to go sometimes."

"What about you?" he asks with a playful glint in his eyes. "Don't you ever like to just go and unleash your inner pop star?"

"Karaoke is usually more of a spectator sport for me," I answer with a laugh.

"Same. Except for that time I had a little too much rum a few years ago at my old chief's retirement party. I serenaded him with 'It's Raining Men.'"

I choke on a laugh. "Oh my."

"Funny, that's what his ninety-seven-year-old mother said when I tripped over my own shoelace midspin and fell face-first into her lap."

My hands fly up to cover my mouth, but that does nothing to stifle the witch cackle/snort combo that rips through me. "I thought you said you were usually coordinated?"

"All bets are off when rum's involved."

"Sounds like it was a once-in-a-lifetime performance."

"Lucky for everyone, it was." There's a lightness in his eyes despite their dark color that puts me at ease and makes my heart race all at once.

"All right, Magic Mike," I say with a sly smile as I begin to step toward the door. "Let me go check on those meds for you."

"Do you have any pets?" he asks before I can leave. "Maybe a dog Ace could run around the dog park with? He could really use a buddy."

Ace sighs and sinks to the floor, no longer interested in our conversation.

"No dog," I say. "It's just me and Catrick Swayze."

"Ah, so you're the infamous 'Baby'?" he asks, not missing a beat. "I promise not to put you in any corners."

"He wouldn't care if you did so long as his food bowl was kept full."

"Do you guys ever practice that dance? You know the one." He mimes lifting someone over his head.

"Yeah, but even after all these years, he still can't catch me," I deadpan, delighting in the way his eyes widen for a split second before realizing I'm messing with him. His smile stretches to his ears, and we explode into a fit of giggles.

Our laughter finally slows, but my heartbeat doesn't.

"Well, I hope you're able to do something fun over the holiday," he says. "Sounds like you deserve it."

My chest aches when I think about how brutally un-fun the next few weeks will be. I used to look forward to the holidays, but that was before my dad died. Before everything changed.

That thought is enough to send my heart and this conversation to a screeching halt. I don't care how cute or funny or ridiculously charming this guy is. Even if I were interested, his job is dangerous. I know all too well the kinds of things that can happen even when your job doesn't require you to risk your life. Sometimes the bad things find you even when you're sitting at home in your favorite chair.

"Okay, I'm going to get Ace's meds," I say, keeping my tone friendly but professional. "One of the techs will bring them in and take you up front to get y'all checked out." I ruffle the fur on top of Ace's head. "It was nice meeting you both. And hey, welcome to Loving. Maybe I'll see you around sometime."

"I hope you do," he says. "I mean, I hope to see you

around. And that you see me too. You know, at the same time."

He waves as I step out of the room and head back to the lab, the remnants of a smile lingering on my lips. Despite knowing this was nothing more than a minor flirtation, I find myself hoping 'sometime' comes sooner than later.

2

___

MJ

EMPTY. THE SPOT WHERE THE CANNED PUMPKIN SHOULD BE IS *empty*. The open space feels like a personal attack, taunting me for having the audacity to search for such a thing this close to the holiday. It's barely 8 a.m. the Friday before Thanksgiving, and I've now been to the only two grocery stores in Loving. I did the very same thing the year after Henry died. You'd think I'd have learned my lesson.

I stare at the manufacturer's label on the shelf as though I can somehow make the cans of orange mush appear by sheer force of will. Pumpkin pie was Henry's favorite. No, he won't be here to eat it—an unfortunate side effect of no longer being on this earthly plane—but we still need to have it. It's not Thanksgiving without it. We've had it every year since he passed away, and we'll have it this year too, even if I have to go to eighteen different stores to find it.

"Can I help you find anything?" a soft voice asks from behind me. I turn to find a woman about Lindsey's age. At thirty-five, she's my oldest.

"I was looking for some canned pumpkin," I say, "but it seems like you're out."

She gives me a regretful smile. "Yeah, I think we ran out last week. We have pumpkin pie filling, and I think there are still a few pumpkin pies in the freezer section. I can go grab one if you like?"

"No, that's okay. Thank you, though." I twist my lips to the corner of my mouth, blinking back the watery film blurring my focus. It can't be just any pumpkin pie. It *has* to be Henry's mother's recipe.

I can at least try to go with the proverbial flow any other time of the year, but the holidays are nonnegotiable. The year after Henry passed, I refused to change anything. His loafers remained by the front door in the foyer. I still made a full pot of coffee every morning, leaving his mug next to mine on the counter. Dinner was on the table promptly at six, though it often went untouched.

Then, on the first anniversary of his death, I packed away and donated most of his things, leaving behind only the most sentimental items and a few of his favorite shirts. I got one of those fancy Nespresso machines and started making myself lattes in the morning. And when cooking for one became too depressing, I switched to a bowl of cereal or popcorn on the couch instead. Maybe a little charcuterie board if I was feeling fancy. Life was going to move on with or without me, so I allowed it to sweep me along with the changing seasons.

Many of our treasured traditions gave way to new rituals, but not during the holidays. This was Henry's favorite time of the year, and for that reason, it will always be sacred.

"Are you sure?" the clerk asks. "They're really good. Almost as good as homemade. My husband loves them."

That's when I lose it. Right there in the middle of aisle

four at the Food Saver. And I'm not talking about a few escaped tears. I mean shoulders shaking, snot dripping, openly *sobbing* in front of God and this precious clerk who's probably regretting asking me a damn thing.

"Oh gosh," she says, a perplexed expression settling over her face. "I'm so sorry, ma'am. I didn't mean to upset you."

"You're fine. I'm not upset." I force what I hope is a reassuring smile, but from the way she flinches, I suspect I look more like a deranged serial killer. "It's me. I'm just having an off day."

I dig in my purse, fishing for the mini pack of Kleenex buried somewhere in its depths. My fingers finally land on the flimsy plastic package, and I pull out a tissue to blow my nose just as my phone blares with a siren that could wake the dead. My grandson changed the ringer months ago, and I have no clue how to return it to its usual chime.

The girl whose name tag reads "Anna" mumbles a quick "happy holidays" and takes that as her cue to leave.

"Hello," I answer.

"You still breathing?" my older sister Rose asks. It's the same question she poses every day during our morning check-ins. It's something she started soon after our father died, when we became the oldest members of our family.

I sniffle, and she immediately clocks it.

"Sister, are you crying?" she asks, her voice wrought with concern. "What's going on?"

"I'm at the Food Saver," I say through ragged breaths. "They're out of pumpkin."

"Oh, for heaven's sake," she says, and I can practically hear the eye roll from here. "It's too early for this, Myra Jean. I haven't even finished my coffee yet. Just go to another grocery store."

"This is the second one I've been to today. What if I waited too long? What if I can't make the pumpkin pie?"

"And?" she asks through a yawn. "Make something else for a change. Or, here's a novel concept, let one of us bring a dessert instead."

I shove the snotty tissue inside my purse and sulk down the aisle, back toward the automatic doors.

"We *have* to have the pumpkin pie, Rose," I say. "It was Henry's favorite."

"Fine." She releases an exaggerated sigh and slurps some coffee. "How can I help? Do you want me to call around to a few other stores? See if I can get someone to hold a couple of cans?"

"You wouldn't mind?" I ask, stepping outside into the mostly vacant parking lot. The air is extra crisp against the dampness on my cheeks as I dig out my keys.

"Oh, I mind," she answers. "But I'll do it anyway."

"Thank you," I say, "I know you don't even like pumpkin pie."

"No, I don't. But I *do* like you." She snorts. "Sometimes."

My call-waiting beeps as I near my car. It's the fourth sedan I've owned in a gleaming shade of pearly white. Henry tried many times to convince me to get something different— an SUV maybe or even just another color—but I never saw a reason to change.

"Rose, Lindsey's calling," I say when I glance at the screen. "Can I call you right back?"

"Yeah, yeah. By the way, if I'm calling these stores for you, you're making me breakfast for my troubles."

"Biscuits and gravy?"

"I'll see you at nine."

I tap the screen to answer Lindsey's call. "Hi, sweetie."

My voice is an octave higher than it was seconds ago as I tap the fob and slide inside the vehicle. "How's it going? How're you feeling?"

"I'm fine, Mom. Same as I was yesterday when you asked," she says with a chuckle. She thinks I worry too much, but I know that while the cooler weather gets many women excited about pie-scented candles and seasonal latte flavors, it does something quite different to her. "Are you in your car?"

"Yes, I'm just leaving the store. What about you? On your way to work?"

"Yeah," she answers before shifting the focus back to me. "Why on earth were you at the store so early? It's Friday. I thought you stopped working on Fridays."

"I somehow managed to forget the pumpkin for the pie, but everyone else in Loving apparently didn't," I say, not bothering to start the car yet. "Went to both stores in town and they're out."

"I have some extra in the pantry. I'll bring it Sunday. *If* you make chicken and dumplins." There's a hint of a smile in her voice.

"Nothing like a little early morning subterfuge," I say with a laugh. "I'd have made them for you even without the pumpkin."

"And I would have given you the pumpkin even without the dumplins."

"Why do you have pumpkin on hand, anyway? You don't bake."

"What?" Her voice sounds funny. Distracted. "Oh, I told Emily and Noah we could make some pumpkin chocolate chip cookies when they come over Tuesday."

That explains it. Lindsey isn't much of a baker, but she'll do anything for her niece and nephew.

"I don't want to take it if you've already got plans for it," I say. "Especially if it's for the kids."

"Don't worry about it, Mom. Trust me, they'll be fine with just chocolate chip. In fact, they probably forgot they even asked for the pumpkin," she says. "Listen, I just got to work, but I'm going Christmas shopping this weekend, and for the life of me, I cannot remember the name of that awful perfume Aunt Rose likes."

"Secret Weapon."

"False advertising," she says with a laugh. "There's nothing *secret* about it. That stuff is so strong it could trip a motion sensor."

"That it could." It *is* a little loud, but to be fair, so is my sister.

"That's what I'm getting her, so make sure you don't get it too. God knows she doesn't need more. She only just ran out from when we all had the same idea five years ago."

"Noted. Let your brother and sister know too."

"I will," she says. "Talk to you later. Love you."

"Love you too, sweetie," I say before ending the call.

I buckle the seat belt and hold my foot to the brake, pressing the button to start the engine. The sense of impending doom I felt moments ago has waned now that the pumpkin pie crisis has been averted. Calm spreads over me like a blanket.

Our well-worn traditions will go on to survive another year. I swallow the lump swelling in the back of my throat as I pull through the empty parking space in front of me and head home.

3

———————

LINDSEY

I reach into the pantry for some microwave popcorn Friday night and spot the pumpkin I promised my mom lingering toward the back. It's been there since the first Thanksgiving without my father, when my mother, still buried under the weight of her own grief, forgot the pumpkin for my dad's favorite pie. It upset her so much that I went to the store the next day and stocked up on a couple of cans just in case this same situation should arise again. I buy some after the holiday rush every year so I'm always prepared.

I pull out the popcorn along with the cans of pumpkin and check their expiration date. Seeing they're still good, I scoot them onto the counter.

"Doing some baking?" Kayla regards me with a wrinkled brow from where she's sprawled on the kitchen floor as June Bug plays tug-of-war with her ponytail. She stopped by my place on the way home from her seven o'clock spin class to try and help me tame the tiny fluffy baby dragon in my care. "Let's hope your skills have improved since that cookie cake you made me for my birthday last year."

I snort. "Listen, I swear that recipe called for four cups of flour."

"That thing could have been used to break a window or commit a felony. We're lucky we still have our teeth."

"It wasn't *that* bad."

"It wasn't that good either," she teases.

"But it was made with love," I say with a grin. "And to answer your question, no. I'm taking these to Mom on Sunday."

My phone rings, the sound distracting the pup long enough for her to drop Kayla's hair. I pry the device from the pocket of my jeans, a number I don't recognize flashing on the screen before I answer the call.

"Hey, Doc," a deep, hoarse voice replies. "It's Ron Phillips."

"Mr. Phillips," I say over June Bug's shrill barks, as Kayla tries to quiet her with a stuffed donut toy. "It's good to hear from you."

"Call me Ron," he corrects me with a soft chuckle. "Mr. Phillips makes me sound old, and heaven knows, I don't need any help with that. Sounds like Junie's showing you her vocal range."

I laugh. "That she is."

"How's she doing?"

I grit my teeth as June Bug drops the toy and heads straight for Catrick Swayze, who's sauntered into the living room. Before my sweet orange fluff ball knows what's happening, the pup is mounting him, but because she's knee-high to a grasshopper, she ends up hugging his back leg.

"No," Kayla shout-whispers. "You're breaking the first rule of being a good houseguest. Thou shalt not hump the cat."

I choke on a laugh as Kayla manages to distract the pup long enough for Catrick Swayze to scamper away.

"She's doing great," I say. "I examined her as promised and got her up-to-date on her vaccinations."

Technically, the little Maltese/Yorkie mix *is* healthy, but I'm convinced the pup is also part alligator. Her mouth is maybe capable of opening two inches wide if she tries really hard, yet she managed to chew the bottom corner off my bathroom door while I was in the shower this morning, and the little devil barked for hours last night. She's the cutest holy terror that ever existed, and I cannot wait for her to go home.

"How are you feeling?" I ask.

"Well, I had surgery yesterday evening." His voice is still raspy, undoubtedly from the breathing tube they'd used during his procedure. "I'm still pretty weak, as you can imagine, but they're kicking me out of here tomorrow."

"I'm sure you'll be glad to get home," I say. "And I know June Bug misses you."

There's a long pause on the other end. "Well, that's actually what I called to talk to you about. My son, Hudson, came down from Cincinnati, and he's insisting I go home with him for a few days while I get back on my feet. He'd stay with me, but that would be a little too long for him to be away from work."

"Oh, okay. Does that mean he'll be picking her up?" I ask.

"That's the thing." Another pause. "His wife is a bit particular and won't allow animals in the house, so I was wondering if you and your sister would mind keeping her a little while longer? And of course, I would pay you for the trouble."

Now I'm the one pausing.

"I can see if I can arrange to have her boarded some-where," he goes on. "I know she's a handful."

"No, no." I wince, summoning all the holiday spirit I can muster. "I'll keep her, and there's no payment needed. You focus on getting better, okay?"

"Are you sure?" he asks tentatively, as Kayla rises to her feet and folds her arms across her chest, wearing a stony expression.

"Absolutely. Just let me know when you're back, and I'll get June Bug home to you."

"I owe you one, Doc." Ron breathes a sigh of relief. "Thank you."

"You're welcome, Ron. Feel better, and we'll talk soon."

I end the call and stare at the phone in my hand for a moment.

"Ow!" Kayla bounces away from the pup who has decided to attack her ankles. "Please tell me the Fluff Ness Monster is going home."

"Um…well…"

She yelps, seeking refuge by jumping on the sofa. "No! How much longer?"

"A while."

"How long is a while?"

"His son is taking him home to Cincinnati for a bit while he recovers, but he can't take the dog because his daughter-in-law isn't a fan of having pets in the house."

"And I'm not a fan of broccoli, but I eat it because it's the right thing to do," Kayla insists. "You cannot keep this dog, Lindsey. I mean, she's sweet, but she's also batshit crazy. Like a baby wolf in a teddy bear costume. Or a Chucky doll. Catrick Swayze is going to pack up his shit and leave."

"She's in a new place, away from Ron, and probably

scared," I say, though to be fair, I'm not sure she's scared of anything. "She just needs some special attention."

Kayla scoffs. "My dating life needs *special attention.* What that dog needs is an exorcist."

"It's not ideal, but it's just for a bit longer. I can make anything work for a few days."

She lifts her brows with a judgy stare.

"What?" I counter.

"What if your fibromyalgia flares up?" she asks. "You already work yourself half to death, and now you're going to spend what little free time you have chasing after a tiny ball of terror?"

"It's not a big deal," I say, waving her off. "I'll be fine."

I don't tell her how worried I am now that the weather is getting cooler. As soon as temperatures start dipping into the forties, that's when that familiar ache settles into my muscles, my joints go stiff as tree trunks, and my brain becomes thick with an impenetrable fog. One of the benefits of living in Tennessee is the extended summer we get. The holidays approaching signals that, like it or not, winter is coming.

"Uh-huh," Kayla says. "Just like you were *fine* a couple years ago after that diabolical snowstorm moved in right after Christmas. You were miserable for more than a month. Granted, part of that was because you refused to take any time off to rest, which is what your body needed most."

"That was different," I insist. "That was, quite literally, the perfect storm of events. Besides, I have better coping mechanisms now. I take my meds when I need them, I get regular massages, and I have my TENS unit. Seriously, I'll be fine."

"At least bring her to the clinic while we're there," Kayla suggests. "We can all help make sure she gets plenty of exercise before you take her home each day."

"Good idea. And maybe Ben and Ellie will bring the kids over to play with her." I rake my teeth over my bottom lip and grin. "You wouldn't want to borrow her for a night, would you?"

She casts a sidelong glance in my direction before pretending to examine her cuticles. "I wish I could, but...oh wait, no I don't."

"You can't blame a girl for trying. I'll call Ben and Ellie and see if they have plans tomorrow night."

THE CLINIC CLOSES AT NOON ON SATURDAYS, SO AFTER WORK, I take June Bug for a walk before crating her so I can venture out for a little Christmas shopping. I start at Laura's Loft where I find a sweater for my sister-in-law, Ellie. Then I visit Heaven Scent, the local perfumery, where I pick up Aunt Rose's Secret Weapon and an organic bath set for Lucy's fiancée, Willow.

It's a drizzly gray afternoon, but downtown Loving is bustling as I work my way up Main Street. Street lamps wrapped in lush garland with white lights line the sidewalk, and storefronts have already been adorned with fluffy red bows. It's overcast enough that the lights are already twinkling. It's almost sixty degrees, but the clouds make it look like it could snow any second. I stretch my neck to the side almost reflexively, and it bends with ease—something I don't take for granted because I know how quickly that can change.

A yawn crawls out of me as I spot The Southern Bean sign up ahead, shining like the North Star, and decide I'll stop for a coffee. I'm about to reach for the door when I spot Oliver, the cute firefighter from the clinic. He's approaching the corner of the street a few yards away, and he's not alone. Clinging to his arm is the cutest little blue-haired lady wearing a festive green pantsuit. With one hand on the small of her back and the other gripping her fingers to support her, she makes the step onto the curb.

My heart lurches, and when he smiles at her, I can't help but smile too. I move to the side of the entrance as Oliver and the lady part ways, and he starts in my direction. He spots me, a grin stretching to his ears just as his shoe snags on the pavement, sending him stumbling forward. He manages to regain his footing before he hits the ground and strikes a pose in front of me, holding up jazz hands.

"I totally meant to do that," he says with a sly smile.

I chuckle. "Of course, you did. Because you're normally very coordinated."

He raises his brows and wags his finger at me. "Right. It's good to see you again, Dr. Haggerty." His voice is instantly familiar, like the first few notes of an old Bing Crosby Christmas tune.

"Yeah, you too," I say. "And it's just Lindsey."

His face beams like sunshine, sending rays of light slicing through the clouds. "Then it's nice to see you, *Lindsey*."

He's standing close enough I can smell him, notes of cinnamon and sandalwood mingling with the fresh scent of laundry detergent.

I clear my throat. "So, you're a firefighter *and* you help little old ladies cross the street. Do you also wear a cape and fight bad guys?"

"Only every other weekend. See, if this was *next* Saturday, you might not have recognized me in my Kevlar-infused bodysuit." He gives me a small wink and folds his muscular arms over his chest, and my brain conjures up an image of him *wearing* said bodysuit that is not at all unpleasant. The sleeves of his flannel are rolled up, giving me a perfect view of the way his forearms tense and flex. I resist the urge to reach out and touch them.

"You okay?" he asks, eyeing me with a puzzled expression.

"Huh?" That's when I realize I've been staring at him like I used to ogle the Backstreet Boys posters on my wall every night before bed, always making sure to kiss the shiny, flat Kevin Richardson, the most underappreciated of the Backstreet Boys.

"I was asking what you were up to when you spaced out on me."

"Sorry," I say through an exaggerated yawn. "I had an early morning. I've been doing some Christmas shopping, but I was just about to stop for a coffee."

"Actually, I was about to do the same." He gestures toward the entrance of the coffee shop. "Up for some company? My treat."

I hesitate for a moment, shifting my bags from one hand to the other. It's just coffee. It's not like it's a date or anything.

"Sure, why not?" I say.

"Great." He bounds for the door and holds it open for me. "After you."

"Thank you," I say, crossing the threshold. The warmth of the coffee shop wraps around me like a hug.

"What do you like to get?" he asks as we join the small line in front of the cashier.

"My favorite is the 'It's Always Fall Somewhere.'"

"I don't know what that is. All I know is, I have to have it." He rubs his palms together and glances around the crowded cafe. "Want to grab us a table while I order?"

"Sure." My arm brushes his as I pass by. Goose bumps pebble my skin, and I'm thankful the sweater I'm wearing conceals the flush I feel rising up my neck.

I maneuver around the tables and other patrons and slip onto the worn leather bench of a vacant booth. The Southern Bean has a cozy, rustic vibe with tables made from reclaimed wood and paintings for sale by local artists hanging on the walls. Soft music plays in the background, punctuated by the sounds of laughter and flatware clinking against ceramic plates.

It's not long before Oliver catches my eye and smiles as he starts toward me with our coffees in hand. He places one in front of me, then slides into the other side of the booth.

"This place is great," he says, glancing around the cozy space.

"You haven't been here before?"

He shakes his head. "I've really only just gotten settled in. The only place I've seen besides my house is the inside of the fire hall and the Food Saver. And the vet's office, of course."

"Where did you move from?"

"Canton, Texas. It's a small town outside Dallas," he answers with his smooth southern lilt.

"Wow, Texas. What brought you all the way to Tennessee? To Loving, no less."

"I needed a change of scenery." He picks at the coffee sleeve with his finger. "I used to spend my summers here as a kid."

"Here, as in, Loving?"

He nods. "My grandfather had a little cottage behind Bowie Park."

"I wonder if we ever crossed paths before."

"We might have. Did you go to Bowie much growing up?"

"Only all the time," I answer. "My dad and I rode our bikes on the trail around the lake a lot."

"My grandpa used to take me fishing there," he says.

"What else did you do when you visited? Did you go to any of the town events like the Founders Day parade or Nature Fest?"

"My grandfather wasn't one for crowds, so we spent a lot of time in his woodshop. He was a brilliant carpenter."

"Did he ever teach you how to make anything?"

"He taught me a thing or two, but I'm nowhere near as good as he was." He takes a sip of his coffee. "What about you? Do you have any hobbies or secret talents you care to share? Can you solve a Rubik's Cube in less than sixty seconds? Or do the moonwalk?"

"Nope. Nothing I can think of."

"Come on, surely there's something."

"Hmm." I ponder the question for a moment, tapping a finger against my chin. "Oh, I know. I can tie a cherry stem in a knot with my tongue, so I guess that's something?"

Oliver chokes on his coffee, coughs sputtering out of him like an engine attempting to start. "Went down the wrong pipe."

It dawns on me what I just said and the implications of my hidden "talent." My cheeks burn like that time I accidentally touched my face while attempting to help Lucy make poblano enchiladas.

"Oh. Oh my God. I didn't mean...um, wow."

"No, it's great," he says with a playful grin. "I just have so many questions, none of which are appropriate to ask someone I've only met twice. So, instead, I'm going to ask if you have any hobbies that don't involve fruit stems."

I chuckle. "Honestly, between the clinic and my family, that's pretty much my life in a nutshell."

"You work with your sister, right? Y'all must be close."

"Maybe too close sometimes," I say with a laugh. "We're always in each other's business. Growing up, Lucy and my brother Ben were basically my best friends. They still are. And our mom…well, she's our world. When we were kids, she always had this way of making little things special, you know?"

"Yeah?" he asks, leaning forward, gaze fixed on me. "How so?"

"She loved to turn an ordinary day into a holiday. She never needed a reason to celebrate. It wasn't unusual for her to set up a blanket fort in the living room for our weekly movie night or for us to come home from school and find she'd prepared a picnic in the back yard on a random Tuesday. But what we were doing was never important. It was just about being together," I explain, taking a sip of my latte. "And we've tried to carry that philosophy into adulthood. Well, minus the blanket forts, but we really should bring those back."

His mouth twists into a wistful smile, and I wonder why. "That sounds nice."

"It is," I say. Well, it *was*. A lot has changed since my dad passed away. It's like we're all kind of going through the motions, but of course, I don't tell him that. I'm sure my troubles are the last thing he wants to hear about.

"What about you?" I ask. "Are you close with your folks?"

Oliver's shoulders hunch, and a flicker of something

resembling sadness flashes across his face so quickly that if I'd blinked, I'd have missed it.

"Not really," he answers. There's definitely more to the story, but I don't pry.

"Do you have any siblings?" I ask.

"I don't, but I wish I did."

"Want to borrow one of mine? For the low, low price of zero dollars, my sister will hound you about your dating life while you play Candy Land with my brother's adorable kids."

He pretends to consider the offer. "Hmm. Can I just stick to the games? That other part doesn't sound so fun."

"Sorry. It's a package deal," I tease, lifting my drink.

"I *do* play a mean game of Candy Land." He rubs his thumb along the smooth edge of his jaw, contemplating. "Well, it's a hell of an offer, but it depends on one thing."

"What's that?"

"Would you be playing too?"

"I would," I say, lowering my cup with a smug grin. "And I would kick your a—"

I somehow misjudge how high the table is and drop my cup, sending what's left of my latte splattering across the wood surface.

"Oh my God. I'm so sorry." I pluck a fistful of napkins from the dispenser on the table in a futile attempt to soak up the coffee.

Oliver grabs a few more of the thin paper squares. "Here, let me help you." We wipe and dab, but it only seems to spread farther. One of the baristas notices our predicament and jumps in with a damp towel, removing every last drop.

"Thank you," I say as she walks away.

I cover my cheeks with my hands and shake my head. "Wow. Can't take me anywhere."

"Well, that's unfortunate for me." Oliver grins, causing adorable crinkles to frame his eyes. "I was going to ask if maybe you'd take a walk with me and show me around town."

My stomach does flip-flops, and I cast a nervous glance down at my watch. This coffee meetup is creeping into what feels like date territory. Part of me is eager to say yes. To see where this afternoon takes me. Because something about hanging out with Oliver makes me feel lighter than I have in years.

But the scar above his lip reminds me of the literal fires he's putting out to save babies and golden retrievers and people on balconies. While noble and brave, it's also extremely dangerous. *Relationships* are dangerous. Too many things can happen, even when you're *not* sprinting into burning buildings.

I must take too long to answer because he follows his proposal with, "But I understand if you're busy."

"I should really get back home and check on June Bug," I say. "You know how puppies are. Tiny bladders and all." A hint of disappointment shadows his face, and before I can stop myself, I add, "But I suppose a quick tour on the way to my car wouldn't hurt."

"Perfect," he says. He grabs his cup, and I loop my bags over my arm as we head for the door.

"Is there anywhere special you remember from when you stayed here with your grandfather?" I ask, starting down the sidewalk.

He falls into step beside me. "He didn't go to a lot of places besides Chappell's Supermarket and the hardware store."

"The Tool Box? It's still there. Just up here on the

right," I say as we stroll down Main Street. "Mr. Isbel's son took it over after his dad retired. You want to stop in and say hi?"

"That's okay," he says. "I'll drop by some other time."

We continue down Main Street, passing by the old movie theater that's been converted into a bookstore, The Magnolia Antique Shop, Lovebird Brews, The Donut Den, and a day spa.

"And that's Bluebells," I say as we approach the flower shop. There's a small table set up outside filled with poinsettias and Christmas cacti. "Loving High School Band Fundraiser" is scrawled on the chalkboard sign beside it.

"Hi," a perky redheaded girl with a spray of freckles across her nose chirps as we approach. "Would you like to support the band today? Your contribution will help us get new uniforms next year."

"We'd love to," Oliver says, turning to me. "I know poinsettias are poisonous to animals, so can I interest you in a cactus?"

I laugh. "A cactus is probably the only plant I could keep alive."

"Sold." He pulls his wallet out of his back pocket and hands the girl a twenty, telling her to keep the change.

"Here you go," she says, giving him the tiny potted succulent.

"For you." He hands it to me with a smile as we walk the last few feet to the corner.

My stomach does a cartwheel. "You didn't have to do that."

"Hey, it's for the kids, right?" He pushes his fingers through his hair, which makes his forearm flex again, and yep —it's definitely time for me to go before I start daydreaming about those arms. Because this can't be more than coffee with a handsome stranger. It just can't.

I clear my throat. "Well, my car's just behind that shop," I say, pointing to the boutique across the street. "But hey, this was fun. Thanks for the coffee, and you know, the company."

"Yeah, I had a good time too," he replies, pushing his hand through his hair again. "Can I walk you the rest of the way?"

"Oh, that's okay. It's not far."

He opens his mouth, and oh my God, he's about to ask for my number, isn't he? I have to get out of here. All rational thinking has gone out the window, and I'm in fight-or-flight mode. On today's menu: flight. So I blurt out the first thing that comes to my mind.

"I think I left my iron plugged in."

I turn away so I don't have to witness the disenchanted look I'm certain has taken over Oliver's face and practically sprint the rest of the way to my car.

Never mind that I don't even own an iron.

"WHEN YOU SAID THIS DOG WAS WILD, I THOUGHT YOU WERE just being dramatic." Ben, the middle Haggerty child, sits on the sofa while June Bug tugs on the leg of his pants as though they'd wronged her in a past life.

"Thanks again for coming." I'm buried in the oversized armchair in the living room of my cozy bungalow later that evening. The electrodes of my TENS unit are attached to my back, sending soothing pulses swimming through my body in an attempt to calm the ache creeping into my muscles. A fresh mug of coffee rests in my hands, and I'm surrounded by my siblings, their significant others, and my two favorite people in this world—my niece and nephew. They came over to play with June Bug and help her expend some energy so that maybe she'd allow me to sleep tonight.

"You feeling okay?" Willow asks, nodding toward the base of the unit clipped to my belt loop.

"Yeah, just being proactive, you know?" I say, though it's only partially true, and she nods.

"Puppy." Three-year-old Emily squeals, waving a stuffed lamb from the doorway with Noah protectively at her side. "Come here."

"Easy," Noah warns a bouncing June Bug.

Noah's only a year older than his sister, but he lives to take care of her. As the oldest of the Haggerty siblings, that's something I can relate to. Even at thirty-five, my instinct is to look after Lucy and Ben.

"Be gentle," Ellie reminds them.

"Okay," the kids sing in unison, and June Bug lets out a high-pitched yip that could wake the dead.

"Trust me, that cute little twerp is made of rubber," Lucy says, taking a bite of the pizza I ordered for dinner as the kids and the pup bound down the hall.

Once Emily and Noah are out of earshot, Ben clears his throat. "The kids want to go to Mistletoe Fest," he announces.

I can't help the sharp breath that escapes from my mouth. Mistletoe Fest is Loving's most-anticipated holiday celebration at Bowie Park. It's a day of festive family fun that includes Christmas-themed food, games, vendors, carolers, karaoke, a gingerbread house contest, and a walk-through light show after dark.

The last time we attended that festival, our collective

worlds fell apart, but before that, it had been something we did as a family. We made a lot of happy memories there.

"But…" Lucy trails off, fidgeting in her seat. "We can't go without Mom."

"I'm not suggesting we go without her," Ben says. "What if we bring it up to her Thursday?"

His hope-filled eyes land on me, and I bark out a laugh. "On *Thanksgiving*? Absolutely not."

My brother's voice softens. "But I thought if you were already going to talk to her about moving where we celebrate Christmas—"

I cut him off. "Ben, I said I would *try*. You know how she gets over the holidays."

"I know," he says with his best sad-puppy face. "It would just mean a lot to the kids."

My chest aches, and I release a heavy sigh. I would give anything to see my niece and nephew get to enjoy Mistletoe Fest. It had been one of my favorite traditions as a child.

"If things go well when we ask about Christmas, I'll *try*," I say, and Ben's frown immediately turns upside down. "You know, it wouldn't hurt for you and Lucy to speak up to Mom every now and then too. I can't always be the bad guy."

"But you're so good at it," Lucy teases, and I shoot her a death glare.

She holds her hands up in surrender. "I'm kidding."

"Look, I'll try, but I make no promises," I say with a pointed look at Ben. "About anything."

"Even if MJ doesn't agree to go to the festival right away, we still have a few weeks to try to convince her," Willow adds with a diplomatic shrug.

"Stranger things have happened, right?" Ben smiles, but I catch a flicker of apprehension in his eyes.

"Speaking of strange things happening," Lucy says, rising to her feet, her eyes laser focused on my mantle. "What the hell is that? Since when do you have plants? You're like the grim reaper of plants."

I nearly choke on my coffee. Of course, Lucy would spot the damn cactus Oliver got me. Why hadn't I hidden it?

"Oh, um, yeah, I thought I'd give being a plant parent a try," I say, heat rising up my neck and to my cheeks. "All those people on the internet make it look so appealing."

Lucy whirls on me and narrows her eyes. "You're lying."

"I am not," I insist, but it's too late.

"You're a terrible liar, Linds," Ben says. "You wear your heart on your sleeve. And your face." He waves his hand in a circle in front of him.

I squeeze my eyes shut and lean my head back. "Fine. I got it from Oliver."

"Who's that?" Willow asks.

"Oliver?" Lucy gasps. "As in, the hot firefighter from the clinic?" she asks, her voice going all gooey around the edges.

"Oliver, as in, the firefighter who assisted us with Ron's medical emergency the other day," I correct her, leaving the *hot* part out, though she's certainly not wrong about that. "We ran into each other in town this afternoon."

Lucy squeals. "You went on a date today!"

"First of all, it was *not* a date," I say. "We ran into each other and got some coffee. Not a big deal."

"Who paid for said coffee?" Ben asks.

I press my lips together, and my silence is all the answer they need.

Ellie waggles her brows. "Kinda sounds like a date to me."

"It wasn't," I insist. "Come on. Aren't we more evolved

than this?" I attempt to soothe the tension building behind my eyes by rubbing my forehead as I give them the rundown of my time with Oliver. "We're just two people who bumped into each other, and we decided to get coffee together."

"Two single, *hot* people," Lucy quickly adds. "The guy is a firefighter, remember?"

"How do you know he's single?" I challenge her. "For all you know, he could have a whole wife and kids at home."

"He doesn't," she insists with a grin. "Because Kayla asked if there were any additional family members who needed to be put on his dog's records and he said no, that it was just him."

Of course, she did. "You two are shameless, you know that?"

"So, how exactly was this not a date?" Ben asks, tilting his head.

I roll my eyes. "Really, Ben? It wasn't a date because I don't need that in my life right now," I say, perhaps a little too defensively. "Is it so hard to believe I'm happy alone?"

Lucy reaches for her mug on the coffee table. "You really haven't dated anyone since Daniel. And that was…a long time ago."

Nearly four years, to be exact. We split almost a year after Dad died.

"I still wish you two could have worked things out," Ben says. "He was a good guy."

They knew my ex, Daniel, as the happy-go-lucky person he was on the surface. What they don't know is that they didn't really *know* him at all.

"Can we drop this, please?" I force a tight smile and rise to my feet. "I'm gonna go check on the kids."

I step into the hall and follow the merry giggles into the

kitchen where June Bug is darting between Noah and Emily, licking their toes. A familiar longing tugs at my heart as I watch them, but I shove it down. Everything I said is true. I *am* happy. I *do* love my life.

I can't entirely fault Ben and Lucy for wanting me to fall in love when their own relationships are so supportive. When Dad passed away, Ellie was the one who stepped up and made lists of everything that needed to be done. She went to the funeral home with us to make arrangements, making sure every detail was perfect. All the while, she single-handedly juggled running the design firm where she still works as our mother's right hand. And Willow, who was Lucy's girlfriend at the time, jumped in and took care of us. She made sure we ate and even helped get Mom's house ready for the wake. Willow had only been with my sister for three months, but she showed up, not just for Lucy, but for all of us.

Even though we'd been together almost two years, Daniel never did any of that, and my family had been too consumed by grief to notice.

But *I* noticed.

I might've been the one to break up with Daniel, but *he* was the one who abandoned me.

4

———

MJ

"So, Lindsey," Lucy says, poking her sister in the arm after our weekly Sunday dinner. "I want to hear more about your date yesterday."

I lean forward, eyebrows raised.

"I already told you everything last night," Lindsey says, whacking her sister with a throw pillow on the tufted sofa in my living room. "And it *wasn't* a date."

Date or not, my daughter is practically glowing. For a moment, she's sixteen again, telling me about her first kiss with Travis Bedford at the homecoming dance.

"You had coffee with a very gorgeous, very available man, for crying out loud," Lucy argues from her spot next to her sister. "If that doesn't scream *romance*, I don't know what does."

I listen and watch with amusement as I take a sip from my steaming cup of peppermint tea, the familiar sounds of my grandchildren shrieking with delight filtering in from the playroom next to us.

"He also got you flowers," Ellie points out from the arm of the La-Z-Boy that Ben is sitting on.

Lindsey never tells me about the men she meets anymore—if she's meeting any at all—so hearing about this is a treat. She had a serious boyfriend—Daniel—a few years prior, and from the outside looking in, their connection had seemed perfect. But about a year after Henry's life ended, so did their relationship. To this day, Lindsey refuses to talk about their breakup, and she hasn't brought anyone around since, always claiming she's happy with her life as it is.

Henry and I may not have always been perfect parents, but we showed our children what it meant to have a loving relationship. We prioritized weekly date nights and weren't afraid to be affectionate in front of the kids, much to their embarrassment. We were the loves of each other's lives, but we were also best friends. So, when Lucy met Willow and Ben met Ellie, they knew. They were able to recognize what true love looked like. I've always wished for the same to happen for Lindsey.

"A Christmas cactus," Lindsey corrects her, but her flushed cheeks give her away. "He got me a cactus from the band kids' fundraiser outside Bluebells."

"Well, that was sweet," I chime in.

"Must be nice," Rose says from beside me. "The last time a man brought me flowers was about seven years ago."

"Fred?" Lindsey grins, already anticipating the answer.

My sister nods. "Yep."

"I don't think I know this story," Willow says, entering the room with two cups of coffee. She hands one to Lucy before taking a seat beside her on the couch. "Who's Fred?"

Rose leans into me, giggling. "He showed up on my

doorstep to pick me up for our date to the Red Lobster with a pall."

"Wait, who's Paul?" Willow asks, and we explode into raucous laughter.

"No, not Paul." Rose snorts. "He brought me *a* pall. You know, one of those floral sprays that go on a casket. He wanted to get me flowers, and this thing was marked down because a funeral got canceled. Turns out the person who was supposed to have died wasn't actually dead."

"No way." Willow's mouth falls open. "You're making this up."

"It would seem like it, but I promise you, that thing stayed on her kitchen table for a month," I choke out.

"I can't believe you kept it." Ben shudders. "Gave me the heebie-jeebies."

Rose shrugs. "Listen, I'm not exactly in a position to be turning away suitors over here. I was just happy to get some damn flowers, even if they were supposed to belong to a corpse."

Lucy shakes her head. "See, Lindsey? Aunt Rose had a guy bring her funeral flowers and even she could see it for what it was. You have a handsome firefighter buying you a cactus, yet you still refuse to believe it was a date."

I perk up. "A firefighter?"

Lindsey rolls her eyes. "There you go getting Mom worked up."

"I'm not worked up," I insist. "I haven't been worked up since I got the flu and couldn't go—"

"See Celine Dion," the kids and Rose say in unison.

"Your heart never did go on from that, did it?" Rose asks, and I pull a face at her.

"Anyway, I want to hear more about this firefighter," I say.

"His name is Oliver," Lucy answers for her sister. "He and his dog just moved to town a couple of months ago."

"And he's *very* good-looking," Ellie says.

A good-looking firefighter named Oliver. Well, this is certainly an exciting turn of events.

"Wait, how do you know what he looks like?" Lindsey asks.

Willow's gaze locks on the mug in her hands. "We may or may not have stalked him on social media after we left your place."

Lindsey side-eyes Willow and Lucy.

"Come on." Lucy turns her empathetic eyes on her sister. "You've hardly even been out with anyone since Daniel. This guy's hot, and so are you. You're a catch, Linds. You need to put yourself out there more."

"It's true," Rose says, taking a sip of her coffee. "Because the next thing you know, you'll be pushing seventy, and the most action you'll get is when you sit on top of the washer on laundry day."

The girls and I shake with laughter.

"La, la, la, la, la." Ben plugs his ears with his fingers, probably willing the recliner to open up and swallow him whole. "I'll take things I do *not* need to know for one hundred, Alex."

"But seriously, the guy is a smoke show," Lucy says. "Dark hair, brown eyes."

Willow nods. "And he's got this cute little scar over his top lip."

"He's gorgeous," Ellie adds with a dreamy sigh.

"I'm sitting right here, you know." Ben playfully pokes his wife in the ribs.

"Oh hush," Ellie chides. "You are too."

"Yes, you are," I say. "You look just like your father."

And just like that, all of the oxygen leaves the room, and the laughter fades as my eyes brim with tears.

"I should go check on the kids," Ben says, coming to kiss my cheek before he leaves the room.

"I'm sorry." I swipe my fingertips beneath my lash line.

"It's all right, Mom." Lindsey moves to sit next to me on the couch and clasps my hand in hers.

"You don't need to apologize," Ellie says.

Lucy gives me a wistful smile. "We miss him too."

"You know what you need?" Rose grips my knee and turns to me with an expression so sincere it makes my eyes well up all over again.

"What's that?" I ask.

"You need to go run a load of laundry." She winks at me, and I immediately roll my eyes. "I'm telling you, sister. A little ride on top of the ole Whirlpool is just what the doctor ordered."

"*I heard that,*" Ben says as he re-enters the room, and we explode into fits of giggles. My tears are forgotten for the moment, but Henry is never far from my mind.

5

LINDSEY

"I HOPE YOU'VE GOT SOME BODY ARMOR UNDER THAT sweater," Lucy says to me as the breeze whips through her rose-gold ponytail, revealing the cluster of stars tattooed on her neck.

I roll my eyes. "I'm talking to our mother, not a mob boss." We're standing on the back deck of our childhood home on Thanksgiving, where we were not even a week ago, while the kids play in the yard. The late afternoon sun is casting a golden glow over everything it touches. It's a pleasant, cloudless day. You'd never know a storm was brewing right here at the Haggerty house.

Ben smirks. "With the amount of cutlery lying around, I'd say this could be every bit as dangerous."

"I think I'd rather meet Al Capone in a dark alley than talk to Mom about changing our Christmas plans," Lucy says with a laugh.

The door to the back patio opens and Ellie emerges with Willow, their wine glasses freshly refilled. A crash, followed by a string of expletives and metal pots clattering, pierces the air outside, and Willow winces, closing the door.

"How's it going in there?" I ask, taking the last sip from my cup of chai that's doing nothing to settle my nerves.

"Food's almost done, but she still won't let us touch anything." Willow grits her teeth. "She wouldn't even let me put ice in the glasses."

"Don't take it personally," I say. "That's how she is."

"It's just been a lot worse since Dad died," Lucy adds, and the air instantly feels ten degrees cooler.

Ellie sighs, leaning her arms over the wood railing. "Should we wait another year? Maybe it's too soon."

Ben shakes his head. "Mom's in a good-ish mood today. I think she's still high on the prospect that Lindsey had a date."

"Happy to contribute to the cause." I roll my eyes. It's true, our mother *has* seemed brighter since Lucy spilled the beans about Oliver over dinner on Sunday, so much so that she was still going on about it over breakfast this morning. I pretended to entertain the idea of seeing him again once I saw the shadows return to her face at the mere suggestion that my afternoon with Oliver was anything *but* a date. We needed all the advantages we could get.

It wasn't hard to act like I have a crush on Oliver because it's not exactly untrue. I just can't act on it. My stomach flutters, but I shove the feeling down when Emily lets out a happy squeal as she jumps into the pile of leaves her brother has been haphazardly gathering for her.

"Whatever. We're doing this for them." I nod toward where the kids have collapsed in a giggling heap.

"Maybe she won't take it as badly as you think," Willow says, brushing a tawny coil off her face. "She could be open to the idea."

"I love your optimism, babe." Lucy threads her fingers through Willow's. "No matter how misguided it is."

"Did you talk to Aunt Rose?" Ben asks, nudging my arm. "Maybe she can get her on board."

"I did," I say. "I called her last night. She's on our side and said she'd do what she can to help. She understands where we're coming from, but ultimately, Mom's going to do what she wants."

"Where is Rose, anyway?" Ellie asks, her pale cheeks pink from being kissed by the breeze.

"She should be here anytime now. She had a Friendsgiving brunch," I answer. "And she was probably hoping to avoid the fifth annual holiday gloom fest."

Ben shakes his head, one of his brown curls falling into his eyes. "I can't handle another holiday like that. I *won't*. It's depressing."

The house is decked out in cranberry garland and gourds with splashes of vibrant orange and burgundy, but the mood is decidedly blue. Since our father died, our mother has been hell-bent on recreating every tradition *exactly* the way we did them when he was alive. The only difference is that now all the joy has been sucked out. It's as though she fears his memory and everything he was will disappear if we don't remain in mourning for the rest of our lives.

That's why we're going to suggest celebrating Christmas at Ben and Ellie's house this year. Because it's not Dad's legacy that's in danger of slipping away from us. It's *ours*.

The patio door opens and Aunt Rose appears, her auburn hair teased so high it would make Dolly Parton jealous.

"The prodigal aunt returns," Lucy says in lieu of a greeting.

"Dinner's ready." Aunt Rose pulls the door shut behind her and lowers her voice. "But are *you*?"

I exhale slowly and start toward her while Ben calls for the kids.

"Got any final words of wisdom?" I ask my mother's older sister. "Anything you think might help?"

"I brought whiskey." She wrinkles her upturned nose, regarding my empty mug and the soggy tea bag inside with pursed scarlet lips. "In case you need something stronger."

MOM LAYS HER FORK ON HER EMPTY PLATE AFTER DINNER. "I need to get the order in for our matching pajamas tomorrow. Do you want buffalo plaid or candy canes?"

Having a conversation with our mother during the holidays is like eating raw cookie dough. We can't *not* do it, but we never know what will set her off, poisoning us all. Talking about the clinic or Mom's design business where Ellie works is always a safe bet, and of course, anything to do with the kids, so that's what we started with. Ben already discussed his latest drama as the designated room parent for both Noah and Emily's classes. Willow told us about her job at the yoga studio in town and the art class she started at the rec center. Then the topic shifted to Christmas.

"I narrowed it down to two that were mostly red since we did the tree print last year," she goes on, mistaking our silence for distaste over her choice in sleepwear. "They did have some Grinch ones, if you all would like those better."

A hush falls over the worn oak table.

"Actually, Mom." I clear my throat. "We wanted to talk to you about Christmas."

Aunt Rose downs the rest of her wine in one gulp.

"Why don't I take the kids into the playroom for a bit and let y'all have a minute?" Ellie says, scooting out her chair. At the mention of the word *playroom*, Noah and Emily bounce out of their seats and skip from the room.

Mom furrows her brow and opens her mouth to say something, but Willow beats her to it.

"I'll come with you." Willow jumps up to help Ellie clear their plates before following the trail of happy giggles.

"Is everything okay?" Mom clasps her hands below her chin.

For a second, I reconsider saying anything at all because it pains me to upset her. Maybe we *should* all grin and bear it another year.

No. Remember why you're doing this.

"We've been thinking about Christmas," I begin, keeping my voice casual. Perhaps if I make it sound like this isn't a big deal, she won't make it into one. "Now that Noah and Emily are a little older and they're able to participate in the holiday more, we'd like to start some new traditions."

"Oh?" Mom's face draws back as though she's been slapped. "Like what?"

Ben gives me a nod of encouragement.

"We'd like to have Christmas at Ben and Ellie's," I answer. "We want the kids to have some holiday memories in their own home, like we do here."

Her frown lines deepen. "And you're *all* on board with this?"

Lucy's smile falters.

Mom purses her lips. "But they've only ever known Christmas *here*. We've always had it at our house. It was your father's favorite holiday."

Her eyes turn glassy, and Lucy shoots me a panicked glance.

"It's ours too," I say. "Because of you and Dad. You made every holiday so special. The house was always bursting at the seams with love because of you. We want the chance to create that same magic for the kids ourselves."

"I don't understand." Mom's voice breaks, sending a hairline fracture down the middle of my heart. "What have I done wrong?"

"You haven't done anything wrong." I reach across the table and touch her arm. "You've done everything *right*. You've given us everything. We just want the chance to do the same for them."

"Wouldn't it be nice to let someone else steer the ship a while, Myra Jean?" Aunt Rose asks. "You'd get to sit back and enjoy all the fun parts of the holiday without any of the hassle."

That's apparently the *wrong* thing to say because Mom's nostrils flare, and her hands ball into fists.

"I happen to love the 'hassle,' as you put it, Rose," she says. "This *is* fun for me."

"We know," I assure her. "And we still want you there for every second. You could stay over so we can all still wake up in the same house. We can drink coffee while Noah and Emily open their presents from Santa. We can still wear matching pajamas if that's what you want."

Lucy holds up her hand. "Actually, do we have to—"

Our mother's mouth drops open, and I cut my sister off with a stern glare.

"I love the matching pajamas." Lucy drops her hand and gives a faint smile. "They're my favorite."

Mom tosses her napkin on her plate. "You hate them. Just

say it. You don't like the way we celebrate Christmas. You want to change everything."

Ben sighs. "That's not what we're saying at all."

"We'd just like a chance to try things our way." I attempt to squeeze her arm, but she yanks it away.

She shakes her head profusely. "This was *our* holiday. Your father was the one who insisted on putting the lights up before the first of December. *He* wanted to take the annual family photo on the porch in our matching pajamas, and he loved nothing more than sitting by the fire on Christmas Eve watching those damn TV movies we all love."

Ben opens his mouth to speak, but I kick his shin under the table.

"He pretended to be surprised every time a big city girl inherited an inn or a goat farm or whatever it was before she moved to some small town in Colorado and fell in love on Christmas." Mom's hands move emphatically, punctuating her every word. "He did that for all of you, and *this* is how you repay him?"

Dad loved Christmas and having us there, but much of what he did was to make Mom happy. He turned the place into a gingerbread house, wrapping every outdoor surface in colorful twinkle lights, even climbing on the roof with a staple gun every year, just to make her smile. Our father couldn't have cared less about us wearing matching holiday-themed pj's. In fact, he confessed to me on multiple occasions how uncomfortable they were since he was so tall and they were always three inches too short, but he wore them with a smile because it brought her so much joy. And Dad's favorite Christmas movie was *Die Hard*. He only watched the ones that played twenty-four seven on cable because Mom was obsessed with them. Truth be told, it was why we watched them too.

I swallow the lump in my throat. "Mom, he did all of that for you."

Her face crumbles like a child whose parents just told her Santa isn't real. "I see."

She pushes back her chair, and it screeches against the hardwood floor as she bolts to her feet and starts gathering the dishes.

"Myra Jean." Aunt Rose blows out a breath. "Sit back down."

"Mom. Can we please just talk about this?" I ask, and she answers by snatching my plate and plunking it on top of her growing stack.

"It sounds like you've already made your decision," Mom says, jutting out her chin. "Anyway, we should have dessert. I've got pecan pie, chocolate meringue, some sugar cookies, and I made your dad's favorite pumpkin pie." She sniffles. "Or maybe he pretended to like that too."

I rub my temples as she storms from the dining room. "That went well."

Aunt Rose gives me an empathetic smile. "Chin up, kid. You handled it the best you could. She'll come around."

I blow out a breath and rise to my feet. "We need to go after her."

Ben and Lucy groan as they stand, but Aunt Rose doesn't budge.

I narrow my eyes at her.

"Do I have to?" Rose pouts, and I reply by raising my brow and propping my hand on my hip.

"Fine." She grimaces and grabs the last remaining roll in the bread basket, stuffing it in her mouth.

I attempt to push through the swinging door to the kitchen but am met with resistance followed by a shrill shriek.

"Oh no," Ben mutters. "That doesn't sound good."

I ease the door open slowly this time. "Mom?"

An ear-splitting wail answers from the floor where my mother sits in a puddle of tears in front of a squashed pumpkin pie, the front of her cream dress covered in orange goo. Some of the custardy filling had even managed to splatter into her sleek, silver bob and onto her fair skin.

"Are you okay?" Lucy asks as we rush to her side.

"It's ruined," Mom answers, sucking in a breath between sobs. "Everything is ruined."

Lucy lets out a soft laugh. "There's no use crying over pumpkin pie. Come on. Let's get this cleaned up."

"No!" Her voice is so sharp it causes me to jump. "What's the use, anyway? So you all can tell me you don't want to spend Thanksgiving here, either? I've had quite enough."

My hands tremble at my sides.

"Sister," Aunt Rose scolds. "What is wrong with you?"

"What's wrong with *me*?" Mom repeats. "This entire day has been a disaster."

"That's not true," Ben begins, but she cuts him off.

"I do everything I can to keep the magic of the holidays alive. To keep your father's memory alive. But apparently, that means nothing to you."

I gasp. "*Mother.*" She's being unfair, and I'm starting to wonder if she dropped the pie on purpose for added dramatic flair.

Lucy's bottom lip quivers, and Ben's face falls.

"You know what," I say. "Maybe we should go and give you some space."

"Yes, that's a great idea," Mom yells. "Maybe you should!"

Ben pulls Lucy and me to our feet, and I reach my hand out to help our mother off the floor, but she pushes it away.

I shake my head. "Happy Thanksgiving, Mama."

It's a calculated move, but a necessary one. When we were little and were sad or hurt, it was never Mom or Mother we called for. It was Mama.

Aunt Rose sneers. "Myra Jean, you're showing your ass."

"I am *not*—"

"Your ass." Aunt Rose points to where my mother's dress has ridden up her legs, revealing a pair of polka-dotted under-wear. "It's showing."

She yanks down the hem of the fabric with a guttural growl, and we back out of the kitchen as though we're escaping a wild bear.

Willow is waiting for us outside the door.

"We need to leave," I say. "Now."

"What?" Willow covers her mouth with her hand. "Why?"

"I'll get Ellie and the kids," Ben says as the rest of us pad into the living room.

I pull a tearful Lucy into my arms. "It's okay, Luce."

"I've never seen her this mad before," my sister chokes out.

Aunt Rose folds her arms over her robust chest. "She's being a childish twat."

"We'll have dessert later. There are cookies at home," Ellie says as she and Ben steer the kids down the hall.

Noah's brow knits. "But we have to say goodbye to Grandma."

"Grandma isn't feeling well," Ben explains. "We'll see her later, okay?"

Together, we make our way outside, and Ellie moves ahead to load Emily and Noah in their minivan.

"I'm sorry, kids," Aunt Rose says. "Your mom loves you, but she's hardheaded. Just give her time."

"Thanks for trying, Linds," Ben says, giving my arm a squeeze.

I force a smile and nod. We all share hugs and *I love yous* before we part ways.

"See you tomorrow?" Lucy calls as she opens the passenger door to Willow's Honda Civic.

"Bright and early," I answer, climbing into my own car. Tears burn behind my eyes as I wait for my family to take their turns pulling out of the gravel driveway.

My mother's harsh words opened up the old wound left behind by my father's death. She knows how important he was and still is to us. I don't think she meant what she said, but it still hurts.

I'd give anything to talk to my dad. He'd know exactly what to do. In the time since he passed, I learned a lot about grief and what it means to lose someone so significant, the most important being that your life becomes firmly divided into two parts: before and after. No matter how hard you try to arrange pieces of the past into the puzzle that is the future, they'll never fit the way they used to.

"Dad, I wish you were here," I say aloud, praying that somehow, some way, he'll hear me. I wipe away the tears spilling down my cheeks with the back of my hand. "I'm a mess. We *all* are. A mess and a half."

I wait for a moment, hoping to hear my dad's voice in my head or get some kind of sign letting me know he's still with me.

The only sound I'm met with is deafening silence.

❄

I push through the door that separates the lab from the lobby of the clinic Saturday morning, where each of the five chairs is already filled with owners and their pets. Mr. Bush is waiting at the front, his arms resting on top of the Formica desk. "Good morning, Mr. Bush. I hear we have another casualty?"

"Yes, Doctor," he answers, whistling through his toothless mouth. Mr. Bush has been a frequent flier at the clinic since he adopted a beagle puppy with an insatiable hunger for Poligrip and resin the year before. "I was in the shower yesterday, and the next thing I knew, Noodle burst through the curtain, grinning up at me like he was in a damn canine Crest commercial."

My eyes fall to Noodle, who cocks his head to one side and lets out a triumphant *rooo, rooo, roooooo.*

"You stop that," Mr. Bush scolds the dog. "Don't you think you've done enough?"

The beagle grunts and begins turning circles, his hind end wiggling.

Kayla kneels to scratch Noodle behind the ears, and he takes the opportunity to give her a big, slobbery smooch.

"Thanks, Noodle," Kayla says. "You're a real ladies' man."

Mr. Bush beams. "Just like his daddy."

"Right." I give him a polite smile. "Okay, you know the drill. I'm going to borrow this little guy for a few minutes to make sure there's nothing lingering in his tummy."

"Okey dokey," he says, handing over Noodle's leash.

I click my tongue, and the pup trots beside me as I lead him to the back with Kayla on our heels. Once we're in the lab, she lifts him onto the X-ray machine so I can take a scan of his abdomen.

Lucy cackles when she glances up from the wall-mounted tub, where she's working up a lather on an elderly Pomeranian, to catch a glimpse of the first patient of the day.

"Noodle," she cries. "You didn't!"

"Oh, but he did," I say, stepping over to the laptop on the counter to view the images from the test. As I suspected, he already passed everything he managed to swallow.

"How many sets of dentures has the man been through now?" I ask as I move Noodle to the steel table in the center of the room to check his vitals. "Four?"

"Eight," Kayla deadpans, giving the pooch a squirt of spray cheese to lick off her hand to keep him still.

"Wow, really?" I raise my brow. "That many?"

"You know he's only coming here for the cheese at this point," Lucy teases.

"Hey, it keeps him calm." Kayla shrugs before turning her hazel eyes on me. "So, how was your Thanksgiving? Did you guys talk to your mom?"

"We did." I sigh as I move my stethoscope along the curve of the dog's belly. "It didn't go like we hoped."

"She's putting it mildly," Lucy says. "It was a disaster."

Kayla gives me a sad smile. "What happened?"

Lucy and I recount the entire fiasco, including how our mother ended up in a heap on the floor with her undies showing.

Kayla shakes her head. "I can't believe it. Your mom has always seemed so…poised."

I remove my stethoscope and sling it around my neck. "Things have been different since Dad died. *She's* been different. Sometimes I think she forgets that losing Dad has been hard on us too. All I know is, we can't handle another holiday where Mom spends the day waxing nostalgic. The holidays are hard enough without Dad, and doing all the things we enjoyed with him only makes his absence feel bigger."

"I'm sure it's difficult for her to think about celebrating the holiday differently," Kayla says, anticipating my every move and handing me the thermometer. "In a way, those traditions probably feel like the last thread connecting her to your dad. She'll come around."

"It'll take a Christmas miracle for that to happen." Lucy turns on the hose to rinse the Pomeranian, which causes it to snarl like a possessed gremlin. "Dad always said she was stubborn as an old goat."

"That must be where you get it from." I stick the thermometer beneath Noodle's tail, and he lets out a dissatisfied whimper, narrowing his eyes at me. "Hey, you did this to yourself, buddy."

"I'm just saying, when our mother is set on something, she cannot be deterred. Case in point: she went to the doctor for a sinus infection and came home with a fiancée for me," Lucy explains.

"Didn't she also set up Ben and Ellie?" Kayla asks.

"She did," Lucy answers before looking back at me. "So, it's inevitable she'll make sure you get coupled up too. Might as well accept your fate now."

I bark out a laugh. "That's never going to happen."

"Oh, that's right. Lindsey Haggerty doesn't believe in love," Lucy teases in a singsongy voice. "She doesn't believe in the fairytale."

"What do you think, Noodle?" I ask, cupping the pooch's face in my hands. "Do you believe in love?"

In lieu of a reply, the beagle unleashes the loudest fart I've ever heard come from a dog, or any living being, for that matter. Truth from the mouths of babes. Or from the butts of mutts.

"My thoughts exactly," I say with a laugh. "Anyway, it's not that I don't *believe* in it. I just don't *need* it to be happy."

I know that kind of love exists because I've witnessed it through my parents' marriage and again through my siblings and their significant others. But for me, it's not worth the risk because it can all be lost in the span of a single breath. At best, when the other person decides your darkest parts are simply too much to deal with. At worst, when the person you love more than life itself is taken from your world with no explanation or goodbyes—when they're alive one minute and gone the next.

"Okay, Mr. Noodle," I say, scratching the pup on top of the head. "You're good to go."

"Let's get you back to Mr. Bush, you little tooth thief," Kayla says, scooping the dog into her arms and placing him on the floor. "How much do you want me to charge him?"

I shake my head. "Nothing. He's on a fixed income. It didn't take that long anyway."

Lucy and Kayla exchange a knowing glance.

"What?"

"It's just no wonder everyone within a seventy-five-mile radius wants to come here," Kayla answers. "You're good at what you do, *and* you have a kind heart."

"And you're almost as cute as me," Lucy quips. "We'll get you married off yet, Linds."

I roll my eyes. "Gee, thanks."

"But first we just need to get you another date with that smokin' hot firefighter," she adds, and Kayla emits a high-pitched squeak.

"Hold up," Kayla says. "What? As in, that super cute guy from the other day? Oliver?"

I huff out a breath and shoot daggers at Lucy with my eyes. "Seriously, how does your head fit through the door with your big mouth attached to it?" I turn to Kayla. "I was going to tell you."

"No you weren't, you dirty little liar," Kayla says with a grin, looping her arm through mine. "Now, spill."

6

———

MJ

It's early Sunday afternoon, and I'm eating the last piece of pecan pie right out of the dish, standing over the sink like a swamp rat. If this had been a normal Thanksgiving, I would have sent the leftovers with the kids, and Lindsey would have called dibs on the pecan pie because it's her favorite. The thought of my eldest daughter sends a sharp pain through my chest, and for a second, I wonder if I'm having some sort of cardiac episode. Wouldn't it be fitting for me to die alone in this house from a broken heart?

I need to return to my lair. After chucking the unwashed dish into the sink, I float up the stairs like a ghost, stopping in front of the collage of photos on the landing. Henry used to tease me about taking so many pictures, but I don't think any amount would have been enough to capture the life we had. My fingers trail along the wall, pausing at the photo we took on Thanksgiving five years ago, not knowing it would be our last one together as a family.

Henry set the tripod up in the living room, and we squeezed together on the couch to fit in the frame. My sister was on the end next to Ellie and Ben. Lucy huddled on the floor with Willow, who'd joined us for their first big holiday together. I was in the middle with Henry, our hands closed tight around one another's. On Henry's other side was Lindsey, leaning her head on his shoulder. They shared the same narrow nose and hazel eyes. But no feature was more alike than their beaming smiles that could light up the darkest room.

My hand drops to my side, and I let that image of the last happy holiday carry me to my bedroom, where I crawl into my king-size bed. The ceiling fan whirls overhead, and I pull the plush comforter up to my chin. Sure, it's almost December, but keeping the fan going year-round is something I'd started in my midforties, when life became one never-ending hot flash. I haven't been cold since Clinton was in office.

A sour taste lingers in my mouth. Did the pie go bad, or did I forget to brush my teeth? Or maybe the mere thought of Thanksgiving is enough to make me miserable all over again.

I spent the entire weekend eating leftovers and wallowing around in my favorite "World's Best Grandma" sleep shirt that my grandkids gave me for Mother's Day a couple years ago. Shuffling through the house, I could still see the kids decorating the Christmas tree when they were little and Henry hanging the stockings on the mantel. I could hear the echoes of my mother's voice from years before telling me that the dressing I'd made, the very same recipe that belonged to my great-grandmother, was the best thing she'd ever tasted.

But I could also see the rooms empty out, one by one, as Lindsey and Ben went to college and Lucy moved into her first apartment. And I could still see my husband being carried away from our home, my sanctuary, the one place that for so long had felt untouchable.

It still amazes me how a house that had once been so loud and full of life could fade to mere whispers.

I pluck my phone off the nightstand, straighten my navy-rimmed glasses, and pull up the photo Ben sent me that morning. I have to give him an A for effort. If anything could get me to crack, it's the smiling faces of my beautiful, perfect grandchildren. I thought nothing could ever top being a mom until I became a grandmother. I wish Henry could see them. He passed only months before Ellie and Ben found out they were expecting.

I swallow the lump that forms in my throat. I've been avoiding everyone since our holiday dinner ended with me yelling at my grown children before throwing a hissy fit on the floor like a petulant child.

My kids and my sister all tried reaching out to me, but I continued to ignore their calls. Partly because I was hurt, but also because I was embarrassed. I'm not proud of the way I acted, but I *am* too proud to admit it.

A *boom, boom, boom* echoes through the quiet house. The vibrating thud of someone knocking on the front door makes me yelp—even though I know exactly who it is, and I knew it was only a matter of time before she turned up.

The key rattles in the lock. "Go away," I mutter.

"Myra Jean!" my sister yells as the door slams shut and she stomps up the stairs with all the grace of a horse in an antique store. "Are you dead?"

"One can hope," I say as Rose's short frame appears in the doorway. What my sister lacks in height, she makes up for with her giant personality and being a big pain in my ass.

"Now you know you're too old to be ignoring phone calls." Rose crosses her arms over her chest. "We're not forty anymore. Avoiding calls is a surefire way to get yourself a wellness check and a possible call to the coroner's office."

I pull the blanket over my head. "Well, I'm not dead, so will you leave me alone now, please?"

Her footsteps clack across the hardwood floor and she yanks off the covers, exposing my threadbare sleepshirt.

"Quit your bellyaching and get out of this bed," she scolds me. "And call your children."

"How do you know I haven't?"

She pins me with a glare. "Because I know you. Henry always said you were a stubborn goat, and you know what? He was right."

"I don't want to call them." I yank the comforter back up, only for her to pull it down again.

"I don't give a rat's ass what you want. This is a family, not a democracy."

I huff. "I ought to take your key back."

She plops on the bed beside me. "You do realize, you've been saying that for over thirty years, and you haven't done it yet."

"There's still time."

A wiry spiral of dyed auburn hair falls into her face. "Then the cops really will have to come bust down your door when you're being a spoiled brat."

"You're my sister. You're supposed to be on my side."

"This *is* me being on your side."

"Well, you're doing a terrible job at it."

"Oh shut up, you old wench." She pokes me square in the ribs. "You love me, and you know it. And even if you don't, I'm all you've got left."

I wince, and I can see her willing the words back into her mouth.

"I didn't mean it like that." She covers my hand with hers.

"I know."

"Henry wouldn't want this."

Tears burn the corners of my eyes. She's right, but that doesn't mean I want to hear it.

"We've just always had Christmas here," I choke out. "I can still see the kids coming down the stairs, their eyes full of wonder, as they spotted what Santa had brought them. And Henry hovering over the damn tripod trying to get the camcorder to work, and Mama drinking coffee in that ugly old La-Z-Boy recliner while Daddy nodded off on the couch." I clasp her hand between both of mine. "And you, showing up in your pj's to open presents with the kids. Is it really so wrong that I don't want that to change?"

"Of course, it's not wrong," she says. "But it's not wrong of Lindsey, Ben, and Lucy to want to do something different, either. You've hosted every holiday, birthday, every gathering this family has ever had. You knitted Christmas stockings and made all the birthday cakes, and nobody does it better than you. But for me, the time spent together is what matters most. If the kids want to host Christmas and start some new traditions, I say, let 'em. It doesn't make a difference to me where we celebrate, as long as we're all together."

My bottom lip quivers.

"Myra Jean, you've been trying so hard to keep Henry alive that I'm afraid you're letting the future with the family you have left die." She takes a piece of my shoulder-length silver hair between two of her fingers. Playing with my hair was something she'd always done to comfort me any time I was upset when we were growing up. "I'm telling you this because I love you, but celebrating the holidays with you has become a real drag."

"That's because it *is* a drag. It's depressing." I swat at her hand. "I'm still grieving, okay?"

"I know," she says, "and nobody is saying you can't do that, but one day, in the hopefully very distant future, all Lindsey and Ben and Lucy are going to have left of us are memories. Photo albums and videos up in the cloud or wherever the hell those things live nowadays. And don't you want them to remember more than their mom crying every holiday, longing for a past she'll never get back?"

I hadn't thought of it that way. "But those past years were so happy," I can't help saying. "Just…filled to the brim with love."

"I know it's hard," she says. "But you don't get the love without the pain. That's not how it works. And one day, the kids are going to be old and gray, and they'll be left with the same hurt you're feeling now. But it'll be worth it for them, just like it's worth it for us." She moves my hand and presses it to my chest. "Because the hurt means love lived here."

I sigh heavily. "Why do you always have to make so much sense?"

"I'm the oldest. Being incredibly wise comes with the territory. Though it's really unfortunate for you that I got the looks too."

I punch her in the arm, and we laugh as she collapses on the bed next to me, resting her head on top of mine. Rose might get on my nerves, but she's also the one person who can help me get out of my own way.

"Now, will you call your children?" she asks. "Please?"

I roll my eyes. "Yes."

She scoots to the edge of the bed and stands. "And brush your teeth, for crying out loud. Your breath smells like roadkill."

I snort out a laugh and toss a pillow at her, nailing her right in the head.

I PRY MYSELF FROM MY BED OF SELF-PITY AND ARRIVE AT MJ Designs a little after 9 a.m. Monday morning. It still makes my heart skip a beat when I see the sleek sign bearing my name out front because it took me so long to get here.

I'd left my first design job when I was eight months pregnant with Lindsey, ready to immerse myself in stay-at-home mom life. Cloth diapering, making homemade baby food—I wanted to do it all.

That lasted for all of five minutes before I realized I didn't have time to take a shower, let alone *pin* a diaper on a wriggling infant, with only four hours of sleep and one measly cup of cold coffee that had been microwaved into oblivion.

As much as I loved being home with my children, part of me yearned to get back to work. I scratched the itch by turning our home into something ripped right out of *Southern Living* magazine. Then, when Lindsey was a senior in high school, one of her friends' moms saw the inside of our house for the first time and wanted to know who my decorator was. I helped her redo her living room, and she was so pleased she told all the ladies in her book club about me.

The great thing about small southern towns? People talk.

"Hey, MJ." One of my favorite young designers, Gabriela, greets me with a blue folder clutched in her hands no sooner than I walk through the front door. Her brow is furrowed, and her face is drawn as though she might burst into tears. "Do you have a second?"

I place my arm around her shoulders. "Is everything all right? Is your mama okay?"

"Yes, she's fine. It's nothing like that," she says. "It's just that I have the Stratford presentation this afternoon. My graphics are ready, but I'm so afraid they won't like it."

"What? Why? I saw those slides you sent me last week before the break. They're some of your best work."

"Thank you." She manages a faint smile. "But I don't know if they'll agree once they see the hand-renderings I did. They're kinda…well, trash."

"They most certainly are not." I narrow my eyes at her before adjusting my glasses and taking the folder from her hand. "I can tell you that without even looking at them."

The drawings are filled with vibrant swaths of color, sharp angles, floor-to-ceiling windows, and built-in bookshelves, all dotted with plush furniture and unique accents. I remember how insecure I'd felt when I finally dusted off my old sketchbook all those years ago, only to find I was practically a dinosaur. Designers were all using computer-aided design software that resembled some sort of high-tech video game. People were less impressed by seeing my portfolio and more drawn to 3D models showing how their spaces could be transformed.

At first, I barely charged for my work because I'd been out of the business for so long, I didn't feel like I was a *real* professional. Then, one night over dinner, Henry asked when I would quit putzing around and start charging what I was worth. The next day, I converted our bonus room into my very first office. Sometimes, all it takes is one person to believe in you.

"They'll love it," I say.

Her eyes light up. "You really think so?"

I nod. "You're going to knock their socks off. I just know it."

With my stamp of approval, she breathes a sigh of relief.

"You've got this, okay? Don't sweat it."

"Thanks, MJ." Her forehead smooths, the stress melting from her deep golden skin. "I really appreciate it."

"Anytime," I say. She heads back to her desk, and I soak in the sunlight pouring through the windows as I work my way through the building.

It's an open space with the exception of my private office and a conference room, but even I have a workstation amongst the other designers. It contributes to the collaborative environment we've all established together, with Ellie and me leading the charge.

Seven years after rejoining the workforce, when the demand for my services increased beyond what I could handle alone, I brought on Ellie, who worked out of my original home office with me. I loved her so much that I set her up with my son. By the time Ellie and Ben got engaged, I'd hired two more designers, and things were getting a little cramped. So when I turned fifty-two, I opened my dream office in a quaint blue house tucked away on a side street of downtown Loving that had been zoned for commercial use.

"Morning!" Ellie is already waiting for me when I enter my office, her tailored red suit popping against her fair skin.

Often, there's some weird sense of competition between mothers and the women who marry their sons. In fact, many women I've known over the years can't stand their daughters-in-law. But I never felt that way with Ellie. I love her as though she were my own, and our family is better because of her. After my Henry died, it was mostly Ellie who kept things going at work while I waded through the never-ending waters of grief, rarely able to make it to the office.

"I got you a latte." She's propped against my desk with a cup of coffee from The Southern Bean that I already know contains my favorite toasted praline latte with an extra shot of espresso. Ellie is thoughtful like that, but the eagerness on her face tells me this cup of coffee carries a little more weight. It's a peace offering—a hope that we can work together without any of the tension from Thanksgiving.

"Thank you, sweetheart," I say, kissing her on the cheek, a wisp of her blonde hair tickling my nose. "By the way, I'm making your favorite pumpkin cheesecake for dessert Sunday."

I spoke with Ben and his sisters last night, just as I promised Rose. Though, I suppose it wasn't really an apology so much as it was me calling and pretending everything was fine and asking what they wanted for our weekly dinner. But that's just as good as saying sorry, right?

"That sounds amazing," she replies.

"How were Noah and Emily this morning?" I ask, placing the coffee on my desk and hanging my coat behind the door. "Ben said you put the tree up Saturday because they were hounding you to death."

She chuckles. "Oh, they were. They're so excited."

I move to my desk and take a seat in my purple velvet office chair. "It's fun, isn't it? Seeing Christmas through their eyes?"

"It is," she says, sitting in one of the tufted chairs opposite me. "Especially now that they really get what's going on. I loved their first Christmases, but now it's extra special."

I sigh, remembering what those holidays had been like in our home.

"Actually, there's something I want to ask you." There's the slightest quaver in her voice.

"Sure. Is everything okay?"

"Oh yes," she replies, her hands fidgeting with the hem of her jacket. "It's just that the kids mentioned Mistletoe Fest coming up next weekend. They saw a sign for it when we went to the store yesterday, and they asked if we could go this year. And I was thinking maybe we could all go as a fam—"

"No," I say, cutting her off, immediately regretting my sharp tone.

"It would mean so much to the kids if—"

"I can't do that, Ellie. I hope you understand." I press my lips into a firm line.

It's selfish. Silly, even. But the last time I went to that festival, I faced the worst tragedy of my life. My entire world was upended and shattered into millions of tiny little pieces that night, and I can't bring myself to ever go to the last place I saw my sweet Henry alive.

Her face falls, taking my heart with it. "Of course."

"But you should still go," I insist, forcing a smile. "Maybe afterward, you can all come by for some hot chocolate?"

"Sure," she concedes, her voice small.

"So, has Lindsey said anything else about the firefighter?" I ask in an attempt to change the subject.

She shakes her head. "Not since Thanksgiving."

Rats. I can't help the face I make.

Okay, maybe I was asking because I actually wanted to know.

"It'd be nice to see Lindsey get back out there, wouldn't it?" I ask.

Ellie gives me a polite nod. "It would," she says, rising to her feet. "Well, I should get to work. I have some emails I need to catch up on."

I know I'm like the Grinch, Ebenezer Scrooge, or some equally awful holiday fun-hater, but I can't go back to that festival.

"Ellie?" I say her name so quietly I'm not sure she'll hear me.

"Yes?" She turns around, her eyes wide.

There are so many things I want to say, but the words get lodged in my throat. "Thanks again for the coffee."

A shadow falls across her face as she forces a smile and leaves my office, pulling the door shut behind her.

My heart sinks, and the corners of my eyes burn. I take a sip of my latte, but apparently, the coffee isn't hot enough to thaw the ice around my cold, dead heart.

LATER THAT EVENING, I FOLD MY LEGS BENEATH ME LIKE A pretzel on the couch and prop my laptop on a pillow in my lap. My fingertips click across the keyboard, typing *Loving Fire Department* into the search bar.

"Let's just see about this firefighter," I say to myself as I reach for my wine on the table beside me.

When the page loads, I scroll until I see pictures from the department's recent food drive. There are several uniformed men and women in the photos—a couple of the guys look like they could be Lindsey's grandfather, and I certainly wouldn't describe them as "hot"— but further inspection reveals a few possible contenders. There's a blond with beefy arms that looks like he could be in that Thunder from Down Under show Rose dragged me to years ago, and a man with whiskey-colored hair and an upturned nose who doesn't strike me as Lindsey's type. Not that I know much about what that is these days.

The captions don't reveal any names, so I continue my scrolling, hoping to see Oliver jump out at me. I pass posts about their annual Trunk or Treat, and I'm watching a short video of them riding in the Loving High School homecoming parade when my phone rings from beside me.

I don't even have to check the screen to know it's Rose doing her nightly check-in, so I swipe and put her on speaker.

"Well, are you still breathing?" she asks before I can even manage to say hello.

I click on a photo from the department's presentation at the high school about the dangers of drinking and driving. Again, some very attractive people, but no one I think would have elicited the glow on my daughter's face when we spoke about him. Lindsey doesn't get excited about just anyone. Whoever this guy is has to be some kind of Prince Charming, and none of these men fit the bill.

"If I wasn't, do you really think I'd be answering the phone? I'm just having some wine." I swirl it in my glass, clicking the trackpad to enlarge another picture.

"What are you doing, Myra Jean?" Her voice burns like an interrogation lamp. "I hear you over there tapping away on that damn computer. You know that thing will rot your brain."

"If you must know, I'm trying to see what I can find out about this Oliver fellow."

"In that case, proceed. Have you found anything yet?"

"Not really. A couple of possibilities, but nobody who—" I stop midsentence when I see him. He's got warm brown eyes and dark hair that's just unkempt enough to tell me he doesn't take himself too seriously. His smile is kind and framed by the tiniest scar above his upper lip. I read the short post that accompanies the picture: *The Loving Fire Department is pleased to welcome Oliver Beckett to the crew.*

"Myra Jean," my sister says. "Did you find him?"

"Yes, I did, and he's cute too."

"A handsome firefighter." She sighs into the phone. "Isn't that the dream? Makes a girl want to fall and not be able to get up, if you catch my drift. Or maybe set a small fire. Not a big one, though, just enough to—"

"That's brilliant."

"Isn't it?" she asks, and then quickly adds, "Wait. What is?"

I snap the laptop shut and plop it on the cushion beside me.

"I want to meet this guy, Rose," I say. "Didn't you see Lindsey? How happy she looked? I think there could be something special about this one, but I want to see for myself. I'll stage a little fall. It's a small department, so the chances of him coming on the call are high, and if he's really as great as he sounds, maybe I can—I don't know—give Lindsey a little nudge in the right direction."

"That's a terrible idea," Rose trills in my ear. "There are about a million and one reasons why this is a disaster waiting to happen. Not to mention *highly* illegal. Besides, you're a *terrible* actress." She sputters out a laugh. "Remember when you tried to tell the kids their goldfish went to live at SeaWorld?"

I do. They were so insistent upon calling SeaWorld to ask Goldie to come home that I finally had to come clean and tell them their beloved fish had made her final voyage straight down the toilet. The kids were traumatized for weeks.

"Come on, Rose. You saw how excited Lindsey was. She

deserves to find someone who loves her—to settle down and be happy. She needs this, okay? *I* need this."

Rose clicks her tongue. "You know you shouldn't meddle in the affairs of others."

"That's certainly never stopped you before," I say, and I can practically hear the smile that forms on her lips.

"Well, if we're doing this, we're going to do it right," she says finally. "In a way that doesn't land us both in the slammer for Christmas. I don't think my book club friends will understand when I send out a card that says, 'Merry Shivmas.'"

"With the stuff y'all read, I think they might. Didn't you read some prison-themed romance last year?"

"Oh, shut up," she says. "When are we doing this?"

"*We?*" I ask. "What do you mean *we*?"

"You didn't think I'd let you have all the fun, did you?"

"Fine, but how are we going to meet him, since you vetoed the fall idea?"

"The old-fashioned way," she says. "With baked goods. 'Tis the season to take our first responders some delicious goodies to show our gratitude, don't you think?"

"Yes! Of course!" Something sparks in my chest, like a pilot light being turned on for the first time in years. "So, when are we doing this thing?"

"I'll meet you for lunch Wednesday, and we'll take them to the fire hall." I can practically see her rubbing her fingers together like the evil genius she is. "And tomorrow night, we bake!"

Rose arrives at my house a little after six Tuesday evening to find me in the kitchen, already working on the brown butter brownies.

"I've got good news." Rose smiles as she helps herself to a cookie from the jar on the counter in the kitchen. "Oliver *is* working tomorrow."

"What? How do you know?"

"I posed as Sharlene from *The Loving Herald*," she says in a thick southern accent through a mouthful of snickerdoodle. "Said I was doing an introductory piece on the new hire and asked if I could schedule a time to speak with him tomorrow."

I gasp. "You didn't."

"I most certainly did." There's a mischievous glint in her forest green eyes as she reaches her hand, adorned with red-lacquered nails, back into the jar. "The receptionist tried to grab him for me tonight, because apparently he was there."

"Did you *speak* to him?" We haven't even put our plan into motion, and already she's blowing our cover.

She waves her hand as though she's swatting away a fly as she dawdles over to the fridge, in search of a drink. "No, of course not. I hung up when they put me on hold."

I'm starting to get anxious. So anxious that when I move to take the butter off the stove, I trip over my own feet, sending the majority of the butter sloshing over the side of the pan and onto the floor.

I toss the pot onto the counter and crouch to dig some cleaning supplies from the cabinet under the sink. "Rose, can you grab me some more butter," I ask over my shoulder. "And don't step over here, all right? I spilled the—"

Rose's scream pierces the air, followed by a loud thud. I nearly give myself a concussion whipping my head out of the cabinet.

"Rose!" I shout. "Are you okay?"

I turn to find my sister on the floor, turned toward me on one side, moaning like a whale.

"Oh my God, Rose!" I rush to her side and help ease her onto her back.

She starts to slowly move one limb at a time, stopping with a yelp when she gets to her left foot.

"I can't move it," she mutters through gritted teeth. "I think it's broken. You've got to call for help."

"Don't move," I say, rising to dig my phone out of my purse on the counter. The adrenaline pumping through me makes me so jittery that the damn thing nearly slips from my hand. I pause mid-dial and gasp. "Oh my God, Rose, what if Oliver comes?"

"Great, I hope he does," she hisses. "You can interview him while he peels my ass off the floor."

"Right. Sorry," I say. I dial 911, and the dispatcher answers on the second ring.

"911, what's your emergency?"

"Um, hi. Yes." I clear my throat. "I need help. Well, it's not me. It's my sister. She's fallen, and she can't get up."

Rose throws her hands up. "God, I'm the old lady in the infomercial."

The sound of clicking on a keyboard comes through the phone. "Okay. Does it appear that she's broken anything?"

"Woman down!" Rose cries. "I need some help here!"

"Her left foot looks pretty swollen," I say into the phone. "I'm scared to try to move her."

"It's best not to move her as long she's stable." *Stable? I definitely wouldn't say that.* "Let EMS take a look at her first. Where did she fall?"

"In the kitchen," I answer. "She slipped on some butter."

"I always knew food would be my downfall, but I never thought it would happen like this." The blue vein in Rose's forehead throbs, and she covers her face with her hands.

The dispatcher must hear her because I swear he stifles a chuckle. "All right. I just need to get a little more information from you."

I give him our names and my address before disconnecting the call. "They're on the way."

"This is all your fault, you know," she hisses. "You brought this plague upon our house when you suggested staging a fall. This is karma."

I don't remind her that *she* was the one who'd planted that idea in my head to begin with.

Less than ten minutes later, the sound of sirens in the distance grow closer. Rose is sprawled on the floor between the kitchen island and the stove with her arms splayed out.

I run to the window in the living room to peek outside, and my heart lurches into my throat when the source of the sirens comes into view.

"Rose!" I snap the curtains shut and hurry back to the kitchen. "I think the whole damn fire department's here. There's two fire trucks *and* an ambulance. And the fire marshal!"

"Dear God," Rose wails. "How do I look?"

A pounding on the door startles us both.

"Shit!" I shake out my hands and rush back to the door, flinging it open. There on the front stoop is the fire marshal flanked by two other firefighters in their department-issued T-shirts—one of whom is Oliver.

"Hi. She's in the—"

A strangled moan worthy of the Ghost of Christmas Past filters in from the kitchen.

"Please," I say. "Follow me."

I lead them to the kitchen where Rose is flopping around like a fish that's washed ashore.

"Help me," she cries out in a voice that falls somewhere between a squawk and a breathy Marilyn Monroe. "Please! Help!"

I clamp my lips together to stifle the nervous laughter bubbling in my throat and instead focus on Oliver, who's surveying the scene.

"It seems you've gotten yourself into a bit of a pickle." The fire marshal kneels beside her, and Rose responds with a groan as she writhes around on the floor.

"I'm like a cow that's been tipped over," she says, touching the back of her hand to her forehead, like a damsel in distress.

"Don't worry. We'll get you right side up in no time." The fire marshal pats her on the shoulder and turns to look at Oliver. "You want to take the lead on this one, new guy?"

"I'd be honored," Oliver drawls.

"I'll send everyone back to the station and wait outside for you fellas. I don't think you need everybody for this one," the fire marshal says, giving me a nod before leaving the kitchen.

"Young man," Rose says, reaching for Oliver's hand and holding on for dear life when he crouches beside her.

"Yes ma'am?"

"Please call me Rose," she insists. "Do you think I'm going to make it?"

"You'll be just fine." His lips quirk at the edges, and he chuckles softly before addressing the other remaining firefighter. "Martinez, you want to get on Miss Rose's other side?"

"Miss Rose," my sister echoes. "You make me sound like royalty."

"A royal pain in the ass," I mutter, and Oliver sputters a laugh.

Rose, on the other hand, is less amused. "Myra Jean, I'm wounded."

"Yes, yes," I say. "I'm sorry."

I watch with amusement as Oliver and the Martinez fellow discuss strategy for how to get my sister right side up, and I push one of the dining chairs into the room. A few moments later, Rose is in the chair, and Oliver has filled out an incident report and checked her vitals.

"I do think you should take her to the emergency room for an X-ray. She could have fractured that foot," Oliver says to me before turning to Rose. "But other than that, I think you're going to be just fine."

"That's all thanks to you," she says, squeezing his arm. "You gentlemen saved me."

"Martinez, grab the transport chair for me, would you?" Oliver asks his colleague, then looks at me. "We'll help you get her loaded in the car safely."

"Sure thing," Martinez says, disappearing outside.

"Did I hear the fire marshal say you're the new guy?" I ask, leaning against the counter.

He nods. "New to the department, not new to being a firefighter. I moved here from Texas a couple of months ago."

"Is that right?" I smile. "Do you have family here? A girlfriend, perhaps?"

"No girlfriend," he answers politely, but there's a flicker in his eyes, like lightning in a storm cloud. "And no family here, either."

"That's a shame," Rose says.

I fiddle with the chain of my necklace. "How are you liking Loving?"

"I like it a lot." His posture is open, friendly. "Everyone is so nice here. I do miss my friends back in Texas, though. I haven't met many people outside of the fire hall."

There it was—my "in." "Well, why don't you come to dinner here on Sunday? I've got three kids about your age. Maybe it would be helpful for you to meet some people outside the fire hall?"

"That's a great idea," Rose chirps from her chair as she stretches her arm to reach the cookie jar on the counter. She finally succeeds and digs another snickerdoodle from the container, shoving it into her mouth.

"Oh, I don't know if I—"

"Besides, we need to thank you for saving my life," Rose says, somehow forming the words around her cookie.

"Exactly," I agree. "It won't be a big to-do. Very casual. And the Titans are playing Sunday afternoon. I've got a big screen that makes you feel like you're on the field."

"It's true." Rose places her hands on her hips. "It's like you're in the huddle."

"Please say you'll come," I add. "It'll be fun. I'll roast a chicken and make some mashed potatoes."

A smile stretches across Oliver's face. "Why not? I love football, and a home-cooked meal sounds nice."

"Wonderful." I clasp my hands together. "Be here at two?"

"Better hurry," Martinez says, rolling a black wheelchair into the room. "Chief just got a call. House fire. We need to roll out."

Oliver transfers her over with ease and starts out the door, while I grab my purse, triple-check that I turned the oven off, and start the car.

Once Rose is tucked safely in the passenger seat of my car, Oliver looks to me. "I better get going, but it was nice meeting you, Myra Jean, is it?"

"Please, call me MJ. So lovely meeting you."

He gives us a polite nod before shutting the door and jogging off toward where the other two men are waiting.

I buckle my seat belt and pull my purse onto my lap. "I should call the kids and let them know." I dig around my bag for a moment, and that's when I remember. "Shit. I left my phone inside. I should go back for it."

"Oh, Myra Jean," Rose says with an exasperated sigh. "Leave it. I'm not dying. You can tell them in the morning."

"Right, sorry," I say, shaking my head. "You're right."

I ease out of the driveway, careful not to jostle Rose around too much.

"I'm so sorry. Are you in a lot of pain?" I ask, just as my tire hits a small pothole.

She winces. "It's okay. It was worth it to see you lose your shit a little."

A hint of a smile tugs at the corner of her mouth.

"Things didn't go according to plan, but I think it went well," I say with a grin. "All things considered."

Rose snorts. "I wouldn't go quite that far. You'll still be in the doghouse when Lindsey finds out you invited him to dinner."

"Hold on a minute. What happened to *we*?"

"*We* left the moment you willed the universe to knock me on my behind."

"Fine," I say. "I'm sure once Lindsey realizes *why* I took such extreme measures, she'll understand."

She'll be so smitten with Oliver that this will be but a minor indiscretion…right?

7

___

LINDSEY

JUNE BUG WATCHES WITH WILD EYES AS I FLUFF THE LIMBS OF my trusty pre-lit artificial Christmas tree in the corner of my living room Tuesday night. The scent of cinnamon and mulled wine wafts from the flickering candle on top of the refinished bookcase beside the tree, making my entire house smell like the holidays.

"Don't even think about it," I say, nudging a stuffed Lamb Chop closer to the pup with my sock-covered foot. Temporarily distracted, she saunters away with her kill wedged between her teeth.

The fire I'd started crackles, casting a soft glow over the room. With June Bug preoccupied, I take the opportunity to open the screen and throw a couple of logs on the fire.

Though the daytime temps are lingering in the upper fifties, at night, it drops to nearly freezing. The colder weather makes my bones feel as fragile as the holly-covered china my mother breaks out for Christmas every year.

I shift the wood with the poker as my phone rings from

the coffee table, so I close the screen and return the tool to the rack before grabbing it.

I smile when I see my sister's name. "Hey."

"So, Mom's really not going to Mistletoe Fest with us next weekend," Lucy says.

"I take it Ellie called you?" I ask. "I'm not surprised. After the way Thanksgiving went, I figured the festival was out of the question."

My sister heaves a sigh into the phone. "I guess I was holding out hope she'd change her mind."

"I know," I say, cradling the phone to my ear as I shuffle to the kitchen to pour myself some spiced cider. "But we're still going to have fun because we'll make it fun for Noah and Emily."

"I guess," she pouts." Anyway, what are you doing?"

I pull down a glass from the cabinet beside the fridge, where I spot my cat hiding beside the insulated bag I use to carry my lunch. "Putting up the tree."

"With the furry hell-raiser there? That's brave."

"Oh, she's fine," I say. "She's been busy playing with her toys and trying to have her way with Catrick Swayze."

"He's never going to forgive you for this, you know."

I open the fridge and pour myself some cider. "Santa's going to be extra good to him this year. New catio and some of those catnip treats he loves that make him act like a stoned college kid listening to *The Dark Side of the Moon* for the first time. I'll even get him a pony if it'll make him happy."

"I'd stick with the cat weed if I were you. I'm not sure he'll allow you to bring another animal around ever—"

A loud crash makes me jump, sending my drink sloshing over the edge of the glass.

"What was that?" Lucy asks as June Bug's shrill bark

pierces the air. A half second later, she appears in the doorway, her paws skittering across the hardwoods as she barrels toward me, whining.

"What happened, girl?" I chuck the glass in the sink and scoop the dog into my arms. "Are you okay?"

"What's going on over there?" Lucy asks.

"I don't know yet." My mind races with possibilities. Did something fall down the chimney? What if someone broke in? What if someone broke in *through the chimney*?

I gulp and take a deep breath, and my heart sinks. It's as though someone has turned up the subtle smoke smell that usually comes from my fireplace. "Oh no. No, no, no, no. June Bug, please tell me you didn't."

"What? Lindsey? Hello?"

With June Bug clutched to my chest, I sprint to the living room, confirming my fears. The Christmas tree has toppled over, which must have knocked the candle off the bookshelf, and flames are starting to crawl up the wall from the floor.

"Fire!" I shriek and run back to the kitchen to find the fire extinguisher that has gone unused since I bought my house seven years ago.

Lucy gasps. "What? Oh my God!"

Do fire extinguishers expire? How long would it take me to Google that? Shit. I don't have time for this.

"Lucy, call 911," I manage, my voice shaking. "I have to try to put this thing out."

"But you need to—"

"Do it! Now!" I throw my phone on the counter and dive for the cabinet below the sink, flinging open the doors as the smoke alarms start to screech their warning. Catrick Swayze yowls his displeasure from his perch on top of the fridge.

June Bug yelps as I stuff her into my hoodie before grabbing the extinguisher, desperately trying to recall the fire safety stuff I'd learned in elementary school a billion years ago.

An eerie sense of calm washes over me, and within seconds, it's over. The charred tree and the floor are covered in white powder, and the air is thick with smoke.

I cough, and June Bug wriggles inside my hoodie. "Settle down, Firestarter. We've got to get Catrick Swayze and wait outside."

MOMENTS LATER, I'M STANDING OUTSIDE WITH LUCY AND Willow as the fire department, including Oliver, finishes up. Willow had the forethought to bring a carrier, in which Catrick Swayze is currently contained, while June Bug trembles in my sister's arms.

"You really think she knocked the tree down?" Lucy asks. "She's like, two pounds."

"Two pounds of pure terror," I mutter, massaging my temples. "But really, it's my fault. I shouldn't have had a candle lit that close to the tree while she was here."

"Don't beat yourself up over it. Accidents happen," Willow says as Oliver exits my front door. The sight of him casually walking out of my sanctuary makes my insides jiggle like they're in a cocktail shaker.

"You really did catch it early," Oliver says, placing a hand on my arm, sending whatever concoction that's been brewing splattering against the walls of my heart. "Are you sure you're okay?"

"A little shaken up," I admit. In more ways than one. "But I'm okay."

He nods, but his gaze lingers on me. "Well, we're finished up here."

I rub my fingers along my arms in an attempt to hide the shiver his touch left behind. "Thank you. Now I can get these animals inside and get some sleep."

"Oh, you won't be able to stay here tonight," Oliver says. "Probably not for…several nights."

"What?" I ask, trying to mask the panic in my voice. "Why not? I thought it wasn't that bad."

"It wasn't," he says. "At least not compared to what it could have been, but you're still going to have some damage. You'll need to have some boards replaced in the floor and some drywall. But more importantly, you're going to need some smoke mitigation done before you can stay here. Do you have somewhere you can go while you're dealing with the insurance adjusters?"

Willow puts an arm around my shoulders. "She'll stay with us."

"Are you sure?" I ask. "Maybe I should see if I can get a room at the Magnolia Inn. It sounds like it could be a while, and I don't want to put y'all out for that long."

Lucy scoffs. "You most certainly will not go to the inn. You'll be staying with us, and that's that."

"Okay. Thank you," I relent, waving my white flag. "Can I at least go in and pack up a few things? Is that allowed?"

"Of course," Oliver answers. "I'll go with you. You know, to make sure you're safe."

My forehead scrunches involuntarily. "The place isn't going to spontaneously combust or anything, is it?"

"No, no," he says, "but better to err on the side of caution, right?"

I nod. "We'll be right back."

It's impossible to miss the satisfied look on my sister's face as we turn to go inside.

"So, how many days do you think I should be prepared for?" I ask over my shoulder, the smoke fumes nearly knocking me over as I cross the threshold.

He hesitates. "Umm…"

"Give it to me straight."

"Normally, I'd say about a month, but with the holidays, things will likely be moving a little slower."

I whirl on my heel. "More than a *month*?"

He winces. "Probably more like two…maybe three, depending on how backed up they are. Your insurance company will have to do an investigation before you can start the mitigation process."

I press the heels of my palms into my eyes until I see stars. "Shit. Okay. *Shit.*" Tears threaten to spill onto my cheeks.

"Hey," he says the word, and then I feel his arms around me. My body tenses for a second because it's been a long time since someone has held me like this. But then my body sinks into his embrace without my permission.

"It'll be all right," he says softly against my ear, sending a shiver through me that collapses my muscles like dominos. "And if there's anything I can do to help, I'm here."

I sniffle, and my gaze meet his for a heartbeat as he gently swipes his thumbs beneath my lashes, as though he'd done so a hundred times before.

Get yourself together, Lindsey. I clear my throat. "This is fine. I'll be fine," I say, withdrawing myself from his grasp.

"I have no doubt you have this under control, but if there's anything I can do to make it a little easier, I'm happy to help.

It's what you do in a small town. You take care of each other, right?"

A smile tugs at the corner of my mouth. "I see what you did there."

"On that note, put me to work. What can I help you with?"

"Do you mind grabbing the stuff for the animals and giving it to my sister? Their food is in the pantry and their bowls are in the kitchen too. Oh, and June Bug's crate and bed are in the corner over there."

He grins. "You got it."

"Thanks," I say. "I'll just be a few minutes."

I run upstairs and dig my suitcase out of my closet and start piling things inside. I'm thankful Oliver can't see me as I take the entire contents of my underwear drawer and dump it in. Once I've got all the clothes, shoes, and pajamas I think I'll need, I head to the bathroom with a duffel and shove everything on the vanity inside before grabbing my products from the shower. I make one last stop at my nightstand to grab my TENS unit and the muscle relaxers I keep on hand for fibromyalgia flare-ups.

About ten minutes later, I'm struggling to drag my bags down the stairs, probably because they're stuffed more than a Thanksgiving turkey.

"Let me get that for you," Oliver says, rushing up to meet me. He lifts the suitcase with ease, which causes me to wonder how easily he could lift *me*.

"Careful with that," I say. "Wouldn't want the bodies to fall out."

He fumbles, nearly missing the last step.

"Are you trying to become an accessory there, Rookie?" I tease, and he flashes a grin over his shoulder. "So, that nickname means you're a new firefighter, right? How long have you been doing this?"

"Almost fifteen years," he answers. "I'm not new to the job, just new to this unit. And in the firefighter world, that makes me a probie."

"Come again?" I stop to grab my purse from the bar that separates the kitchen from the den, making sure my phone is inside before stepping into the dining room to get my laptop from the kitchen table.

"A probie is someone who's new to the department. Basically, it means I do all the grunt work until someone even more new than me comes along. So not only am I a firefighter, but I'm also a chef, a janitor, and I'm a hell of a dishwasher. Comes with the territory."

"Yikes."

"What?" he asks.

"I mean, it's Loving. People aren't exactly moving here in droves. You could be the new guy for...well, a really long time."

"Yeah," he says somewhere between a laugh and a sigh as we step outside and I lock the door. "I know."

"Got everything?" Lucy asks.

"I hope so," I say with a shrug.

"I'll pop the trunk," Willow says, and we follow her out to the car.

Oliver hoists my suitcase inside, and I drop my duffel and purse beside it, next to the supplies he'd gathered before he snaps the trunk closed.

"Crap. Wait. I need to get my purse." I grip my hair at the roots. "My keys are in there. I've got to drive my car."

"We'll come back and get the car after work tomorrow," Lucy says. "You've had a rough night."

"But—" I begin to protest.

"No buts," Lucy insists.

I hold up my hands in surrender. I'm too tired and too cold to argue. "Thank you."

"Now, I'm gonna get this little nugget in the car where it's warm." Lucy holds June Bug's paw up as though she's waving to Oliver, while Willow climbs in the driver's seat.

I pull the sleeves of my sweatshirt over my hands. "Thank you for coming to my rescue. You're getting the reputation of being quite the hero around here."

"To be fair, you did most of the work before we got here," he says with a chuckle. "We just finished it."

"Well, that doesn't make me any less grateful."

"And I meant what I said. If you need anything, I'm happy to help."

"Thanks," I say with a smile.

His brown eyes spark something inside me, and I know I need to get out of here before I start any fires I can't put out.

He opens his mouth to say something, but I beat him to it.

"I guess we should get going," I say. "But seriously, thank you."

His face falls a little, but then he nods and opens the back door of Willow's SUV for me.

"Good night," I say, sliding inside next to a meowing Catrick Swayze.

Oliver's gaze lingers on me for a few seconds, and he opens his mouth as though he's going to say something else. My breath catches in my throat, and the moment passes us by.

"Good night, Lindsey," he says before closing me inside the car.

"So, when's the handsome firefighter taking you to dinner?" Lucy asks no sooner than the door has shut.

"He isn't," I insist. "It's not like that."

Willow snorts. "Maybe not for you, but that man is definitely feeling it."

The darkness conceals the flush creeping onto my neck. "He's not *feeling* anything."

"Oh, but he'd like to," Lucy quips, and she and Willow dissolve into a fit of giggles.

"Okay." I let out an exaggerated sigh. "Knock it off, you two."

"Fine. I'll let it go. For now, anyway," Lucy says, passing her phone back to me. "You should probably call Mom and tell her what happened, though, before she hears it from someone else and freaks out."

"She's going to freak out regardless, but yes, I should." I dial my mom, and it rings several times before going to voicemail.

"Hey, Mom," I begin, "Everything's fine, but there's been a small incident…"

8

———

MJ

I WAKE WITH A START TO THE SOUND OF "GRANDMA GOT RUN Over by a Reindeer" being played at an earth-shattering decibel. My glasses are halfway down my face, which is smushed into my pillow. I sit straight up and wipe my hair out of my face. A string of drool clings to my bottom lip as I push myself up and take in my surroundings. I'm in my bed on top of the comforter with all of my clothes on from the night before and the lights still on.

The room comes into focus when I shove my glasses back up my nose. Where on earth is the music coming from? Am I dreaming? Is this a message from God?

A squawking sound rises above the music, and I swing my legs over the side of the bed so fast I nearly throw out a hip. The memories from hours before trickle in. I got home from the emergency room with Rose a little after 2 a.m. It took me a few minutes to get her settled and comfortable on the couch. The last thing I remember was sitting on the bed to take my shoes off. A quick glance down tells me I was not successful.

The screeching continues, but this time I make out actual

words. "Myra Jean, I'm sixty seconds from peeing my britches!"

"Oh no! Rose! I'm so sorry! I'm on my way," I shout, jumping to my feet and hustling downstairs, gripping the railing as hard as I can. We'll really be up shit's creek if I manage to fall too. "God, where is that music coming from?"

No sooner than I land on the bottom step, the song comes to an abrupt stop.

"What the…" I'm losing my mind. "Did you hear that? Please tell me you heard that too."

I enter the living room to find my sister wearing the night-gown I'd put her in and a smug smile.

"I had to get your attention somehow," she says, already attempting to rise on her own. "It took me half an hour, but I finally figured out how to connect my phone to those fancy Bluetooth speakers the kids got you last year."

"Why do you think I gave you Mama's old dinner bell?" I hiss, rushing to her side.

"I rang the damn bell," she argues as I help her stand. "Do you know how many angels got their wings while I was down here waving that thing around like an air traffic controller? I probably summoned Jimmy Stewart from the dead."

"I'm sorry," I say, securing my arm around her. "I was so exhausted, I must've just passed out."

She winces as we slowly creep toward the bathroom, a crutch on her right side and me on the other keeping her steady. The giant brace on her left foot scrapes the hardwoods with every step.

"The pain's bad, isn't it?" I ask. "I don't even know what time it is. You're probably long overdue for your medication."

"Oh, I'm fine," she says as we make it to the bathroom. "I've felt worse. Remember the time I fell out of the tree trying to sneak back in the house the night Martin Boswell popped my ch—"

"As much as I love listening to you reminisce about the good ole days, can we at least wait till I've had some coffee?"

"I've got it from here," she says, easing herself onto the toilet. "I'd like to keep a shred of dignity."

"Too late," I reply with a grimace.

If she hears me, she chooses to ignore me. "Go make the coffee. We have a lot of ground to cover on this trip down memory lane. Like the time Bart Sanders handcuffed me to—"

"Can't wait," I mutter under my breath, closing the door behind me before she can finish. I trudge into the kitchen on autopilot to prepare the coffee. The clock on the wall lets me know it's a little after 7 a.m.

I still haven't called the kids to fill them in on what happened, and I was so tired when we got in that I didn't even think about it. My phone catches my eye from the counter while I wait for the machine to brew, and I pick it up to dial Lindsey when I see I already have a voicemail from her.

"You still good in there?" I call out to my sister.

"Yep," she shouts back. "Need another minute."

I cradle the phone between my ear and my shoulder, pulling mugs from the cabinet as the message starts to play. I'm half listening until I hear the word *incident*.

Within thirty seconds I'm in hysterics, and I practically carry Rose back to the couch, blubbering as I tell her what happened. I try Lindsey, Lucy, and Willow, to no avail, as I give Rose her coffee, a muffin, and her pain medicine.

"Lindsey, this is Mama, honey," I say on my third voicemail two minutes later. "Please call me back. I'm worried."

"What are you waiting for?" Rose asks, shooing me with her hand. "Go! Go check on her!"

"I can't leave you here like this."

She rolls her eyes. "You're not fleeing the country. I'll be fine."

I nod and scramble back to the kitchen for my purse. "Don't try to get up on your own. You have to promise me you won't."

"I won't."

"Rose, I mean it," I say, pausing on my way out the door. "You cannot move."

"Dammit, woman," Rose snaps around a mouthful of muffin. "Will you just go already?"

"I'll be right back." The front door shuts behind me, and within seconds, I'm on the road.

"You know I appreciate this, but it really wasn't necessary," Lindsey insists as I help her up the stairs and into the room she grew up in with her bags and Catrick Swayze later that evening.

"Nonsense." I place the cat carrier and a duffel bag on the floor. "This will be much better than staying on the sofa at Lucy and Willow's. Especially with your fibromyalgia. You need somewhere comfortable to rest."

She wheels her suitcase to a stop. "I can still stay at the inn or get a temporary rental. The insurance adjuster said they'd cover it."

"It's the holidays. Everything will be booked," I say, though I don't know that for certain. All I know is I want my daughter here. I want to take care of her. "It'll be like old times. We can make cocoa and watch movies and put up the tree together. You can keep me from strangling your aunt. It'll be great."

"Poor Aunt Rose. I still can't believe she fell. You two have had a rough twenty-four hours."

"So have you."

"And you're sure you don't mind the cat being here?" she asks. "Lucy offered to keep him *and* June Bug, but I think she's going to have her hands full with that one and her own dogs. I can take Catrick Swayze to work with me during the day if you'd rather."

"I don't mind at all," I promise. "There's no need to cart him back and forth. I've already cleared a place for his litter box in the laundry room. Hopefully he can get settled in here, and so can you. There are fresh sheets on the bed, and I put that old afghan of your grandmother's that you used to love over the quilt because I know you get cold at night. Is the temperature okay in here? I can turn the heat up or I can bring you the electric blanket."

"No, it's perfect. Thank you, Mom." She gives me a small smile. "It's nice to be home."

"Oh sweetie," I say, pulling her into my arms, the corners of my eyes stinging. "It's so good to have you here. And I owe you and everyone else an apology. I'm sorry for how I behaved on Thanksgiving. It's been hard for me to think about doing things differently because the old ways connect me to your father and a lifetime of happy memories." I pull back and smooth my hand over my daughter's hair. "But when I got the voicemail from you this morning…it made me realize how silly I was being. What I'm trying to say is, I'm open to discussing it. I might not be ready to make the change this year, but I *am* open to making it."

"I love you, Mom."

"I love you, too."

"Myra Jean," comes the squawk of my sister's voice from down the stairs. "I have to tinkle!"

I squeeze my eyes shut and sigh. "I'll be right there," I call back.

"Remember, she's injured," Lindsey says with a laugh.

"I know," I say through a yawn. "I'll go take care of Rose and let you unpack, but after that I thought I might make a meatloaf for dinner. How does that sound?"

"Mom, you don't need to go through a bunch of trouble. You're exhausted. Why don't we order in Chinese?"

I can practically feel my droopy eyes brighten. "And watch *The Preacher's Wife*?"

It was one of our favorite holiday movies, so much so that we went through at least three copies of the Whitney Houston classic over the years because we inevitably wore them out.

She nods. "You read my mind."

THANKFULLY, THE REST OF THE WEEK PASSES WITHOUT ANY additional disasters or mishaps. With Lindsey and Rose staying at the house, I don't have time to feel lonely or sad because I'm having so much fun. Sure, Rose gets on my nerves on occasion, and I fully regret ever giving her that damn bell, but it's nice feeling like I'm taking care of someone again. Like I'm needed.

Rose is flipping through the channels while we drink coffee on the couch late Sunday morning when Lindsey bounds down the stairs in her scrubs.

"Where are you off to in your work clothes?" I ask. "It's Sunday."

She shrugs on her coat. "One of my clients called and is having a problem with his goat."

"A goat emergency?" Rose says. "What on earth?"

"I'll be back in time for dinner," she promises, lowering herself to plant a kiss on each of our cheeks. "I don't think I've ever looked forward to a family dinner more. With the stress of the fire and dealing with insurance adjusters, I'm beyond ready for some normalcy."

I choke on a sip of coffee as the consequences of my own actions pop up like a jack-in-the-box and sock me right in the nose. This family dinner will be anything *but* normal with Oliver in attendance. How could I have forgotten?

"You okay?" Lindsey asks while Rose eyes me suspiciously.

"Of course," I say, gesturing to my mug. "Yes, sorry. We'll have a good time. Dinner will be great."

"See y'all later," she calls on her way out the door, closing it behind her.

I slam my cup on the coffee table with one hand and grip Rose's knee with the other.

"I forgot we invited Oliver," I blurt out.

After a moment, my sister throws her head back in a rich cackle.

I jump to my feet. "Crap, Rose! We can't uninvite him because that would be rude, and even if I was willing to do that, I don't have his number."

"Sounds like quite the predicament, doesn't it?" she says between fits of laughter.

I pace the floor, my arms flailing at my sides. "Rose, this is serious. What are we going to do?"

"*We?*" My sister flashes me a smug smile. "I don't know what *you're* going to do, but *I'm* planning to sit back and enjoy the show."

"Gee, thanks for the show of solidarity," I say. "What happened to you not letting me have all the fun?"

She points to her braced ankle. "This was the extent of my fun, and I learned my lesson. Guess it's time for you to learn yours too."

I let out a heavy sigh. As much as I hate it, she's right. The only way out of this is through.

9

LINDSEY

"I can't do this anymore," Lucy wails through the Bluetooth on my car as I drive to Mr. Greene's farm. "Our dogs are terrified. This puppy is on another level. She's destroyed every pair of socks we own. She chewed a hole in the wall. *The wall,* Lindsey. How is that even possible?"

"I'm sorry," I say. "My hands are tied. I checked in on Ron this morning, and he said it would be a few more days."

"Willow is going to divorce me."

"You're not married yet," I say with a chuckle.

"And if this dog stays here one more day, I never will be," she pouts. "How's Ron doing, anyway?"

"He sounded like he was in better spirits," I answer. "But I know he misses June Bug and can't wait to have her home."

"That makes two of us," she mutters.

"Listen, I'll ask Kayla if she'd be willing to help, but it'll have to wait till later because I'm almost at the farm."

"Maybe Mr. Greene could use her to keep the goats in line."

I chuckle. "I'll see you at dinner."

"Fine," she says, but I can hear her smile through the phone as I end the call.

I turn onto the long gravel drive that leads to Mr. Greene's farm, winding up a wooded hill. Once I hit the clearing, I gasp. The three-story home and rustic barn come into view, but they're not what catches me off guard. Parked alongside Mr. Greene's worn pickup with the attached trailer is a fire truck. And there, on top of the roof above the second floor balcony, is a very pregnant goat.

I park and head up to where Mr. Greene is standing amongst a handful of firefighters, yelling obscenities up at the animal who looks down, unimpressed.

"Hey, Mr. Greene," I say as I approach.

He turns to greet me, but I barely notice because I catch a glimpse of another familiar face: Oliver.

"Well, look who it is," Oliver says with a smile that could melt ice caps.

"Dr. Haggerty, thank goodness you're here," Mr. Greene says. "The kids left the back door cracked again, even though I've told 'em over and over again to make sure it shuts behind them when they come inside," Mr. Greene explains around the toothpick he has wedged between his teeth. "Anyway, me and the missus was out tending to the chickens when we heard our youngest, Bobby, screamin' bloody murder because Agatha showed up outside his bedroom door. The sound must've startled her, 'cause she somehow managed to push through the window to the roof before I could get inside."

I cock my head and study Agatha, who is pressed against the shutters of the third story window.

"So, I called you and the fire department because I didn't know what to do," Mr. Greene continues. "We tried to lure her back in the house, but she wasn't having it."

A firefighter with bronze skin, whom I recognize from the day Ron fell ill, speaks up. "I say we just go up on the ladder and carry her down."

"That won't work, Martinez." Oliver shakes his head. "You'll spook her, and she could fall off."

"Then what do you suggest, Probie-Wan Kenobi?" Martinez quips, folding his arms over his broad chest.

"I've got to admit, this never happened back in Texas." Oliver turns to me. "You have any ideas?"

I chew my lower lip for a moment, lost in thought as I weigh our very limited options.

"I don't know," I say, "but we need to act fast because I'm pretty sure she's in labor."

"How can you tell?" Oliver asks.

I gesture toward Agatha with my head. "Look how crooked her tail is and how prominent her hips are. That tells me the kid has dropped into the birth canal. And you see the way she's kind of hugging the side of the house? She's probably experiencing some contractions. Goats tend to pull away and hide when those start up."

Mr. Greene turns to me. "What should we do?"

I glance back at the rig, where the engine is still running, before catching Oliver's eye. "You can make that thing into a crane, right?"

A flash of confusion passes over his face before his mouth settles into a knowing smile.

"I like the way you think," Oliver says, leading me toward the truck. "Come on. I'll get the sling."

Moments later, I'm on the roof with a bucket of feed, speaking to Agatha in soothing, hushed tones.

"It's gonna be okay, girl," I say to her as the crane inches toward where I'm standing. The ropes and hooks swing slightly in the breeze.

I harness Agatha in the sling, making sure to keep the pressure off her belly. Though she doesn't love me poking around as I hook her up, she seems to sense I'm there to help and allows me to continue.

Once the rig is close enough, I fasten the sling to the rope, pulling to make sure it's secure.

"We're ready," I call down to Oliver, who gives Martinez the go-ahead. In a matter of seconds, Agatha is lifted into the air and placed gently on the ground. She bleats her displeasure as Oliver dashes to unhook her, and she darts toward the barn no sooner than the harness hits the ground.

I ease myself back through the window and rush downstairs to the sound of cheers from the rest of the firefighters and Mr. Greene's neighbors who have now gathered in the yard to watch the spectacle.

"That was incredible," Oliver says, meeting me at the bottom of the front porch steps with open arms. It's the second time this week I've found myself in his embrace, and I'm afraid I like it a little too much. "*You* were incredible."

The way he lowers his voice so that only I can hear him stirs something deep inside me and causes me to take a step back.

"You guys did great too," I say with a tight smile. "But I should go check on Agatha."

"You want me to help you with—" Oliver starts to offer his assistance, but I cut him off.

"I've got it from here. Thanks."

"Hey Rookie, don't you have somewhere to be?" Martinez asks Oliver as I start toward the barn.

I don't hear his response, but I glance back just in time to see the doors to the rig close with him inside.

LUCY RACES OUTSIDE TO MEET ME AS I TRUDGE UP MOM'S sidewalk after getting back from the farm Sunday afternoon.

"Sorry I'm late," I say, glancing back at the unfamiliar pickup parked on the street in front of the house. "Mr. Greene's goat was on the roof, and then she went into labor."

"I've been trying to call you," she shout-whispers.

"Did I mention I was dealing with a pregnant goat on a roof?"

She runs up the stairs and blocks the door. "Before you go inside, I need to tell you something, and I want you to know that Willow and I had nothing to do with it."

I narrow my eyes at her. "Did you guys try to bring up Mistletoe Fest again? Y'all know that's a bad idea."

"Trust me, I wish that's all it was." A nervous laugh bubbles out of her. "No, it's something else. Or rather *someone* else that's joining us for dinner."

"There's nobody Aunt Rose could invite to a family dinner that would surprise me," I say. "Her ability to shock me went out the window when she showed up to my birthday brunch with that Elvis impersonator."

I start to push past my sister, but she grabs my arm. "I'm pretty sure this isn't Aunt Rose's guest."

I study her worried expression, and then it hits me all at once. "Oh my God. Does Mom have a date in there? She does, doesn't she?"

Why didn't she say something earlier? I've been staying with her for days and she hasn't uttered a word about it. Maybe she felt it best to wait until we were all together, but still, I'm hurt she didn't give me a heads-up.

Lucy opens her mouth to speak, but I maneuver around

and head toward the sound of laughter in the kitchen. I can't say I didn't hope that our mother would date again, but I expected there would be some sort of conversation about it first.

I enter the kitchen to find my mom in full Martha Stewart hosting mode, laughing with none other than Oliver while the rest of my family looks on in amusement.

My mouth is frozen in an *O*, and Oliver's gaze snags on me, looking almost as stunned as I do.

"Come on, kids." Ellie's voice is an octave higher than normal. "Let's go to the playroom."

She and Willow herd Noah and Emily out of the room, tossing worried glances back in my direction.

"Oh good, you're here!" My mother's smile falters as she dashes to my side and slides her arm around me. "Oliver, this is my oldest daughter, Lindsey. Lindsey, this is Oliver."

Lucy steps in warily behind me as Oliver crosses the tile floor to greet me. Ben leans against the counter, his eyes wide and his hand covering his mouth.

"Yes," Oliver says, his eyes sparkling like a moonlit lake. "We've already met. In fact, we were just on the same call at Mr. Greene's farm."

"Well, isn't that something," Aunt Rose says from where she sits in the rolling office chair we'd put her in to help her get around. She pokes a cookie in her mouth, holding the jar in front of her like a shield.

"Um…hi." My cheeks are on fire, I am on fire, and *the entire room is on fire*. "It's good to see you again but, um, what…what are you doing here?"

Oliver opens his mouth to answer, but my mom jumps in.

"You two know each other?" Her voice has turned to

molasses, which is one of the tells my mother is lying. "What a small world. Isn't it, Rose?"

"It sure is," Aunt Rose mumbles, reaching her hand inside the Tiffany blue porcelain container.

My mom places her hands firmly on my shoulders, as if she's Vanna White and I'm the prize she's presenting.

"You see," she says, "when I called the fire department the other night to help Rose, it was Oliver here who saved the day. He mentioned he was new in town, and I suggested he come over for dinner, both as a thank-you and to meet some young folks his age."

I smile at Oliver. "That's my mom. She's big on southern hospitality." *And absolutely, certifiably insane.*

My brother clears his throat. "Listen, Oliver, would you mind coming and talking to the kids for a second? Noah is obsessed with firefighters. You're like a rock star to him. He's going through this phase where he doesn't want to eat his vegetables. I know this is probably a weird request, but maybe it would help if—"

"If he knows firefighters get big and strong by eating their broccoli?" Oliver asks, completing the thought with a chuckle.

"Exactly," Ben says as he leads Oliver out of the room, but not before he throws one last wide-eyed glance at me over his shoulder.

Lucy gestures after them. "I'm just gonna…" She trails off before scampering from the room.

"Are you feeling okay? You look flushed," Mom asks. "Rose, doesn't she look flushed? Is your fibromyalgia acting up, sweetheart?"

I swat her arm. "No, it's not. What is the matter with you?"

"What?" My mom presses her palm to her chest.

"I expected better than this from you."

Aunt Rose snickers as she pulls a glass off the counter and fills it with chardonnay. "Well, *that* was your first mistake."

"I know how this looks, Lindsey," my mom says with a casualness that tells me she, in fact, does *not* know how this looks. "But maybe this can be an opportunity for you and Oliver to get to know each other better."

"Did it ever occur to you that I would prefer to do that on my own terms?" I whisper loudly. "You are off your rocker!"

Aunt Rose shrugs. "I tried to tell her."

"Oh, don't act like this wasn't at least partially your idea," I hiss before turning back to my mom. "This is wildly inappropriate."

She squeezes me around the shoulders. "Honey, I was only trying to help. I *know* you, okay? And if left to your own devices, I was afraid you'd never give this Oliver fellow a fair shot. I just want you to be happy."

I push my fingers through my hair and blow out a breath. "I realize the boundaries in this family get a little fuzzy sometimes, but you have *got* to stay out of my personal life."

"I'll ask him to leave if that's what you want," Mom says.

I squeeze my eyes shut. It's not what I want, but I don't want to give her the satisfaction of telling her so.

"No," I finally say. "But only because you'd look like a lunatic, which would, in turn, make me look like one."

"The apple never does fall far from the tree." Aunt Rose raises one perfectly painted-on brow.

"I'm going to go upstairs and change real quick," I say, attempting to soften the scowl on my face.

Mom grabs the bread basket from the counter. "Don't be long, sweetie."

"I won't," I say, bounding up the stairs.

I'm glad to see Oliver, even if I'll never admit it to my mother. But she has to learn it's not okay to interfere in my life.

I smile to myself, a plan already forming in my mind. I whip my phone out of my pocket and fire off a text to Lucy, even though she's just downstairs.

I think I figured out how to get June Bug out of your house.

The bubbles pop up almost instantly.

Say less. What do you have in mind?

I shut the door to my room and bite back a grin as I tap out my response.

Perhaps Mom could use a furry companion for a few days to fill the free time she's spending meddling in my love life. What do you think?

10

MJ

"Our plan appears to be working," Rose whispers as I pass her the pot I just washed in the kitchen sink.

"*Our* plan?" I ask. "I thought you absolved yourself of all responsibility."

"Well, I did," she says, drying the dish with a towel. "Until I saw how brilliant my idea turned out to be."

Echoes of laughter waft in from the living room, and my heart swells. Lindsey might have been surprised, or even a little upset at first, but from the way she smiled and giggled next to Oliver on the couch, I could tell that any frustration she felt had already melted away.

"He's a good egg, that one," Rose says, reading my mind.

"That he is," I agree, busying myself by scooping toasted hazelnut coffee into the filter and filling the carafe with water.

Oliver is more amazing than I imagined. In fact, I'm not sure I could've found someone as perfect as him if I'd been given the opportunity to handpick a match for Lindsey myself. He's the kind of guy who doesn't just *ask* if he can help with the dishes. Instead, he gets up and starts *doing* them.

When he asks Lindsey questions, you can tell he genuinely cares about her answers and that he's filing the information away for safekeeping.

"Grandma!" Emily's voice tinkles like a bell. "Can I have a cookie?"

I give her tiny cherub cheek a squeeze. "Why don't you let your dinner settle a bit longer and then I'll bring some dessert into the playroom?"

She sighs. "All right."

I turn long enough to pull some mugs from one of the upper cabinets, and in that amount of time, I hear the sound of porcelain scraping and the snickers of two people who think they've pulled one over on me.

""Rose!" I whirl around just as Emily scampers from the room with a fistful of cookies.

"What?" my sister asks, pushing off the cabinets with her good foot, sending the office chair she's sitting in gliding across the room. "Did something happen?"

"You think you're so sneaky."

"Dammit, Myra Jean. You have eyes in the back of your head or something?"

"Of course, I do. I have three kids."

"Let's get back out there." Rose tugs the sleeve of my cardigan. "Things were just getting good."

The coffee maker starts to hiss, and I roll her back into the living room.

"Coffee's on," Rose announces as I wheel her to the love seat, and I take my place beside her, curling my legs beneath me.

"Did you ever play?" Oliver asks Ben, motioning to the football game on the television.

Ben leans forward in the recliner, resting his elbows on his knees. "Nothing more than some pickup games with friends. I did play some soccer in high school, though."

"No kidding? Me too." Oliver's eyes brighten. "What position?"

"Keeper," Ben says. "You?"

"Center fullback." Oliver laughs easily. "But I wasn't very good."

"What about you?" Oliver asks, turning his attention to Lindsey. "Did you play any sports in school?"

She presses her hand to her chest, eyes wide. "Who, me? *Nooo.* I'm not very athletic. In fact, my PE coach in high school requested I sit out because I accidentally knocked him in the crotch with a golf club while he was teaching me how to swing."

"That's my girl," I say with a chuckle, and Oliver laughs.

"You've learned a thing or two since then," Ellie begins. "It's because of Lindsey that the kids had a soccer program this past spring."

"Really?" Oliver angles himself toward Lindsey, and my inner body-language-armchair-expert has a field day. "Is that so?"

Lindsey, ever humble, ducks her head. "It wasn't a big deal."

"Oh, it was," Ben says. "Coach Morgan tore her ACL right before the start of the season, and the rec center couldn't find a replacement on such short notice."

"They thought they were going to have to cancel the whole season," Ellie goes on. "The kids were crushed. So, this rock star stepped in to help with zero knowledge of the sport."

"You should have seen her." Lucy moves forward and looks past her sister at Oliver. "She watched soccer-for-beginners videos at work on her lunch break for two weeks straight."

Lindsey runs her hand through her hair and shakes her head. "It was nothing, really. I saw a need, and I filled it. That's all."

"Well, it meant the world to Noah and Emily." Ellie regards Lindsey with a warm smile.

"Ref Caldwell, on the other hand, was glad when the season ended," Ben says with a laugh. "Lindsey gave him so much hell."

Lindsey throws up her hands. "Um *yeah*, because he *never* called offsides, and why would he when his daughter was playing for the other team? Nepotism at its finest."

Oliver breaks into a grin. "Please tell me you'll be doing it again next year, because I need to witness this in person."

"Lucky for everyone, Coach Morgan will be taking back her spot next season," Lindsey says.

Lucy blows a puff of air through her lips. "The only person benefiting from your absence is that toad of a referee."

Ben rubs his palms together. "You know, Nashville has their own soccer team now."

"I wanted to go to a game when I first moved here," Oliver says, "but I never did make it."

"We should go when the season starts in February," Ben adds, clearly over the moon to not be the only guy in the fold anymore. "All of us."

"Hell yeah, we should." Oliver turns to Lindsey, his eyes flickering over to her sister and Willow seated on her other side. "Would y'all be up for that?"

Rose and I exchange wide-eyed glances as we wait for Lindsey's answer. Luckily, we don't have to wait long.

"That sounds fun."

Lucy shrugs. "I'm always down for an excuse to drink overpriced beer."

"Count us in," Willow says.

My heart is overflowing, like the shimmering bows in my Christmas gift wrap organizer.

"And what about you guys?" Oliver turns to me and Rose. "You'll come too, won't you?"

"Of course, we will," Rose answers before I can even attempt to bow out. That's all right—there'll be plenty of time for that.

"It's a shame we have to wait till February. This one" — Lucy pinches her sister's arm— "works entirely too hard. She needs a little fun."

I silently praise my youngest daughter for playing right into my hands.

"She certainly does," I agree. "And then add to that the stress of the fire incident. You really do need a break, sweetheart. You need to get out and blow off some steam."

Warning lights flash in Lindsey's eyes.

Oliver clears his throat. "Well, maybe we could grab dinner together. We could even finish up that town tour we started."

"Oh. Um…" I can almost see her wheels turning to spin out an excuse.

Oliver adds, "I have tomorrow night off."

"I was supposed to get the stuff to make cookies and gingerbread houses with the kids after work, remember?" Lindsey says with a pointed glance in my direction. "They've been looking forward to it."

"Rose and I will do it," I insist. "We'd love to. And this way Noah and Emily will still get to have fun while you go on your date."

Lindsey's cheeks turn pink at the mention of the word *date*.

Oliver peers at Lindsey expectantly. "Well, what do you say?"

Her eyes flash over to mine so quickly it's imperceptible to anyone else but me, and I give her an encouraging nod.

"I'd love to."

I clasp my hands together as my daughter gives me a tight *are-you-happy-now* smile. "It's settled, then."

AFTER THE GAME, EVERYONE IS GETTING READY TO GO HOME when Lindsey and Lucy pull me aside in the kitchen.

"Mom, can we talk to you?" Lindsey asks, and I brace myself for a stern lecture.

"Sure," I answer. "Is everything okay?"

"We need your help with something." Her face is pinched with worry as she tugs on a lock of her milk chocolate hair.

"We're in a bit of a bind," Lucy adds. "It's kind of a big ask, though."

My mind races with possible scenarios. Are they having trouble at the clinic? Do they need money?

"You know I'll do anything I can to help you," I say. "Now, what's this all about?"

Lindsey sighs. "You remember the puppy I was keeping for my client, Mr. Phillips? You met her the other day."

"Oh, June Bug," I say. "She was there during the fire, wasn't she?"

"She was," Lindsey answers.

I remember the little furball. She was curled up, asleep in Lucy's lap, the morning I went to check on Lindsey.

I nod. "Her owner's the man who got sick while he was at the clinic, right?"

"Yes," Lindsey says. "Oliver was there when it happened. That's how we met. He's Mr. Phillips's neighbor. Anyway, it turns out, he's going to be gone a bit longer than anticipated."

Lucy nods. "And she's so tiny and sweet that I'm afraid our dogs might hurt her. They haven't taken too kindly to having their space invaded. Noah and Emily love her. We'd ask Ben if he wasn't—"

"Allergic," I finish for her, the big ask clicking into place. "So, you want to keep the puppy here until this Mr. Phillips gets back."

"Can we, Mom?" Lindsey's eyes are pleading, and it reminds me of all the times she presented her case to me and Henry when she was growing up, begging to adopt whatever homeless, or in some cases, wounded animal she'd found. "Just for a few days. It would be such a big help. We can't really give her the attention she needs while we're at work during the day."

"Of course," I say as Ben comes bounding into the room to place a couple of empty mugs in the sink. "I'd be happy to. I'll work from home for a few days so I can look after her. A puppy would be good company for me."

Lucy smiles. "Oh, she will."

"You're getting a dog?" Ben asks.

"No," Lindsey answers. "Mom has kindly agreed to help me by keeping June Bug until Mr. Phillips gets back."

"Huh?" Ben blinks. "The baby dragon?"

"I, uh, put her in a dragon costume the other day," Lindsey explains quickly. "And she was the cutest little dragon, wasn't she, Ben?" She shares an inscrutable glance with her brother, who tilts his head like a confused Saint Bernard.

"Um, yeah," he says finally. "One might even say *aggressively* cute."

I have to admit, I'm excited. I considered adopting a pet after Henry died, but I knew it'd be yet another loss I'd have to endure one day, so I ultimately decided against it.

"You'll love her," Lindsey adds, squeezing my arm.

"It's a puppy," I say, thrilled that even though my kids are grown, they still look to me for help. "What's not to love?"

11

LINDSEY

"I can't believe Mom still hasn't texted you," Lucy says as she and Kayla file into my office Monday after lunch. "She's bound to have figured out by now that we left her with a puppy grenade."

"Not a word," I say with a shrug as they plop into the chairs across from my desk. "Maybe she got the rowdiness out of her system already."

Lucy shakes her head. "Ain't no way. She's probably holding Mom and Aunt Rose hostage in the garage with their hands and feet bound with tinsel."

Kayla opens a bag of cheese puffs and offers some to Lucy and me. "Forget Rosemary's Fur Baby. I want to know where Oliver's taking you tonight."

I reach my hand across the desk and into the bag of chips, plucking out a handful.

"First of all, he isn't taking me anywhere," I say. "I'm meeting him. Second, I don't know where we're going. I told him I'd show him more of the city. I was thinking I'd take him to a few of the stores in town for some Christmas shopping.

We'll probably grab a burger or something low-key. This is so not a big deal."

Lucy scrunches her nose. "I don't know. I'm pretty sure Oliver thinks it is." She turns to Kayla. "You should have seen him yesterday. It was adorable."

Kayla blows a wisp of her honey-colored hair from her eyes. "I don't get it, Linds. Why are you being so stubborn about this? This guy is awesome and clearly into you. What's the deal?"

"Seriously," Lucy adds. "It's not like you're *not* into Oliver. You get all giggly-wiggly with him. It's cute. A little nauseating, but cute."

I take my time chewing a cheese puff, brushing the orange dust off my hands. They're not wrong. I *do* like Oliver. But I also like the sense of stability I have in my life without any romantic connections. You can't get left at the party if you never show up.

"He's great," I admit. "But y'all, he's a firefighter. I'm not saying he's not extremely brave, but his job is also dangerous. I can appreciate what he does without wanting to be a part of that life."

"What do you mean?" Kayla asks. "It's not like you have to join the department too."

"No," I reply, "but let's say we get together. I would never have a moment's peace while he's working. Part of me would always be waiting for that other shoe to drop, for that phone call telling me something horrible has happened."

"That could happen with anyone, though," Lucy says.

"Don't you think I know that?" I snap and immediately wince. I didn't mean to sound so harsh. "I'm sorry. All I'm saying is, I don't want to take any more risks than I have to. Oliver is lovely, and I'm sure he'll make a great friend."

Kayla and Lucy exchange dubious glances.

Even as the words leave my mouth, I wonder how realistic it is to think we could just be friends. How long would it take for lines to blur and feelings to develop? How long until I let my guard down and share too many pieces of myself, only to find I can never get them back?

"If that's really how you feel, you need to make sure he knows that," Lucy says. "Because he's definitely into you."

"You're right," I say. "Maybe I should cancel."

"Wait a second," Kayla says. "Look, it's just a date. It's not a lifetime commitment. What if you go into the evening without any expectations and see what happens? For all you know, you could find out he has really bad breath or that he braids his leg hair and this will all resolve itself."

"Or maybe you'll realize that some risks are worth taking," Lucy adds.

I open my mouth to protest, but she cuts me off.

"Can you have an open mind about this? Please? Consider it a Christmas gift to me."

I lift my brows. "So you changed your mind on the Taylor Swift vinyls you asked for?"

"I'm serious," Lucy says. "This is what I want. I want you to spend the evening with him, but I want you to be present on this date. No having one foot already out the door. No thinking ten steps ahead and psyching yourself out. Just be in the moment with him, and if by the end of the night you're still not feeling it, I'll never mention him again."

I fold my arms over my chest. "Swear on Taylor Swift's entire discography?"

My sister nods. "Even the ten-minute version of 'All Too Well.' And you know I don't mess around when it comes to Taylor."

It's true. The girl once battled Ticketmaster for nine and a half hours for nosebleed seats and then stood out in the pouring rain with thousands of other Swifties during a four-hour concert.

I throw my hands up. "Okay. Deal."

Lucy and Kayla share a victory high five.

"If you'll excuse me, I need to get back to work so I can leave on time," I say, shooing them from the room.

Kayla bounces. "Leave on time for what?"

"Yes, what's it called again?" Lucy asks, a mischievous sparkle in her eyes.

"My hangout," I answer.

Lucy makes the sound of a gameshow buzzer. "Wrong. Try again."

I huff out a breath. "Fine. My date. Are you happy now?"

Their squeals are my answer as I close the door behind them. If they're excited about tonight, maybe I can give myself permission to get a little excited too.

12

———

MJ

"June Bug, *no*," I say, edging closer to the puppy who has one of my favorite loafers in a choke hold in the living room. "Leave it alone."

She lets out a playful yip, because of course, she thinks this is a game. It doesn't matter to her that this is my favorite pair of shoes or that I haven't been able to find any like them since the early aughts.

"Come on." I take another step toward her, and she hunkers to the ground, raising her cute little butt in the air. "Who's a good girl?"

The puppy pauses to scratch before unleashing a series of excited barks, bouncing around in a circle like a wind-up toy, right on top of my loafer.

"That's right. You are." Another step, and then I snatch up my loafer.

"You know, sister, if I didn't know any better, I'd think you've been bamboozled," Rose calls from the kitchen where she's eating lunch.

"Really, Captain Obvious?" I say, my voice flat. "What on earth gave you that impression?"

June Bug was here about twenty minutes before I realized she was clearly my punishment for meddling. The dog has already managed to pee on my cream-colored rug, leave teeth marks on the leg of my coffee table, and play tug-of-war with my cashmere scarf. But I can't even be mad because Lindsey's going out with Oliver tonight, and that's what matters.

I saw the way she glowed when she talked to him last night. She hasn't smiled like that in far too long, and that's how I know that even if she *is* a little annoyed with me, I did the right thing.

I know my daughter better than she thinks I do. She expected me to call her the second the puppy peed on my rug, while making unusually strong eye contact with me. I'm sure she and Lucy are at the clinic right now, placing bets on how quickly I'll crack so they can tell me that this is what I get for not minding my own business.

They can bet all day long. This cookie isn't going to crumble. Sometimes mother really does know best, and what I *know* is that my daughter's happiness is worth the retribution.

"Listen here, girlfriend." I pick up the puppy. She twists and contorts herself in my hands, reminding me of that scene in *The Exorcist* when Linda Blair's head spins while she's possessed by an ancient demon. I turn her to face me, holding her so we're nose to nose. "I don't care what you pee on or how many things you chew to bits. I'm not calling Lindsey. So, we may as well make the most of this situation and find a way to coexist until your papa gets back. Think we can do that?"

She wags her tail and nibbles my chin.

"You're lucky you're cute," I say, sticking June Bug in her

crate so I can feel safe enough to turn my back for more than three seconds while I get some water and the little rugrat's food.

"I take it this isn't making you want to adopt one of your own anytime soon," Rose says as I enter the kitchen.

"Definitely not."

"So, this is payback for the stunt you pulled," Rose says with a knowing smile.

"We," I clarify. "The stunt *we* pulled. Speaking of, I'll need you to keep an eye on the pup while I go pick the kids up from school."

She nods, chewing quietly for a moment before speaking again. "He really is a sweet guy. Handsome too."

I take a sip of my drink. "He is."

"I think Henry would approve."

A fist tightens around my heart. "Me too," I say, scooping up some kibble from the container Lucy brought with the little she-devil this morning and carry it to the living room where I stop midstep.

The crate door is wide open, and there isn't a June Bug in sight. "Shit."

"What?" Rose calls.

"The little Houdini got out of her crate." I set her bowl down and scan the room. "June Bug! Where are you, you little stinker?" I mutter, looking beneath any piece of furniture she could have hid herself under, which to be fair, is most of what I have.

After having no luck in the den, I check the spare bathroom, the kitchen, and the dining room, but she isn't there either, and it's quiet. Too quiet. I call her name, to no avail, and a pit forms in my stomach. What if she got wedged under something or put her paw in a damn light socket?

Holding my breath, I move to the playroom and immediately let out a sigh of relief. There's June Bug, curled up on a teddy bear, fast asleep. I tiptoe over to where she's snoring softly and scoop her up. She barely stirs as I settle into the rocking chair in the corner of the room. The same chair I rocked my babies to sleep in. It's also where I eventually read *Charlotte's Web* to my grandbabies.

She nestles her sweet face in the crook of my arm, and for a moment, we call a truce.

"Grandma, can I have a snack?" Noah asks as we make our way to the front door.

"Me too," Emily says, bouncing beside her brother.

"Of course," I say, letting the kids inside. "How about you grab some string cheese to tide you over until I order the pizza?"

The children screech as they bound into the kitchen.

"Oh my word," my sister shouts from the living room over a collection of other voices. "Can you believe that?"

"Rose?" I drop my keys into a bowl on the entryway table and head toward the sound of her voice, the bag of gingerbread house fixins' I got at the store clutched in my arm. "Who are you talking—"

I choke on a laugh. Rose is sitting entirely too close to the television in her office chair with the puppy stuffed in her sweater, her little paws hanging over the front. They pry their eyes from an old *Dateline* episode playing at an earth-shattering volume when they hear me snort.

Rose clicks the remote, silencing the TV. "Sorry, we didn't hear you come in."

June Bug wriggles in Rose's ample bosom, and she plucks her out to reveal her teeny-tiny tail twirling in circles.

"Looks like someone is happy to see you," she says, holding her out to greet me.

"Hi, girl," I coo, letting the pup kiss my cheek. "How did she do?"

"She didn't want to sit still while I watched my shows, so I stuffed her in my shirt." She pats her boobs. "These boulders could secure a rottweiler in place."

"That's not weird at all," I say in a tone that lets her know it definitely is.

"It worked, didn't it?"

"Aunt Rose," Noah shouts as he and Emily bound into the room, cheese in hand, to give their great-aunt a hug.

"Hey, kiddos." She ruffles their hair and gives them a squeeze. "Who's ready to make gingerbread houses?"

They screech a chorus of "meeee."

"And we're going to do that very soon," I say. "How about you two go play for a few minutes while I order the pizzas and get set up?"

"Will you play with us, Aunt Rose?" Emily asks, smiling up at Rose with her cherubic cheeks. "We can play princesses."

"Yeah!" Noah pumps his small fist in the air. "I want to be Ariel this time."

"Oh, I don't know." Rose purses her lips, pretending to consider their offer as she always does. It's part of their game. "I'm feeling a bit tired this afternoon."

"Pleeeeeeease," they beg.

"I'm afraid I'm just too tired." Rose gets a mischievous glint in her eyes and crouches down, hooking her fingers into claws. She lowers her voice to a creaky rasp. "But lucky for you, Rosanna the sea witch wishes to feed on the souls of young princesses.”

No matter how many times I've witnessed this exchange, it still makes me laugh every time. The kids shriek with delight and June Bug wags her tail furiously.

“Come, my faithful sea urchin companion,” my sister says, tucking the dog back into her bra. “We must feast. Princesses, please push my boat to the playroom.”

“Don't eat *too* many souls. We'll be having pizza soon.” I chuckle as Rose winks and the kids push her rolling chair out of the room.

I take my bag of goodies into the kitchen and place them on the island along with my purse. I dig in my bag for my phone and pull it out to order dinner. But before I do, I tap out a quick text to Lindsey:

Can't wait to hear about your date! 🩶

13

LINDSEY

"The Curious Heart." Oliver reads the name on the sign above the door aloud as we step inside that evening, the cozy store restoring some warmth to my cheeks. It's getting colder, and every day the ache in my muscles spreads a little wider, and I feel like I'm playing pain Russian roulette. Will this be the day my fibromyalgia rears its ugly head again, condemning me to bed for days on end and making it damn near impossible to think through the brain fog?

"I love this place," I say, pushing the thoughts from my mind as we make the next stop of our extended tour of Loving.

The Curious Heart is decorated for the holidays, but not in the traditional sense. The Christmas tree in the corner is made entirely from books stacked at least six feet high. Sparkly purple garland is strung from the ceiling with quirky ornaments dangling from it. I spot a ceramic disc painted to look like a pepperoni pizza and another designed to look like van Gogh's *The Starry Night*.

"Oh wow." Oliver glances around the cozy space, packed

to the gills with every kind of gift you can imagine and plenty you can't. "This place is incredible."

"It's chaotic in the best way." There's handcrafted jewelry and paintings done by local artists, and a section filled with rare toys. In the middle are racks of vintage clothing and a few costumes.

"Welcome in," the busy clerk greets us with a wave from the checkout counter.

"Hi," I call out, maneuvering around pieces of vividly painted furniture to get to an especially garish nutcracker costume. I pluck it off the rack and hold it up so Oliver can see. "I think I just found the perfect outfit for you."

He raises his brows and lifts the attached plastic package. "It even comes with a mustache."

I stretch out one of the sleeves and try to maintain a straight face. "I think this green would really bring out your eyes."

"Really?" He arches a brow and cocks his head, casting a dubious glance in my direction.

"What? You don't like your nutcracker costume with sequins?"

"Of course, I do," he says with an amused grin. "But the mustache ruins it. Makes it way too over-the-top."

"Oh, *that's* what ruins it?" I plunk the hanger back on the rack with a laugh, and we set off in pursuit of a small tabletop tree with dozens of ornaments attached. I gingerly trail my fingers along a pink unicorn, a hamburger, a turtle with dove wings, and a tiny record player.

"Did you see this?" He shows me one of a gift box with a small puppy inside. "It looks like Ron's dog. How's she doing, by the way? Is she a handful?"

"She's got lots of energy. You know how puppies are." I

leave out the cat humping and penchant for destruction. I don't want him to think I'm complaining. "Maybe I'll get that for him as a little get well present."

He places the trinket in my hand. "I think he'd love that."

I return my focus to the ornaments until I find a tiny fire truck and pluck it off the tree. There's a button on the side that I press, which causes the lights to blink. "Look at this one."

"How cool is that?" He reaches for it, and our hands touch, sending a shiver vibrating through my body. "I should get it for the tree at the fire station."

"It's perfect," I say as we continue browsing.

"What made you decide to become a firefighter, anyway? Was it something you always knew you wanted to do?"

"Yeah, since I was eleven," he answers. "I was actually in Loving when I realized that was what I wanted to be when I grew up."

"Really?"

"I was here with my grandpa that summer, and one night he started having chest pains," he begins. "I got scared and called 911. By the time I heard the sirens coming around the corner, Grandpa had collapsed. His heart had stopped beating. When the firefighters arrived, one of them jumped off the rig and ran inside. He did CPR and ultimately saved his life. Because of that firefighter, I got another ten years with my favorite person."

Tears blur my vision. I know first hand what a beautiful gift time can be and how devastating it is to lose it.

"After that, I just knew I wanted to be like them one day, and now, here I am."

"That's incredible, Oliver," I say, "but don't you ever get…scared? Running into burning buildings and all?"

I picture him bursting through a window to save someone,

flames coiling around him like poisonous snakes. It's admirable and brave, but it's also terrifying. As great as Oliver seems, his job is a hard-line for me. One I won't dare cross. Too many things can happen, even when someone *isn't* putting their life on the line, let alone when they're sprinting toward burning buildings.

"I can't even tell you the last time I saw a big fire. Yours was the first fire call I've been on since I moved here," he says with a shrug. "The majority of what the fire department responds to is medical, *especially* in small towns. Where I moved from was even smaller than Loving."

My mind replaces the image of Oliver surrounded by flames with one of him helping animals stuck on rooftops, little old men who tumbled down the stairs, or women who've gone into labor.

My brows shoot up. "Wait, really?"

He nods. "Before yours, I think the last fire I responded to was a couple years ago on Thanksgiving. This old-timer started a grease fire while frying up his turducken."

"Was he okay?"

"Oh yeah. The turducken, not so much," he says. "Though, if you ask me, those things are weird anyway. They're just so…meaty."

"I think that's kind of the point." I chuckle. "What do you say we check out so we can continue our tour?"

We head outside, and the scent of garlic and simmering tomatoes fills the air as we get closer to the sleek white "Antonio's Cucina" sign.

"Oh wow, that place looks fancy. It smells amazing." He peers into the window, where a few patrons are dining. "You ever been?"

My breath catches in my throat. Antonio's is a sweet little

Italian spot known for its warm, homemade bread and share-able pasta dishes. It has an intimate vibe and is the kind of place that books out months before Valentine's Day.

"I have," I answer. "It's been a while, though." With my ex, Daniel, about a month before my dad passed, and it hadn't exactly gone well. I'd had a rough day at work after having to tell one of my favorite patients that her beloved dog with cancer was out of options. I wanted to cancel our date night, but he insisted we go. When I broke down and cried into my linguine, he told me I was humiliating myself.

I didn't *feel* humiliated. At least, not until he said that.

"How is it?" Oliver asks.

Like an old wound that's been scratched open, visions of Daniel bleed through my mind. The worst of them are the ones where he wasn't present at all. The ones where I was left alone, crying on my bed in the fetal position, during one of the worst times of my life. Just as quickly as the flood starts, though, it stops. My sister's voice and the deal I made with her slap a Band-Aid over the hole in my heart. Tonight isn't about the past.

"Good," I say. With the right company, it could even be great.

"Maybe we can go there together sometime," he says, shoving his hands in his pockets.

"Maybe," I say, and I'm surprised to find I actually mean it. "Speaking of food, there's a really cool place around the corner. How do you feel about nachos?"

He grins. "Are you kidding me? If you don't like nachos, then I'm *nacho* type."

"Wow," I say with a laugh. "How long have you been waiting for the right moment to use that in a normal conversation?"

"Long enough that I should probably be embarrassed by the answer."

"But you're not," I say. It's not a question or a judgment. It's more that I'm…impressed—fascinated by this guy who doesn't take himself too seriously.

"Not even a little," he says with a smile I can't help but return. I like how comfortable Oliver is in his own skin. He doesn't seem concerned about what other people think, and that intrigues me.

We walk the short distance to Chips on the Table, a hole in the wall nacho bar that has shelves filled with every board game under the sun and a wall lined with retro arcade games.

Oliver's eyes widen, and a soft gasp escapes him as we step inside. "No way."

"What do you think?" I ask.

"I think I'm going to kick your butt at some Skee-Ball."

Hands on my hips, I lift my chin. "Game on."

"TABLE SIX," THE CASHIER CALLS, SLIDING A TRAY THE SIZE of a trough onto the counter.

"That's us," Oliver says, jumping up to retrieve our order.

We've already played three rounds of Skee-Ball, which I won before we moved on to the off-road racing game where Oliver proceeded to beat me twice. I enjoyed every second of it. My mind never wandered. My thoughts didn't spiral to all the dark possibilities that have been lurking in my head like shadows. I was having too much fun for that.

After a round of Pac-Man, we decided to stop long enough to order some dinner and drinks.

"These look amazing," Oliver says, placing the mountain of nachos on the table.

My stomach growls, and I reach for a chip piled high with buffalo chicken, tomatoes, onions, jalapeños, cilantro, a drizzle of blue cheese dressing, and of course, lots of melty cheese.

My eyes practically roll back in my head when I take that first bite. "To call these nachos almost seems like an insult. These are more like a religious experience."

He pops a loaded chip into his mouth, then presses his hand to his chest. "Wow. Oh *wow*. These are good."

"They'll definitely ruin all other nachos for you."

"I haven't had one of those in ages," Oliver says, gesturing toward my drink.

"A Shirley Temple?" I ask, and he nods. "I love these things. They remind me of my dad."

"Was that his favorite drink?"

"Yeah," I say with a smile. "He used to make them for me when I was a kid. Whether it was after a bad day or if I was celebrating something like a good grade on a test, he'd make Shirley Temples, and we'd just sit and talk. We called it 'bartender time.' Now I understand it was because bartenders are such good listeners."

"That's sweet," he says.

"When Ben and Lucy came along, he continued the tradition, only sometimes, I was allowed the coveted position of bartender, which I loved. At the time, I thought I was cool because I got to make the drinks, but of course, it was never really about the drinks. It was about the time we spent together, supporting each other on the hard days or celebrating the good ones."

"I love that," he says. "So, what's today?"

"What do you mean?" I ask.

"Is it a good day or a bad day?"

"A good one." My lips curl into a grin. "I mean, how could anyone have a bad day while eating nachos?"

"Ah, so it's just because of the nachos," he teases.

"*Well,*" I say, drawing out the word. "The company's pretty great too."

"Yes!" He pumps his fist in the air before folding his arms on the table and leaning forward. "Okay, I want to learn more about you."

I take another loaded chip. "What would you like to know?"

The adorable crinkles that frame his eyes when he smiles reappear. "Everything."

Before I can register what's happening, he reaches across the table, his finger brushing the corner of my lip. "You have a little something there."

Reflexively, my hand moves to cover the spot he touched, a rush of warmth passing through me, as though I've just had a glass of expensive wine.

"If you were a sandwich, what kind would you be?" he asks.

I snort out a laugh. "I'm sorry—what?"

"I told you, I want to learn about you," he says. "And while knowing things like your favorite color or holiday are nice, they don't tell me a lot about *you.*"

"This may come as a shock to you, but I've never considered this before," I say, resting my chin on my hand. "Are you sure I can't interest you in my favorite color—blue—or my favorite holiday—Christmas?"

"While I do love blue and Christmas, and even 'Blue Christmas,' no. This is important."

I chuckle, then pause to consider the question. "Well, my favorite is ham and cheese."

"But are *you* ham and cheese?" he asks with mock seriousness.

"No," I say, shaking my head. "I don't think so. Ham and cheese is too effortlessly good. It's simple and doesn't feel the need to try too hard. I would be a club sandwich."

"And why's that?" The way he listens intently, eyes focused on me, makes me want him to ask me questions all night long.

"A club has something for everybody. Depending on who you're feeding, you can add or take away as much as you like. It aims to please. A club isn't too spicy or bland, and it's dependable. It'll always fill you up."

"I feel like I need a minute to digest that answer."

"Which is fine, because club sandwiches are easy on the stomach," I say with a grin. "Same question for you. What sandwich would *you* be?"

"Peanut butter and banana."

"And why's that?" I ask.

"It's reliable, sturdy. But it's also got something a little unexpected; something fun."

"Wow, that is wildly accurate."

"But," he says, lowering his voice, "now I kind of wish I was ham and cheese."

"Don't we all," I say, plucking the cherry garnish from my drink, biting the sweet fruit from the stem.

Oliver clears his throat, his eyes traversing down to my mouth. "So, are you going to show me your secret talent?"

"Huh?" I ask.

He gestures toward the cherry stem I'm rolling between my fingers.

My cheeks burn.

"You don't have to," he adds quickly. "Unless, of course, you want to. In which case, please do, because truly, I am fascinated."

I let out a giggle so high-pitched, I don't even recognize the sound as my own.

"Sorry, but that's something I reserve for a third or fourth date," I say.

Oh. My. God. Am I...*flirting*?

"Well, I am nothing, if not committed to the cause," he says with a laugh. "So, any chance you'd let me take you to dinner Wednesday? We could go to Antonio's."

What am I doing? This was *not* part of the plan. This was supposed to be a one and done thing, but there's something so freeing about being in Oliver's presence that makes my heart feel lighter. It's something I haven't felt in...well, ever.

I smile, twirling my straw in my drink. "It's a date."

14

———

MJ

"I wonder if she's having fun," I say to Rose. It's just after 9 p.m., and June Bug is snoozing between us on the couch. My sister has some reality show playing in the background. "Do you think she's having fun?"

Rose is zeroed in on the TV. "I'm sure she is." Her foot is out of the boot, and she's got one flannel-covered leg propped up on the ottoman.

"I hope she's having a good time," I say, taking a sip from my mug of tea. "She must be having a good time, right? She'd be home by now if she wasn't."

"Mm-hmm," she mumbles.

"Where do you think they went?"

Rose huffs and mutes the television. "Myra Jean, how am I supposed to find out if this delicious piece of man candy finds a wife if you won't quit yammering?"

I pull my robe tighter around me. "Aren't you even a little curious?"

"Of course I am, but until Lindsey gets back from her date, there's nothing I can do about it."

I drop my head against the back of the sofa and sigh. "You're right."

"Always am. It's one of my most endearing qualities."

"Yeah, okay." I roll my eyes. "Are you sure you don't want me to get you some ice for your ankle?"

"I told you, I'm fine," she says. "The swelling has gone down a lot, and I'm getting around a lot better. I'm going back home tomorrow."

"You don't think it's too soon?" I ask. "You're welcome to stay as long as you need."

"If I wasn't nosy and dying to find out about Lindsey's rendezvous with the hot firefighter, I would have left today."

I swat her arm. "Gee, thanks."

"Well, it's true. I love you, and I would take a bullet for you," she says, "but I do *not* want to live with you or anyone else. Why the hell do you think I'm single?"

"You do like your space."

I'm glad Rose is feeling better but knowing she's going home tomorrow makes my chest ache. Yes, she gets on my last nerve sometimes, but it's been nice having her here.

"And you love having someone to take care of," Rose says, giving June Bug a pat on the head. "You know, maybe a dog wouldn't be the worst idea. Think we could dognap this one?"

"I don't think her owner would appreciate that," I say with a laugh. "Besides, I'm fine. With the business, I'm not usually home enough to warrant having a pet."

"Just take the dog with you. This one would fit in your purse. You'd be like Paris Hilton."

"Because Paris and I have so much in common."

I'm about to finally give in and watch whatever ridiculous dating show Rose has on when I hear the sound of a car pulling in the driveway. The noise is enough to rouse June Bug from her slumber, and she launches into guard mode, ready to take on any intruder.

"That must be her," I cry, bouncing to my feet with the puppy hooked under my arm, peering out the window in time to see my daughter getting out of her SUV.

"How does she look?" Rose asks.

"What do you mean? She looks like Lindsey. She looks happy."

"How happy are we talking?" Rose continues. "Is her hair mussed up? Are her cheeks rosy from exertion?"

"Oh, for heaven's sake, Rose," I snap. "She's a normal amount of happy."

Before Lindsey can get the key in the lock, I fling open the door, and she yelps.

"Geez, Mom," she says, crossing the threshold. "What were you doing? Just lying in wait for me to get home?"

"No," I say at the same time Rose says, "Yes."

I shoot my sister a glare before grabbing my daughter's hand. "Come sit with us. Tell us about your date."

She allows me to drag her to the couch, and a wiggling June Bug crawls onto her lap to give her kisses.

"How'd it go with this one?" Lindsey asks in a tone that suggests she already knows the answer.

"Fine," I say.

Lindsey lifts her brows. "Really?"

"Of course," I say.

"So, she was on her best behavior?" Lindsey deadpans. "A perfect angel?"

Rose snorts. "Sure, if that angel's name is Calamity Jane."

"Oh fine. She was a little...destructive," I admit. "But we

got on just fine, and I received your message loud and clear that I shouldn't have meddled."

"You did?" she asks, casting a doubtful glance at me.

"Yes," I say, "but I'm hoping you had such a good time with Oliver that maybe a small part of you will be glad I did?"

"You probably should have stopped at 'yes,' Myra Jean," Rose quips.

"You are incorrigible." Lindsey laughs and shakes her head. "Both of you."

"Not me," Rose says. "I was perfectly content to sit here and find out if this rich farmer finds himself a wife."

"But are you?" I ask, ignoring my sister. "At least a little glad?"

"I would have agreed to go out with him on my own. In my *own time*," Lindsey says. "We did have fun, though."

I squeal and squeeze her knee. "What did you do?"

She tells Rose and me about their tour through town and their evening at Chips on the Table. She even tells us the heartwarming story about how Oliver became a firefighter.

"His job does make me nervous," Lindsey says. "But if it's really as low-key as he said, maybe it's not so bad."

"I'm sure it's not," I say. "Just think about what happened with Rose. I bet most of the calls he goes on are like that."

Lindsey trails her fingers along June Bug's back. "That's kind of how he put it—that most of the calls they get are medical."

"So, how did you leave things?" I ask. "Are you going out with him again?"

She gives me a nonchalant shrug. "He did ask me to dinner on Wednesday night."

"And?" Rose and I blurt in unison.

A smile spreads over her mouth. "I said yes."

The three of us are screeching with delight, and June Bug lets out a squeaky howl to match our energy.

"Tell us the rest," Rose insists. "Did he kiss you?"

Lindsey shakes her head, her cheeks flushing pink. "Not yet. I think he wanted to, though. And if he'd tried, I think I would have let him."

Our squealing commences once again.

"Oh, that's wonderful, sweetheart," I say.

Lindsey picks at the hem of her sweater and sighs as June Bug toddles over to my lap. "There's just something about him. Being around him makes me feel…lighter, somehow. Like I can just be silly and have fun."

"You need that in your life," I say. And she does. After the loss of her father, and then her subsequent break up with Daniel, my eldest daughter retreated inside herself. It took me a while to notice because I was so swallowed up in my own grief. But once I waded through the thick of it, I returned to find Lindsey a little less whole.

"Yeah," she says. "I think you're right." A soft meow comes from the top of the steps, and Lindsey rises from the couch. "I should check on Catrick Swayze and get some sleep. You want me to tuck in the little heathen first?"

"No, that's okay," I answer, stroking the silky hair of the pup's ear. "I've got it."

Lindsey grins. "If I didn't know better, I'd think you actually like having her around."

"She certainly kept me on my toes today," I say. But I *have* enjoyed having her. Yes, she's a little destructive, but she's also a sweet little thing with a feisty personality all her own.

Rose eases onto her feet. "I suppose I should hit the hay

too. I've got physical therapy in the morning before I head home."

"You don't want to find out what happens with the farmer?" I nod toward the television.

"Nah." She gives a disinterested wave toward the show still playing silently in the background. "He's got goofy ears, anyhow."

We say our goodnights, and Lindsey and Rose each head off to their respective bedrooms, leaving me, June Bug, and Farmer Gary in total stillness.

15

———

LINDSEY

"Thank you," I say as Oliver pulls my chair out at Antonio's Wednesday evening, the scent of his woodsy cologne forcing me to swallow a dreamy sigh.

"Of course." He sits across from me, and I catch a blissful glimpse of the way his forearms flex in his rolled-up button-down. "You look beautiful tonight."

"You said that already." The girlish giggle that tumbles out of my mouth surprises me.

"Not that you don't always look amazing," he says. "Because you do. But…wow."

My cheeks pink. "Thank you. So do you."

I give silent praise to Kayla, Lucy, and Willow, my own personal glam squad for the evening. Their efforts made me look good, but they made me *feel* even better. Confident, flirty, a little sexy—though that may have also been a result of the glass of wine I pregamed with. Willow worked her magic on my makeup, and Kayla fussed over my hair with a curling iron while they peppered me with questions.

Once they were finished, I shimmied into my outfit—a

loan from Willow. The emerald green dress fits me like a glove, dipping in a soft V below my collarbone. It's the perfect balance of structure and flow with its long, drapey sleeves, hip-hugging body, and a slit in the center that adds a little edge to its midcalf length.

"This place is nice." Oliver glances around the restaurant, lit only by the votives on the tables and the ornate chandeliers that hang from the high ceilings. A crystal bud vase with a single red carnation sits at the center of the pristine white tablecloth, and goblets of water were waiting for us on the table, along with two leather-framed menus. It occurs to me how long it's been since I've been somewhere to eat that didn't coat their menu in thick, cloudy plastic.

A server approaches with a pen poised over his notepad. "Good evening. I'm Parker, and I'll be taking care of y'all this evening. Can I get you started with something to drink while you..." He trails off, focusing on me. "Dr. Haggerty! It's so good to see you."

"Oh, hi." I study him a moment, running through my mental files, trying to place him and the pet he belongs to. He's short, a little more salt than pepper in his hair, especially at the temples.

"You probably don't remember me." His deep drawl drips off his tongue like the honey I get at the farmers market. "But you helped me with my cat, Itty, after he had his lil nads snipped off."

Oliver nearly chokes on the sip of water he's taking as my eyes widen with recognition.

"Oh my goodness, yes. Parker Rhodes," I say with a chuckle. "How's Itty doing? And your grandpa?"

"You know Itty. He's a firecracker." He waves his hand as though he's swatting a fly. "And well, Grandpa is too. If a hip replacement can't keep him down, I don't reckon much ever will."

"I'm glad to hear it," I say as Parker shifts his attention to Oliver.

"A heart of gold, this one." Parker gestures his thumb toward me. "'Bout four years ago, my grandpa Chuck fell and broke his hip at the church sock hop where he lives back home in Mississippi." Except when he says it, it sounds more like *Missippi*. "The man is ninety-one years old and *still* thinks he's got the moves of Elvis Presley. *Anyway*, this all went down the day of Itty's surgery, and I was distraught because I wanted to be there for Grandpa's procedure. Not to be morbid, but you just never know when somebody gets to be that age. So, Dr. Haggerty here offered to keep Itty at her house for an entire week while I was in Biloxi. Told me to focus on my family, and she'd take care of everything else. Didn't charge me a cent, neither."

"Is that right?" Oliver beams, and a rush of heat sweeps up my neck, knowing where this story is heading.

Please don't say it. Please, please don't say it.

Parker nods. "And Itty ain't no regular cat. He's high-maintenance. Thinks he's from New York City or somethin'. He has a very specific evening routine, and Dr. Haggerty followed it to the letter. Itty can't fall asleep without being rocked like a baby, and he wants you to sing him 'Purple Rain.' You know, the ole Prince song? And he don't want that radio-edited version, neither. It's gotta be the long one. If it's anything less than eight minutes and forty seconds, he'll spend the night yowling in your ear."

Oliver presses his lips together, stifling a laugh, while I pray for the floor to open up and swallow me.

I clear my throat. "I'm just so glad that Itty and Grandpa Chuck are doing well."

"Goodness gracious. Listen to me, rambling on," Parker says, "when I should be taking your drink order. What can I get y'all?"

"How would you feel about sharing a bottle of wine?" Oliver asks.

"I'd love that. Merlot okay?"

"Perfect," he says, turning to Parker. "Can we get a bottle of your best merlot?"

"Absolutely. Are we celebrating anything special this evening?"

"Oh, nothing—" I start to say, but Oliver speaks up, his gaze lingering on mine.

"Actually, this is our first date. Well, our first official date."

My heart leaps like a dog making a break for it, off the exam table.

"Oooh," Parker purrs. "Love that for you. Wonderful. Well, y'all take a gander at those menus, and I'll be back with your wine."

"I'm sorry," Oliver says. "Is it okay that I said that?"

"Yeah." I fiddle with the hem of my dress, a bundle of nervous energy. "It is."

"I'm glad." He bites his lip, hesitating a moment. "So. 'Purple Rain,' huh?"

I bury my head in my hands. "Oh my God."

He laughs and reaches across the table to pry away my fingers. "I think that might be the cutest damn thing I've ever heard."

My skin still prickles from his touch after he removes his hand.

"Okay, but seriously," I say, lowering my voice barely above a whisper. "He's not joking. I thought this was just something that Parker made up or did of his own accord, so on that first night, I didn't do it, and that cat howled for seven hours straight. I didn't miss his nightly lullaby after that."

Oliver's shoulders shake with laughter. "But how did you sing that song for eight minutes? Isn't, like, half the song a guitar solo?"

I nod, giggling. "Uh-huh. A guitar solo that I hummed quite terribly, I might add."

"I'm going to need to hear this."

"Here we are," Parker says, returning with the wine, pouring it into our glasses. "Have you had a chance to look at the menu? What's sounding good to y'all this evening?"

"Oh," I say, lifting the single page from the table, scanning it quickly. "I'm sorry. We haven't even looked."

Parker gives a good-natured laugh. "That's okay. I get it. Y'all are busy getting to know each other. How about I bring you some of our crostini to munch on while you decide?" He gives me a wink that's about as subtle as a puppy pretending it didn't just chew a hole in the sofa. "It's on the house."

"Thank you," Oliver says as Parker disappears once more.

I return my focus to Oliver. "Okay, now you need to tell me something embarrassing about yourself so I can feel less like a loser, please."

"Only cool people can sing 'Purple Rain' *with* the guitar solo." He takes a sip of his wine. "That's a fact."

"You wouldn't think that if you'd been forced to witness it."

He grins and shakes his head. "Okay. Something embarrassing."

"Humiliating, even."

He taps his fingers along the table for a moment before raising his pointer. "I wanted to be in New Kids on the Block when I grew up."

I take a pull from my wine, giddy with this new information. "Does that mean you can sing?"

"Not even a little. And definitely not in public, so I'm not sure how I thought that was gonna work." He leans back in his chair, his picket-fence-straight teeth gleaming. "But that didn't stop me from learning every one of their dances. Honestly, I still remember them, which is kind of impressive, considering I don't know where I put my car keys half the time."

"Stop." I cover my mouth with my hands. "No, you don't."

"Oh, I do. And I may or may not still sing 'Hangin' Tough' in the shower."

My giggles become a full-on cackle. "Oh my God."

He blushes, his smile still intact. "Now you think I'm crazy."

I shake my head and take another drink. "I used to pretend to be Dolly Parton."

He leans forward, folding his hands on the table. "Okay, I'm going to need to hear more about that."

"I used to dress up like her when I was a kid. I'd sneak into my mom's makeup drawer and smear lipstick on my face, put on her heels, and stuff my shirt with a throw pillow. I used a turkey baster as a microphone."

"Not a hairbrush?"

I shrug. "Five-year-old me thought a turkey baster more closely resembled a microphone."

"I bet you were a cute kid."

I press my palm to my forehead, warm with embarrassment. Though this time, I didn't have Parker to blame for spilling the beans.

My laugh fades into a contented sigh. "I was a mess and a half. That's what my dad used to say whenever I dressed up, pretending to be Dolly, or I invented some silly game he'd play along with. He'd laugh and say, 'Lindsey Loo, you're a mess and a half.' I guess I still am."

Since he died, every moment of joy has been stained by loss, like red wine spilled on a white tablecloth…no matter how much time passes or how much I try to wash it out, it lingers.

"A beautiful mess."

I drop my gaze to the menu, my heart eyes blurring the words into happy swirls before I look at him again.

"Listen, Lindsey…" Oliver clears his throat and rubs his hand along the back of his neck. "Maybe this is forward of me to say, but I've learned that when you feel something, you've got to say it. Life's too short not to. I really like you."

"I like you too." It's a big admission, one I can't believe I'm making. I wait for the cloudiness to settle in. The inevitable sadness that follows the moments I'd give anything to be able to call and share with my dad. But this time, it doesn't come.

"I wonder what song Ace would want as his lullaby," Oliver says as he opens the passenger door to his truck for me after dinner. The buzz from the wine has faded, but I'm drunk on Oliver's smile and the way his eyes almost disappear when he laughs.

"Well, 'Purple Rain' does have a track record of being pet-approved." I grin, buckling my seat belt. There's a cold, misty rain falling that makes the street lights reflect off the pavement. It's the kind of weather that often causes me to have a flare, but even that can't dampen my mood.

He chuckles as he climbs into the driver's side. "I don't think Ace is a Prince guy."

"How do you know? Have you asked him?" The fun, playful side of me had come out of her hiding place, a little dusty from years of being hidden in the basement of my heart. I'm surprised at how quickly it comes back and how easy it is to be that version of myself with Oliver.

"This may come as a shock to you, but I haven't."

"He might like show tunes, for all you know."

"Well, I don't know any, so I'll need you to come over and sing some to fully test that theory." He glances at me with a mischievous glint in his eyes before he pulls out of the lot and onto the road, Christmas music playing softly on the radio in the background. "I think he's probably more of a classic rock guy, though. Like 'Bohemian Rhapsody.'"

I give him a nod of approval. "Clearly, Ace has great taste."

"He does," Oliver agrees, tossing me a smile. "He did pick you as a vet, after all."

"Did Ace pick me as a vet, or did *you*?" I tease.

"I guess we both have great taste, then."

I'm thankful for the darkness that hides the flush of attraction that washes over me. For a moment, I shift my gaze out the window, watching as the town's Christmas lights pass us by, and I'm overcome with joy. Too often I'm the one in the driver's seat, focused so intently on the next stop that I don't get to enjoy how magical our small town looks after dark, wearing her holiday best.

The familiar notes of an old Ramones Christmas song pierces through the sounds of the windshield wipers as Oliver's hand reaches for the dial.

I squeal. "Turn that up. I haven't heard this in forever."

He stops before touching the button and closes his hand into a fist before opening it again and raising the volume.

I tap my fingers against my knees to the beat. "I used to love this song. It's one of the most underrated Christmas songs, if you ask me. Have you heard it before?"

His smile is replaced by a hardened jaw, and his Adam's apple bobs before he responds.

"I have," he answers. "It was, um…It was my wife's favorite. Before she died."

The admission knocks the wind out of me. Not because I'm upset—it would be ridiculous of me to think a man this wonderful had never loved or been loved before. Instead, I'm overcome with empathy.

"Oliver, I'm so sorry. I didn't know." I place my hand on his arm. "We can turn it off."

"No, it's okay. It's a great song, and it's tied to a lot of good memories for me. Sometimes that grief just hits you when you least expect it, you know?"

God, do I know.

I want to ask about her because I know how much talking about Dad helps me feel close to him still, but I don't want to overstep.

"Do you…want to tell me about her?" I finally ask. "If you do, I'd love to listen."

He sighs and gives me a faint smile. "Jess and I had just celebrated our fifth anniversary when she passed away four years ago."

"How did you meet?"

"She was a bridesmaid at my buddy's wedding, and I was the best man. I remember seeing her walk down the aisle with one of the other groomsmen, and I just knew she was someone I wanted to know."

"Did you ask her out after that?"

"I didn't, actually," he admits, raking his teeth over his bottom lip. "I was too shy. But then, as luck would have it, we both ended up at my friend's house for a Super Bowl party a few months later. And I wasn't about to squander my second chance. I asked her to dinner, and the rest was history." He clears his throat. "I'm sorry. Is it weird that I'm telling you this?"

I shake my head. "Not at all. I asked. We all have a past, Oliver."

He nods and pauses for a moment before continuing. "We were about to start trying for a family when we found out she had triple-negative breast cancer. But by the time the doctors discovered it, it was too late."

"I'm so sorry." I try to think of what to say next, and then I remember what makes me feel better when I miss my father —thinking about how he lived.

"What was she like?" I ask.

He peers at me, a question written in his eyes. "Are you sure?"

"I'd be honored to hear about her."

He gazes ahead, lost in thought a moment before he answers. "She was a grilled cheese—warm and kind, and she always knew how to make everyone feel comfortable and at ease. And she was loud."

I chuckle. "Okay, explain."

His smile returns, making my chest squeeze. "Jess didn't know how to do anything quietly. Every morning she'd hop out of bed, pots and pans clanging as she made breakfast, singing songs she'd made up about whatever mundane task she was doing. She used to sing to Ace when he was a pup too."

"That's absolutely precious," I say, certain that if I'd known Jess, I would have liked her. But a small part of me does wonder how I could ever hope to live up to such a special person in his life. If we were together, would he always be left disappointed?

"She found joy in the simplest things, you know? And since she died, I've tried hard to do that too."

"I think finding Ace's lullaby is more important than ever," I say with a chuckle, and after a beat, I add, "Have you dated anyone since?"

He nods. "About a year after Jess died, I started seeing someone. She wanted something serious, but at the time, I just didn't want to be alone. We dated for about six months until I broke it off. I was nowhere near ready for a relationship, and it wasn't right for me to keep going when I didn't see a future with her. I needed time to find myself again before I could even begin to think about getting back out there."

"Of course, you did. That's understandable."

"Okay, I've told you about my last relationship," he says. "What was yours?"

I watch the raindrops dance along the windshield. Am I really going to get into this? Do I *want* to? He's willing to be vulnerable, so I should be too.

"His name was Daniel," I say. "We met at this networking event for young professionals in Nashville, back when I actually did that kind of thing. Honestly, we had a good relationship. He was…" I trail off, unwilling to lie and say he was great, but equally reluctant to tell him the truth. "We were together almost two years, but we, um, broke up a few months after my dad passed."

He turns to me, his brow creased. "Wait, he left you after you lost your dad?"

"No," I say quickly. "No, I broke up with him. A relationship was just too much to handle after my dad died. Overnight, I lost my father and inherited the clinic. It was a lot to process at once."

I leave out the rest of what happened, because it doesn't matter anyway. It was still my choice, even if he ended up hurting me far more than I could have imagined.

He gives me a solemn nod of understanding. "Are you happy you were able to take over the business?"

"I am," I say. "That business meant everything to my dad, and he meant everything to me. If I can be even half the vet he was, I'll have succeeded."

"You're an excellent vet." His lips stretch into a grin as he pulls into my mom's driveway, parking behind my SUV. "In fact, I've heard you're the best in town."

I can't help but laugh. "It's easy to be the best when you're the only one."

"You'd be the best in any town."

I lock eyes with him, and my heart beats wildly, like an erratic bird flapping its wings.

"I had a really great time tonight," he says.

"Me too."

"I'd like to do it again."

"I would too." I suck in a breath. "Actually, I'll be at Mistletoe Fest on Saturday. It's the Christmas festival they have in town every year. Lots of good food, karaoke, carnival games. Lucy and Ben are going too. The whole gang. Well, everyone except Mom." My smile falters. "Would you…like to come with us?"

"I'd love to." He's close enough that I can smell his cologne.

Is he going to kiss me? Does my breath reek of garlic? I knew I should have grabbed a mint on the way out of the restaurant like Oliver did.

Before he can make a move, I reach for the handle. "I should probably go. I've got an early morning tomorrow."

"Right. Yes," he says, popping open his door. "Let me get that for you."

He helps me out of the car, and I pull my coat tighter around me before digging my keys out of my purse.

"Thank you again for tonight," I say as he walks beside me to the front door. "I had fun."

"Me too." He nods as I shove the key into the lock. "Good night."

"'Night," I reply, but before I can open the door, he places a hand on it.

"Lindsey?"

I turn, and his eyes shimmer like two twinkling stars.

"Yes?" My voice is almost inaudible.

He steps closer and touches my cheek with his hand, stroking it with his thumb. Longing rushes through me, taking down every single reservation and insecurity. He leans in to me, and I'm lost in his gaze, drifting in space. Our lips touch and stars glitter behind my eyes. He tastes like peppermint and feels like everything I ever wanted. For one single, perfect moment, I'm soaring high above the clouds.

16

MJ

"Are you ready to go home to your papa?"

June Bug wriggles in my arm while I pack her things with one hand Thursday morning. Lindsey called from work to let me know the puppy's owner is back in town and on his way to pick her up.

The pup sneaks a kiss on my chin, and my heart gives a little tug. "I know, girl. I'm going to miss you too."

I have to admit, I'm sad to see her go. That first day was rough, but we found a rhythm together. She only peed on my rugs a couple more times and *did* manage to leave some pretty impressive bite marks on one of the legs of my dining table, but she made up for it with lots of kisses. I enjoyed holding her while she slept, curled in a tiny ball in my lap. It was nice to have some company during the day, and I kind of dread the familiar echoes of emptiness that are sure to return once she and eventually, Lindsey, go home.

About twenty minutes later, I'm soaking in our last cuddles when the doorbell chimes. June Bug lets out a shrill bark to warn me in case I somehow failed to hear it.

I tuck her into the crook of my arm and head to the door, swinging it open. My stomach jumps into my throat when I lock eyes with the man waiting on my doorstep.

I didn't expect him to be so…attractive. He has a strong nose and jaw. His sturdy build is clothed in a pair of gray slacks and a cozy sweater, and he has the kindest eyes I've seen since…well, in a long time.

"There's my girl," he says with a grin, and June Bug's tail spins like a ceiling fan. "You must be Ms. Haggerty. Ron Phillips."

"Please, call me MJ." I hand the squirming pup over to her dad and smile. "Nice to meet you, Ron. You want to come in? I've got her stuff all packed up and ready to go."

He wrinkles his brow. "She didn't have anything when I left her with your daughter."

I laugh and clasp my hands together. "Well, now she does. That's Lindsey for you. Between her and Lucy, they made sure June Bug would have lots of toys and things to go home with. There's a crate here too."

"Your daughters are special people," he says, following me inside. "And so are you. Lindsey told me she needed your help to take care of little Junie after the fire, and you were quick to pitch in. I'm just so glad everyone's safe and that her house will be okay. When I saw my neighbor this morning, he told me about it. He's a firefighter here in town."

"Oh, yes," I say. "I know Oliver. He's such a like a lovely young man. I think he's taken a liking to Lindsey."

"Ah, that makes sense. He definitely got a little flustered talking about her," he says. "Well, I haven't known Oliver long, but he's a good kid. He introduced himself when he moved in and let me know he was around if I ever needed anything. I've had to take him up on it a couple times."

"He really is a sweet guy. Lindsey thinks so too."

Ron nods. "Life's dealt Oliver a tough hand. It's nice to hear that Lindsey sees how great he is. That kid deserves some happiness."

I smile. "They both do."

"Well, I don't want to hold you up. I'm sure you're a busy lady, but I can't thank you all enough for everything you've done. "

I lead him to the living room where I've gathered June Bug's things. "It was my pleasure."

"I hope she didn't cause you too much trouble."

"Just enough." I decide not to mention the rugs or my loafers. "Honestly, I'm going to miss her. This house gets quiet now that I'm the only one in it."

"No Mr. Haggerty?" he asks. "Or Mrs.?"

"My husband Henry passed five years ago."

"I'm sorry to hear that."

"Thank you."

"That's why I got Junie here." He scruffs the top of her head. "Living alone can be, well, *lonely.* I'm divorced, and my son and daughter-in-law moved to Cincinnati to be closer to her family, so I don't get to see them as often as I'd like. I have friends around here, but it's not quite the same as having someone that shares the day-to-day with you, is it?"

I shake my head, and June Bug stretches her tiny paws toward me. "No, it isn't." I scratch behind her ears, and my hand accidentally brushes Ron's, sending a shiver up my arm.

He clears his throat. "Well, I appreciate your kindness, MJ. I can tell you took great care of my girl. Looks like she might rather stay here with you."

A giggle bubbles up from inside me, originating from a place I thought I locked up years ago.

"She's a doll." I beam, leaning over to let the pup lick my cheek.

"So, um, MJ, maybe you'd let me take you to dinner?" he says. "As a thank-you."

"Oh, you don't have to do that," I answer, raking my fingers through my hair and pushing it forward in an effort to hide the blush that's crept onto my cheeks. "Truly, it was my pleasure."

Even if he *is* offering to be polite, he's still the first man to ask me out since Henry died. And for reasons I can't explain, that makes my stomach turn squishy like the Play-Doh the grandkids leave all over the house when they visit.

"Really, I'd like to," he insists. "You'd be doing me a favor. I just got back in town from staying with my son, and I've gotten spoiled having company at dinner. While I love having June Bug, she's not the best at holding a conversation."

I chuckle and smooth my hands over my blouse. It's just dinner. Sharing a meal with someone close to my age that isn't Rose or one of my few girlfriends. This isn't a big deal, yet it *feels* like it is.

Sensing my hesitation, Ron speaks up. "I'm sorry. I didn't mean to make you uncomfortable."

"I'm not," I say quickly. Flustered, maybe. Twitchy like June Bug's tail when she's excited, but not uncomfortable. "You didn't. Make me uncomfortable, I mean."

He gives me an amused grin. "How about Lovebird Brews, then?"

"Sure," I say finally, resting my hand on my cheek. "Dinner would be lovely. Thank you. When would you like to go?"

He shrugs. "How about tonight?"

"Tonight?" I blink. "Don't you need to get settled in?"

"Nah," he says with a wave of his hand. "It'll be nice to get out. I love being with my son and his wife, but well, they make me feel kinda old sometimes."

I laugh. "Well, we can't have that."

"Pick you up at six?"

My insides, which are *clearly* far more limber than I am, are having a full-on dance party.

"Six it is," I say.

"Well, I should let you get on with your day."

"Can I help you get everything out to your car?"

"Tell you what," he says, holding June Bug out to me. "You carry her, and I'll handle the rest."

"Deal." I kiss the pup's muzzle as I take her in my arms.

Ron gathers her things, and I follow him down the path to his car.

Once he has everything loaded and the puppy secured in the crate, he opens the driver's side door, his eyes lingering on me.

"It was nice meeting you, MJ."

"Likewise," I say. "I guess I'll see you tonight."

He nods and climbs into his car.

"It's a date." The snap of the door clicking shut is the exclamation point on the sentence.

I wave as he backs out of the driveway, then run inside and shut the front door, leaning against it, my hands on my cheeks.

What did I just agree to?

Am I going on...*a date*?

"TOASTED PRALINE LATTE WITH AN EXTRA SHOT FOR MJ?" the barista at The Southern Bean calls out.

"Thank you," I say, grabbing the cup from the counter.

After Ron left with June Bug, I wasn't able to stop pacing. So, I brought my laptop to the coffee shop to catch up on emails to prevent myself from wearing holes in the floor.

I take the mug back to my table and resume staring at my computer screen, but all the words are blurring together.

Did I actually agree to go on a date? No. That's crazy. I wouldn't—couldn't. My heart belongs to Henry. It always will. I can't go on a date. Oh God. What am I doing?

"MJ?"

The deep voice that materializes next to me causes me to jump and give a loud screech.

"Oliver," I say, peering up at his wide grin.

"I didn't mean to startle you."

"No, it's so good to see you. How are you?"

"I'm fine—just on my way to the fire hall and thought I'd stop in for a coffee," he says. "I'm glad I ran into you, though. I was wondering if…Could I talk to you about something?"

I scrunch my brows together. "Me? Sure."

"Mind if I sit for a second?" he asks.

"Of course." I gesture to the chair across from me. "What's going on?"

"Lindsey invited me to Mistletoe Fest on Saturday." He folds his hands on the table in front of him. "She mentioned the whole family was going."

My heart hammers an erratic beat in my chest. The news comes as a bit of a surprise, even though I told Ellie they should go without me.

"Everyone except you." He pins me with a concerned

stare. "And anyway, I don't know if you already have plans, but I would love it if you could come, even just for a bit."

"Oh." I take a long sip of my coffee, hoping to quell my dry throat, but I may as well have been drinking a spoonful of sugar. "I, um, it's not that I have plans, per se."

I can't tell him the real reason I'm not going. I'll be a blubbering mess, and my insides are already mixed up enough as it is, like a deck of cards scattered on the ground.

"I hope I'm not overstepping here," he says. "But when Lindsey mentioned you weren't going, she looked kind of… disappointed. Sad, even."

Fingers wrap around my heart, giving it a squeeze. "She did?"

He nods. "MJ, I really like Lindsey, and I want to keep getting to know her. Part of that means getting to know the people who mean the most to her. And that's you."

I blink, a rush of emotion jolting through me like a power surge. "Really?"

"Well, yeah," he says with a soft chuckle. "You're her mom."

I run my fingertip along the edge of my cup.

"So, would you come to the festival?" he asks.

I open my mouth to protest, but he cuts me off.

"Please. It would mean a lot to me, and I know it would mean a lot to Lindsey too."

His fixes his hopeful brown eyes on me, and all I can see is Lindsey. My first daughter, the second love of my life. I swallow the lump that forms in my throat. Her happiness means the world to me, and this precious man in front of me just wants to make her smile.

Guilt washes over me. Maybe I've been selfish in not agreeing to go. This festival brings back painful memories as so many things do. My entire life has become a never-ending reminder of what I had. What *we* had. But how can I expect Lindsey to think about her own future if I'm not willing to take even the tiniest step forward? I've always prided myself on leading by example. I need to do this and take one for the team.

"Okay," I finally say. "I'll go."

His eyes brighten. He stands and reaches for my hand, giving it a squeeze. "Thank you, MJ. Seriously, we're gonna have a great time."

The box I've kept locked deep inside rattles, the Ghost of Christmas Past clamoring to be let out.

I swallow hard. "I'm looking forward to it."

He heads to the counter. Once I know he can't see me, I drop my head into my hands.

What am I doing? In the span of mere hours, I've agreed to go to dinner with a man who isn't my husband *and* go back to where my dream life became a nightmare.

My phone buzzes, vibrating the table, and it's a text from Lindsey.

Having a movie night with Kayla. Be home around ten.

At least I'll get to keep one of my questionable choices to myself tonight.

"Mr. Ron," a young hostess greets us from behind the podium at the front of Lovebird Brews. "It's good to see you. I was wondering where you'd been."

"I was visiting my son in Cincinnati," he says. "I had a minor medical issue a couple weeks back, and he insisted I stay with him until I got back on my feet."

Her blonde ponytail bobs as she leans across over the stand, gripping the edge. "Are you okay?"

"Fit as a fiddle." Ron smiles and places a hand on my arm. Even through my coat *and* my turtleneck, my skin prickles. "MJ, this is Kerry."

Kerry reaches for my hand. "Nice to meet you."

"You too, Kerry."

"I come here for dinner once a week," Ron explains. "Kerry here is studying to be a nurse, and she's gonna be a damn good one."

Ron beams at her like a proud father or grandfather, and something about the gesture makes my heart turn soft, like a marshmallow.

"We all love Mr. Ron," Kerry says as a nearby server looks up from his table and waves in our direction.

"Hey, Ron," he shouts. "What's good, my man?"

Ron raises a hand to him. "Nice to see you, Owen."

"You want your usual table?" Kerry asks, grabbing a couple of menus and handing them to us.

"Sure," he answers. "If it's available."

"Head on back." Kerry gestures with a nod to the right. "Owen will be with y'all in just a minute."

"Thank you, dear." Ron places one hand on the small of my back and guides me through the cozy, dimly-lit pub. He pulls a chair out for me at a high top by a window that looks out on Main Street. It's a breathtaking view. I forgot how magical our little town becomes at Christmas, decked out like a holiday postcard.

"I've been coming here once a week for the last two years," he says. "After I retired, I quickly discovered how much I missed being around people. I found myself coming in for dinner once a week just for the conversation. Not that the food isn't spectacular too, because it is."

"What did you do?" I ask, folding my hands on the table.

"I was a high school music instructor out in Franklin. But Loving's been home for most of my life."

"So, retirement, huh?" I say. "What's that been like?"

He chuckles, his eyes crinkling at the corners. "I started teaching private piano lessons six weeks after my last day of work, if that tells you anything. I was bored out of my mind. What about you? Are you still working?"

"I have my own interior design business, MJ Designs. Aside from my kids and my grandkids, it's my whole life. Honestly, the idea of retiring makes me feel panicky. I know it's the thing people do when they get to be our age, but God, what am I supposed to do all day? I can hardly sit still as it is."

"There's only so much daytime television one can take. And naps. God knows, I took enough naps to last me a lifetime. I got caught up on fifty years' worth of lost sleep."

"Look what the cat dragged in." The man I recognize as Owen appears beside our table and gives Ron's shoulder a squeeze. "We missed you these last couple weeks. You go on vacation or something?"

"Nothing quite that glamorous," Ron says. "My appendix ruptured, and I had to have surgery to get the thing taken out."

"Oh no." Owen folds his arms over his broad chest. "Are you okay now?"

"I feel great," Ron replies. "Truly."

"You should, with this lovely lady sitting across from you," Owen says, directing his attention to me.

Ron smiles. "Owen, this is my new friend MJ. She and her

kids helped me with June Bug while I was recovering. MJ's daughter is the veterinarian in town."

Owen's eyes light up. "Dr. Haggerty?"

"That's my girl," I say.

"My dog loves her, and he's a crotchety old fart, so that's saying a lot." Owen chuckles. "And her sister, the groomer."

"That would be Lucy." I love when I meet clients or chat with a new acquaintance, and they find out who my kids are. The information is always met with a compliment or anecdote that fill me with pride.

"That's right." Owen nods. "Well, my friends, we need to celebrate. We have the famous Dr. Haggerty's mom in the house *and* Ron is back in action. What do you say we start with some drinks?"

"That sounds great," Ron says. "I'll have my usual."

"One Bowie IPA coming right up." Owen turns toward me. "And for you, MJ?"

"What would you recommend for someone who's more of a cider girl?" I ask.

"How do you feel about wassail?" Owen counters with a grin.

"I love it. I haven't had that in ages."

"Then I'm bringing you a Hallelujah! Holy Shit cocktail," Owen says. "It's my family's own wassail recipe mixed with bourbon and frozen cranberries. Tastes like Christmas."

"Sold," I say.

"Coming right up." Owen rubs his palms together and heads toward the back.

Ron folds his hands on the table. "So, what does MJ stand for, anyway?"

"Myra Jean," I answer. "It's painfully southern."

"Myra Jean." He repeats my name like he's contemplating something impressive. "I think it's lovely."

"Thank you. My older sister Rose is the only person who calls me that. Do you have any siblings?"

He shakes his head. "Nope, and I only have one child. I always wanted a big family, but it wasn't in the cards for me. My ex, Mary Ann, didn't have a very big family, either. I still keep up with her brother from time to time, though. And I usually see Mary Ann at least a couple times a year."

"That's nice. Does that mean things ended on good terms?"

"We're great friends now," Ron says. "Our situation is unique, I guess. There was no big falling out. One day, after our son, Hudson, went to college, Mary Ann sat me down and confessed that she loved me, but she wasn't attracted to me, or any man, for that matter. She was distraught, and well, I was too. My whole world fell apart."

"I'm so sorry," I say. "That must have been devastating."

He nods. "It was. It took me the better part of a year to get to a point where I could even begin to look at what happened rationally. The split felt personal, but in reality, it had nothing to do with me." He drops his gaze for a moment. "I completely shut her out during those first few months, and I have a lot of regrets about that. But she gave me time to process how I felt."

"I imagine that was hard for both of you."

"She was worried I'd hate her, but once I finally got it, I just remember thinking how much courage it must have taken her to tell me."

I pressed my hand to my heart, thinking of Lucy. I knew early on that she liked girls because she felt safe to share that part of herself with her family and friends, but I've lived long enough to know that safety isn't something guaranteed for everyone.

"To be honest, I always knew ours wasn't some epic love story," he says. "We were best friends, and I'm thankful for the life we had, but I'm equally grateful she finally found the love of her life. She and Sadie got married and retired to Hawaii."

"Have you ever wanted to find someone else? Remarry?" I'm not sure what surprises me more—the fact that I asked the question out loud or how badly I want to know the answer.

"I'd love to, if the right person comes along. I figure I'm young," he says with a small wink. "There's still time."

Before I can react, Owen returns with our drinks and places them in front of us. Mine is in a copper mule mug, and it's beautiful. The frozen cranberries are mingling with a cinnamon stick and a sprig of rosemary, and it does, indeed, smell like Christmas.

"Thanks, Owen," Ron says, taking a swig of his beer.

"This looks delicious." I bring the cup to my lips. The first sip is a contented sigh of crisp cider, orange peel, and nutmeg. "Oh my. This is heavenly."

Owen dips his head and holds out his hand. "And *that's* the *hallelujah*."

I scrunch my brows. "Wait, what's the *holy shit* part?"

"Ask me again after you finish a couple of those." Owen flashes me a mischievous grin. "I'm going to let you two look over your menus and I'll be right back."

Ron holds his beer out toward me. "Cheers."

"Okay," I say, touching my mug to his glass. "What are we toasting?"

"To dinners with new friends. Thank you for joining me tonight, Myra Jean."

"It's my pleasure," I manage before taking a gulp of my drink. "Cheers."

"You know what? Screw my cholesterol," I say, plopping the remaining quarter of my burger back on the plate. "If loving something this good is wrong, I never want to be right. I want to eat this every day for the rest of my life."

I pop a fry into my mouth and close my eyes, savoring the crunch from the initial bite that gives way to salty, pillowy-soft goodness. Red meat and fried food aren't things I indulge in often these days, especially in light of what happened to Henry. I became hypervigilant about my heart health after that, but I forgot how good a cheeseburger and fries can be.

"I've never had anything here I didn't love," Ron says, finishing his last buffalo wing. "Not to be macabre, but I want their biscuits and gravy to be my last meal. That's on their weekend brunch menu, and they're the most amazing thing I've ever tasted."

I shake my head and take a healthy swig of my second cocktail. "You haven't had mine yet. Not to toot my own horn, but they'll change your life."

"Toot, toot," he teases. "I'm not so sure. These are pretty good."

"I'm serious. My biscuit recipe was passed down from my grandmother. In fact, I'm fairly certain it's what made my grandfather fall in love with her."

"That's a glowing endorsement. I guess I'm going to have to try them and judge for myself. But don't think I'll take it easy on you just because I like you, Myra Jean."

"I'd be offended if you did." My insides swirl like the

dregs of my drink when I slosh the mostly-thawed cranberries around in the cup before polishing it off. "Holy shit. That bourbon really sneaks up on you." I snort out a laugh. "Oh. I get it now."

"That Owen knows how to make a mean cocktail."

"Oh, I don't know." I thread my fingers together and stretch my arms over my head. "Seems pretty *nice*, if you ask me." My limbs are bubbly and tingly, like somebody filled them with champagne. I haven't felt this good in a long time. The cocktail helped to loosen me up, but what I find myself enjoying most is the company.

Ron's lips quirk, and he lifts his salt and pepper eyebrows.

"What?" I chomp into my burger, swiping my thumb over my chin to catch the dribble of grease trickling down my skin.

He chuckles, and an almost imperceptible flush creeps onto his cheeks. "I'm not quite sure how to say this because it's been a very long time, but Myra Jean, you are... *something*."

"Something?" I echo, cocking my head to one side. "And what does that mean?"

"You're spunky," he says, "and fun."

My breath catches in my throat. Fun isn't something I've been accused of being for the last five years, but right now, I feel like I could simply sail away on a cloud of bourbon, carbs, and good conversation.

"*This* is fun," Ron continues, his eyes shimmering with the reflection of the twinkle lights outside. "Spending time with you."

My heart feels like it's reached the highest point on a Ferris wheel, where you can see for miles, and it's almost as if you're flying.

"I'm having a good time too," I say.

He gives a single nod and grins. "So, biscuits and gravy would be my last meal, but what would yours be?"

"You mean besides this burger?" I ask, resting my elbow on the table and my chin on my hand. "When Henry and I went to France on our honeymoon, there was this little patisserie that had the most amazing chocolate croissants. I must have eaten at least a dozen of them on that trip. Anytime I find *pain au chocolat* on a menu, I have to try it, just in case, but I've never had another pastry that even comes close to how good those were. So, if I get to pick, that's what I want."

A familiar yearning tugs on my heart as it always does when I think of my husband. But for the first time since he died, the feeling doesn't pull me deep into an ocean of despair. The thought makes me lighter somehow. Instead of being sucked beneath the current, unable to catch my breath, I'm drifting along the surface of a lifetime of beautiful memories, each one keeping me afloat.

"Y'all still doing okay?" Owen asks as he approaches the table. "Did the *holy shit* kick in yet?"

"Why yes, I believe it did," I answer with a laugh. "Well worth it, though. It was delicious."

Owen leans against the table. "How about another?"

"You know, I might if I thought I'd still be able to stand afterward," I joke. "So I better not."

"How about some dessert?" Owen asks, and Ron gives me a questioning glance.

I hold up my napkin. "I'm waving the white flag. I don't think I could eat another bite."

"We'll take the check, then," Ron says.

Owen shakes his head. "Not tonight, my friend. This one's on the house. We missed you around here."

"You don't have to do that," Ron insists. "Please, let me pay. Besides, this was a thank-you dinner for MJ."

Owen gives me a subtle wink. "I guess you'll just have to bring this lovely lady in again then, huh? Maybe next week?"

Ron focuses on me, and I squirm beneath his gaze.

"Well, Myra Jean, what do you say?" Ron asks. "Will you come to dinner with me again?"

My heart flutters—a side effect of the alcohol, or maybe it's just delightfully intoxicating to have Ron's eyes on me.

I attempt to keep my tone cool and casual and *not* like a giddy girl with a crush. "I'd love to."

17

LINDSEY

"So, Mom's really coming to the festival? Of her own free will?" Lucy asks Friday afternoon, running the shears over a goldendoodle named Finch. "This isn't some bait and switch thing where we say we're taking her to see *The Nutcracker* on ice or something and then we're like, 'surprise'?"

"Nope," I say, propping my elbows on the table, allowing Finch to kiss my nose. "Oliver said she's actually going."

"How?" Lucy wipes a bead of sweat off her forehead with her arm. "I mean, that's great, but *how*?"

"No clue, but Mom confirmed it this morning before I left the house." I was just as shocked when Oliver texted yesterday evening to let me know he ran into Mom at the coffee shop and convinced her to go to Mistletoe Fest. I was even *more* shocked when she told me this morning how much she was looking forward to it. I was hoping to ask her about it last night, but she was already in her room with the door shut by the time I got home.

"And you didn't ask him to do this?"

I shake my head. "He did it all on his own. I didn't even tell Oliver *why* Mom wasn't going. All he knew was that she wasn't coming."

Oliver already proved he *can* hang with my family, but this showed me that he *wants* to. My family is the most important part of my life and quite the spirited bunch. That can be intimidating for some people. But not Oliver.

"If I wasn't already Team Oliver, this would certainly seal the deal," Lucy says. "I don't think just anyone could talk her into this, Linds. There's something special about him. I feel it in my bones."

I rake my teeth over my bottom lip. "I think you might be right."

"I'm going to need you to put that in writing and sign it, please."

"Hey, Linds," Kayla says, poking her head into the room. "You have a special visitor."

My eyes widen, and Lucy squeals.

"Sorry, it's not Hottie McHotterson," Kayla continues. "It's Ron."

"Oh! I have something for him. I'll be right there," I say, darting toward my office.

Once I retrieve the gold gift bag, I head to the reception area and smile when I spot him with a small vase filled with an assortment of red and white flowers, accented with pops of green and frosted pine cones.

"Ron," I say. "It's good to see you. How are you feeling?"

"Wonderful," he answers, holding the bouquet out toward me. "These are for you, Doc. I just wanted to thank you again for all you did to help me and June Bug."

"You didn't need to do that." I take the blooms, inhaling the sweet scent of carnations.

"Trust me, it's the least I can do. I know June Bug can be a handful."

"They're lovely. Thank you," I say, placing the flowers on the desk. "And I have a little something here for you too." I hand him the bag with sparkly tissue paper spilling over the top.

His smile stretches to his ears. "For me?"

"Consider it a 'get well' present. It's from me and Oliver."

"You *and* Oliver, eh?" He raises his brows before plucking out the small ornament. "Oh my goodness. Look at that. It's June Bug."

"We saw it when we got together the other day and knew you had to have it."

"I love it, Doc. Thank you. I can't wait to show June Bug and put it on my tree at home."

"How is the little rascal?"

He chuckles. "If I could bottle up her energy and sell it, I would be a very rich man."

"That's for sure."

"She really took up with your mom," he says. "After having dinner with her last night, I can see why."

Excuse me, *what*? "Dinner?"

He hesitates. "I took MJ to Lovebird Brews last night as a thank-you."

My face must reflect how shocked I am because Ron winces.

"Oh dear. I hope that was okay for me to say. I just assumed you knew since you're staying with her."

"Of course," I lie with a wave of my hand, trying to pretend this wasn't news to me. "It just slipped my mind."

Relief burrows into the lines of Ron's forehead. "Whew. Good. Had me worried I'd told you something you didn't already know."

"I'm so glad you two had a good time," I say, hoping he'll divulge a little more. I talked to my mother before I left for work this morning, and though she was a little more high-strung than usual, she didn't once mention their dinner.

"I can't think of another time in recent history when I smiled that much." He drops his gaze to his brown loafers.

I blink. Am I losing it, or does he *like* her?

"Your mom is a special lady," he goes on, and the reason my mother failed to mention her outing with Ron becomes crystal clear.

Ron might not be the only one with a crush.

"Yeah, she is." I swallow hard, the realization washing over me like a splash of cold water. It's hard to imagine my mother with anyone but my dad. Sure, I hoped she'd get back out there one day, but I guess I didn't think that day would be *today*.

As soon as the thought forms in my mind, I'm kicking myself. I've been hell-bent on Mom moving forward, and the second she might actually be doing it, I freak out? My mother has a whole life left to live. It hurts to think of her living it with anyone but Dad, but it's more painful to imagine her spending the rest of her life alone.

"I'm looking forward to seeing her again next week," Ron says, tucking his free hand in the pocket of his slacks, a bashful expression on his face. He clearly likes her. As he should. My mother is a catch.

"Ron, are you busy this weekend?" The words leap from my mouth before I can question voicing them.

He tilts his head, his brow furrowed. "I don't think so. Why?"

"Mistletoe Fest is tomorrow. My siblings and their families are going, and Oliver's coming. And my mom will be there too. You should come."

"Really?"

"Of course. Mom would be thrilled if you joined us." I have no idea if that's true or not, but I'm going with it.

He nods and smiles, and the look on his face is so sincere I could cry.

"In that case, I'd love to," he says. "When should I be there?"

"I'll meet you by the entrance at two."

"Perfect. I'm looking forward to it, Doc. Well, I better let you get back to it." He holds up the ornament. "And thanks again for this."

"See you tomorrow," I say with a wave.

Once the door closes, Kayla clears her throat from behind the reception desk where she's leafing through our next patient's file.

"Do my ears deceive me or did you just *meddle* in your mother's love life?" She lifts her eyes from the manila folder. "The very same thing you were upset with her for doing to *you*."

"Um." I press my lips together. "Maybe."

She narrows her eyes at me and slaps the file onto the counter.

"What can I say? I guess I get it from my mama."

A grin tugs at the corner of her mouth, and she rubs her hands together.

"What?"

"Oh, nothing. I was just thinking about the extra caramel

popcorn I'm going to get at the festival." She gives me a little smirk. "I want to make sure I have plenty of snacks for the show."

"I still can't believe Mom went out with the baby dragon's dad," Ben says with a laugh at Mistletoe Fest Saturday afternoon. I'm standing off to the side with my brother and Kayla, watching Ellie, Noah, and Emily get their faces painted by someone dressed as Buddy the Elf outside Santa's Workshop. "And that you *invited* him. Isn't this exactly what you got mad at Mom for?"

"That's what *I* said." Kayla pops a piece of popcorn into her mouth from the bag clutched in her gloved hands and gives me a smug grin.

"It's not *exactly* the same. It's…*similar*." I shove my hands in the pockets of my tweed coat. A familiar ache is scratching at my bones, but I'm determined not to let it ruin this day.

Kayla raises an brow at me.

"Okay, fine." I huff out a breath. "You're right. I meddled, but I had a good reason. You should've seen Ron. He looked like a kid with his first crush. He was giddy over her."

Kayla nods. "He was. I was eavesdropping on the entire conversation."

"I think that's why Mom didn't mention it," I continue. "I think she likes him too, and that probably scares her."

Ben narrows his eyes at me. "And you thought the best way to handle that would be to invite him today?"

"Can't help you out of that one, Linds," Kayla says.

I shrug. "Honestly, I didn't think that far ahead. I saw a

wonderful man who appreciates how amazing Mom is, and I think she needs that. Maybe I shouldn't have done it."

"I'm sorry," Ben says, touching my arm. "I don't mean to give you a hard time. I guess it's a little strange for me to think about Mom dating, but we want her to move forward, and this is part of it, right?"

I swipe my hair from my face. "Look, if this goes south, I'm willing to admit defeat and beg for forgiveness. But I just have a feeling, Ben. I think this could be a good thing."

"I believe you," he says. "What time is he getting here, anyway?"

"Two. Oliver's bringing him since he lives next door." I pull my phone from my pocket and glance at the time. "Oh, shoot. That's right now. I have to go meet them out front."

"When are Lucy and Willow getting here with MJ and Rose?" Kayla asks.

"Any minute now. They're supposed to meet us in time for the *Do You Want To Build A Snowman* contest at two thirty," I answer.

"Good," she says with a smirk. "Gives me time to grab more popcorn."

I roll my eyes as I back away. "I'll meet you guys over by the activity tent."

"THANKS AGAIN FOR INVITING ME," RON SAYS AS WE WEAVE through the bustling crowd. "This is nice."

It's overcast, making the forty-five degree day feel far cooler. People are dressed in festive colors, puffy coats, and sweaters. Some are even decked out in holiday costumes or full caroler garb. Despite the chill, the air is warm with the scent of cinnamon and roasted chestnuts.

"I'm glad you came," I say, glancing up to Oliver, who's fallen into step beside me. "I'm glad you did too."

"Same." He reaches for my hand, and electricity buzzes through me when he threads his fingers through mine.

"So, what's this competition you said we're participating in?" Ron asks. "Something about building a snowman?"

Oliver cocks his head. "Wait, how do we do that? It's cold, but definitely not cold enough for snow."

"We divide into teams, and we have to build a snowman using only what they provide us," I explain. "Toilet paper, bubble wrap, tissue paper, garland, things like that. And the most creative snowman wins."

"That sounds fun," Ron says.

I nod. "It is. It's one of the most popular events we—"

"Lindsey! Hey, Lindsey!"

We stop at the sound of someone shouting my name behind us and turn.

Lucy and Rose are waving their hands wildly while Willow watches my mom like she's a bomb that could detonate at any moment.

Mom's eyes fall on me and Oliver and she smiles, but that look vanishes when she spots Ron standing next to me.

"Good to see you again, Myra Jean," he says.

The color drains from my mother's face, and in a matter of seconds, her expression morphs from confusion to panic to surprise.

"Ron?" she says, masking her shock with a smile.

"Who's Ron?" Rose shout-whispers to Lucy.

My mother's throat constricts as she swallows. "Wh-what are you doing here?"

Ron gestures toward me with his thumb. "Lindsey invited me."

Mom pins me with her eyes. "Oh, she did." It's a statement, not a question. She clasps her hands together in front of her chest, shifting her focus back to Ron. "Well, it's good to see you again."

Rose mouths, *Again?* to Willow with wide eyes.

"We should get over to the tent," Lucy says. "We don't want to miss the contest."

"Wouldn't be the only thing I'm missing today," Rose mutters.

"It's nice to see you guys." Lucy smiles at Ron and Oliver, hooking one arm through each of theirs. "How's June Bug? How's the fire hall? Tell me everything."

Oliver flashes me a puzzled grin as Lucy steers them away, and I give him what I hope is an encouraging smile as Mom grips my shoulder.

"Care to explain what's going on, dear daughter?"

"To all of us, please," Rose says with a huff.

"Rose, maybe we should go with Lucy," Willow says. Aunt Rose attempts to argue, but Willow pries her away, leaving me alone with my mother.

"What do you mean?" I feign innocence once everyone is out of earshot.

"Why is Ron here?"

I shrug. "He's a friend."

"Oh?"

I peer at her through slits. "Why does that surprise you?"

She can't meet my gaze. "He...He's, uh, a stranger, really."

"A stranger, hmm?"

Her cheeks flame red, like two little Rudolph noses. "Well, I…I met him the other day. Briefly."

"Was it?" I ask. "Brief?"

She squeezes her eyes shut and takes a breath. "We also had dinner together."

"And did you have a good time?"

When she finally looks at me, there's a brightness to her face I haven't seen in a long time.

"I did," she says, barely above a whisper.

"Doesn't sound like he's much of a stranger to either of us then, does it?" I wrap my arm around her shoulders and give her a squeeze. "I'm glad you're here, Mom."

Her face softens. "Don't think you're getting off that easy, young lady. You pulled a fast one on me."

I grin and loop my arm through hers. "Why don't we just call it even?"

"THE WINNER OF THIS YEAR'S *DO YOU WANT TO BUILD A Snowman* contest is…" The mayor of Loving pauses for effect. "The Butts Family!"

"What?" Rose's voice slices through the air, bringing everyone's attention to her. She throws her hands up. "I'm just saying what we're all thinking. This competition's rigged."

Several people from neighboring teams nod and clap their agreement.

"Small-town politics," Lucy mutters.

Willow stifles a laugh. "Or maybe it's because our snowman looks a little" —she lowers her voice so Noah and Emily can't hear— "phallic."

"Oh God, it does," I whisper, clasping a hand over my mouth.

Our snowman ended up with no arms and two large wads of bubble wrap at the bottom to add additional support because he kept toppling over. Even the Santa hat we put on him at the last minute couldn't save him.

"I think it adds a little something, if you ask me," Rose says. "Jolly Old Saint Dickolas is standing tall."

Ben snorts. "One might even say *erect*."

"Butts family," the mayor continues, "you can come collect your hundred-dollar gift certificate to Lovebird Brews."

"I get to take you back there this week," Ron says to my mom, and my heart lurches. "If you ask me, I already won."

"What's next on the agenda?" Kayla asks as the volunteers come around to collect our snowmen.

"The karaoke contest starts in half an hour," Ben answers.

I sense my mother stiffening at my side, and I touch her arm.

Dad used to love the karaoke competition. He looked forward to it every year, and he always had to have a spot right by the stage. For as much as he loved to watch, he never actually competed.

But Mom did. Every year, she sang just for him because he loved it so much. Because he loved the sound of her voice. I haven't even heard her hum since Dad passed away. Not in the kitchen, not in the car, not anywhere. When Dad died, the music in our lives did too. One second, we were singing along to our favorite song. The next, we were right in the middle of the best part when it just stopped, never to be heard again. The words linger on the tips of our tongues, but the melody is always out of reach.

"What do you say we all hit the refreshment stand?" Oliver asks. "I noticed The Southern Bean is serving coffee up there."

"There's also spiked hot chocolate and Mistletoe Margaritas." Kayla bounces her shoulders. "And funnel cake."

"Actually, a drink sounds nice," Mom says.

Ron smiles. "Lead the way."

About ten minutes later, with our drinks procured, we push through the crowds toward the main stage where the community bell choir is finishing an enchanting rendition of "Carol of the Bells." The tinkling of the chimes carries through the audience, flickering above the hushed voices like fireflies. The song finishes with a flourish, and everyone erupts into applause, including those passing by who've been stopped in their tracks by the performance.

"Give it up for the Loving Bell Choir," a deep, velvety voice belonging to a short man with jet-black hair and a five o'clock shadow booms into a mic. Eddie O'Donnell hosts a popular morning radio show in Nashville, but he's lived here for years and brings his adorable pit bull, Dolly, to the clinic. He's something of a local celebrity.

Eddie claps along with the audience as the choir files offstage with smiles and waves.

"We're going to take a five-minute break, but when we come back, it's time for some holiday karaoke," Eddie says. "The beautiful Agnes from The Knitting Post is manning the sign-up booth to the left of the stage. Give us a wave, Agnes." He looks to where a woman about my mother's age with a white-blonde chignon and an emerald green coat is sitting, and she wiggles her fingers in the air. "Remember, there's a three-night stay at a gorgeous cabin in Gatlinburg up for grabs, so you better run like Rudolph to register."

"I'll scope out some good spots," Ben says, starting for the seating area where people are beginning to disperse.

"Woo boy." Kayla takes a slurp of her margarita. "I better get my name on the list before the tequila wears off."

"Wait for me," Aunt Rose says, reaching for Kayla's arm. "Maybe I'll put my name in."

I twirl my finger at her. "You're not fooling anyone. You just want to check out Eddie."

"Of course, I do." Aunt Rose lifts her chin, giving me a sly smirk. "I'm going to need a handsome suitor to accompany me to the mountains when I win."

Oliver leans his head toward mine, his voice low as Kayla and Aunt Rose disappear through the crowd. "Your aunt is…" He trails off, searching for the right words.

"A man-eater? A shameless flirt? Likely to one day set off her Life Alert bracelet so a bunch of hot firefighters show up to rescue her?"

"Exactly." He chuckles and takes a sip of his coffee. "So, your aunt has a thing for firefighters?"

"Any man in uniform, really. Why?" I ask. "Know someone at the fire hall you can set her up with?"

"I don't," Oliver says. "I was just wondering if this is something that runs in the family."

I cock my head. "You want to know if I have a thing for men in uniform?"

His lips quirk. "Firefighters, specifically."

I touch my finger to my chin, pretending to think about it. "You know, I've always been partial to park rangers."

"It's the hats, isn't it?" he says with a grin. "I get it."

This time, my fingers are the ones finding his. "But there's one firefighter I think is pretty cute."

"Over here!" Ben waves from the end of the third row.

Noah is already bounding toward him with Ellie and Emily on his heels, leaving the rest of us to follow suit.

"After you." Ron smiles, gesturing for Mom to walk ahead.

"Half of us can sit here, and the other can sit in front of us," Ben says as we get closer.

"I'm sitting in front of you," Lucy says. "I don't want anything to block me from seeing Kayla butcher that Mariah Carey high note."

Oliver and I file in behind her and Willow, leaving two seats for Kayla and Rose, while Mom and Ron settle in behind us next to Ellie.

"We could do our famous duet," Lucy says to me, leaning over Willow's lap.

"Don't you mean infamous?" Ben wrinkles his nose. "I didn't think 'Last Christmas' could get any worse."

"Hey!" I whip around and fix him with my eyes. "Those are fighting words."

"And what we lack in talent, we make up for with our dazzling stage presence," Lucy adds, wiggling her fingers.

Ben narrows his eyes. "I think we need someone with *actual* talent to sing."

"Don't worry," Kayla says as she and Rose squeeze past us to their seats. "They'll be calling my name soon."

"I've got my earplugs right here." Ben pats his coat pocket. "I meant we need Mom to get up there."

"You're a singer?" Ron asks.

Mom shakes her head. "No, not at all."

"Of course, she is. Where do you think we get our charisma?" Lucy asks.

"Not from me," Mom insists.

Willow nudges Lucy with her elbow. "I'm beginning to

think your mom singing is some kind of urban legend. Nobody else can back up your claims."

"It's true," Ellie says. "I've heard it."

Oliver shifts in his seat, resting his arm over the back of the chair. "You should get up there. I want to hear you sing."

"That makes two of us," Ron agrees.

Willow raises her hand. "Three."

"You should do it, Myra Jean." Rose gives her an encouraging nod. "For old times' sake."

"She used to sing 'Santa Baby' every year," Ben says. "Always got the crowd going. She even won a couple times. The prizes weren't near as good back then, though."

"Is that right?" Oliver asks, a mischievous glint in his eye. "You should do it, MJ. I'll even sing with you."

My mouth falls open. "Really?"

"Oh, I couldn't," Mom says, her gaze dropping to her lap.

"Please, Grandma," Noah begs. "Please sing."

Mom smooths the invisible wrinkles in her holly-green cashmere pants. "Sweetheart, Grandma hasn't sung in a long time, and I just don't think I'm up for it."

"C'mon, Grandma," Emily pleads. "I want to hear 'Baby Santa.'"

Mom chuckles and scrunches her nose. "I don't think so, sweetie."

Lucy stands with a sigh. "Well, I guess you guys are stuck listening to me and Lindsey, then. I'm going to put our names in."

"I wanna go too, Aunt Lucy," Noah pipes up. "I want to sing."

"Oh yeah?" Ellie asks. "What song?"

Noah presses his lips together, his eyes squinted. "Mmm…'Jingle Bells'!"

"No way," Lucy says, pressing a hand to her chest. "That's my favorite. Come on. Let's sign up."

I glance back at Mom, and she gives me a wistful smile as Eddie O'Donnell returns to the stage.

"How're we doing, Loving?" Eddie asks and is answered with raucous applause.

Oliver places a hand on my knee, and when our eyes meet, all is calm and bright for the first time in what feels like forever.

"GIVE IT UP FOR GRUFF, EVERYONE! I DON'T BELIEVE I'VE ever heard a more, um, *enthusiastic* version of 'The Little Drummer Boy,' Eddie says with a polite smile as a balding man in a leather jacket, motorcycle boots, and a pair of reindeer antlers exits the stage with a guttural yell.

"Enthusiastic?" Kayla shout-whispers in my ear. "All I got was a 'great job' and Mr. *Sons of Anarchy* is *enthusiastic*?"

"I'm not so sure he meant it as a compliment," I say. Gruff's performance consisted of him screaming the words like he was fronting a metal band.

Aunt Rose cocks her head to the side. "Is it just me or is Gruff kind of sexy."

"It's just you," Lucy, Kayla, and I say in unison.

Oliver shakes beside me with laughter.

"That'll be a tough act to follow, but someone's gotta do it, and that someone is..." Eddie opens the folded red paper in his hand and laughs. "This is cute. Next up, we have someone by the name of Grandma MJ singing 'Santa Baby.'"

The audience chuckles, and I gasp.

"What?" Mom inhales sharply, and we all turn to look at her. "Lucy!"

"Yay, Grandma!" Noah claps, and his sister joins in.

Lucy clamps a hand to her mouth. "Oh *shit*. Mom, I swear I didn't know."

"Noah, did you put your grandmother's name in?" Ellie asks, and he nods. "You shouldn't have done that, honey. Grandma doesn't want to sing."

"Now, where's Grandma MJ?" Eddie squints, peering into the crowd with his hand shielding his eyes.

"Here!" Noah shouts, pointing at my mother, whose face has turned the color of a cranberry.

"There she is. Come on up, Grandma MJ," Eddie says, and the crowd cheers.

Mom freezes, and Ron places a hand on her shoulder. "Myra Jean? Are you all right?"

A few more seconds pass, and Eddie tries again. "Don't be shy, Grandma. We're all friends here, aren't we?"

The audience's cheers grow louder.

Aunt Rose glances at me, a question dancing in her eyes.

I open my mouth to speak for Mom, to tell Eddie there's been a mistake, but before I can get the words out, Oliver is on the stage.

"Sorry, Eddie," he says, his voice trembling slightly. "There's been a change of plans. I'm Oliver, and I'll be performing in MJ's place."

The women in the crowd scream their excitement. Meanwhile, my heart is gooey, like the icing on my mother's famous caramel cake.

"Sounds like they approve," Eddie says. "Let's hear it for Oliver singing 'Santa Baby.'"

I watch with wide eyes as the opening notes of the song

begins to play, and Oliver shimmies his hips to the rhythm, eliciting a series of hollers and giggles that turn his cheeks pink.

"Um, what exactly is happening right now?" Kayla asks, her mouth dropping open when Oliver begins to sing, terribly off-key in a wobbly tenor.

I'm laughing with tears in my eyes as he croons about asking the big guy in red for a convertible and a yacht. He catches my eyes and gives me a subtle wink, and I smile, shaking my head in disbelief. Oliver saw how uncomfortable my mother was and didn't hesitate to take the attention off her. His voice quivers, and beads of sweat are dotting his hairline. I think back to the day we went to Antonio's, when he told me how he used to want to be in the New Kids on the Block but didn't like to sing in public. Oliver isn't comfortable on stage, but he got up there anyway. He did it for her. He did it for *me*.

I turn to find my mother quaking with laughter, her hands tucked under her chin. She locks eyes with me and smiles, and for a second, it takes my breath away. I'm not shrouded in grief or nostalgia or longing for days past, and neither is she. We're right here, in *this* moment, with the soundtrack of Oliver's wonderfully awful singing in the background. She's here with us at a place she swore she'd never return. It's a step I didn't think she'd make, but I'm so thankful she did.

Mom leans forward and squeezes my shoulder, and before I can register what's happening, she's strutting toward the stage. The audience cheers in delight as Oliver takes her hand and gives her a twirl. Eddie appears from the side to hand her a mic, just in time for her to start the next verse.

A lump forms in my throat as her rich alto fills the air. I look to Lucy, who is smiling and wiping tears from her eyes, and then to Ben, who hoots, pumping his fist in the air. Ron is watching her, wonderstruck, as though she's the most enchanting person he's ever seen. It's a look I've seen before.

"She's incredible," Willow says in my ear. "And she looks so happy."

I nod, swiping my fingers beneath my lashes as my mom sings the song Dad always requested of her. I never really understood why *that* was the song he asked for instead of something prettier like "The Christmas Song," but as I watch my mother throw her head back in laughter between verses, without a care in the world, it becomes clear. Dad loved it because this is Mom at her best—silly and bursting with joyful energy.

My mom is leading Oliver in a box step, and when he catches my gaze, I swear my heart skips, like a prized record I've listened to so much I wore it out. Oliver is the reason Mom came to Mistletoe Fest to begin with, and he's the reason for the smile etched across her face.

The song is drawing to an end, and Kayla puts her arm around me.

"You okay?" she asks.

I give her a nod as Mom and Oliver take their bows to wild cheers and a standing ovation. She wraps him in a bear hug, and they exit the stage, catching high fives and pats on the back as they return to their seats.

"Grandma MJ and Oliver, everyone," Eddie booms. "Keep that applause going. Wasn't that incredible?"

"You were amazing," I say with a chuckle.

"I'm glad you think so because I was *terrified*," Oliver admits. "Do you think your mom had fun?"

"Definitely," I say, unable to take my eyes off this beautiful, thoughtful, dream of a man, for fear that if I do, he'll disappear, and I'll find he's been a figment of my imagination all along.

"Hey," he says, touching my cheek. "What's that face for?"

I want to thank him for helping to bring the best parts of my mother back to life—for caring about me enough to see how important she is to me. But my words get lodged in my throat.

So I do the next best thing and kiss him instead.

18

———

MJ

"It's time to crown our holiday karaoke champion," Eddie O'Donnell's voice booms into the mic at the center of the stage where he's holding a large red envelope. "I've always known Loving's got talent, but y'all really showed up this year."

"You certainly did." Ron chuckles, nudging my arm.

"Oh, stop," I say with a wave of my hand as Eddie opens the envelope, pulling out the piece of paper that holds the name of the winner. I grip the edge of my chair, shocked to find I'm actually nervous, though Oliver and I probably don't stand a chance. There were twenty-one entries, and Eddie's right. There's a lot of talent in this town.

"Our champions were selected based on stage presence, vocal talent, and crowd participation, and for the first time in our town's history, the judges were *unanimous* in their decision." Eddie waits while the audience cheers. "I'm sure you'll all agree that these particular performers were especially captivating."

The crowd goes silent, and I look at Ron, who has his

fingers crossed. In the row in front of me, Lindsey's holding hands with Oliver on one side and Kayla on the other.

Rose turns around to give me a little wink. "You've got this in the bag, sister."

"Our holiday karaoke champions are" —Eddie pauses for effect— "Oliver and Grandma MJ! Come on up here!"

Everyone, including our two rows, erupts into wild cheers as Oliver jumps to his feet and spins to face me.

"We did it," I say as I stand up, my hands on either side of my face.

He gives me a gentle smile. "*You* did."

When Lindsey turns, her eyes are glistening. Even my sister's cheeks look a little damp.

Ron squeezes my hand as I exit the row, sending a rush of warmth through my limbs.

Oliver meets me in the aisle, and I take his arm, allowing him to guide me up the stairs and onto the stage.

"Congratulations," Eddie says, standing between us. "You've won a three-night stay in Gatlinburg in a gorgeous cabin, big enough for the whole family."

My kids and the grandchildren are screaming their heads off, which causes the rest of the crowd to join in.

"It looks like you two have quite the cheering section, Grandma MJ," Eddie says with a laugh, holding the microphone out to me.

"We do," I manage, overcome with emotion from the abundance of love staring back at me. My entire family is on their feet, and I can't remember the last time I saw them so happy.

"As you should. That was a heck of a performance, and I hope you and your family enjoy the mountains." Eddie pats me on the back. "Stop by the booth, and Agnes will get your info so you can collect your prize."

"Thank you," I say, reaching for Oliver. I hold up his hand, and the crowd loses it once again.

Once we climb off the stage, I turn to Oliver. "You should take the trip. You did most of the heavy lifting, anyway," I joke.

He shakes his head and grins. "It's all yours, Grandma MJ."

"Really," I say, nodding toward where my kids are sitting. "Seeing the looks on their faces is the only prize I'll ever need."

"I imagine the looks on their faces when they find out they're going to the mountains will be pretty amazing too." He gestures at the booth. "Come on. Let's give them your information."

Once we finish, we head back to our cheering squad.

Ben wraps me in a hug. "You were great, Mom."

"Yay, Grandma!" Emily cries.

"You did good, Myra Jean." Rose nods, dabbing beneath her eyes.

"It was the performance of a lifetime," Lucy says as she and Willow envelop me between them. "I'm so proud of you."

Over Willow's shoulder, I see Oliver wrap Lindsey in his arms, lifting her off her feet, and the sound of her laugh tugs on my heart.

"I'm hungry," Noah whines, and Ellie shushes him.

"What do you guys say we hit the food trucks before we see the lights?" Kayla asks.

"Yum," Emily says as Lindsey finally makes her way to me.

Lindsey opens her mouth as though she's about to say

something but closes it, folding her arms around me. The crisp, sweet scent of her hair takes me back to when she was just a little girl and I used to comb her dark locks, the smell of her apple detangler tickling my nose.

Lindsey knew I needed this. Ben and Lucy too. They tried repeatedly to pull me from the depths of grief, but I'd swatted their hands away every time. When had they all grown up? When had they started knowing better than me?

"I love you," Lindsey whispers in my ear.

I kiss her cheek. "I love you too."

"I'm so happy you're here," she says.

"Me too," I say, and I mean it.

Ellie gives my arm a squeeze. "We're going to start toward the food before these two try to gnaw off their own arms."

Ron extends his hand to me. "Shall we?"

"Actually, you all go on ahead," I say. "I'd like to speak to Oliver for a second if he doesn't mind."

Oliver's brows shoot up in a question. "Me?"

I nod, and Lindsey smiles, placing her hand on Ron's shoulder.

"Looks like you're stuck with me," she teases him.

"Always happy to be stuck with you, Doc," Ron says. "We'll see you two in a bit."

Oliver falls into step with me as we watch the group scamper off toward the food trucks.

"Is everything okay?" Oliver asks. "I hope you're not upset that I—"

"Upset?" I echo, placing my hand on his arm. "Heavens, no. I wanted to thank you."

"For what?"

"For…well, everything," I answer. "For starters, I haven't seen my daughter smile with such happiness in a long time."

He gives me a bashful grin.

"Did you know we used to come to this festival together as a family every single year before my Henry died?" I ask as we continue slowly toward the smell of funnel cakes and barbecue.

He shakes his head. "No, Lindsey never mentioned that."

I sigh. "After Henry passed, I couldn't bring myself to come back. I guess I was scared. I thought it would be too hard, too painful. That I'd only be able to remember the hard stuff."

"I had no idea," he says, dropping his gaze. "I'm sorry, MJ."

"Don't be. Today's been a gift. You showed me there was nothing to be afraid of. I got to relive some of my happiest memories today and make some new ones too. And I have you to thank for that."

He lifts his eyes to meet mine. "I'm glad I could help."

I smile up at him. "And you know what else?"

"What?"

"You made me laugh like I haven't laughed in years," I say. "*And* you helped me realize I don't want to be sad anymore. Henry wouldn't want that, either. I think he'd want me to live."

"I didn't know Henry, but based on what I've heard, I think he would too," Oliver says, holding out his arm to me. "Now, how about we celebrate our win with funnel cakes? My treat."

"Not this time, mister. They're on me. Besides, I kind of owe you for more than just tonight."

His brow crinkles. "What? Why?"

"Remember the first day we met? When I asked you to dinner?"

"When Rose fell?"

"Yeah," I say with a chuckle as I loop my arm through his. "About that…"

WITH EVERYONE'S BELLIES FULL, WE VENTURE OFF TO PLAY some carnival games before it's time to head over to the walk-through light show. Lucy, Willow, and Ellie are helping Emily play the Santa's Cookies Beanbag Toss, while Ben and Noah search for a restroom. Ron and I are watching as Oliver, Lindsey, Rose, and Kayla compete in a water gun game, each trying to move their reindeer to the top of the chimney the fastest.

"C'mon, Blitzen," Rose shouts, pumping the trigger on her water pistol. "Get yourself together. Santa's got shit to do."

"I think my reindeer's drunk," Lindsey says through fits of giggles as her little guy starts to lean to the left before turning completely upside down. This gets Oliver laughing, and before long, his reindeer's looking a little tipsy too.

"Yes!" Kayla shrieks as her reindeer hits the top of the chimney.

"Oh hell," Rose pouts.

"Let's go again," Kayla says, rubbing her hands together. "I'm feeling lucky!"

I shake my head. "Never a dull moment with this bunch."

"I love it." Ron grins, sending my heart galloping like Santa's reindeer across a roof. "I'm having a great time."

"Me too."

"Look." Ron leans into me and points to the game set up just a few feet from where we're standing. "No one's in line for the Pop-a-Balloon. What do you say we give it a whirl?"

"Sure. I can't hit the broad side of a barn, but why not?"

"On that note, I'll make sure to stand behind you." He places his hand on the small of my back and steers me toward the wall of festively colored balloons.

"Wise decision," I say.

The teenager working the game barely looks up from his phone. "It's a buck a shot. If you pop a balloon, you get a prize." He gestures to the narrow wall behind him, lined with various holiday-themed stuffed animals.

I point at a lone penguin wearing a snowflake-printed scarf. "That one's cute."

"We'll take five." Ron gives the boy the cash, who in turn places five darts into my hands.

"Fire away, Myra Jean," Ron says.

I stand behind the marked line, though the boy probably wouldn't notice if I walked right up to the wall and stabbed the balloon, as though I were a jilted mistress on *Snapped*. I pinch the dart between my thumb and forefinger, closing one eye to zero in on my target, before letting it fly.

"Whoops." I wince as the dart bounces off the wall and skitters to the side. "See, I told you I have terrible aim. Maybe you should do the next one."

Ron takes the dart from my hand, his skin brushing mine. Despite the chill in the air, my cheeks turn hot.

"We've got a winner here," he says. "I can feel it."

He steadies himself before throwing the dart with one swift movement, and it plows into the center of the board.

I clap my hands. "That was a warm-up shot."

"I'm a little rusty," he says with a chuckle. "You take the next one."

"You sure?" I ask. "I don't want to take anybody's eye out."

"Here," he says, moving to stand behind me. "Let me help you."

I take the dart between my fingers, and Ron covers my hand with his own. His cheek is so close to mine I can smell a hint of cinnamon on his breath, and it makes my pulse quicken. He guides me over a few steps.

"The trick is that you want to face your target head-on," he explains. "Now, relax your shoulders."

"Okay." Admittedly, it's hard to relax with the warmth of his breath tickling my ear, but I try to do as he says.

"You want to hold the dart with your thumb and first three fingers," he continues, helping position my hand. "And when you throw it, you want to follow through, extending your whole arm."

"I can do that," I say, miming his directions, giving myself a little run-through. "I've got this."

"I know you do."

"Okay, here we go." I take a deep breath, and when I release the dart, it at least makes it onto the board this time. "I did it!"

"Yeah, you did!" He smiles. "Look at you."

"Your turn," I say, beaming back at him as I hand him another dart.

He shoots again, narrowly missing one of the balloons. "Well, damn."

"We still have one more." My lips curl into a grin, and I give him the last dart. "And I think this is the winning shot."

"You know, I believe you're right." He pauses a moment, sniffing the air. "Do you smell that?"

I wrinkle my nose. "No. What does it smell like?"

"Victory," he says, and I can't help but laugh. "I'm getting you that penguin, Myra Jean. Here goes nothing." This time, he aims for a spot on the bottom row, shooting the dart at a downward angle. A loud pop causes me to jump, and the remnants of the balloon sag.

"You won!" I throw my arms around him. The gesture comes as easy as breathing, shocking us both.

"I told you I was gonna get you that penguin," he says into my hair.

When we pull apart, the teen barely glances up, reaching for the stuffed animal behind him.

"Here," the kid says, shoving it in Ron's direction.

"Thank you, young man." Ron is unfazed as he turns the penguin in his hands and grins. "Cute little fella, isn't he?"

My cheeks ache from smiling so much. "Yes, he is."

"For you, Myra Jean. I think you might be my lucky charm."

Ron presents me with the stuffed toy, and I hug it close.

"Thank you," I say. "I love it."

I look down at the penguin, my own little talisman of hope that I might be lucky enough to have years of good memories still ahead of me.

"You want to take a walk while the kids are finishing up?" he asks.

He offers me his arm, and I take it. Despite the excited atmosphere, I'm at peace. My limbs are loose, and my mind is still.

"Would you believe that as long as I've lived here, I've

never been to Mistletoe Fest?" he asks. "I'm glad I came. It's nice."

"We came every year before Henry died. Nothing could keep us away. Henry looked forward to it every year. We all did."

"Was it just too painful after losing him?"

I nod. "I thought the bad memories would be too overwhelming, because the last time we came five years ago was the night my world got turned upside down." I laugh to myself. "Henry was teasing me because I'd taken forever deciding which sweater to wear. I remember how he held my hand when we got out of the car, and the way the air smelled. Like pine. It was a perfect day."

Ron studies my face as we walk, his forehead scrunched into little worried lines.

I blow out a breath. "Later in the day, Henry started feeling sick. Said his stomach hurt and that he was going to head home and lie down. I told him I'd go with him, but he insisted I stay. The kids were having such a good time, and so was I. He didn't want to rain on our parade. Ben and Ellie said they'd take me home, and Henry said 'it's settled, then.' He kissed my cheek and left. I didn't even watch him go. Instead, I got swept up in the fun and moved on to the next thing. I think I stopped at a booth selling homemade snow globes."

We slow to a stop a few yards away from the entrance to the light show, out of the way of passersby.

"We had such a good night," I say, Ron's figure blurring in my watery eyes. "The lights were so beautiful, we went through the display twice, and we stopped for a cup of coffee after because we were cold. Ben and Ellie drove me back to the house. They wanted to walk me to the door but I waved them off. It was late. They needed to get home."

I sniffle. "I went inside, and I could hear the TV. The end of *A Christmas Carol* was playing. I was hungry, so I stopped in the kitchen to get some crackers." My voice broke, and Ron placed his hand on my arm. "I shouted to Henry and asked if he wanted anything, but he didn't answer. I went into the living room. It was dark except for the glow of the television, and he was so still, I thought he was asleep. So, I said his name once. When he didn't answer, I said it again, louder this time. But he didn't move, and that's when I realized something was wrong."

Ron's hand covers his mouth as he waits for me to speak, to tell my story in my own time.

"I called 911. The paramedics did everything they could. They tried all the way to the hospital, but he was gone. It was a heart attack," I say. "While I was looking at Christmas lights and having the time of my life, my husband was dying."

"Myra Jean, I'm so sorry."

"This festival became a shadow lurking in my mind, like a monster under the bed," I say. "I was so afraid if I looked, I'd find nothing but my worst moments."

He touches my arm. "Is that what happened when you came here tonight? Did it bring it all back?"

I shake my head. "Not at all. The monster turned out to be a shoebox full of some of the happiest memories of my life." I remove my glasses and wipe beneath my eyes with the sleeve of my coat. "This is the first time I've been able to talk about what happened without feeling bitter and sad. Coming here has been…cathartic."

He gives me an earnest smile.

"I'm sorry," I add quickly. "That was a lot to unload on you. I don't know why I did that."

"Don't apologize," he says. "I'm glad you felt comfortable enough to tell me."

"And I'm glad you're here," I say, holding his gaze. "Really glad."

"Me too, Myra Jean. Me too."

19

LINDSEY

"I hope she also informed you I had no idea what she was up to," I say, covering my cheeks with my hands as we walk along the trail for the light show. "I can't believe she told you."

Oliver chuckles. "She did, and she made sure to mention you had nothing to do with it."

The trees are shimmering overhead, bathed in the glow of warm fairy lights. They're so beautiful, they almost don't look real. The rest of our group is several feet ahead.

"I don't know what's more embarrassing—the fact that Aunt Rose fell while they were scheming to meet you, or that she *told you* that's what they were doing."

"It's hilarious. I think your mom is a hoot."

"And a *teensy* bit overbearing sometimes," I add.

"Maybe," he concedes. "But her heart's in the right place. I really think she just wants you to be happy."

"I know," I say. "And I am. I have been. My parents had this beautiful love story, and then Lucy and Ben found their perfect matches, and I think that made it hard for my mom to understand why finding someone stopped being a priority for me. It's not that I don't see how amazing it can be, because I do. It's just…"

I trail off, becoming nervous about where I've taken the conversation.

"You said it stopped being a priority, so does that mean it *was* at one time?" he asks, his arm touching mine as we walk.

I press my lips together, trapping my words inside.

How much is *too much* to say? Too much of myself to give away?

"It was," I admit.

His face softens as he peers down at me. "What changed?"

"I guess *I* did." I sigh, dropping my gaze to my boots crunching along the gravel path. "I didn't want to invite someone in only to be let down again."

"That's understandable."

"And after my dad passed so suddenly, the way I looked at life shifted. I realized I didn't need someone to sweep me off my feet in order for my life to begin. I already have everything I need."

"You do," he agrees. "It's one of the things I like most about you. You're not looking for anyone to complete you. You already have a life you love."

His fingers find mine, and my skin tingles with electricity.

"I just want the chance to be a part of it," he says.

My entire body vibrates. "I'd like that."

"Really?" he asks, and suddenly he trips, lurching forward and narrowly avoids falling on his face.

"Are you okay?" I ask, grabbing onto his arm.

He stops walking and pulls me off to the side, taking my

hands in his. "You make me nervous. In a good way. You have this uncanny ability to turn me into a bumbling fool, and I love every minute of it. I haven't felt like this about anybody in…well, a long time. Not since Jess."

My breath catches in my throat. "I haven't, either."

"Look, Lindsey—cards on the table—I'm not seeing anyone else. It's okay if you are. I don't want you to feel pressured in any way, but I want you to know, I'm serious. I care about you."

"I'm not seeing anyone else," I say, squeezing his fingers.

Oliver gives me a smile that makes my heart flutter so fast I think it could carry us up into the trees.

"Good," he says. "All right, then."

"All right," I echo, turning my eyes skyward. I chuckle to myself when I realize where we're standing.

"What's so funny?"

"Look up," I say, and he does.

We're standing beneath one of the many glowing trees, and hanging from its lowest branch is a sprig of mistletoe wrapped in twinkle lights.

"You know, one of the secrets of Mistletoe Fest is that this stuff is strung all along the path," I say. "There's probably hundreds of those things around here."

Our eyes meet again, and he tucks a piece of hair behind my ear. "Then I hope we find every single one."

BY THE TIME WE MAKE IT THROUGH THE LIGHT DISPLAY, we're all exhausted and start heading our separate ways.

"It's been fun, everybody," Kayla says as we approach the exit. "But I'm gonna head on out."

A chorus of goodbyes and good nights follow her.

"Dinner at two tomorrow?" Lucy asks.

Mom smiles. "Yep."

"See y'all then," Ellie says as she and Ben carry a sleepy Emily and Noah to the car.

Rose yawns, tossing a wave over her shoulder. "Good night, y'all. Nice meeting you, Ron."

"You too," he calls. "G'night."

"Well, Ron, are you ready to hit the road?" Oliver asks, his fingers still laced through mine.

"Sure am," Ron says. "Myra Jean, Doc, it's been wonderful."

"What do you say we do it again tomorrow?" Mom asks, causing me to turn my head so quickly it nearly gives me whiplash.

Ron chuckles. "I'm pretty sure the festival is a one-day-only event."

"Come to dinner at my house tomorrow," Mom says. "Both of you. Ron, you can bring June Bug too, if you like."

"You should," I add. "It'll be fun."

Ron's lips quirk into a grin. "I'd like that. Count me in."

"Me too," Oliver agrees.

Mom gives a single nod. "We'll see you tomorrow, then."

Ron hugs me and then my mother, and Oliver kisses my temple before the two of them start toward the parking lot.

"Come on," I say, gesturing to the right. "I'm over that way."

Once inside my car, I turn the ignition and get the heat going. The chill I've tried to hold off has burrowed its way into my bones and made itself comfortable, causing my entire body to throb.

I rub my hands together to warm them but stop because

even my fingers hurt. "It might take me until next year to thaw out."

"You mean all those kisses from Oliver didn't warm you up?" Mom asks, buckling her seat belt. "I saw you two canoodling all through the light display."

I snort. "What does that word even mean? Do regular people canoodle? I feel like I only ever hear about that word in reference to famous people. Like George Clooney. Or Leonardo DiCaprio."

"I bet George is a good canoodler."

"I say again, what does that mean?"

"You know," she says, moving her hands as though she's pulling her thoughts from thin air, "it's like a cuddle. A snuggle."

"You sure about that?" I arch an eyebrow at her, biting back a grin. "Because remember that time you said you had an out-of-control beaver?"

She gasps and swats my arm. "How was I supposed to know people used that word to describe their hoo has?"

"You said it so seriously too." I dissolve into a fit of giggles. "And it wasn't a beaver, it was a groundhog."

"Well, whatever it was, the little shit tore up my flower beds and ate all my herbs," she chokes out through her laughter. "Okay, forget the canoodle. You two seemed like you were having a good time."

"We were," I say, glancing in my rearview mirror as I back out of my spot. "Speaking of, you and Ron looked pretty chummy."

"I still can't believe you invited him." She's shaking her head in feigned annoyance, but joy radiates from her rosy cheeks.

I peer over at her while I join the long line of cars, waiting for my turn to pull onto the highway. "You didn't seem to mind all that much when you asked him to dinner tomorrow."

"I did do that, didn't I?" She grits her teeth as she smooths her hands over her pants.

"You did."

"Is that…Was it weird for me to do that?" she asks, her voice small and uncertain.

"What do you mean? Weird how?"

She shrugs and shifts in her seat. "These dinners are usually reserved for family. Ron's not family."

"Well, neither is Oliver, and this will be his second dinner with us."

"But you like him."

"And you like Ron," I say, and her gaze drops to her lap. "Don't you?"

She nods.

"It's not a marriage proposal," I say, my tone gentle. "It's just dinner."

"You don't think it'll upset Ben and Lucy by inviting him, do you?"

"What? Why would you think that?" I massage the back of my neck, attempting to dislodge the rock that's formed there.

She leans her head against the seat. "Will they think it's too soon? Will they think I've lost my mind?"

"Of course not."

"I'm serious, Lindsey," she says, facing me with wide, worried eyes.

"Oh my God, Mom. Stop. You're spiraling." I reach over and squeeze her arm. "I think we all want the same thing."

"And what's that?" she asks as I inch the car forward.

"For you to be happy," I answer, giving her a faint smile. "Are you? Happy?"

She sighs. "Today was one of the best days I've had since…well, you know."

"And that's all it has to be," I say. "There doesn't need to be any pressure, okay? We had a good day as a family with a couple new people we really like."

She takes a deep breath. "Yes. Okay. You're right."

I turn the knob on the radio. "You need something else to focus on. How about some Christmas music?"

"*Or* you could tell me more about Oliver."

"What do you want to know?" I glance out the window nonchalantly, as though I'm not bursting at the seams.

"Just one thing, really," she says, pinning me with her gaze. "Are you going to give this thing between you and Oliver a chance?"

I open my mouth to answer, but she keeps talking.

"Because he's such a great guy, Lindsey. He's everything I could have ever dreamed of for you and more. He's kind and thoughtful and brave. And not just in the obvious runs-into-burning-buildings sort of way. He got up on that stage because he knew I didn't want to. He did that for me, and I've seen how he is with you. So tender and gentle and—"

"Mom."

"Sorry." She holds out her hands, pumping the breaks on her own thoughts. "Anyway…are you? Going to give this a shot?"

I twist my lips and wait, as though I need even a second to consider it. As though my heart isn't firing off like a confetti popper.

"Well?" she asks again.

"I am," I answer finally.

"I knew it," she screeches, her feet dancing against the floorboard. "Oh, I'm so glad. He really is a sweetheart, and he clearly knows what a catch you are."

"There's something else," I say, holding up my finger. "But you have to promise you're not going to freak out if I tell you."

She squeals. "Okay."

"I mean it."

"Right. Yes." She shakes out her shoulders and releases a slow breath. "All right. I'm not going to freak out."

"Oliver told me he's not seeing anyone else."

"Really?" She presses her hand to her chest, trying to contain herself. "And what did you say?"

"I told him I'm not seeing anyone, either."

"Really?" This time, the question comes out as a squeak.

I chuckle and roll my eyes. "Oh fine. Go on. Let it out. You know you want to."

And she does, loudly shrieking her excitement. "I feel good about this, Lindsey," she says. "And your father would have too. He would have liked Oliver."

My chest constricts, and I tighten my grip on the steering wheel. "You think so?"

"I do."

I blow out a breath, a smile tugging on my lips. "We had a good day today."

"A damn good day." She places her hand on my knee and gives it a squeeze. I flinch, and her eyes crease with concern. "Oh no, sweetheart. Your fibro is acting up, isn't it?"

"A little." It's a white lie, but I don't want her to worry. "I was just out in the cold too long. I'll feel better after I get warmed up."

"I'll make you some hot cocoa when we get home," she says, already devising a plan to make me feel better.

"That'll do the trick." Another untruth, but I don't want anything to dampen my mother's mood tonight. Reality will just have to wait.

20

———

MJ

"Oh my," Ron says, taking his seat at the table. I'm standing at the head, in the spot Henry used to sit, and he's to my left. "This looks wonderful."

June Bug barks from her crate in the corner of the room.

Oliver chuckles. "I think June Bug agrees."

Ron gives me a subtle wink. "That's because she has great taste."

"Thank you." I adjust the platter of homemade rolls, making sure everything looks perfect. The pot roast is placed center stage with roasted potatoes, carrots, and a tossed salad. I also made some macaroni and cheese from scratch for the grandkids.

"Looks great, sister." Rose plops in the chair at my other side, immediately reaching for the bread. "You know these are my favorite."

The sound of chairs scooting against the wood floor fills the room as everyone takes their seats. Oliver pulls Lindsey's chair out for her, and it makes my heart sing. It's a simple gesture, but he does it with such ease that it seems almost second nature—like he's done it every day for years.

I clasp my hands together. "Dig in, everybody."

The chatter is lively as everyone serves up their plates. My worries about the kids being upset that I invited Ron were unfounded. From the second they walked in, they were nothing but welcoming.

"I'm glad you could come today, Ron," Ben says, passing the mac 'n' cheese down the table.

"Yes," Ellie agrees, scooping a spoonful of beans onto Noah's plate."How long have you lived in Loving?"

"I grew up just south of here," Ron answers. "In Columbia."

"And what are your intentions with my sister?" Rose ask, and I nearly choke on a carrot. Lindsey exchanges a wide-eyed glance with Oliver, while Ben hides his face behind his water glass.

"Oh no," Lucy says.

Ron raises his brows. "Come again?"

"Your intentions." Rose nods in my direction. "With her."

"Rose," I hiss.

"What?" Rose asks. "You're my only sister, and I don't want you to end up on one of those Netflix documentaries."

"I've been trying to tell you, you've got to lay off the true crime, Aunt Rose," Lucy teases. "It'll make you crazy."

I snort. "Too late."

"There are all kinds of horror stories about women our age being taken advantage of." Rose lifts her glass of wine. "I just want to know what his intentions are and what type of person he is. You like her, don't you?"

"Do we really have to do this?" I ask through gritted teeth.

"It's okay," Ron assures me. "It's a fair question, and it's simple to answer. I enjoy Myra Jean's company, and I want to get to know her better." He holds up his fork with a cubed potato speared on the end of it. "The delicious food is just a bonus. I'm a semiretired music teacher. I teach piano lessons part time now. I have a son, and I don't own any weapons or windowless white vans. However, I do enjoy cooking and watching reruns of *Friends*."

"I see." Rose nods, narrowing her eyes. "And which *friend* would you say you're most like?"

He takes a bite of his potato and chews, a contemplative expression on his face.

"I'd have to say Chandler," Ron says finally. "I can be a little dry at times, but I like to think I have a good sense of humor. And I'm a bit of a romantic."

Rose taps a red nail against her wine glass, glancing from Ron to me, then back to Ron again. Finally, she points at me with her fork. "Well *you*, Myra Jean, are as Monica as they come," Rose says. "You're an amazing chef, and you love playing hostess. You're everyone's caretaker, but you're also a little uptight. So, I approve."

"Well, I appreciate that, but there's nothing to approve of." I squirm in my seat, the implication of us being compared to two characters that make up one of the show's most iconic couples not lost on me.

Rose opens her mouth, likely to protest, but Ron cuts her off.

"And who would you be, Rose?" he asks.

"Rachel, obviously," she answers, and Ben, who's sitting next to her, nearly chokes on his water.

I chuckle. "Has anyone ever told you self-awareness isn't exactly your strong suit?"

Lindsey, Ben, and Lucy snicker.

"What?" she asks, chomping into her roll. "Who do *you* all think I am?"

"Phoebe," we say together, bursting into laughter.

She gasps. "I am not."

I stifle a giggle. "Have you met you?"

"I have to agree," Ron adds. "She's one of those characters that grows on you more with every rewatch. She's free-spirited, blunt, but she's also kindhearted and unapologetically herself. Now, I haven't known you long, but I think that sums you up pretty well."

I give him a small smile. Not only has he described my sister to a T, but he's just highlighted the many reasons I love her so beautifully. Rose is my best friend as much as she's my sister, and she's one of the biggest parts of my life. And Ron understands her.

More and more, I think Ron understands me too.

Rose considers his explanation for a moment, mulling it over as she picks up her glass, swirling the liquid inside.

"I see your point." Rose nods once and sighs. "I mean, I *am* pretty great."

"We couldn't agree more," I say.

Rose spears a carrot with her fork. "Have any of you heard anything about that Eddie O'Donnell fellow? He sure is a cutie. Do you think he's single?"

I shake my head, stifling a laugh, and Ron catches my eye. There's something comforting about his gaze. It's steady but exciting—familiar, yet completely new.

And somehow, that makes me feel new too.

"THOSE TWO SEEM TO BE GETTING CLOSE," RON WHISPERS IN the kitchen after dinner, gesturing toward the back door where we can see Lindsey and Oliver huddled together on the deck with steaming mugs of coffee in their hands.

"They do," I agree, snapping the dishwasher shut. "Are you sure you don't want some coffee?"

"I'll be up till next Sunday if I have caffeine this late," he says with a laugh.

"You can head into the living room if you want. I'll be in there as soon as I finish washing up these pots and pans." Lindsey and Oliver tried to do them for me, but I insisted they get some coffee and enjoy themselves. The rest of the kids and the grandkids are in the living room playing with June Bug, their laughter carrying through the house.

"I have a better idea," Ron says, grabbing the towel off the hook by the sink. "You wash, I'll dry."

I open my mouth to argue, but he beats me to the punch.

"I'm not taking no for an answer."

"Okay, then." I dunk my hands into the sink and set to work.

"Thank you again for inviting me and June Bug tonight. I've had a great time."

"I'm glad you came," I say, handing him a freshly-washed saucepan.

"So, I still owe you dinner this week."

The citrus scent of his aftershave and the warmth of his presence make me jittery, like I've had one too many toasted praline lattes.

"You know, you really don't have to," I insist, scrubbing the roasting pan with more vigor than I need to, just to have something to do with my hands.

"You're not trying to get out of our date, are you? What is it the kids call it these days? Ghosting?"

I chuckle. "Of course not."

"Good," he says. "When are you available?"

"This may come as a surprise to you, but my calendar isn't exactly packed with social engagements."

He grins, glancing over at me as he rubs the towel in every crevice of the skillet I just handed him.

"That does surprise me, actually. But hey, maybe that means I won't have to wait long to see you again," he says. "How about tomorrow night?"

The back of my neck prickles. "Tomorrow?"

"Sure. If you're not busy, of course."

"Tomorrow it is, then."

"I know I said I was going to take you out, but I was wondering how you'd feel about letting me cook for you."

I must have looked like he'd suggested we book a table to dine on the moon, because he starts to laugh.

"I take it you're used to being the one who does all the cooking."

"I am," I admit. "It's not that other people don't offer. The kids offer all the time, but it's just kind of my thing. What if I cook something and bring it ov—"

"I'm sorry, but this is a full surrender of kitchen responsibility."

"Oh…I, uh…" My words get lodged in my throat as I hand him the last dish.

"Myra Jean, it would be my honor to prepare a meal for you," he says. "Will you let me do that?"

With no more cookware left to scrape clean, I suddenly feel exposed, so I busy myself by ripping some paper towels off the dispenser by the sink to dry my hands.

"Sure," I answer. "I'd like that."

"Good." He places the last pot on the rack. "I'll pick you up at five tomorrow."

"I thought you were cooking at your place? I can just drive myself."

"I'd like to pick you up and bring you some flowers," he says, keeping his tone casual. "If that's okay with you, of course."

Heat rushes into my cheeks, and I nod. "That sounds… lovely."

"Perfect." His eyes linger on mine. "You ready to get back in there with the kids? Sounds like June Bug is giving them hell."

"Yes, I'm just going to pour myself a cup of coffee."

"I'll see you in there, then," he says, heading for the door.

I open the cabinet to pull down a mug, but Ron's voice stops me in my tracks.

"Oh, and Myra Jean?"

"Yes?" I say, turning toward him.

"Monica was always my favorite."

21

LINDSEY

"MJ, your tree is gorgeous," Oliver says, touching one of the shiny gold ornaments adorning the seven-foot faux spruce. My siblings have already gone home, and I'm standing in the living room with Oliver, June Bug, and Ron as they prepare to leave. "Actually, your whole house looks amazing."

"Isn't it beautiful?" I say. He's right. Sometimes, it's easy to take the magic of the home I grew up in for granted because I've seen my mother's holiday decorations every Christmas of my life. Her collection has grown over the years, but she's always maintained the perfect balance of cozy and simple elegance.

Lit garland rests atop the mantle where the stockings Mom knitted for us hang. Slender, flocked trees and glowing vines are placed throughout the house, and the banister leading up the stairs is swathed in greenery.

"Thank you, Oliver." Mom beams.

"When we were kids," I begin, "she and Dad used to

decorate the outside with so many colorful lights. It looked like a gingerbread house."

"We loved the look on your faces every year when we plugged them in for the first time. Gosh, I haven't seen the house like that in ages. It got to be too much for your father to climb up that rickety old ladder as we got older." Mom's smile turns nostalgic, and her eyes shine as she rubs a strand of my hair between her fingers. "We had some good times, didn't we, kid?"

"Yeah, we did," I say.

"Anyway." Mom sighs. "I'm so glad you both could come." June Bug wags her little tail at the sound of my mom's voice, and she kisses the pup on the nose. "You too, you precious thing. And I suppose, I'll see you both tomorrow night."

"I don't know who's looking forward to it more," Ron says, gesturing at June Bug. "Me or her."

"Are you sure I can't just drive myself?" Mom asks. "I hate for you to have to get out and—"

"I insist," Ron says, cutting her off.

"Okay, then," Mom says. "I'll see you tomorrow."

"Thank you again, MJ." Oliver gives my mom a hug. "Dinner was delicious."

"Anytime, hon," Mom says. "Y'all drive safely."

I step out onto the front stoop, the chilly night air stinging my cheeks, and Ron continues on to Oliver's truck with June Bug in tow.

"Good night, Ron," I say, and he throws a wave over his shoulder.

"So," Oliver says. "Tomorrow night, I'm meeting some guys from the fire hall for dinner and Monday night football at Snappy's Pizza. A couple of them are bringing their significant others, and I was wondering if maybe you'd want to come?"

I know what I should say. That as much as I want to spend time with him, I really need to stay home and rest. My fibromyalgia hasn't let up since yesterday, likely a result of too much cold exposure and simply pushing my body to the limits recently. But I don't want to tell Oliver that. He doesn't need to be worried about me, and I certainly don't want him thinking I'm making an excuse not to see him.

"Yeah, that would be fun," I answer finally. "I can meet you there after work."

"Perfect." He brushes my cheek with his thumb and presses his lips to mine. "I'll talk to you tomorrow."

"Good night."

I watch as he walks away, somehow managing to hold in my squeals of excitement until he's tucked safely inside his truck.

Nerves roll around in my stomach like dice. Oliver easily became a part of my world, but now, I was going to find out what it was like to be a part of his.

I CHANGE CLOTHES AND AM ABOUT TO LEAVE THE CLINIC WHEN Kayla pokes her head into my office a little after six thirty p.m. Lucy's already gone for the day, but we stayed behind to get everything prepared for the next day.

"Oliver's here," she says with an apprehensive smile on her face.

"Huh?" I glance down at my phone, and there are no missed texts or calls. "I thought I was meeting him at Snappy's."

She shrugs. "I dunno. He's up front."

"Maybe I misunderstood," I say, grabbing my coat and purse, but she stops me at the door.

"Are you sure you're okay to go tonight? You know I'm all about this thing with you and Oliver, but you've felt like garbage all day."

"I'm fine," I insist, though that isn't exactly true. I'm so exhausted that I fell asleep at my desk during lunch and had to rinse mustard out of my hair. My body aches all over like I have the flu. Except I know it isn't and there's no amount of time or medication to rid me of this feeling once and for all.

"Okay, but did you at least take your muscle relaxers?" she asks.

My silence is her answer.

"Lindsey," she hisses. "Seriously?"

I hold up my hands. "Fine. I'll take them." I dig in my purse for the tiny pill container I keep stashed inside and grab one.

She grabs my trusty water bottle from my desk and hands it to me so I can gulp down the medicine.

"You have got to start taking better care of yourself," she says with an accusatory glare.

"I'm fine," I lie again because it's easier than admitting she's right.

"Uh-huh."

"Well, I'm committed to faking it until I make it, okay?" I say, pushing past her and out into the lobby where Oliver is waiting.

"Hey you," he says with a smile.

I give him a peck on the cheek. "Everything okay? I thought I was meeting you."

He smiles. "Yeah. Actually, I was hoping I could catch

you before you left so we could ride together. There's some-where we need to stop on the way there."

"Oh, okay. Sure." I push my arms through the sleeves of my coat. "Kayla, I'll see you tomorrow."

"Y'all have fun," she says with one last stern glance in my direction that adds a silent *But not too much fun.*

"See ya later, Kayla," Oliver says as we step out into the cold.

"So, where are we going?" I ask as we stroll toward his truck hand in hand.

"It's a surprise," he says, his eyes glittering in the glow of the lamplight overlooking the parking lot.

"Hmm." I raise my brows at him. "I'm intrigued. Can you give me a hint?"

"Nope. But I think you're gonna like it."

Once inside his truck, we set off in pursuit of our mystery destination, but the path quickly becomes familiar.

"Wait…where are we going?" I ask as he turns onto the street I know like the back of my hand. The closer we get to my childhood home, the more confused I become.

"Wait…" I trail off. "Are we going back to my mom's?"

He grins over at me. "Yes, we are."

We roll to a stop in front of my mother's house. It's completely dark except for the porch light illuminating the front stoop.

"She's not here," I say. "I'm pretty sure Ron picked her up a while ago."

"He did. We're not here to see her, though." He unbuckles his seat belt and opens his door. "C'mon. I have something to show you."

"Okaaaay," I say, stretching out the word as I join him in the driveway. "What's this all about?"

"You'll see." With his hands on my shoulders, he leads me to the center of the yard. "Wait here. I'll be right back."

"What in the world?" I chuckle as he jogs up the walk and onto the porch. "Oliver, what is going o—"

I'm silenced by the buzz of thousands of lights coming on, their glow so bright I have to shield my face for a few seconds to allow my eyes to adjust. Oliver is back at my side by the time the spots in my vision fade to reveal the perfect gingerbread house.

"Oh my God." I cover my mouth with my hands as tears spring to my eyes. "How? When?"

"I had a little help," he says. "I knew Ron was picking your Mom up at five, so I asked a few of my buddies at the fire hall to pitch in. You'd be surprised how many Christmas lights six guys can put up when they have access to the ladder on a fire truck."

I shake my head in disbelief, speechless. It reminds me so much of the way my parents decorated the house when I was a kid that my heart aches. It's the perfect blend of past and present.

"Do you like it?" he asks.

Tears stream down my face, making the lights look as though they're in soft focus.

"Oliver, this is…" I trail off because no words seem big enough to describe how much this means to me. "This is the best gift anyone has ever given me. And Mom…She's going to love it." I fold my arms around him, and he holds me close. For a moment, I just stare at the house that built me, the home that held my family through better and worse.

"After hearing you and your mom talk about the way your dad used to decorate the house, I wanted to try and give you some of that magic again."

I rise on my toes to kiss him softly.

"You did," I whisper. "Thank you."

"You're welcome," he says, hooking an arm over my shoulders. "Come on. Let's get you out of the cold and go get some pizza."

We walk arm in arm back to the truck, the lights of memories past guiding the way.

22

—

MJ

"ARE YOU SURE I CAN'T DO ANYTHING?" I ASK RON WHILE HE stirs the saucepan simmering on the stove. The smell of basil and freshly grated parmigiana-Reggiano makes my stomach growl.

He nods toward the sleeping puppy in my arms. "You're on June Bug duty. That's a very important job."

"Well, this hardly seems like work." I run my fingers along her silky hair.

"Besides, dinner's almost ready. I've just got to throw this sauce over the pasta."

Ron and I lingered over salads and glasses of pinot noir before he set to work on dinner. While he started the prep, I looked at the collage of photos hanging in the entryway of his townhouse. Since we met, Ron has been the one submerged in my universe, so I enjoyed finally getting a peek inside his.

There were pictures of his son, Hudson, who looked like what I imagined Ron did in his thirties. He showed me his daughter-in-law and photos of his friends from when he was a teacher. He even had a plaque from when he was named Teacher of the Year a few months before he retired.

His home is exactly as I imagined—comfortable and full of reminders of a life well lived. June Bug's toys are scattered along the floor, and there are a few presents tucked under the modest live fir in his living room. It smells like clean laundry and coffee, which for some reason, feels like home.

Ron clasps his hands together. "Okay, Myra Jean. Dinner is served."

I gently place June Bug in her crate while he plates our food and tops off our wine glasses. He lights the small candelabra at the center of the small bar-height table that sits to the side of the kitchen, then pulls a chair out for me.

"Thank you," I say, my stomach fluttering as he takes a seat next to me. "This smells incredible."

"I'm excited for you to try it."

I place my napkin in my lap and pick up my fork, digging into the perfectly-cooked pasta. When I take a bite, I close my eyes, the mixture of tomato, garlic, heavy cream, and fresh basil converging together in a hallelujah chorus on my tongue.

"Oh my." I dab at the corners of my mouth with the napkin. "This is heavenly."

He gives me a satisfied smile. "I'm glad you like it."

"I *love* it," I say, taking another bite. "You certainly can cook."

"Thank you. I enjoy it. It relaxes me."

"Don't forget, I still owe you some biscuits and gravy."

He chuckles. "Trust me, I won't. I've been dreaming of those things since you told me about them."

"I'm going to have to step up my game if all your dishes are this good." I take a sip of my wine to pace myself so I don't inhale the entire dish. I was so nervous about our date that I'd barely eaten the sandwich Ellie picked up for me while she was out, and our pre-dinner salads hadn't done much to stifle the growls of my stomach.

"I'm good," he says, "but trust me, you're the only pro here."

"I don't know about that."

"Did Henry like to cook?" he asks. "And if that's at all uncomfortable for you to talk about with me, I understand. But he's an important part of your life, so I want to know about him."

My breath catches, and I clear my throat, resting my fork on my plate.

"I apologize," he adds quickly. "I didn't mean to overstep."

"You didn't," I say. "It's just, I'm not used to hearing people talk about him in the present tense. It's always 'he *was* a good husband' or 'he *was* a big part of your life,' so it caught me off guard is all."

He nods, his eyes fixed on me for a moment before he speaks again.

"I'm not good at this, so forgive me if I'm a little direct," he begins. "I've grown quite fond of you since I showed up on your doorstep to pick up my puppy, whom you kindly allowed to terrorize your home, though we'd never even met."

I can't help but chuckle. "She wasn't *that* bad."

He smiles. "When I first laid eyes on you, I thought you were the most magnificent woman I'd ever seen. But as I started to get to know you, I discovered your heart is somehow even more beautiful."

I lower my gaze and swallow hard, willing my racing heart to slow.

He hooks his finger beneath my chin and lifts my head up so he can look into my eyes.

"Myra Jean, I mentioned your husband in the present tense because I know he's very much still a part of you, and I don't want to change that. You don't get to be our age without living a whole lot of life. We've both got a good bit of mileage behind us, but I never want you to feel you have to leave your husband in the rearview. I don't need to be in the driver's seat or even the passenger seat. I'm just happy to be in the same car with you, if you'll let me."

I blink, sending the tears that formed in my eyes cascading down my cheeks. The nerves that kept me company all day have slipped out the side door, leaving me and Ron alone at last. I didn't realize how much I needed to hear what he said, how much I needed to know that it was still okay to love my husband. That perhaps it was somehow possible for me to miss him and love him and even grieve him while still moving forward.

He wipes away the moisture on my face with the pad of his thumb, and I grasp his hand before he can pull it away.

"Okay," I say finally. "But I've got to warn you, I've been told I drive like a bat out of hell."

A grin stretches across his face. "Guess I better buckle up."

AFTER DINNER, RON AND I TALK ON THE COUCH WHILE throwing a ball for June Bug. He tells me tales about his years teaching and about the time he talked to Johnny Cash in a bar ages ago without knowing it was him until The Man in Black was already out the door. We talk about our kids, and when

Henry comes up as he often does in many of my stories, Ron is unbothered. Instead, he asks me questions, content to get to know Henry as an extension of me.

When the time comes for Ron to drive me home, my heart and belly are full, but my limbs are light and airy like cotton candy. He takes the scenic route so we can look at the homes decked out in Christmas lights.

"Look at that." I point out the window to a house that has an alarmingly real-looking Santa that appears to be stuck in their chimney headfirst. "I don't know if that's cute or traumatizing. If Lindsey had seen something like that as a kid, she would have been convinced it was real and that we needed to save him. I would have had to knock on their door with a weeping five-year-old and beg them to prove Santa wasn't actually stranded up there."

He laughs. "Why do I get the feeling you're speaking from experience?"

"Because I am," I say. "We had a neighbor for a few years that went all out for their holiday displays, and they had a similar decoration one time. Only theirs was the back end of a reindeer that looked to have crashed into an upstairs window. Lindsey was so distraught when she saw it that she managed to call 911 without me knowing. Imagine my surprise when two very confused EMTs showed up at my door after getting a call about an injury."

"That kid of yours sure has a good heart. I believe she'd help anyone."

"She would, and she does. Lindsey is like her dad, through and through."

He glances over at me and smiles. "I think she's a lot like you too."

We pull onto my road, and I see the glow of a massive light display up ahead.

"Oooh, I wonder whose lights those are," I say. "They must have just put them out. I thought I'd seen everyone's decorations on this street."

Ron doesn't say anything as we approach my house, bringing the lights closer and closer into view.

"Wow. That's beautiful. Whose house *is* th—" I cut myself off with a gasp when I finally see the source of the holiday cheer. "That's *my* house."

Ron pulls into my driveway as I shake my head in bewilderment.

"What on earth?" I press my fingers to my open mouth as we climb out of the car, and he follows me as I walk toward the middle of the yard so I can take it all in.

"How? Who could have done this?" I ask, the corners of my eyes stinging. "It couldn't have been the kids because they would've had to do it while I've been with you, and there's no way they could have finished something like this in that amount of time."

Ron chuckles, curling an arm around my shoulders. "It was Oliver. He called and told me about his plan because he wanted to make sure I was still picking you up."

I have no words as I stare ahead at my perfect gingerbread house. I blink rapidly, my vision becoming a viewfinder of the past. Each time my eyes close, there's a flash of Henry and me, standing in this very spot with the kids whose tiny faces are tipped back in awe. It was beautiful then, and it's beautiful now.

"Of course it was," I say, unable to stop smiling. "That precious boy."

"He really outdid himself, didn't he?"

"Did he ever." Laughter bubbles out of me as I loop my arm through Ron's and start up the walk.

With every step, I notice something new. The giant lollipops that stand out from behind the shrubs, the snowman that tips his hat, and the way the hundreds, if not thousands, of lights on the roof twinkle like a starry night sky.

"This couldn't have been a more perfect night," I say as we climb the porch steps.

But standing with Ron in the soft glow of the Christmas lights, I know that's not entirely true. There is one thing that could make it even more special, only I'm not sure I have the guts to do it.

Just then, out of the corner of my eye, I catch a glimpse of something green hanging above the center of the doorframe: mistletoe. Maybe it's a sign. Or maybe Oliver knew exactly what he was doing when he put it there. Either way, it's the push I need.

"Actually, now that I think of it, there is something that could make it better."

"What's that?" he asks.

I don't say a word, I don't overthink. To be honest, I'm not even sure I'm breathing when I close the distance between us, take his face in my hands, and kiss him.

23

———

LINDSEY

"Beckett," says Joe, the fire marshal, patting Oliver on the back and taking a swig of his beer. "Good thing you're better at being a firefighter than you are at playing pool."

Oliver gets a mischievous gleam in his eyes. "Or maybe I've been letting you win because you're my boss."

"Guess we've got to play another round and find out," Joe says with a wink. "Ladies, if you'll excuse us."

Oliver leans down to kiss me on the cheek before they head back to the vacant pool table.

We watched the game on the big screens at Snappy's, and at halftime, Oliver and the guys decided to hit the pool table. Their buddies Martinez, Sanders, and his girlfriend tapped out after the Green Bay Packers won, leaving me and Joe's wife, Tessa, sitting at a table nearby, munching on the remainder of the cinnamon dessert pizza we ordered somewhere around game three.

"Oh no. The trash talking has begun." Tessa turns back toward me, shaking her head. "Joe has a bit of a competitive streak, in case you didn't notice."

"Really?" I tilt my head to the side, feigning surprise as the guys start their sixth game. "I never would have guessed."

"So, how long have you and Oliver been together?" Tessa asks, twirling a piece of her long blonde hair around her finger.

"Um." A nervous laugh bubbles out of me. "We actually just started dating. This is very new."

Her eyes widen. "No way. Really? Wow, I would have thought y'all had been together for years. I just assumed you moved here with him."

"Why's that?" I ask, taking a sip of my soda.

"I don't know." She taps a short, sparkly nail against her chin. "It's just the way you are with each other. Comfortable."

I drop my gaze to the table, picking at a piece of the sugar-dusted crust left on my plate. It *does* feel like I've known Oliver for ages, even though it's not quite been a month.

"Joe and I were like that," she says, glancing at her husband, who's crouched over the pool table, preparing to make his next shot. "You know, I was married before to my high school sweetheart. We were together six years, married for one, and let me tell you, that was one year too long. Thought I'd never get married again in a million years. I spent the rest of my twenties single as a dollar, not looking for change. It wasn't long after my thirtieth birthday that Joe came into the salon for a haircut, and that was all she wrote. We went down to the courthouse and got married two months later. That was ten years ago."

"Wow. Two months?" I ask. "Were you nervous at all?"

"Oh yeah." She chuckles. "I got cold feet and almost called it off the morning of. My mom wasn't on board with her little girl getting married so fast, especially after what I went through with my ex, and it just got in my head."

"What made you decide to go through with it?"

"He showed up at my apartment to talk things out about an hour later, and he brought my favorite coffee," she recalls with a nostalgic smile. "Which may not sound like a big deal, but even after all the years my ex and I were together, he *still* couldn't remember what I liked. I ordered coffee in front of Joe *once*. He paid attention. Hell, he still does. Sometimes that looks like having dinner made when I get home because he could hear in my voice while on the phone that I had a rough day at work. Other times, it looks like him watching my silly reality shows and pretending to be interested simply because I love them."

"Anyway, we got married, and I never looked back," she continues. "I think I always knew he was my person. Call it intuition. Or maybe it's an instinct we have that becomes sharper after being with the wrong people. Maybe it becomes easier to identify the right one. Whatever it was, I think sometimes we just know."

"Maybe you're right," I say.

"Hey, babe," Joe calls over to Tessa. "You mind closing out our tab? Beckett here just sank the eight ball."

"Sure thing," Tessa answers. "Anyway, we should do this again. Maybe we could go on a double date sometime."

"I'd like that."

"We'll set something up for after New Year's," she says, rising to her feet. "I'll be right back."

Oliver catches my eye from across the room and starts toward me, making everything around us fade.

"I sank that ball on purpose," he says, sliding into the seat next to me. "I was hoping to have you to myself for a bit before I take you back to your car, if that's okay. I know it's a work night."

"I think I can manage to stay out a little longer before I turn into a pumpkin. Is there somewhere you'd like to go?" I ask, hoping that wherever it is, it'll be warm. Even with all of my layers, my body is still chilled.

"Actually, there is." He leans in closer. "Are you afraid of heights?"

I shake my head, but concern is tiptoeing inside my brain. Maybe he wants to take me to a really tall…building?

"Why?"

He reaches for my hand. "There's something I'd like to show you."

"THE FIRE HALL?" I ask with a laugh as Oliver turns into the lot. "You do know I'm from here, right? A visit to the fire hall was customary every year when I was in elementary school."

"I promise you've never seen this," he says, pulling to a stop near one of the rigs out front.

He opens the door for me, and I realize someone is waiting by the fire truck. As we get closer, I recognize her as the woman who responded to the call with Martinez when Ron got sick.

"Evening, Beckett," she says with a smile, and he greets her with a wave. "Nice to see you again, Lindsey."

I nod, still unsure of what we are seeing her for. "You too."

"Thanks again for doing this, Helen," Oliver says. "I know it was kind of short notice."

"No problem," she says. "Better than watching Smith kick Tucker's ass at chess again."

Oliver chuckles. "When will Tucker realize he can't Uno reverse himself into beating Smith? He's the only one here that remains undefeated."

"Who are you telling, Rookie? I've been here for eight years," she says. "There's always some dingleberry that can't accept defeat. Anyway, y'all heading up?"

"Up?" I ask. "Up where?"

Helen motions toward the fire truck and then toward the sky.

I whip my head toward Oliver. "Um, I don't know. Are we?"

"We sure are," he says. "There's something I want you to see, but you can only see it from up there."

My muscles are already throbbing, and I'm so cold, it physically hurts. Why didn't I tell him I needed to get home? That I have an early morning tomorrow.

Of course, I know why. What if he sees I'm not exactly the perfectly put-together version of myself he's gotten to know? It was a problem for Daniel, so how can I know it won't be one for Oliver too?

"You said you're not scared of heights, right?" he asks.

"No," I say quickly. "Definitely not."

"I'll be with you the whole time." He presses a kiss to my forehead. "I won't let you fall."

"Are you sure this is okay?" I ask, stalling, hoping someone will call with a barnyard animal stuck on a roof and need this very rig.

"Actually, it was Joe's idea," he admits.

The fire marshal has stamped his seal of approval on this activity, so I don't think I'm getting out of it.

Unless I just tell him the truth.

"See those supports?" Oliver asks, pointing to the metal

legs attached to the rig. "Those keep the truck stabilized, and Helen will be right here just in case we need anything. You'll be secure at all times."

I force a tight-lipped smile to cover my chattering teeth. "Let's do this."

We step onto the bucket, and he latches the door behind us.

"First, we've got to fasten you in." He wraps a large belt around my waist and tightens it, drawing me closer. Even as crummy as I feel physically, I love being next to him.

After putting on his own belt, he pulls me into him with one hand and maneuvers the control panel with the other.

"Elevator going up," he says, and with a small jolt, we're on our way.

I nestle into his chest as the view around us starts to shift, and it feels like we're closer to the stars than to the ground. In a matter of seconds, we're above the buildings, high above the trees. That's when I see it.

"What do you think?" he asks as we crawl to a stop.

I draw in a breath. "It's beautiful."

From up here, Loving is a cluster of colorful constellations. The Christmas lights scattered all throughout town resemble fireworks. Forever suspended in the night, never burning out.

"It's magical, isn't it?"

I nod. And it is. I only wish this magic could make the pain that's seeped into my bones disappear.

He must feel me tremble because he moves his hands up and down my arms to warm me.

"I clearly didn't think this through with the weather," he says, holding me tighter. "I should have stopped to get us some hot chocolate."

I laugh, but my voice shakes. "To be fair, I'm not sure I could hold anything because I can't feel my fingers. It was worth it, though."

"We should get you back to your car so you can get home to your mom's and warm up."

He reaches for the panel, but I stop him. "Wait. Let's stay just a little longer."

I know that tomorrow, I'll regret every minute spent in the cold, every second I haven't rested, despite my body begging me to. I might hate myself in the morning, but tonight I want to enjoy the perfect view with the perfect man because I know moments like this don't last forever.

"Penny for your thoughts?" he says, peering down at me.

I slide my arms up his chest and around his neck. "Kiss me."

"LINDSEY, SWEETIE, ARE YOU OKAY? LUCY JUST CALLED. Lindsey? It's after eight."

"What?" I bolt upright, sending a sharp pain through my neck. "No, it can't be."

I blink hard, desperate to clear the fog that's settled around my brain, and snatch my phone off the nightstand. Sure enough, it's 8:13 a.m., which means I'm late for work.

My mom sits on the edge of the bed, petting Catrick Swayze who hasn't so much as lifted his head. "Honey, you don't look like you feel well. Maybe you should reschedule your appointments for the day."

"I can't," I say. "They need me. I'll be fine. Just tired is all."

"Your fibromyalgia is flaring up, isn't it?" she asks as I

slide out from under the covers. "You really should take a day to rest. You know your father would want—"

"Mom, I'm okay. I've got everything under control," I insist, knowing full well I do *not*.

My mother opens her mouth to protest, but I grab my scrubs and run to the bathroom to change. I brush my teeth just long enough to knock the morning breath off my tongue and swish around some mouthwash while I throw my hair in a haphazard bun.

When I return to my room, my mom is waiting outside the door.

"Is there anything I can do to help?" she asks as I rush by her to grab my purse, phone, and keys. "You look exhausted. Maybe I could just drop you off at the clinic? I'm on my way into the office now."

"I've got this, Mom." I pause long enough to peck her on the cheek. "Thank you, though. Love you," I call as I dash down the stairs and out into the cold.

Thankfully, my drive to work is even shorter from my mom's house, allowing me to make it there in six minutes.

I burst through the door to find two clients in the lobby and Kayla eyeing me as though a wild animal just strolled in wearing a top hat.

"Sorry I'm late. I got held up this morning." I turn to address the waiting pet owners in the lobby before I push through the entrance to the back. "I'll be right with y'all."

Before the door can close behind me, Kayla's on my heels.

"Lindsey, how about I reschedule the rest of your day?" she asks, following me into my office.

"No need." I toss my bag on the desk and grab my lab coat from the back of the chair. "Just let my next one know

I'm running a little behind, but I should be able to catch up."

Kayla body blocks me as I try to leave the room. "Lindsey, you know I love you, right?"

"Yes, but I need to get to work," I say, attempting to step around her, but she holds out her arm to stop me.

"I don't think you understand," she says, lowering her voice. "You look a little like a feral possum fresh out of the dumpster."

"Lindsey, is that you?" I hear Lucy's voice before she appears in the doorway. "Are you—" She cuts herself off with a sharp intake of breath. "Oh my God, what happened to you?"

"She got *held up*," Kayla answers for me.

"At gunpoint? Because I guess that would explain it," Lucy says. "Seriously, you look like shit."

"Gee thanks, y'all." I roll my eyes. "I just overslept and didn't have time to get ready. It's not a big deal."

"You're having a fibro flare, aren't you?" Kayla asks. "I knew it. Lindsey, you need to rest. You can't keep burning the candle at both ends."

"Sure, I can," I quip. "Because now I have a hot fire-fighter boyfriend that can put out the flames."

Kayla folds her arms over her chest. "I suppose he could if he knew about your illness, but he doesn't, does he?"

Oof. Checkmate.

"Look, I'm fine." Kayla and Lucy lift their brows, so I clarify. "I'll *be* fine. I just need some coffee, and I'll be good to go. Promise." I grip Kayla's arms. "Will you please, please, *please* grab me a cup? I'll get it after I see the first patient."

She sighs. "*If* you agree to go straight home after work tonight and rest. Do not pass go, do not collect two hundred dollars, and definitely do not go out with your superhot boyfriend, no matter how superhot he is."

"Okay, okay." I hold my hands up in surrender. "Coffee. Pretty please?"

"I mean it," she says as I squeeze past her.

"And the insurance adjuster called here for you," she adds before I can make it far. "Said she's been trying to reach you."

"Shit," I mutter under my breath. I intended to call her yesterday, but it slipped my mind. The insurance company completed their investigation, and now I need to pick a company to handle the smoke mitigation. I just wish I could clear the smog in my head long enough to get my act together.

"Okay, thank you," I say and scurry away before either of them can remind me of anything else I've forgotten to do.

I'M CATCHING UP ON EMAILS WHILE I FINISH SCARFING DOWN the lunch my sister got me when a knock on my office door causes me to jump, nearly knocking over my soda.

"Oliver?" I say, rising to my feet. "What are you doing here? I thought you were working today."

He's handsome as ever with two Southern Bean coffees in his hands. I'm grateful I took the time between patients to borrow some mascara from Kayla and also dotted some rosy-pink lipstick on my cheeks. It didn't work miracles, but it did return some life to my face. Now, instead of sick and tired, I just look tired. I'll take what I can get.

"Well, I was," he says, coming around to kiss me on the cheek before handing me one of the cups. "But I ended up with the day off. I hope you don't mind me dropping by. Kayla told me I could head on back."

"Of course, I don't mind," I say as he sits across from me. "So, what are you going to do with the rest of your day?"

"Well, that's kind of why I'm here." He shifts in his seat and clears his throat. "The chief sent me home when he found out it was my birthday. Said he had plenty of people on and to consider it a gift."

"Today's your birthday? Oh my God! Happy birthday," I say. "Oliver, why didn't you tell me before?"

"I don't like to make a big deal about them, mostly because there was only ever one person in my life who made them special." He gives me a faint smile. "But I was thinking that if you don't have plans tonight we could get dinner together. Maybe watch a movie. It doesn't have to be anything special."

"Of course, it does," I say. "You deserve to be celebrated. I'm taking you out tonight."

"You don't have to—"

"How about I pick you up at seven and take you to Opryland Hotel for dinner," I say, leaning forward with my head on my hands. "We can see the lights, maybe do some ice skating. It'll be fun."

His eyes brighten. "Really?"

A flutter beyond the entrance of the door catches my eye. Kayla is a few feet from the opening, waving her arms like a mad woman. When she has my attention, she shakes her head, points to me, and then mimes sleeping.

I ignore her. "Of course."

Kayla slashes her finger across her throat and pins me with a death glare before disappearing from sight.

"I'd love that," Oliver says with a grin. "Thank you."

"You don't need to thank me. I want to spend the time with you." I can rest tomorrow night. This is more important.

"Well," he says, rising to his feet. "I guess I should let you get back to it. I have a couple errands I need to run."

"Thank you for the coffee." I maneuver around my desk to wrap my arms around him. "I needed a little pick me up, and seeing you was the icing on the cake, birthday boy."

His lips find mine in a tender kiss. "It's been a long time since I've even done anything for my birthday, so it just…it means a lot."

"I'll see you tonight," I say, and with one more kiss, he's out the door.

Before I can even get back to my chair, Kayla is in the room, closing us inside.

"What the hell was that?" she hisses.

I plop down and press the heels of my palms into my eyes. "Kayla, what was I supposed to do? It's his birthday. I'm not going to let him be alone."

"How about a smidge of honesty?" she asks. "I'm not feeling so hot. How about a movie on the couch? Or better yet, let me take you out this weekend after I've gotten some rest?"

"A movie on the couch isn't enough," I say. "Oliver deserves more."

"And so do you," she shoots back. "You deserve better than the way you're treating yourself. It's not noble to hide your pain from everyone, Lindsey."

"Not everyone needs to know," I say. "I don't want to bother people with my problems."

She draws back with an incredulous glare. "Your problems? You mean your *life*?"

I massage my temples with my fingers. "I will tell him eventually. When the time is right. But I've been down this road before, Kayla. You know how Daniel—"

"Was a pretentious asshat?" she asks, cutting me off. "I'm well aware. We've been through this. What happened with Daniel had nothing to do with you. It wasn't because of your illness or your grief or any other stupid excuse he gave you. He did what he did because he's an insufferable piece of shit."

I rake my hands over my face and sigh. "I need to do this, okay? I'll rest tomorrow night."

She props her hands on her hips. "I'm moving up your last appointment of the day so you can leave a little early. If you're doing this, you're going home to take a nap beforehand."

I open my mouth to argue, but she beats me to it.

"So help me God, I will look in Oliver's records for his phone number and call him myself if you—"

"Okay, okay," I relent. "Fine. And I'll go straight home after work tomorrow to rest. I swear."

Her nostrils flare as she breathes out. "I'm sorry I got testy. I love you, you ding-dong."

"I love you too," I say with a faint smile.

"I know," she says softly. "I just wish you would also give a little of that love to yourself. But anyway, finish your coffee, and I'll go call your last client."

"Thank you," I say as she backs out of the room.

This is good. This is more than good. I'll go home, take a quick nap, and that'll get me through the night so I can make sure Oliver's birthday is one he won't forget.

24

———

MJ

"*You* kissed *him*?" Rose asks as we sit in my living room Tuesday night. We're curled up on the couch with a giant bowl of popcorn and two glasses of wine under the pretense of watching *White Christmas*, but so far, all we've done is talk. Lindsey's upstairs asleep, having looked like death warmed over when she got in early from work. She wouldn't even let me make her something to eat, saying she just needed to lie down for a bit, but that was hours ago. I know she needs the rest, so I didn't dare disturb her.

"Yes," I say, pushing my hand through my hair. "I'm freaking out here, Rose. I *kissed* someone. Someone who is not my husband."

"And I think that's great. But I also think it wouldn't be the worst thing in the world for you to consider a time when perhaps you might do *more* than kiss someone."

"What's that supposed to mean?"

She raises her eyebrows. "You know."

"Clearly I don't."

"You know." Rose lets out an exasperated huff. "Sending Ron on a spelunking mission down south."

I gasp. "Oh my God, Rose. What is wrong with you?"

She holds out her hand, examining her perfect red nails. "I ask myself this every day."

"That is the last thing I want to think about."

"Why?" she asks. "You're not dead yet, woman. You mean to tell me you don't miss it? Not even a little?"

My cheeks are on fire, but I refuse to give her the satisfaction of admitting she's right. I *do* miss it, but I also miss Henry.

"Look, I know Henry was the love of your life," Rose says, as though reading my mind. "But what if you get more than one?"

"Doesn't that kind of defeat the purpose? If you get more than one, they're not really *the one*, are they?"

"Aren't we more evolved than that, Myra Jean? You can love Henry for the rest of your life, *and* you can still move on and love someone else. It doesn't have to be either/or," she says. "And maybe Ron won't be the right guy, but I think you should be open to the idea that there's more than one person on this planet for you."

I blow out a breath. "I don't know. It's so hard to imagine."

My sister pins me with her eyes. "Is it really? Because I'm not so sure it is. In fact, I think you *have* imagined it, and that's why you've got your panties in a twist. The very idea has you petrified."

I drain the rest of my wine in one gulp. "Well, can you blame me?"

"Of course not." Her face softens. "It's okay to be scared. I'd be worried if you weren't. But you can't let fear rule your life. We may not be spring chickens anymore, but we've got a lot of years left. And if you get the chance to be loved twice, you should take it."

"This, from my perpetually single sister."

"You know the whole relationship thing has never been my bag, but it *has* been yours," she says. "I have all the companionship I want, and I'm happy with my life as is." She hoists herself off the couch and takes my empty glass. "But are *you*?"

I open my mouth but close it again.

Am I happy? Will I be happy if this is all there is?

"I'm going to get us a refill," she says. "I'll be back."

I nod, staring ahead at Henry's stocking that I still hang from the mantle.

If she asked me the question just days ago, before I met Ron, I would have said no. I wasn't happy, and I couldn't imagine a time when I would be again. There were fleeting moments of something resembling joy, but they were inevitably swallowed whole by grief.

Grief not only for the loss of my husband, but also for the years we lost, a future we would never see together.

However, something's changed since I met Ron. I've smiled and laughed more than I have in a long time. He's unearthed parts of me I thought were buried in a cemetery, left behind, along with the rest of my heart. But maybe they were never really gone. Maybe it just took them a while to find their way home.

"Okay," Rose says, returning to the sofa with our drinks. "I need details about this kiss. Tell me everything."

I snort as she hands me my glass. "Absolutely not."

"Oh, come on. Humor me." She kicks at my leg with her sock-covered foot. "What was it like?"

I toss a handful of popcorn in my mouth. "Like leaping off a building," I garble.

"You know, you're not exactly selling this," she says, wrinkling her nose.

I chuckle, taking a swallow of wine. "I wasn't finished. I was going to say it was like leaping off a building, being completely terrified, only to find out I could fly."

"Aw." Rose presses a palm to her chest. "That might be the cutest, most disgusting thing I've ever heard."

I swat her arm with a throw pillow.

"When are you seeing him again?" she asks.

"Tomorrow. We're meeting for lunch at The Southern Bean."

She rolls her eyes. "Oooh, a lunch date. How sexy."

I throw up my hands. "What would *you* have me do? Make out with him in the back row of a movie theater like a teenager?"

She smirks. "I mean…yes."

25

LINDSEY

BELLS. WHY ARE THERE SO MANY FREAKING BELLS? THE noise pries me from my dreams as I wipe sleep from my eyes.

The sound stops, and I feel for my phone on the nightstand. I peer at the screen through slits. It shows seven unread texts and four missed calls, all from Oliver, and that it's now 8:03 p.m.

I shoot upright, my breathing turning shallow as my phone rings again. Oliver's name flashes across the screen.

"Oliver, I'm so sorry," I answer immediately.

"Oh, thank God," he says, and I can hear the relief in his voice. "Are you okay? I started getting worried when I didn't hear from you."

"Yes," I say quickly, trying to think of any excuse to make this okay. "I'm fine. We had an emergency…um, at the clinic. Someone brought in a dog with…uh…a broken leg."

"Wow. Really?" he asks.

I clear my throat. "Yep. That's right. Poor thing took a tumble off the bed. Anyway, I'm just about to leave now and grab a change of clothes, and then I'm headed your way."

The line goes quiet, and I think we've been disconnected. "Oliver?"

"That's weird because I'm outside the clinic right now, and no one's here," he says, and my heart sinks. "I finally drove over when I didn't hear anything. I was worried something was wrong—that you had a flat tire or God forbid, an accident on the way home."

My throat goes dry, and my stomach churns. "I'm sorry. It's not what it looks like."

"Really?" he asks, the hurt in his voice so palpable I can feel it oozing from the phone. "Because what it looks like is that you lied to me."

That's exactly what I did, but it's not for any of the awful reasons he probably thinks.

"Oliver, please. I can explain—"

"Are you hurt?" he asks.

"No," I answer.

"Are you okay?"

"Yes."

"Good," he says softly. "Did you lie to me?"

Tears well in my eyes, blurring my vision. I can't bring myself to answer. To hurt him more than I already have.

"Okay," he says.

"Please forgive me. I swear, it's not what you think," I plead. "Let me make it up to you."

"The thing is, it's *exactly* what I think. I'm sure you have a reasonable explanation, but instead of giving it to me, you lied. You lied like it was easy. And honestly, my experience with people who lie is that they usually do it because they have something to hide."

Only myself. "I'm so sorry I hurt you. Can we talk about this?"

"Not tonight," he says. "I need time to think and sleep this off. We can talk tomorrow."

"Okay," I say, barely above a whisper. "I really am sorry."

I hear him sigh. "Me too. Good night, Lindsey."

The line goes dead, but I cradle the phone to my chest as though doing so might keep our connection alive a moment longer. As though somehow, he will feel my remorse through this little rectangle.

I allow myself to fall against the mattress and curl my legs against my chest. How did I let this get so messed up? I was trying to keep him from seeing me like this. Because what if it's too much?

What if *I'm* too much?

There's only one person I want to talk to right now, but he's also the only person I can't reach. I wish heaven had cell reception because I'd give anything to hear my father's voice. For him to tell me everything will be okay. Instead, I settle for the next best thing. I get up and tiptoe to my mother's home office next door where she keeps the family photo albums.

Stretching on my toes, I run my fingers along the tops of the built-in shelves until I feel the soft leather of the one I'm searching for. I pull down the photo album, hugging it to my chest as I carry it back to my bed.

The binding cracks slightly when I open it, and my breath catches in my throat. On the first page is a collage of pictures from when I was a little girl. In the first, I'm sitting on my dad's shoulders with fistfuls of his hair clutched in my hands while he watches TV. In another, Dad is asleep on the couch, holding a baby Lucy. Then he's in a rocking chair, reading to me and a diaper-clad Ben. We're snuggled into his arms, back when we believed no harm could come to us as long as Dad was around. Somehow, we never considered that harm could come to him.

I suck in a breath and turn the page, taking in memory after beautiful memory. Like that summer when I was eleven, when a hummingbird flew into the back door so hard, it stunned itself. Dad scooped the little guy up, running his finger along the bird's belly. Mom snapped a picture of me watching him, my eyes wide with wonder, the moment before the tiny creature flew away. I thought my father must be magic. And to me, he was.

By the time I get to the last page, tears are dripping onto the thin plastic sheets protecting each memory. I swipe my thumb over the portrait of my dad on the funeral program tucked inside the back of the book. It still knocks the wind out of me every time I see it.

I shut the album and lay it beside me before crawling under the covers, bringing my knees to my chest. My shoulders shake, and my breath comes in shuddered gasps. I weep for my father. For the lessons he hadn't gotten around to teaching me yet. For the little girl locked inside that photo album, who doesn't know what it means yet to have a broken heart. And for me, the woman who does.

I SENSE MOVEMENT BESIDE ME, AND IT STARTLES ME AWAKE.

"I'm sorry, honey," my mother says softly. "I was heading to bed when I noticed your light still on. I was going to turn it off, but I saw the album and thought I better move it so you wouldn't roll over on it in your sleep."

"Oh." I nod and rub at my puffy eyes as I sit up.. Catrick Swayze's warmth is tucked against my hip.

"Sweetheart, are you all right?" Mom faces me as she sits on the edge of the bed, lightly scratching the cat's head. "You don't look like you feel well."

"I don't." I shake my head. "I've ruined it."

"Ruined what?" she asks.

I sniffle. "Everything with Oliver. I messed it all up."

She places a gentle hand over my arm. "I can't imagine that's true. He's crazy about you. I'm sure whatever happened is a misunderstanding."

"It's not," I insist. "I know it's not because I lied to him."

"What?" She shakes her head in disbelief. "How? Why?"

She listens as I explain the events from the day, including the stupid cover story I made up that exploded in my face.

"Why didn't you tell him the truth to start with? I can't imagine Oliver being upset over something like this."

"I know," I say, raking my hands down my face. "He's wonderful. Hell, he probably would've sent *me* a care package on *his* birthday if he knew. But that's the thing. We just started dating. I don't want to drag him down or be this huge burden on his shoulders. This should be fun. Especially this early in the game. He should see me as happy and fun and carefree."

"You are *not* a burden," she says. "And if he or anyone else thinks that, they're not someone you want in your life. But I don't think Oliver will feel that way. You should talk to him, sweetie. If you tell him what you've told me, I truly believe he'll understand."

I shrug. "I tried. He didn't want to talk about it anymore tonight, and I can't say I blame him. He caught me in a blatant lie, Mom. The reason I did it doesn't matter."

"Sure it does. You were scared. That's all," she says, cupping my face in her hands. "Your illness is a deeply personal part of you, and it's not something you share with everyone. Anyone worth their salt will get that."

I swipe the moisture from beneath my eyes, then reach for the album on the bed, running my fingers along the binding. "I miss Dad."

"Me too." She gives me a bittersweet smile. "Your father had a way about him. Just his presence was enough to comfort you kids. When y'all were little, he could walk in the room when one of you was having a total meltdown, and you'd crawl right into his arms. He'd have you smiling again in no time."

"Yeah, he did."

"It was a lot simpler then. Back when your biggest problems were petty fights with your friends or being told to do your homework." She sighs and covers my hand with hers. "There was little that couldn't be fixed with a pep talk and a Shirley Temple."

I smile. "I miss his pep talks. And the ice cream he let us sneak before dinner sometimes."

She snorts. "You only *thought* you were being sneaky. I always knew."

We sit together in silence for a moment, the only sound coming from Catrick Swayze's soft purrs, each of us lost in our own memories.

"You should get some rest," she says finally. "It'll help you feel better, and you'll wake up with a clearer head tomorrow. You and Oliver will work it out. This is just a small bump in the road."

"I hope you're right," I say, lying back against the pillow.

She pulls the covers up to my chin, tucking them around me like she did when I was a kid. The gesture makes my eyes well with tears again. It reminds me of the many nights she and my father did this, despite my insistence that I was far too grown-up for it. Then, one night they tucked me in for the last time. I didn't think much of it then, probably so dead set on acting more mature than I was. But now, I wish I could go back. To savor those moments a little longer and carve them into my mind because one day, those memories will be all I have left of them both.

"You want the light on or off?" she asks, picking up the album.

"Off is good," I say. "Thank you."

The mattress shifts as she stands and turns off the lamp.

"Sweet dreams," she says before padding out of the room, pulling the door closed behind her.

There, wrapped in darkness, I allow my mind to drift to a time when I was young and held close. When words and a sweet fizzy drink could fix anything. Long before I felt suffocated by the weight of my broken pieces.

26

———

MJ

"WILL YOUR SON AND DAUGHTER-IN-LAW BE VISITING FOR THE holiday?" I ask Ron, taking the last bite of my soup. Admittedly, I'm only half present for our lunch date. My mind keeps drifting back to my eldest daughter.

"They will," Ron answers. "They won't be here till early Christmas morning, but they're going to stay through New Year's."

"That'll be a nice visit." I take a sip of my coffee.

"Maybe you could meet Hudson while he's here?"

I sputter and cough, choking on my drink. It shouldn't come as a shock, but somehow, it does. It's not like Ron hasn't met *my* kids, but that's different. My connection to Ron came through Lindsey. Ron wanting me to meet Hudson carries a different weight. That implies seriousness. That implies *commitment*. Am I ready for that? I'm not *not* ready, but...

"Are you okay?" Ron asks.

I nod and flutter my hand as though I'm not on the cusp of

258

experiencing a medical emergency, while Ron jumps up and firmly pats my back.

"Yep," I manage to choke out, now garnering the attention of other customers.

I gasp, and a new wave of uncontrollable hacking hits.

"Easy does it, Myra Jean," Ron says in a low, calm voice. "Try to breathe."

How am I supposed to breathe when you asked me to meet your son? When I might be falling in lo—

I take in a deep, shuddering breath and clear my throat so hard it scrapes the bottom of my stomach.

Ron rubs my back. "There you go."

Despite the chill inside the coffee shop, I'm now sweating. I swallow down some water and steady myself.

"Oh my," I say, as Ron returns to his seat across from me. "Sorry about that."

He chuckles. "Are you apologizing for choking?"

Yes. No. I'm apologizing for mentally freaking out about meeting your son so much that I almost died here at this table. I'm apologizing because everything about that and the way I feel for you scares the living daylights out of me.

"No, I suppose I'm a bit on edge. Lindsey's not feeling well," I say, changing the subject. "She was in rough shape last night. She has…well, she has some health issues, and when they flare up, it can get bad fast. To add insult to injury, she and Oliver had a little row. I think it was all just a big misunderstanding, but I'm worried about her. I didn't see her this morning. She left for work before I got up."

Ron's forehead creases. "Well, of course, you're worried. No matter how old she is, she's still your kid. Do you want to try to call her?"

"Actually, I think I should swing by the clinic and check on her."

"You should. It's still lunchtime. Maybe you can catch her while she's not too busy."

"Are you sure?" I ask. "I hate to leave so soon, but—"

"Don't you worry about me," Ron says, cutting me off. "Family comes first. Go on and get out of here. Make sure Doc is okay."

"Thank you." I reach across the table and squeeze his hand before rising to my feet, shrugging on my coat.

"I'll give you a call later. I'm going to take June Bug for a walk around the block while it's sunny out."

"Give her kisses for me," I say, already starting for the door.

Outside, I suck in a lungful of cold air before striding toward my car to make the short drive to the clinic.

I need to make sure Lindsey's okay. That's the *only* reason I'm leaving my date with Ron early. It has nothing to do with the fact that he wants me to meet his family or any feelings I may or may not have for him.

Nothing at all.

"KNOCK, KNOCK," I SAY, TAPPING ON THE OPEN DOOR OF MY daughter's office. My chest tightens because I can almost see Henry hunched over his computer at this exact desk the many times I brought him lunch over the years.

"Mom," Lindsey says, placing her uneaten sandwich back on a plate on her desk. "What are you doing here?"

I glance around the room at the office that feels so familiar but also different. "I was in the neighborhood having lunch with Ron and thought I'd stop by and see my girls."

"Lucy stepped out for lunch with Willow," she says, furrowing her brow. "Is everything okay?"

"Of course, it is." I smooth invisible wrinkles from my cream-colored slacks. "Why wouldn't it be?"

Her chair creaks as she shifts her weight, leaning forward. "It's just…you never come by here anymore. Not since… well, you know."

"It's about time I start, don't you think?"

I move to the shelves hung on the wall and run my finger along the framed photo taken of Lindsey and her father at her veterinary school graduation.

I chuckle softly. "He was so happy that day. Remember how he almost got kicked out—"

"For bringing in a cowbell," she finishes for me. "He said, 'if you can't bring a cowbell to a vet school, where *can* you bring one?'"

"He'd be so proud of you, kid. You know that, right?" I ask, taking a seat in one of the chairs across from her.

"You came here to check on me, didn't you?"

"Well, yes," I answer. "How are you feeling? I didn't get to see you before you left this morning."

"Not great," she admits. "The rest helped a little, but I still feel like a terrible person."

"Have you talked to Oliver yet?"

"Only via text." She releases a deep sigh. "I think the conversation we need to have deserves to be had in person, so I'm meeting him for coffee when I leave here."

"Good. I think you'll be glad you did," I say, crossing one leg over the other. "And you can put all this behind you."

She rubs her thumb along the cuticle of her ring finger. "So, how was lunch with Ron?"

I pick at some imaginary lint on my coat. "It was nice. He, uh, wants me to meet his son while he's in town for the holidays."

Her brows stretch to her hairline. "And how do you feel about that?"

"Oh, I don't know," I say, not quite meeting her eyes. "It seems a little soon, doesn't it?"

She shrugs. "Ron's met all of us."

"That's different. I met him because of you."

"That's true. But you were the one who invited him to our family dinner."

She has a point. I can't explain why it feels different, but it does. Him meeting my kids was important, but something about meeting his makes this feel more…real.

"It doesn't have to mean anything," my daughter says, as though reading my mind. "It can, but it doesn't have to if you're not ready for that."

"You're right. It doesn't have to be a big deal unless I want it to," I say more to myself than to her. "Well, I'll get out of your hair and let you finish your lunch. I should be getting back to the office. I have a staff meeting this afternoon."

"I'm glad you came by."

"Tell your sister I said hello," I say, rising to my feet. "And don't stress over this thing with Oliver, okay? It's all going to work out. I'm sure of it."

"Thank you." She stands and leans over the desk to kiss my cheek.

"You're welcome, honey. I love you."

"Love you, too," she says. "And Mom?"

"Yes?" I ask, pausing in the doorframe.

"I think it's all going to work out for you too."

27

LINDSEY

My stomach flutters when I enter The Southern Bean to find Oliver already in a booth waiting for me with two cups on the table. He gives me a little wave, and I start toward him, shrugging off my coat before sliding in across from him.

"Thank you. For meeting me."

He nods. "I got you an 'It's Always Fall Somewhere.'"

"Thank you," I say again. An invisible fist tightens around my heart. He remembered my favorite coffee. But I can't even think about drinking it right now because my heart is too strung out.

I reach across the table and take his hand. Thankfully, he doesn't pull away.

"Oliver, I'm so sorry I lied to you. It was a stupid thing to do, but I guess I was just too embarrassed to tell you the truth."

"Embarrassed?" he asks.

I sigh, my gaze dropping to our entwined fingers. "When I told you I wanted to take you out for your birthday, I meant that. I wanted so badly to make your day special. I've been worn out recently, so I left work a little early to take a nap before picking you up. But I was so exhausted, I forgot to set an alarm, and apparently, I also slept through your texts and calls until that last one woke me up."

It's not the whole truth, but it's close enough.

A slight smile tugs at the corner of his mouth. "Wait. All you did was fall asleep? Why didn't you tell me that instead of making up some story about an emergency? I would have understood."

"I know it was ridiculous," I admit. "I should have come clean right away, but I felt terrible because I was the one who asked you to do something big for your birthday, and then I let you down."

He squeezes my fingers. "It's okay. I wouldn't have been upset. In fact, I'd have been happy taking a nap with you for my birthday."

I chuckle. "A nap isn't exciting or special."

"But the girl I'd have been napping with is."

The last layer of ice around my heart starts to melt.

"Lindsey, the reason I got so upset yesterday is because the only person who ever made a big deal out of my birthday was Jess. I didn't grow up with the kind of family you did. There weren't birthday parties or presents. I was lucky if my parents remembered to get me a cupcake. I grew to dread my birthdays because it was just a day that reminded me of what I didn't have." He pauses, taking a deep breath. "Then Jess came along. She never said as much, but I think she was always trying to make up for what my family lacked. After I lost her...I ignored my birthday because there was no one I wanted to share it with."

I blink back tears.

"Until I met you," he says, his voice hoarse.

"I'm so sorry I hurt you, Oliver," I say.

He touches my arm with his other hand. "I forgive you. I just…please be honest with me from now on, okay? Maybe I haven't been clear enough about my feelings, but I'm crazy about you. I'm in this."

I swallow hard. "I'm in this too, and I want to make it up to you, if you'll let me. Any chance you're free tomorrow night?"

A grin spreads over his face. "I think I can free up my schedule."

I laugh. "I'll set my alarm now. And a back up alarm. You know, just in case."

"Good idea," he says, taking a sip of his drink. "Anyway, tell me about your day. How was work?"

"It was good," I say, and I tell him all about every detail.

Well, all but perhaps the most important one—the real reason I slept straight through our date.

"I'M GLAD TO SEE YOU'RE IN BETTER SPIRITS. MUST BE because you're seeing Oliver tonight," Kayla says in my office late the next afternoon. Everyone else has gone home for the day, so the clinic is quiet. "Was that you humming 'White Christmas' earlier or a very off-key ghost?"

"Listen, not all of us can be Mariah," I tease.

"But with the help of tequila, all of us can try." She sighs and eases into the chair across from me. "Anyway, are you feeling better?"

I rub my palm over my forehead. "A bit. Taking it easy the last couple of nights helped."

She feigns shock. "It's almost like I was right."

"Yeah, yeah. Rub it in."

She laughs, her eyes falling on the picture of my father and me on the wall. "He was always good at knocking some sense into you and talking you off the ledge." Her lips tug into a faint smile. "I know it's not the same, but you know you have me, right? I'm always in your corner."

I nod. "I know. Thank you."

"I'm pretty sure Oliver's in your corner too," she says. "When you talked to him last night, did you tell him about your fibromyalgia?"

I twist my lips to the corner of my mouth. "Not exactly."

She drops her head back and huffs out a breath. "Seriously?"

"Kayla, you know what happened with Daniel, and that was after we'd been together a while. I'm just being cautious."

She leans forward, her elbows poised on her knees. "There's a fine line between being cautious and straining yourself through a filter, leaving only the bright and happy parts. Why bother if you can't be yourself with the guy?"

"I can." I cast my gaze downward. The truth in her words needles at my heart, as though it's digging for a stubborn splinter. "Well, I want to."

She peers at me through hooded eyes. "So do it."

"Fine. I will," I add. "Tonight."

"Attagirl." She pushes herself up from her chair, drifting toward the door. "Okay. Well, I'm going to wrap things up out front. Do you need anything?"

"No." I shake my head. "I'm all set."

She nods once and pivots on her heel, but I call out her name, stopping her midstep.

"Thank you," I say. "For caring about me. For being such a good friend."

"Of course." Her face relaxes into a smile. "Have fun tonight."

"Good night," I say, before she pads out of the room.

I finish my paperwork for the day and spend an hour catching up on emails before changing to get ready to pick up Oliver. After what happened the other night, I was too nervous to go home and run the risk of falling asleep. Instead, I opted to bring what I needed to get ready in the office bathroom. Once I'm satisfied with my reflection, I pack up my things and sling my purse over my shoulder. Just as I'm locking the front door, my phone rings. I fish it out of my bag and smile when I see Oliver's name on the screen.

"Hey, you," I answer. "I was about to head your way."

"Lindsey, it's Joe. Beckett gave me his phone to call you." His urgent tone causes my stomach to knot, and my words lodge themselves in my throat.

"There's been an incident," he continues. "There was a five-alarm house fire caused by a gas leak. We had to call everyone in. A couple of the guys were injured, and Beckett's face shield was compromised."

The blood in my veins slows to an icy trickle, chilling my bones. "Joe, is he okay?"

I brace myself against the brick, painfully aware of the familiar shock seeping into my limbs like bitter-cold sludge. This wasn't the first time the voice on the other line didn't belong to the person I thought was calling me.

It had been a little late, but that hadn't been unusual. Sometimes Dad would think of something he needed to tell me, usually related to a patient, and he'd call me so he wouldn't forget.

Hi, Dad. I'd said. *Are you feeling better?*

Lindsey, it's Mama. Sweetheart, I need you to come to the hospital. Your father...

In a cruel twist of fate, my mother called from my father's phone because her battery was dead. I'm not certain how I got to the Vanderbilt emergency room that night. I don't remember some long, agonizing drive. It was as though I blinked, and when I opened my eyes, I was somewhere else. Somewhere my father didn't exist.

"He got a lungful of smoke," Joe says, keeping his voice steady. "The doctors are with him right now."

I fire questions at him in rapid succession. "Where are you? Is he at Vanderbilt? Can I see him?"

"Yes, he's at Vanderbilt," he answers. "And I'm not sure. They're still working with him."

I don't know if I managed a goodbye or a thank-you as I end the call and run to my car. My body is on autopilot as I peel out of the lot and shout at my Bluetooth to call my mom.

She answers on the third ring. "Hey, sweetheart. I was just—"

"Mama." I choke on the word, tears making my vision turn fuzzy. "I need you."

I spot Tessa when I sprint through the entrance of the emergency room, and she rushes toward me. My jaw clenches as the smell of bleach and antiseptic hits my nostrils, transporting me back to the last time I blew through these automatic doors.

My mother had floated toward me like a ghost, her skin pale and her eyes blank.

They did everything they could, sweetheart. It was too late.

"Hey," Tessa says, pulling me into a tight embrace. "It's okay. Oliver's gonna be okay. They have him on oxygen right now. The doctor's keeping him overnight just to be safe, but they said he'll be discharged in the morning."

Relief wooshes out of me in a long exhale. "Thank God."

Over her shoulder, I see the waiting area is filled with firefighters in uniform and their loved ones wearing weary expressions. I imagine this scene isn't entirely uncommon for them.

"We all came when we found out," Tessa explains, motioning toward the small crowd holding vigil nearby. "It's what we do when something like this happens. We're a family. We take care of each other."

"Joe said a couple other people were hurt. Are they okay?" I ask. "And the family whose house it was?"

"Everyone's going to be fine. They were able to get the family out. One of the guys got a concussion, and another has a broken leg," she says. "It could have been much worse."

Her eyes darken, and I suspect she's witnessed a time when the outcome *was* worse.

"Right." Knots form in my stomach.

Tessa squeezes my arm. "We got lucky."

"Lucky," I echo.

This time. The implication hangs in the air between us, lingering like ashes.

"When can I see him?" I ask.

"Soon. Joe's back there checking on everyone." She places her hand on my back. "Come on. Let's get you some coffee."

I nod and allow her to steer me toward the refreshment area.

I remember thinking when I was here before how odd it was. That people could casually pour themselves cups of stale coffee, watering it down with powdered creamer, while others' lives are changing forever.

While some lives are ending.

A television playing a twenty-four-hour news station provides a muffled backdrop to the tired, hushed voices in the lobby. Tessa places a Styrofoam cup full of grainy black liquid in my hands, and I know I should be thankful that this time, I get to drink the coffee. It's not my life changing forever in a room beyond these walls. Everyone I care about is okay. This time.

But there *will* be a next time. There's always a next time. With a firefighter like Oliver, there would be *many* next times.

And what then?

28

MJ

THE BOTTOM FALLS OUT OF MY STOMACH AS I ENTER THE hospital. It's like when the kids used to insist Henry and I go on those gravity-defying rides at the spring carnival the school hosted every year. All we could do was hold on tight and pray the rusty bucket we were putting entirely too much trust in wouldn't snap off, sending us crashing to our untimely ends. And we did it all without letting on we were afraid. We held their tiny hands and promised everything would be okay, that no harm would come to them.

But the truth is, we never *really* knew. We only hoped.

I still hope.

Before I have time to scan the room, Lindsey is rushing toward me. Her eyes are puffy and mascara has shadowed the hollows of her eyes. I gather her in my arms, rocking her gently.

"How's Oliver?" I ask. "Have you seen him?"

"Not yet," she answers, blowing out a breath. "He's okay. They're treating him now. I should be able to see him soon. They're keeping him overnight, just to be safe."

My shoulders sag in relief. "Good. That's good news."

She scrubs her hands down her face before tucking them under her chin. "Yeah. Yeah, it is."

"And how are you?"

A glossy film covers her eyes, and her lower lip trembles.

"It's okay, honey. How about we find a restroom?" I ask, curling my arm around her. "Splash some cold water on your face."

She nods, allowing me to lead her down the short corridor where the overhead signs direct me. I push the door in, the heels of my boots clicking along the tile floor. There are only a few stalls, all of which are empty at the moment.

I wave my hands in front of the automatic dispenser until I have a couple of paper towels clutched in my fingers and dampen them under one of the faucets.

Lindsey is leaning into her reflection, palms on the counter. "Mom, I'm a mess. A mess and—" She chokes back a sob, unable to finish her sentence.

I turn her so she's facing me and dab the towels beneath her eyes, removing the small black flakes clinging to her bottom lashes.

"I know, sweetheart," I murmur. "But Oliver's okay."

"What if he wasn't, though? What if—"

"But he *is*," I cut in. "He's going to be fine."

"I don't know if I can do this." Her voice comes out weak and childlike.

"Do what?"

"This," she cries, throwing up her hands. "Being with somebody. Especially when that somebody risks their life for a living. He told me this didn't happen—that they mostly answered medical calls and got cats out of trees. I let myself fall into this false sense of security that somehow

Oliver was exempt from bad things happening. But he isn't."

I swallow hard, but my throat is dry.

"When his number showed up on my phone and I answered it and it wasn't him…I can't do that again." She shakes her head. "I can't get another call like that. If anyone can understand how I feel, it's you."

I *do* understand.

Losing someone you love changes you. It alters you on a cellular level. It's not like loss is new, of course. We know it happens. I felt it when Rose and I lost our parents. I've felt it when I lost friends over the years to illnesses or car accidents. After each one, I swore to live each day like it was my last. And I did, for a moment, anyway. Then life inevitably got busy again and I'd get buried in the minutia of the day to day until the next loss happened, when I'd start the cycle over. I'd promise myself this time would be different. *This* would be the turning point, when I'd stop viewing life as a promise that couldn't be broken. But with every day that stretched between losses, the seconds blurred until the next death snapped everything back into focus. We think we still have time, that we have tomorrow.

We're always surprised to find out we don't.

"I get it," I say finally. "I do."

"What do I do?" She shakes her head, folding her arms over her chest like a shield. "Tell me what to do, Mama."

I give her a sad smile. "I wish I had the answers, kid. Contrary to what I've let you and your brother and sister believe, I don't know everything." That elicits a small chuckle from her, so I continue. "I can't tell you what to do. I can tell you what I wish for. I want you to have someone to grow old with. Someone who'll rub your feet after a long day, who you'll want to strangle sometimes because they snore like a bear. I want you to have every frustrating, magnificent, heartbreaking moment that comes with falling in love with the person who becomes your best friend."

I scrape my teeth over my bottom lip and sigh. "But what you have to understand is that love comes at a cost that *someone* must pay, and as much as I want you to have that kind of love in your life, only *you* can decide if it's worth the price. I always thought your father and I would go out like they did in *The Notebook*, old and moments apart, but life isn't as kind as fiction."

She blows a strand of hair from her eyes. "My mind is a mess. I'm so afraid of making the wrong decision."

"I don't think you need to make any decisions tonight. It's been an emotional evening. Sleep on it. The important thing is, Oliver's okay," I say. "Listen, sweetheart, I don't know if he's the man for you, but I *do* believe he's a good man. I know it's only been a short time, but it's clear he cares about you. And I know you care about him too."

"I do. That's what makes this so hard."

The bathroom door opens, starling us both, and a petite blonde woman comes in.

"Lindsey, they just got Oliver in a room," she says. "You can go see him now."

Lindsey nods. "Thanks, Tessa."

The girl gives her a warm smile and acknowledges me with a small wave before ducking out of the room.

Lindsey steeples her hands in front of her mouth.

"Go see him," I say. "I'll wait here as long as you need me to."

"Will you come with me?" she asks, her words unsteady.

"Of course, I will." I smooth my hand over her hair. "Come on. Let's go."

LINDSEY REACHES FOR MY HAND, AND I GIVE HER AN encouraging smile to conceal the tremble of my own lips.

The fire marshal leads us to Oliver's room, deep in the bowels of the hospital. I hate this place so much. Nurses are milling around and people are talking softly on cell phones outside of closed doors. So many stories are taking place in this building, each on a different page. Some are just beginning while some are coming to an end. Some will even stop in the middle of a sentence. Those books will be closed and put away, only to become one of the many tales that linger in these halls. The greatest story of my life ended here, within these walls. The echoes of my worst moments exist here.

Despite the grim scene I witnessed then—the paramedics shouting orders and statuses I didn't understand—I still held hope. I told myself that miracles happened all the time, and that if anyone deserved one, it was my Henry.

I'm so sorry, Mrs. Haggerty. We did everything we could.

"Here we are," Joe says once we reach Oliver's room. He knocks before sticking his head in. "Beckett, you've got some visitors."

Joe holds the door and nods. "I'll be outside if you need anything."

"Thanks, Joe," Lindsey says as we enter the room.

"Hey." Oliver's voice is a bit scratchy, but he still greets us with a smile, his gaze focused on Lindsey. "Aren't you a sight for sore eyes? I'm sorry about our date."

"That's the last thing I'm worried about," Lindsey says, rushing to his side. "How are you feeling?"

I stand back to give them a moment. My heart aches, seeing Oliver in that bed—seeing Lindsey bear witness to that, knowing the turmoil her heart is going through. *Love comes at a cost that someone must pay.* God knows, I've paid dearly, but if I had it to do all over, even knowing how it would all end, I'd still do it in a heartbeat. The cost was steep, but the life Henry and I had together was worth every penny.

But is it a price I'm willing to pay again with someone else?

"MJ, I'm so glad you came," Oliver says, reaching a hand out to me.

I step forward and take it, giving it a squeeze. "And *I'm* glad you're okay."

"It's nothing, really," he insists. "It could have been much worse."

My daughter's back stiffens where she's seated on the edge of the gurney.

"I'm just grateful everyone made it out safely," he continues, "and I'll be able to return to work in a couple days."

Lindsey wavers. "Are you sure you ought to go back so soon? Maybe you should take some time off. Make sure you're feeling a hundred percent."

"After I get some rest and fluids, I'll be just fine," he says. "This kind of thing is par for the course, and what I experienced tonight was minor. The guys got me out of there fast."

Lindsey's jaw tightens, and I know she's imagining a future time when they don't.

"Promise." He reaches for my daughter's hand and threads his fingers through hers, as though he can see the thoughts flashing through her mind. "I'm not going anywhere, okay?"

She nods like she believes it, but I know she doesn't. Because she can't. Because *I* can't. Life doesn't work that way.

I lean forward and pat Oliver's shoulder. "I'm sure you're exhausted. Maybe we should let you get some rest."

"I can stay," Lindsey offers. "In case you need anything."

He touches her cheek. "You should go on home with your mom. It's late, and I'm afraid I won't be very good company anyhow, unless you like watching people sleep with the TV on. I'll text you as soon as I get discharged."

"I'll come back and take you home in the morning," she says.

"Joe and a couple of the guys are going to break me out of here tomorrow," he jokes, but Lindsey remains stone-faced. "They need you at the clinic. I'll be okay. Maybe you could come by my place after work?"

"Sure," Lindsey answers.

"Let me know you made it home, okay?" he says to Lindsey.

"I will." She pinches her lips shut like she's trying to trap her emotions inside.

My mind drifts to our conversation in the bathroom. Did I say the right things? Maybe I said too much. I didn't mean to add to her already mounting fears. I want my daughter to have someone to spend her life with, but I don't want her to fall in love and have regrets one day if the cost becomes too great. Whether she chooses to walk this path with Oliver or not needs to be her decision. Part of making a choice like that is understanding the risks.

Lindsey gives him a quick kiss, and I wave as we head out the door. Joe leads us through the labyrinth and back out the way we came. He and the blonde from earlier, who appears to be his wife, walk out with us, followed by the rest of the crew, who was waiting in the lobby. We wearily bid everyone a good night in the parking lot, heading in the direction of our cars.

"How do you feel?" I ask when we reach her SUV.

She fixes her eyes on the sky as though she's seeking guidance from the stars.

"I know what happened to Oliver tonight is just part of the job for him, and he's so brave." Her eyes turn glassy when she meets my gaze. "But I don't know if *I* am."

"I understand, sweetheart. I do." Because I don't know if I'm brave, either. Of course, I don't tell her that. "Whatever you decide, I'm here for you. Do you want to ride back with me? I can bring you to your car tomorrow."

"That's okay," she says. "I think I'm going to drive around for a bit. Clear my head."

I envelop her in my arms, lingering a moment longer than usual. I'm searching my brain for something, *anything*, I can do or say to make her feel better. Then it hits me.

"Lindsey, about what you said on Thanksgiving," I start. "About celebrating at Ben and Ellie's. Maybe we could try—"

"Actually, let's just forget about that for now."

I blink. "What? Why? I thought this was what you wanted."

She shrugs. "I thought it was too. But maybe you had it right all along. I mean, why change something that's perfect as it is?"

I press my lips together and nod, but there's a pit growing in my stomach. *Was* I right? *Is* it still perfect? Now I'm not so sure.

Lindsey kisses my cheek. "Love you, Mom."

"I love you, kid. Don't ever forget that. I'll see you back at the house."

She gets in her car and I go on my way. I check my phone before driving off and see a missed call from Ron. In all the commotion, I didn't have a chance to fill him in. Once I'm on the road, I use the Bluetooth to give him a call and let him know what's happened.

"Geez. That's terrifying," he says. "But he's okay? You saw him?"

I try to keep my tone upbeat. "Lindsey and I got to see him briefly, but we left so he could get some rest. He was in good spirits. Already talking about going back to work."

Ron chuckles. "Suppose that's a good sign. How's Doc? I imagine tonight must have shaken her up quite a bit."

"It did. I…I think tonight has given her a lot to consider—about how much she's prepared to handle, I mean."

"Oh?" Ron asks, concern creeping into his voice. "You think his job might be too much for her?"

I heave a sigh. "It could be."

He clicks his tongue. "That's too bad. I gotta say, I thought they'd be in it for the long haul."

"Mm-hmm. Me too."

There's a momentary silence on the other end of the line.

"Myra Jean," he says. "Are you okay?"

"Hmm? Oh yes. Just a bit tired."

"Are you sure that's all?" he asks. "I assume hospitals aren't exactly the easiest place for you to visit. I'm sure being there dredged up a lot of feelings."

My thoughts travel the inky black highway to my daughter and the forlorn look that had taken up residence in her eyes. The ease with which she gave up on the idea of changing how we spend Christmas, knowing how important it was to her.

What kind of life will she lead if she never does anything differently, never lets anyone in, never takes another risk?

I swallow hard. The answer feels dangerously familiar.

"I'm fine." A lump forms in my throat, and I mentally begin putting my walls back up, brick by brick. Having only had them down for a short time, the task is easy, as though I'm relying on muscle memory.

Ron pauses, and for a moment, I think he's going to press the issue.

"Okay," he relents. "I'll let you go so you can focus on the road. Call you tomorrow?"

"Yes. Tomorrow," I say. "Tomorrow is good."

"Perhaps we can grab dinner together?"

I clear my throat. "Um, maybe. I'll have to let you know."

Another pause. "All right, then. Sleep tight, Myra Jean."

"You too," I say before ending the call.

My mind races, stopping only long enough to wrestle with my heart, letting me know sleep won't be in the cards for me.

29

———————

LINDSEY

"Hell*ooo*," Lucy's voice rings out in the lab at the clinic late the next afternoon. "Earth to Lindsey."

I jump, nearly dropping the chart I'm looking at. "Sorry, what?"

"Are you sure you're okay?" she asks, ambling over to me with the extra-floofy Cavapoo she's just finished grooming.

I press my tongue to the inside of my cheek. I'm not okay, and I haven't been since I got the call from Joe last night that Oliver was in the hospital.

"I'm fine," I insist. "Just exhausted. I didn't sleep well."

At least the last part isn't a lie. After I left the hospital, I drove around for over an hour, my mind running wild with possibilities of what might have been, each vision more gruesome than the last. When I finally got home and crawled into bed, I spent hours staring at the ceiling. My mother's words sat heavy on my chest, making it hard to breathe.

Love comes at a cost that someone must pay.

"You act like I haven't known you my *entire* life," she says, playfully rolling her eyes. "I know what happened last night freaked you out, but it seems like there's more going on in that head of yours."

I drop the chart on the counter and press my fingers into the back of my neck in an attempt to ease the pressure that's been building there.

"I can't do it, Lucy. I have to call it off."

"Call what off?" she asks, scratching the pup she's holding behind the ear.

My throat feels like it's coated in sand. "This thing with Oliver."

Her eyes go wide. "Wait, really? Are you serious?"

"Lucy, Gizmo's owner is here to get him," Kayla calls, entering the room. She catches a glimpse of the gloomy expressions on our faces and frowns. "You guys all right?"

"Kayla, do you mind taking Gizmo up front for me?" Lucy gives her a pleading look.

"Of course," she says, taking the pup from her arms. "Come on, Gizmo Bo-bizmo. Let's get you back to your mom."

She disappears from the room, and Lucy shifts her focus back to me.

"Let's go into your office," she says, already steering me in that direction. Once inside, I sit behind my desk and she closes the door before settling into the chair across from me.

"Now, talk to me," she says, leaning forward. "What's going on?"

I suck in a breath to try and calm my nerves.

"When Oliver's name showed up on my phone last night, I thought he was calling to make sure I was on the way to his house, that I hadn't fallen asleep again or something," I say. "But it was Joe, telling me Oliver was in the hospital. Lucy, that phone call took me right back to the night Dad died. I thought Dad was calling me, but it was Mom and…"

I don't have to fill in the blanks. She knows because she got the same call.

"Being at the hospital, seeing all the crew and their families waiting for answers. It was so clear this wasn't as uncommon as Oliver let me believe," I continue. "Or maybe that's just what I wanted to believe because I liked him so much. I was stupid. He literally came to my house because of a fire. Of *course*, firefighters go out on fire calls. That's the job."

My sister frowns, her brows drawing together with concern.

"I'm a terrible person, Lucy. What kind of coward breaks up with someone because their job's too scary?"

"A person who knows what it's like to lose someone," she says. "And that doesn't make you a bad person. I know his job is dangerous, but Lindsey, these things can happen to anyone. Just look at Dad. I mean, something could happen to me or Willow. Nobody's immune. It's a chance we take."

"How?" I prop my elbows on the desk, shoving my fingers through my hair. "How do you do that when the stakes are this high? Don't you ever feel scared?"

"Well, yeah. Of course, I do." She gives me a resigned shrug. "But it sure beats the alternative, you know?"

I twist my lips to the corner of my mouth. "I'm not so sure."

"So, what are you going to do? What are will you say to Oliver?"

"I'm not sure I'll truly know until I'm standing in front of him." I hit the button on the side of my phone to illuminate the clock and let out a sharp exhale. "Which I'll be doing in just a few minutes because I'm headed over to his place. I've got to get going."

I rise to my feet and gather my things, powering down my desktop.

Lucy stands. "You know if you need me, I'm only a phone call away."

"I know."

She pulls me into a hug. "I mean it. Let me know if you need anything. I'll be there in a heartbeat."

"I will," I say, starting toward the door.

"Hey, Linds?" Lucy calls.

"Yeah?"

"Being afraid doesn't make you a coward. It makes you human."

I pick up chicken soup for Oliver from the deli in town. Even if I had an appetite, which I don't, I know I won't be staying for dinner. Telling Oliver how I feel isn't going to get any easier, so I might as well just rip off the Band-Aid.

"Hey, beautiful. Get in here. It's raining cats and dogs out there." He answers the door looking handsome as ever, and my heart aches for a time when I believed love never died. For a time when I wasn't waiting for the other shoe to drop, no matter how naive I might have been.

Naivete, I've realized, is a luxury.

"You look like you're feeling better," I say as he kisses my cheek, taking the bag and cup from my hands. I reach down and pet the top of Ace's head. "You've been taking good care of your dad."

"He's a pretty good nurse." Oliver chuckles. "Thanks again for bringing dinner."

"Of course." I do my best to force a smile.

"I'll take it into the kitchen and plate it up," he says, walking ahead.

I try to speak as I trail behind him, but my words can't claw their way out of my chest. My feet come to a stop in the kitchen doorway, unwilling or unable to move any closer. This is the first time I've been to Oliver's home, and it's as cozy and warm as I imagined it. Just like Oliver.

"The food smells delicious, by the way." He unpacks the bag and frowns. "I think they forgot part of the order. There's only one container in here."

My heart is beating so fast I think it might shatter.

"That's okay." He reaches into an upper cabinet and pulls down two bowls. "We can share."

"Oliver, I can't stay." My voice comes out strained, the weight of my emotions is crushing my windpipe.

"What? Why?" he asks, placing the bowls on the counter. "Do you need to get back to the clinic?"

"No," I say, the answer getting strangled in my throat. "It's not that."

He tilts his head, stepping toward me. "Is everything okay? You seem tense."

I slip my bottom lip between my teeth.

"Lindsey, talk to me. What's going on?" He reaches out and squeezes my arm. "Honesty, remember?"

"Oliver, um, there's no easy way to say this," I say, blinking back tears. "I like you. A lot. Getting to know you has been so special for me. Not just for me, but for my family too."

"Why do I feel like there's a 'but' coming?"

"I think we need…that *I* need to take a step back."

His hand drops to his side. "I'm confused—I thought things were going great between us. Did I misread something?"

"No," I say. "You didn't. This is all on me."

He shakes his head. "I don't understand. Can we talk about this? It seems like this is coming out of nowhere and—" A knowing look settles over his face, and he rubs his thumb along his jaw. "This is about last night, isn't it?"

I open my mouth but close it again.

"I knew it. It freaked you out." He takes my hands in his. "Lindsey, this kind of thing happens sometimes. It's part of the job, but I'm safe. You don't have to worry. I know what I'm doing. I'm gonna be okay."

I withdraw my fingers from his grasp. "I want to believe you. I do. But you can't know that. Too many things can happen."

"You say that like I haven't lost someone," he says, his voice rising as he shoves his hand through his hair. "Like I don't know how it feels to have the ground ripped out from under me."

"I know you do, and that's why I hope you'll understand that I need to take a step back."

"And what does that mean to you, exactly?"

I drop my gaze to the floor.

He nods once. "You don't want to see me at all."

My chest is hollow, as though my heart has simply fallen out. Maybe it has.

"I'm sorry." I look up at him with pleading eyes. "This has *nothing* to do with you."

"Like hell it doesn't," he snaps. "You're backing off

because of my job. Kinda sounds like it has *everything* to do with me."

"No," I choke out. "This is all on me. I think you're amazing. You're kind and thoughtful and brave."

He throws up his hands. "So be brave *with* me, Lindsey. It doesn't have to end like this."

My lips tremble, and silent tears roll down my face. "I...I can't."

"Can't or won't?"

My silence is all the answer he needs.

"You weren't the only one taking a risk here," he says, his mouth flattened into a hard line. "I let you in. I trusted you."

"I care so much for you. I need you to know that," I say, "and I'm so—"

He holds his hand up to stop me. "Don't."

I nod and take a step back.

"Listen, Lindsey, I don't need you to try to soften the blow or explain it away. If you don't want to be here, leave."

My throat constricts. "Okay."

"Okay." He scrubs his hands down his face, and I retreat back to the front door with him on my heels.

I pause on the front stoop to look at him once more, and the light in his eyes has dimmed.

He shuts the door with a thud, leaving me standing on his porch, the rain mingling with my tears.

This is how it has to be. I'm better off this way. We both are.

I repeat these thoughts over and over like mantras. If I say them enough, maybe I'll eventually believe them.

30

——

MJ

The office is a ghost town Tuesday afternoon, despite the fact that I told Ron I'm swamped, which is the reason I gave when declining every invitation he's made since Thursday. After finishing my Christmas shopping, I found myself here. My laptop is open, but it's been so long since I've touched it that the screen has gone black.

The quiet is occasionally punctuated by the sound of a ringing phone or someone venturing to the break room for a cup of coffee. The normally bustling space more closely resembles a library with most of the staff getting an early start on their holiday break. We're technically closed the week of December, so anyone who's in the office now is here because they want to be.

Perhaps there's also something or some*one* they're avoiding.

The truth is, this is a slow time of the year for us. People are busy decking the halls and spending time with those they love.

Love.

The word hangs from the center of my mind, dangling like a new air freshener from the rearview mirror, permeating the space around me. I can't escape it, no matter how hard I try.

"What are you doing here?"

The sudden presence of my daughter-in-law in the doorway of my office makes me jump and let out a high-pitched yelp.

"It's Christmas Eve Eve," she continues. "I'm surprised you're not already baking up a storm."

"Oh my God, Ellie," I say with a chuckle, holding my hands to my chest. "You scared me half to death."

She sits across from me and unwinds the plaid scarf from her neck. "Sorry. I didn't mean to startle you. I was out running errands and saw your car here, so I thought I'd stop by."

"Taking care of some last-minute Christmas shopping?" I ask.

"Yeah. I had to pick up stocking stuffers for the kids," she answers. "And I got some snacks for tonight."

"Lucy told me earlier that y'all are having a girls night to try to cheer Lindsey up. That's sweet of you. I know she'll appreciate it."

Ellie gives me a sad smile. "I was sorry to hear she stopped seeing Oliver."

"Me too."

"He seems like such a great guy, and it's obvious they care about each other," she says. "From what Lucy told me, Lindsey's pretty torn up."

"She is," I admit. "What happened the other night really rattled her."

"I can only imagine, but…" She trails off, closing her mouth before opening it again.

"What?" I ask. "What were you going to say?"

Ellie presses her lips together, a contemplative expression on her face. "I understand if she's not quite ready to take the leap into a relationship. That's completely valid." She pauses, shifting in her seat. "But if she keeps running away from love, eventually there won't be anywhere left for her to go. There's not a type of love in the world that doesn't come with a risk."

She didn't intend those words for me, but they cling to me like shrink-wrap. If *I* choose to walk away from Ron or even the possibility of love, where does it end?

I've been running since I lost Henry, only I haven't been running away so much as I've been running in circles. Somehow, I thought if I put everyone I love in a time capsule, I could keep them safe, and I could also keep Henry alive in some way. It's why I've held on to every moment of the past so tightly.

I fold my hands on my desk and sigh. "You know what, Ellie? You're absolutely right."

"Anyway, you never said why you're at the office" —she raises an accusing brow at me— "three days before Christmas. I know you're in demand, but we're not *that* busy this time of year."

"You're right," I say, holding my hands up in surrender.

"How about you pack up and get coffee with me before you head home?" she asks.

I snap my laptop shut. "On one condition."

"What's that?" she asks.

"I'm buying."

"You know, you're supposed to be helping," I say to Rose as she gingerly grabs another of the snowflake-shaped cookies I've been icing and takes a bite. After I got home, I was feeling antsy, so I asked if she wanted to come over to wrap presents and do some baking.

"I *am* helping," she insists around a mouthful of cookie. "I'm quality control."

I chuckle and roll my eyes. "Right."

My phone pings from the counter, but I ignore it.

"We both know you don't *actually* want my help, anyway," she says, refilling both of our wine glasses. "If memory serves, the last time you allowed me to actually bake something was when you got the flu and were supposed to be baking cupcakes for Lindsey's thirteenth birthday."

"And can you blame me? They looked like little boobs."

Lindsey's favorite color was pink, and she wanted that on top of the vanilla frosting. Did Rose really have to put the little Hot Tamales in the center, though? To be fair, they *are* Lindsey's favorite candy.

"You said that was Lindsey's favorite birthday," Rose said.

"It's true," I admit, handing her a freshly-frosted cookie. "The kids thought it was hilarious and that she had the coolest aunt ever."

My phone chimes again.

"Well, she does." She chomps into the snowflake and leans her elbows on the counter, glancing over at my phone. "So, how's Ron?"

I fix my eyes on the next batch of icing I'm mixing. "We haven't really talked much since Oliver went to the hospital last week."

The heat of her gaze is burning holes into my skull.

"Uh-*huh*. And why's that?" she asks.

"I haven't had time."

She snorts. "You have nothing *but* time."

"I've been busy."

"Have not."

"Have so. I've been at the office a lot."

"Doing what?" she asks.

"Things," I snip.

"What kinds of things?"

I toss the spatula I'm holding into the mixing bowl with a clatter. "Avoiding Ron things, okay?"

She wags a finger at me. "I knew it. I was worried this might happen."

"Worried *what* might happen?" I huff.

"That being at that hospital would bring back some difficult memories and you'd freak out and overanalyze everything."

I open my mouth to speak but she cuts me off.

"I'm not saying you don't have every right to freak out, because you do. Though, you could stand to chill on the overanalyzing part," she says.

"It's not just that, Rose. He wants me to meet his son."

She throws up her hands. "So? He's met your kids. He's met me."

"That's different."

"How?"

"I don't know. It just is." I press my fingertips to my temples. "That feels like a big commitment, doesn't it? I don't know if I'm ready for that."

"For Heaven's sake, Myra Jean. We're not twenty-five anymore. We're too old to not communicate with the people we care about. You need to tell him what's on your mind. He deserves to know where your head's at."

"I know." I run my tongue over my teeth, my mouth suddenly dry. "I've been trying to figure out how to tell him what I'm feeling."

Her tone softens. "Which is?"

"That I don't know what I want. I'm scared." I blow out a steady stream of air. "God, Rose. Let's say I *do* get together with Ron or anyone else and we commit to each other. What happens if history repeats itself? I wouldn't survive another loss like that."

"Of course, you would."

I scoff at her. "That's a callous thing to say."

"No. It isn't." She presses her palms flat on the counter. "It's the truth. You thought you wouldn't survive losing Henry, yet here you are. You made it because you had to. Because that's what people do."

"I haven't exactly been thriving."

"Maybe not at first," she says. "But now? I think you're doing pretty damn good." She holds out a hand to stop the rebuttal I'm ready to launch at her. "And that's okay. That's a good thing. It means you're healing."

I grab the cup towel beside the sink and wipe my hands. "Maybe I don't want to be healed."

"Sure, you do." She reaches across the counter to touch my arm. "Why would you say that?"

I blink back the tears burning at the corners of my eyes. "If I'm all healed and better, what does that mean for Henry?"

"Uh." She juts her chin forward and scrunches her brow. "Nothing, I suppose. It's not like he can really be a part of it."

"Exactly. If I move on, Henry is really gone."

"He's gone either way, sister."

"I know," I snap. "Don't you think I know that? I *meant*, if I were to move on with someone else, *that* becomes my life, and Henry just disappears into the ether."

"That's not how it works."

"Oh really," I bite back, sarcasm dripping from my voice. "Enlighten me, then. How *does* it work?"

"You don't keep someone's memory alive by shutting down and folding in on yourself, Myra Jean." She reaches for my hand. "You keep them alive by *living*. By living so loud that wherever Henry is, he can hear you."

I rub my fingers over my forehead, attempting to smooth out the dozens of wrinkles I'm certain have formed in the duration of this conversation.

"What do I say, Rose?" I ask. "What do I tell him?"

"Tell him what you told me," she says. "That you're scared and you're not sure what you want this thing between you two to be just yet. Be honest with him."

I rake my teeth over my bottom lip and nod slowly. "Okay. You're right. I'll do it."

She narrows her eyes at me. "When?"

"The next time he calls."

She taps a manicured nail to her chin. "Fine, then. Since I'm already on your nerves, you should know I got you a spa package for Christmas."

"Why would that get on my nerves? That's a lovely gift. Thank yo—"

"Well, actually, *I* got a spa package," she says. "From Lester. It's got a massage, a pedicure, something called a vampire facial, and a bikini wax, so I thought I'd give *you* the wax."

I roll my eyes. "How thoughtful."

"A little maintenance never hurt anyone. When was the last time you got checked out under the hood?"

"It's not gonna happen, Rose. Not now. Not ever."

"What if I throw in the vampire facial? I heard they use your own blood."

I pop my lips together and grab my phone. "You know what? Maybe I'll go call Ron now."

"Yeah." Rose flashes me a Cheshire cat grin, pawing at another cookie. "You do that."

I pad up the stairs to my bedroom and shut the door, dialing Ron's number.

"Myra Jean." His voice is chipper when he answers the phone. "How's the design emergency? Did you finally come up for air?"

"You scare me," I blurt out.

Oh my God. What am I doing? I couldn't even say *Hi* first or *How are you*? I slap my palm to my forehead and flop onto my bed. If I have to die from embarrassment, I at least want to go out comfortably.

I curse Rose under my breath. This is all her fault.

"Excuse me?" Ron asks, taken aback.

"That's not what I meant," I say. "I mean, it is, but it isn't."

"Okay," he says, drawing out the word. "I'm going to need some clarity on what you *do* mean."

"Yes. Right." I draw in a long, slow breath. "Ron, there was no work emergency. I've been...I was avoiding you."

"I had a feeling," he admits.

"Oh..."

He heaves a sigh. "I don't know a lot about design, but it seemed unlikely there would be an emergency this close to Christmas. You were a little off when I mentioned introducing you to Hudson, and after the way you sounded on the phone the night of Oliver's accident, I got the impression you might be having second thoughts."

"It isn't that. Well, I guess it is, but not because of you. It's because of *everything*."

He chuckles softly. "Is that supposed to make me feel better?"

I run my hand down my face. "I'm really messing this up, aren't I?"

"You're not messing up anything, Myra Jean. Tell me what's on your mind."

I can do this.

If that's true, why do I feel like I'm going to be sick?

"Okay." My heart performs an erratic tap dance against my chest while my stomach contorts itself into a pretzel. "Ron, I like you. A lot. And that's terrifying to me because I thought Henry and I would be riding our electric scooters around the grocery store together when we were ninety, lamenting about the price of eggs. I never considered the possibility of anything different. I wasn't supposed to have this much of a future left without him in it."

"I get that, Myra Jean. I do," he says, "and no matter where this thing between us goes, I'd never expect to replace Henry. Nor would I want to."

"I know," I assure him. "The thing you have to understand is that I spent the last five years trying to keep him alive. *That* was my life until you came along and showed me there might be other ways to live. But I'm still wrapping my mind around what that looks like and what I *want* it to look like. What happened with Oliver the other night scared Lindsey, but it also shook me up. It reminded me how quickly things can change, and if I'm going to be brave enough to let someone in my life, I've got to make sure I'm brave enough to lose them too."

A beat of silence passes between us.

"How can I help you not be scared?" he asks. "What do you need from me?"

"Time," I say. "I just need a moment to catch my breath."

He pauses so long, I have to look to make sure the call didn't disconnect.

"Okay," he says.

"Really?"

"Yes, really. I'd be lying if I said I'm not disappointed, but I don't want you to do anything you don't want to do."

A lump forms in my throat. "Right."

"Take all the time you need," he continues. "When you're ready to talk, you know where to find me."

"Wow," I say with a nervous laugh. "So, it's just that simple?"

"Nothing about you is simple," he says, and I detect a trace of sadness in his voice. "And if you ask me, that's one of your best qualities."

"Thank you." I hold the phone closer, as though somehow that would bring *him* closer.

"Good night, Myra Jean. And if I don't talk to you before then, Merry Christmas."

I swallow hard. "Merry Christmas."

31

———

LINDSEY

Determined not to let me mope alone, the girls insist on having a pre-holiday sleepover on Christmas Eve Eve at Lucy and Willow's to cheer me up. Kayla and Ellie arrive just after I do with a smorgasbord of goodies in an effort to cheer me up, including tacos from the little food truck that comes to town a couple times a week, which I pick at, despite how delicious they are.

"I got you some Hot Tamales," Willow says, handing me the colorful box of candy as she takes a seat beside me on the couch. "I know they're your favorite."

I give her a weak smile. "Thanks, Wil."

"Lucy told me you got some good news today," she says. "I know you'll be glad to be back in your house again."

"Oh. Yeah," I say. "It'll be nice." I've been in such a funk that I couldn't even muster a speck of excitement when the insurance adjuster called with the news that I'm clear to move home at the end of January. In a few short weeks, I'll be on my own again. A couple months ago, that might've made me happy, but now all it does is remind me of how alone I am.

Lucy bounds into the room with a flowery tote. "I got sheet masks and some of those treatments that make your feet shed like a snake."

"Ew." Ellie wrinkles her nose as she enters with a charcuterie board full of movie candies, placing it on the coffee table. "I'll pass on that part."

"Gimme one of those foot thingies," Kayla says, flopping at my other side. "I'm going out for New Year's Eve. I want these puppies to be baby soft, so that when I take my heels off after wearing them for approximately five seconds, my feet won't resemble the claws of a velociraptor."

"Where are you going?" I ask.

"My cousin invited me to some fancy shindig in Nashville. Thought you might want to be my plus-one?" She nudges me with her elbow. "If you're feeling up to it."

"Maybe," I offer, though at the moment, the idea of going out is about as unappealing as yanking out my own tooth with a pair of pliers.

"So, what movie should we start with?" Ellie asks, grabbing the remote. "*The Holiday* or *Love Actually*?"

"Maybe we should steer clear of rom-coms tonight," Lucy suggests. "We'll be subjected to enough of those tomorrow at Mom's, anyway."

Ellie nods. "*The Nightmare Before Christmas* it is."

"Thank y'all for doing this," I say. "I know this probably isn't how any of you wanted to spend the night before Christmas Eve."

Kayla squeezes my knee. "There's nowhere we'd rather be."

"How are you holding up?" Willow asks.

"I'm kind of a mess," I admit. The corners of my eyes are

already stinging with fresh tears. How I still have any moisture left in my body is beyond me.

"Talk to us. That's what we're here for." Lucy sits cross-legged on the floor, unwrapping a foot mask and sliding it on.

I press the back of my head into the cushion and blow out a breath before filling the girls in on what happened the night Oliver went to the hospital and the memories that dredged up for me.

"I care about Oliver, and the idea of something like that happening to him is terrifying," I explain. "And the closer we get, the harder it'll be if something bad happens, you know?"

Ellie nods. "I understand why this whole thing would shake you up and make you rethink what you're ready for."

"But do you think it's possible you might have jumped the gun on pulling the plug?" Willow asks, a hint of trepidation in her voice as she places her hand over mine.

My chin falls to my chest, and I press my hand over my heart in an attempt to dull the ache that's been throbbing just beneath the surface since I walked away from Oliver last week.

"No. I did it because I had to." My words aren't convincing to anyone, least of all me.

"Did you, though?" Kayla asks gently.

"I really need you guys to support me right now."

"We do," Ellie says. "No matter what."

"Linds, when you were with Oliver, you were happier than I've seen you since…well, maybe ever," Lucy admits. "We just want to make sure you're doing what's best for you and that you're not making this choice based on some hypothetical situation that hasn't happened yet. Something that may *never* happen."

"Please don't hate me for what I'm about to say." Kayla

props her elbow on the back of the sofa and leans against her arm. "But I think you've been looking for a way out. You're self-sabotaging."

"I am not," I argue, heat climbing up my neck.

"You never told Oliver about your fibromyalgia and why you overslept on his birthday," Kayla points out. "You were afraid for him to see any part of you that wasn't sunshiny and happy and perfect. Then this whole thing happened and you ran. But the truth is, you already had one foot out the door."

"That's not true," I protest, but as the words leave my mouth, I know they're a lie.

Kayla gives me a knowing look, and I drop my gaze. She's the only one here who knows the full extent of what happened with Daniel. I never told my family because it would've done nothing but add more hurt to an already painful time. It would have shifted attention to me when the focus needed to be on our mother.

"I think you have to really get honest with yourself about why you decided to walk away," Willow says.

I worried about my shadows being too much for Oliver because they were too much for Daniel. Sometimes they're even too much for me. I feared getting too close because of how suddenly I lost my dad. His death showed me how easily my world could come to a screeching halt, throwing me out of orbit, sending me hurtling through the darkness.

If I could just keep him at arm's length, I could avoid the anguish that came from being too much for Oliver or too close to him.

To anyone.

"The bottom line is, we love you," Lucy speaks up. "We're here for you."

"But you clearly think I made a mistake," I say. "You all do."

"We don't know that," Ellie replies. "We *can't* know that."

Kayla leans her head against mine. "But even if you did, it doesn't matter. We're always going to be in your corner."

"She's right, you know." Willow pokes me in the arm. "We love you."

"I love y'all too," I say.

"Me most of all, of course." Lucy beams, rifling through her sack of goodies. "Look, we're here to help you feel better, and I think I have just the thing." She plucks out five thin packages, holding them up proudly.

"Whatcha got there, Mary Poppins?" Kayla asks.

Lucy flashes us a mischievous grin and tears open one of the packets, placing a printed sheet mask on her face that I think is supposed to look like the Grinch but more closely resembles an alien.

"That is...truly frightening," I say with a laugh.

"Oh, just put them on." Lucy passes out the remaining masks before squeezing in next to Willow on the couch, resting her feet in her lap.

We do as she says, and Kayla reaches for a Red Vine. "You guys ready to start the movie?"

They look to me, and I manage a weak smile. "Sure."

THE NEXT MORNING, I STOP BY THE OFFICE ON THE WAY BACK to Mom's for Christmas Eve under the guise of calling to check on a patient whose number I forgot to bring home. Lucy knows there's no such patient but goes along with the story, letting our mother know I'm going to be a little late.

Even after Ellie and Kayla left to go home, Willow and Lucy stayed up to watch movies with me. Once I finally convinced them to go to bed, I laid on their couch in the dark beneath a pile of blankets for hours. Their words haunted me like a ghost lingering in the corner of the room. The pain in my body had finally subsided, but the hurt in my heart had only grown.

Did I react too quickly? *Was* I just self-sabotaging? And even if I was, does that mean my actions were wrong? Maybe I did blow everything up, but I did it to avoid an even bigger explosion later. I'd rather deal with the fallout from a bottle rocket than a stick of dynamite.

The bells hanging from the front door jingle loudly as I enter through the front lobby, closing the door with a thud. The office is silent, but I can still hear the echoes of my father's robust laugh. It's harder to hear when the clinic is abuzz and filled with patients, but when everything is quiet, that's when his memory comes alive. And right now, I just want to feel close to him.

In some ways, this place looks different, a byproduct of five years of growth. But then there are the things that remain the same. The artwork left exactly where my father hung it. A small gash in the wall from the time he tried to move one of the exam tables by himself. The pen marks etched in the desk where he used to fill out paperwork. So many pieces of him linger here.

Of course, I feel his presence in my childhood home, but there's something special about this place. Something that's so completely him. I can almost smell the scent of his coffee as I bounded into his office after school when I was sixteen, working as the receptionist. I can almost see him round the corner in his white coat, his wire rim glasses sliding down his nose.

I step into my office, the one that was once his, and pick up the picture of the two of us. I study his broad smile and the lines that map his face, every road where laughter and sorrow intersected on display.

"I'm a mess, Dad," I say to his image, frozen in time. "I wish you were here."

My phone buzzes from inside my coat pocket, and for half a second, I hope it's Oliver. But reality sets in when I pry it out and see my sister's name on the screen.

You okay?

I tap out a quick reply.

Yeah. About to head that way.

I go to lock the phone, but stop, hovering my finger over the button. Instead, I swipe my finger over my message threads until I find Oliver's name. Is he okay? Is he working or home alone? Did he decide to fly back to Texas last minute? So many questions to which I don't have the right to know the answers.

I know he probably doesn't want to hear from me, but I can't allow this day to go by without letting him know he's on my mind.

I'm sorry. I miss you. My thumbs tap out the words, only to delete them. I start and stop about a hundred sentences before I finally land on one.

Merry Christmas, Oliver.

Almost immediately the bubbles pop up to let me know he's typing, and my heart leaps into my throat. What is he typing? Will he simply acknowledge the text and move on? Does he miss me too? What if we can work this out? Maybe I just need some time and we can start over. With every possibility, my hopes rise until they're threatening to burst through the ceiling.

But after a moment the bubbles vanish. I wait in that spot for nearly five minutes, barely blinking for fear I'll miss something.

They never appear again.

I BUSY MYSELF MOST OF THE DAY BY PLAYING WITH NOAH and Emily while made-for-TV holiday movies play in the background. Occasionally, other family members sit in with us before returning to the kitchen for more snacks or returning to whatever sappy Christmas flick happens to be on. Focusing on numerous rounds of Candy Land and Chutes and Ladders makes it easy to tune out the love stories on the television while the fireplace crackles.

After a seemingly endless amount of games, Emily yawns and leans her head against me, the citrus scent of her detangler so sweet and familiar. I swipe an errant curl from her face.

"Are you tired, sweet girl?" I ask, and she gives me a sleepy nod.

Ellie rises from the couch. "How about we go lie down?"

Emily peers at me through her thick lashes.

"Aunt Lindsey take me," she mumbles, and my heart squeezes.

"Of course, I will," I say, scooping her into my arms

"Thanks, Linds," Ben says.

Ellie gives me an appreciative smile as Emily rests her head on my shoulder.

I carry her upstairs to the room she and Noah share when

they stay at my mom's, tucking her into the small bed. She's so tired she doesn't fight it. Instead, she snuggles under the covers, and I smooth my hand over her silky hair.

"There you go," I say, pulling the quilt tight around her. "You want Jasper?"

She murmurs a "yes," so I grab Jasper, the teddy bear she's slept with every single night since I can remember, from the dresser and nestle him beside her.

"You want me to stay till you fall asleep?" I ask, and she nods.

I lay beside her, gently rubbing her back the way I've always done. When Noah and Emily were both babies, this was how I got them to sleep when they stayed with me or if I babysat them. Noah has already outgrown this type of affection, so I soak up as much of this time with Emily while I still can.

My phone vibrates in my back pocket, and my chest blooms with hope that it's Oliver. I reach for it, careful not to disturb Emily, who's already fast asleep. I illuminate the screen, and my heart aches. It's Kayla checking in to see how I'm doing. I swipe over to Oliver's text thread, which still shows my last message as *read* with no response from him. I doubt there ever will be.

A knot forms in my stomach. I ruined the best shot I ever had at love, at having the kind of happiness my mom and dad had together, all because I was too much of a damn coward to take a leap of faith. Oliver sprints into burning buildings, while I run at the first sign of trouble.

Silent tears slip down my cheeks, leaving tiny pools of regret staining the pillow. I've spent these last few years convincing myself I didn't want anyone else in my life because it was easier than opening myself up to potential heartbreak. I told myself I was okay with the clinic being my baby and just being a cool aunt—that I didn't need anyone.

And I don't. But maybe I *want* someone.

Even as the thought forms in my mind, I know I don't just want *someone*.

I want Oliver.

But it's too late. For all I know, he may have already moved on. Maybe there was someone waiting in the wings who already snapped him up—someone who wasn't afraid to walk through the fire.

32

MJ

I'M IN THE KITCHEN, POURING MYSELF A CUP OF TEA, WHEN Lindsey comes back from tucking Emily in. She pads into the kitchen barefoot and retrieves a glass from the cabinet.

"How're you holding up, sweetheart?" I ask as she gets herself some water from the dispenser.

"Fine," she answers, though we both know she's not.

I point to a foil-covered platter. "I have some brownies over there. Your favorite." It's a recipe I make every Christmas that I found in a cookbook I bought at an estate sale nearly thirty years ago, one that quickly became Lindsey's favorite. And Henry's.

"Thanks." She gives me a weak smile. "I'm not really hungry."

"Okay." I nod as she leaves the room, a dark cloud looming over her head, and I can't shake the feeling that I helped put it there. That my advice, coupled with the way I've lived these last five years—how I've forced us *all* to live— has hardened her.

I follow behind her with my steaming mug in my hands and pass Ben, who's taking Noah up to bed.

"I wanna go home and wait for Santa," Noah whines.

"We can't do that, buddy," Ben says. "We're staying here."

Noah pouts. "But why?"

"Because we always spend Christmas with Grandma." Ben's tone is vaguely annoyed, suggesting this probably isn't the first time the subject has come up.

"But—"

"Tell your grandmother good night, please."

"'Night, Grandma," Noah says, his little mouth turning downward.

Ben gives me an apologetic smile, and a twinge of guilt pokes me in the side.

"Good night, sweetheart," I say before taking my spot on the love seat next to Rose, where yet another Christmas movie is playing. I can't remember a single thing about the plot of any of the films we've watched today. It's hard to focus on anything with Lindsey looking so heartbroken. She arrived late because she had to drop by the clinic on the way over. Something about checking on a patient. When she got here, her eyes were red and puffy, and I began to suspect there wasn't a patient at all.

She went through all the motions of a typical Christmas Eve with the family. We grazed on the snacks I prepared and ate lasagna for dinner. Lindsey picked at her food just enough to make it look like she was eating. She's avoided having much in the way of conversation, opting to play no less than seventeen rounds of Candy Land with Noah and Emily.

The light that's been shining in my daughter's eyes for the last month has dimmed to a mere flicker.

"Didn't we see this one already today?" Lucy asks, munching on a handful of Chex Mix. "That girl looks familiar."

Willow rests her head on Lucy's shoulder. "I think that's because she was the lead in the one we watched two movies ago."

"Can't they find anyone else to star in these things?" Lucy pops a pretzel in her mouth. "How am I supposed to believe she's serious about this guy running the bakery when she's supposed to be with the guy that owns the goat farm?"

Rose yawns. "That two-timing hussy."

"Actually, I'm pretty sure goat guy and bakery guy are the same person too," Ellie says. "He just shaved his scraggly beard."

"Well, he was a goat farmer," I say. "I think the beard kind of suited him."

Rose nods. "He's welcome to farm this old goat any time."

Lucy wrinkles her nose. "Ew."

"What do you think, Linds?" Ellie asks. "Beard or no beard?"

It takes a moment for Lindsey to register that Ellie's question was directed at her.

"Hmm?" she says finally.

"The guy." Ellie points to the TV. "Do you like him better with the beard or without?"

Lindsey stares blankly at the screen, and I'm positive she still has no clue what we're talking about.

"Oh. Um, without's fine, I guess," she says with a shrug before rising to her feet. "I'm pretty tired. Too much Candy Land for one day. I think I'm going to go on up to bed."

"Are you sure?" Willow asks. "If you stick around long enough, we might get to see this guy own a rundown inn."

"Yeah, I'm beat." Lindsey forces a smile. "But I'll see y'all bright and early."

"Of course, sweetheart," I say. "Get some rest."

She leans down to kiss my cheek. "G'night."

A chorus of "good night" follows her as she leaves the room.

"I wonder what facial hair he'll have in the next one," Rose says. "A goatee? Maybe a Tom Selleck mustache?"

And they're off on another tangent, the goat farmer and the bakery owner forgotten. I make a concerted effort to nod at appropriate intervals and contribute an occasional *uh-huh*, but my heart is with my eldest daughter, who's climbing the stairs to her childhood bedroom.

Her footfalls on the steps grow farther and farther away, until they disappear. The sound used to bring me comfort because I was once naive enough to believe that as long as my children were close, I could protect them from anything.

In my own grief and desire to keep things the way they were, I lost sight of what matters: the people I love that are still here. Lindsey asked me what she should do when we were in that hospital bathroom, and I failed her. I told her about the cost of love, but I didn't tell her about the reward. Maybe because I've been so focused on everything I was missing that I lost sight of what I have.

Everything I *still* have.

My sister, my beautiful children and grandchildren, and a life well-loved.

But there's something else too. Ron's face and kind smile fills my mind, warming me from the inside.

There's a new story waiting to be written, if I can just be brave enough to grab a pen.

I RISE JUST BEFORE THE SUN ON CHRISTMAS MORNING, GET dressed, and tiptoe downstairs so as not to wake anyone while I brew the first of many pots of coffee. Normally, I'd be starting the French toast casserole we have for breakfast every year and prepping the sides and Christmas dinner. I'd be in a tizzy all day to make sure everything is perfect. But not today.

Today, I've decided, will be different.

I fill a travel mug with coffee and shrug on my coat before grabbing my purse and keys from the kitchen counter. Frigid air slaps me in the face when I step out into the dawn and trudge toward my car. The leather seats are so cold, they send chills through my body, but I don't have time to let it warm up. I want to get out of here as inconspicuously as possible.

Thankfully, the drive is short. It's not one I've made in years, but I know it with the intimacy of a worn love letter, the ink faded from decades of retracing the words with my fingers.

When I arrive at Harpeth Hills Memory Gardens, I drive up the winding path that leads to where Henry is waiting for me. We bought our plots in our late thirties, back when the idea of needing them seemed eons away. We told the guy at the funeral home we liked the magnolia trees along the back of the property, and when he said he had two plots together beneath one of the sprawling giants, we bought them and promptly put the whole thing out of our minds.

I pull to a stop a few yards away and climb out of the car

with my coffee, grabbing a blanket from the trunk before making the rest of the journey on foot. Henry insisted I keep one there in case of emergency after the Mid-South got hit with a massive ice storm in the late nineties. He always thought of things like that.

The air is still and peaceful, other than the light wind rustling against the trees and the echo of tires on asphalt in the distance from the occasional car passing along the highway. The sun is rising over the tree line, casting a golden glow over the headstones. I never considered cemeteries to be anything but sad, but right now, this place is beautiful.

"You've got a nice view here." The warmth of my breath fogs up my glasses as I approach Henry's resting place. With one hand, I wrap the thick blanket around me and sit, grateful to have the extra layer of protection from the frosty ground.

I take a long pull from my coffee. The sight of Henry's marker still makes my stomach sink. It's hard to comprehend how a life so vibrant can be reduced to a simple inscription:

Loving Husband, Father, and Friend to All Animals.

"Merry Christmas, sweetheart," I say. "I'm sorry I haven't come to visit. It's still hard for me, and if I don't come, I can play these mind games with myself and pretend you're somewhere else, away at one of those vet med conferences you used to speak at. That's a lot easier than accepting that you're really gone."

"I'm afraid I've made a mess of things," I admit. "Rose told me after Thanksgiving that celebrating the holidays with me wasn't fun anymore, and I think she's right. I've been hanging on to you so tight, I didn't leave room for, well, anything else. All I've managed to do is make myself and everyone around me miserable. I couldn't see it before, or maybe I just didn't want to."

I slide my thumb over the edge of my mug and sigh.

"I'm worried about Lindsey," I say. "She met someone. You'd like him. He's everything you ever wanted for her. I think she was starting to feel something for him, but she got scared and ended things. She chose feeling safe over being loved."

I place my hand on the cold bronze stone bearing my husband's name, as though maybe wherever he is, he'll feel it.

"We both know safety is an illusion, don't we?" Tears brim my eyes, and I place my cup on the ground so I can remove my glasses and dab beneath my lashes. "We were supposed to have many more years together, you and me. In fact, I believe I was promised forever, and now, here we are. But how lucky were we to find someone we loved so much that even forever wouldn't have been long enough?"

God, we were so lucky. I sniff, pulling the blanket tighter around myself.

"I've been in a holding pattern since you died, Henry. Our entire family has, and that's my fault. They only stayed that way because of me. They wanted to help me not be sad, when the truth is, I'll never not be sad about losing you."

"This is a beautiful sunrise. It's perfect." I lean my head back and squint, my eyes adjusting to the growing light. It looks as though someone sliced a blood orange and used its juices to paint the sky. "I wish I could have this sunrise—this exact one—every day for the rest of my life."

"But I can't. I get to enjoy it while it's here, but that's it. That's all I get." I squeeze my eyes shut, the colors staining the backs of my eyelids. "I can sit here every morning and wait for that same exact sunrise to come again, with those same vibrant colors, but I'll never be satisfied. I'll always be disappointed because some mornings it'll be overcast or maybe it won't be quite as pretty. Or maybe it'll be stunning, but in an entirely different way. As long as I'm sitting here waiting for *that* sunrise, I'll never find what I'm looking for."

My tears leave icy trails down my cheeks. "Or I can decide right here and now to remember this sunrise for the rest of my life. To accept there will never be another one like it, but that doesn't mean the one that comes tomorrow won't be beautiful in its own way."

I close my eyes, and I can almost feel my husband next to me, his hand covering mine.

"And I think that's what I want to do, Henry. I want to chase sunrises for as long as I can. Or maybe I'll become partial to sunsets or midnights."

Warmth builds in my chest, as though the sun is shining directly from the center of my heart.

"I want you to know, I'll carry you with me no matter where my story ends, because you are where it began and you'll always be my most favorite part."

I kiss the tips of my fingers and place them to the headstone before rising to my feet.

"I love you, Henry. I always will, but it's time for me to go chase some more sunrises."

33

LINDSEY

"WHAT DO YOU MEAN MOM'S *GONE*?" I ASK, STILL BLEARY-eyed and half asleep.

Ben woke me up in a panic because our mother was nowhere to be found when he and Ellie went downstairs for coffee.

"I mean she's not here, Linds."

"Well, did you call her?" I stifle a yawn as I pour some creamer into my steaming mug. "She probably forgot something for the French toast casserole and went to find a drugstore that was open."

Catrick Swayze saunters into the room and meows, as if to ask why on earth we're all awake at this ungodly hour.

"I got her voicemail," he says.

I reach in the pocket of my robe for my phone and try her myself. Straight to voicemail.

"There's got to be a note somewhere," I insist, checking the dry-erase board she keeps on the fridge. "She wouldn't leave without telling someone."

"There's no note," Ellie says.

Ben shoves a hand through his hair, his glasses askew on his face. "We already checked everywhere. We even looked in her room. She didn't even make the bed."

That, in and of itself, is enough to fire off a warning shot.

"What's going on?" Lucy asks as she and Willow pad into the room, making a beeline for the coffeepot.

"Mom left this morning," Ben says. "We got up, and she was gone."

Willow's eyes widen. "Gone? For how long?"

"We don't know for sure," Ellie says. "We only woke up about thirty minutes ago."

"But we don't know how long she could have been gone before that," Ben continues. "None of us heard her leave."

Lucy's wide awake now. "What do we do? Should we call the cops?"

"Cops?" Aunt Rose's voice comes from the doorway. "Why are you calling the cops? And where's Myra Jean?"

"That's what we're trying to figure out," I say. "Did she mention anything to you last night about needing to go somewhere this morning?"

She shakes her head.

"Where could she have gone?" Lucy asks, pressing her fingers to her lips.

"I don't know, but I'm going to go look for—" Before I can finish my sentence, the front door clicks shut and we race to the foyer to find my mother hanging her coat in the closet.

"Where were you?" I demand, equal parts relieved and annoyed. "Are you okay?"

"Of course," she answers, as though that was the silliest question she's ever heard.

"We tried calling, but it went straight to voicemail," Ben adds.

Mom digs in her purse for her phone. "I'm sorry, sweetheart. Looks like I forgot to turn it on."

"You had us scared to death," Ben says. "Where on earth did you go this early in the morning? And on Christmas, no less."

Ellie touches his back. "The important thing is, she's okay."

"This is entirely too much excitement this early in the morning," Rose mutters.

"Where were you?" I ask again as she starts toward the kitchen with all of us on her heels.

"I just needed to run a quick errand," she says.

Our voices collide in an accusatory chorus. "On Christmas?"

She drops her purse on the counter and her travel mug in the sink before grabbing one of the festive Christmas tree mugs out of the cabinet and filling it from the carafe.

"Yes," she says, blowing a puff of air through her lips. "I went to see your father."

Any frustration we've been feeling dissipates in an instant.

"Oh." I frown, my heart sinking into my stomach. "I'm sorry, Mom. Are you okay?"

She nods and smiles, a peaceful expression smoothing the lines in her skin.

"I really am," she says. "I feel great."

Before we can press her any further, tiny footsteps come bounding down the steps.

"Mom!" Noah shouts as he and Emily barrel into the kitchen. "Dad! It's Christmas!"

Emily flies into my brother's leg. "Presents!"

"Not yet, Em. You know Grandma likes for us to have

breakfast first," he says. "Mom, do you mind if I put the French toast casserole in the oven?"

"Actually, I didn't make one." Mom clasps her hands together in front of her mouth, a playful glint in her eyes.

Lucy taps her forehead. "Am I dreaming? Are we in the twilight zone?"

"Very funny," Mom says, wagging her finger. "I was thinking we'd do something different this year."

The room is so quiet, I can hear myself blink.

"Mom, are you sure you're okay?" Ben asks. "Do you need to lie down?"

"No, I don't need to lie down," she answers with a laugh. "I was thinking maybe we could make breakfast together as a family."

"You're gonna let us help you in the kitchen?" Willow asks, her brows touching her hairline.

Mom takes a sip of her coffee. "Only if you want to."

"We'd love to," I say, exchanging bewildered glances with Ben and Lucy.

"Yeah," Ben agrees. "What are we making?"

Mom shrugs. "Anything you want."

Noah gets a wild gleam in his eyes. "Chocolate chip pancakes!"

"Yeah?" Mom asks, matching his energy.

"With whipped cream?" Aunt Rose adds.

Noah nods emphatically.

"What about you, Em?" Mom squats down to her level. "Anything you want."

Emily tilts her head, her teeth clamped on her bottom lip. "Pizza rolls!"

Mom chuckles. "Okay, then. Pizza rolls and chocolate chip pancakes, it is. Any other requests?"

"Froot Loops!" Emily yells.

"I believe I have some of those from the last time you stayed the night." Mom crosses the room to the pantry and reaches for the cereal box. "What else?"

Aunt Rose leans against the counter. "You know, I'd love a mimosa."

"Ice cream sundaes," Lucy says, and the kids cheer, bouncing up and down.

Willow wrinkles her nose. "For breakfast?"

"Why not?" Lucy asks. "It's Christmas."

Ben makes his way to the fridge. "How about I fry up some bacon and eggs? Maybe some hash browns?"

My stomach growls. I haven't felt like eating much the last couple of days, but this all sounds surprisingly good.

"I could make some biscuits and gravy," I offer. "Mom's recipe."

Ellie speaks up softly. "Maybe some Pop-Tarts?"

"Yes, yes, yes," Mom says, clapping her hands. "That's the spirit. What about you, Willow?"

She taps her finger to her chin. "What about some breakfast quesadillas?"

Her suggestion is met with enthusiasm from the entire group.

"Perfect," Mom says, a playful glint in her eyes. "Now, who wants to open presents before we eat?"

Noah and Emily's hands shoot up, and Lucy squeals.

"Me!" the three of them say together, and I raise an eyebrow at my sister.

"Really?" I ask with a laugh.

Lucy grins. "What? A thirty-year-old can't be excited about presents?"

*

"I couldn't possibly eat another bite," Aunt Rose says, popping one last piece of bacon into her mouth.

Mom snorts and raises an brow at her.

"What?" Aunt Rose garbles. "It's a palate cleanser."

I pat my stomach. "Thinking I should have requested some Tums."

"I've definitely got some of those," Mom says with a laugh.

The house is a disaster, but I can't recall a single moment in the last five years when our family has been more relaxed and happier.

"What would y'all like to do next?" Mom asks.

Lucy's brows pinch together as she chances a confused glance in my direction.

Ben scratches the side of his head. "You normally want to watch home movies all day."

Mom raises her shoulders and drops them. "I think we've seen those enough, but I'll be happy to grab them, if that's what you want."

"No," we answer together, perhaps a little too quickly.

Mom laughs. "That's what I thought."

"What if we went to the actual movies today?" Ben asks, snapping his fingers.

"Hmm, yes. That's an idea." Mom purses her lips and adjusts her glasses on her nose. "I like it. But on one condition."

Ben pouts. "What's the condition?"

"We go get Chinese for dinner afterward," she answers with a sly grin.

"Who are you and what have you done with my sister?"

Aunt Rose squints. "Myra Jean, are you in there? Blink twice if you need help."

"Seriously," I say. "Are you sure you're okay with all this?"

Mom nods and reaches across the table for my hand, giving it a squeeze. "I haven't been this excited about Christmas in…well, a long time."

As it happens, neither have I. It's almost enough to take my mind off how much I miss Oliver.

"I, for one, think this is awesome," Lucy says.

"I'll go start cleaning the kitchen," Ellie offers, but Mom holds out a hand to stop her.

"You most certainly will not," she says. "There will be no cleaning done today. We have a much more pressing issue at hand."

"What's that?" Willow asks.

"We have to go to Noah and Emily's house to see what Santa brought them," Mom says.

"Well, come on!" Noah jumps up with a squeal. "What are we waiting for?"

Everyone rises from the table with Noah and Emily leading the charge.

I lag behind and pull my phone from the pocket of my pajama pants, hoping I've somehow managed to miss a text from Oliver. If he responded to my message from before, maybe that would mean the door to our relationship could be reopened.

My heart drops when I hit the button to light up the screen. There are no missed calls or texts, and the last message I sent him was still left on *read*.

There's no indication Oliver has thought of me at all.

✳

After seeing what Santa brought the kids, we catch a double feature and eat our weight in lo mein before ending up back at Ben and Ellie's. Noah and Emily have long since passed out, proclaiming this as the best Christmas ever, leaving the rest of us to enjoy some wine and Cards Against Humanity.

It comes as no surprise to anyone that Aunt Rose wins every round.

Lucy slaps her cards on the eat-in dining table. "Damn it! I was so close!"

"Let's go again," Willow says, shuffling the cards. "This is fun."

Aunt Rose takes a sip of her wine. "Ready to admit defeat again, I see."

"You're gonna have to count me out on this one, kids," Mom says with a yawn as she stands. "I'm beat. I think I'm going to head on out." She peeks at the clock on the microwave above the stove. "It's already after eight."

"Are you sure?" Ellie asks. "You can stay in the guest room, if you like."

Mom leans down to kiss her cheek. "You're sweet to offer, but when you get to be my age, you need about seventeen pillows to sleep and not wake up feeling like you've been bludgeoned with a bat."

"It's true," Aunt Rose agrees as Lucy and Willow rise to give Mom a hug.

"Merry Christmas, Mom," Lucy says.

"Merry Christmas to you, my dear." Mom leans over to plant a kiss on top of Ben's head. "To all of you."

She moves to give me a hug, but I push out of my chair. "I'll walk you out."

"Thank you, sweetheart."

Everyone sings out their goodbyes as Mom and I shrug on our coats, and I walk her outside while my siblings' laughter carries out into the silent night.

Mom curls her arm around my shoulders and smiles. "That's my favorite sound, you know? When you were younger, you three used to laugh yourselves silly. You loved playing little pranks on us. And each other, of course. Your father and I used to stand outside the room, just out of sight, and listen to your giggles."

"You did?" I ask. "How did I not know this?"

"We nearly gave ourselves away *many* times," she says as we reach her car. "We'd be shaking with laughter, tripping over ourselves, listening to y'all carry on."

I grin and lean into her shoulder. "Today was a good day, Mom."

"It sure was, kid." She rubs her hand along my arm. "You should go back inside. It's cold out here. Do you want me to come back and get you in the morning?"

"No, that's okay. I'll have Ben bring me over after this next round."

She nods and moves to open the car door.

Before she can even climb inside, I blurt, "Do you think I made a mistake?"

"What?" she asks, her hand frozen on the handle.

"With Oliver. Do you think I ended things too quickly?"

She takes a beat and presses her lips together. "Do *you* think you did?"

"Yes. No. I don't know," I admit, grinding the toe of my boot into the gravel driveway. "I just really miss him."

She opens her mouth as though she's going to say something but shuts it and nods.

"Take some time and think it over," she says. "Listen to what your heart's telling you."

"That's just it. I don't know. I'm a mess and a half."

She places a gloved hand on my cheek. "You've never been a mess. Not now. Not ever. One thing about you kids is, you've always known exactly who you are and what you want. Gosh, when you were younger, we had to beg you to stop studying and go outside to play during the summer. Do you remember that?"

I give her a small smile. "I do."

"You got so annoyed with us. All you wanted to do was shadow your father at the clinic."

"But that's different. That's what I do, it's not who I am."

"You're right," she says. "A veterinarian isn't who you are but being determined and sure of yourself *is*. But I think somewhere along the way, you stopped trusting in that." She takes my hand in hers and presses it to my heart. "You stopped listening to this."

"I don't know how," I admit. "I can't hear it anymore."

"It's still there. You just have to quiet the rest of the noise so you can listen to it."

"But how?" I ask. "How do I do that?"

She kisses my temple and pulls me into her arms, her voice barely above a whisper. "I'm a fan of watching the sunrise. The world makes a lot more sense there."

34

———

MJ

I'M ONLY IN THE CAR FOR A MOMENT WHEN I KNOW I'M NOT going home. There's one more stop I need to make.

The way to Ron's house is thankfully seared in my mind because if I had to call first, I might lose my nerve. I might be tempted to take the easy way out, but this conversation needs to happen in person.

My fingers tap the steering wheel in an off-tempo beat to "It's Beginning to Look a Lot Like Christmas" playing on the radio. I take a deep breath through my nose and let it out through my mouth in a futile attempt to soothe my nerves.

It doesn't take me long to get to Ron's, but I argue with myself the whole way.

Is this the right thing to do? Am I being crazy? Is this *crazy?*

The porch light is on when I pull into the asphalt driveway, and there's still light seeping out from around the curtains. I cut the ignition and get out of the car, shutting the door with a soft thud. It's not too late to back out. I can just go home.

But I don't go home. I tread carefully up the shrub-lined walk, the tap of my boots against the concrete mingling with the laughter wafting outside from the house.

I release a sharp exhale as I hit the top step. My finger is hovering centimeters from the doorbell when I drop my hands back to my sides.

This is crazy, I'm being a crazy person. It's Christmas. He's with his family. This can wait till tomorrow.

"What are you doing, Myra Jean?" I mutter, backing down the steps. "You need to—"

An ear-piercing bark startles me and I yelp, tripping over my own two feet, landing butt-first in one of the bushes.

June Bug appears in the glow of the window, her head hooked around the curtain, squawking like a deranged goose. She must be standing on top of the couch, unless she's grown giraffe legs since I saw her last.

The laughter inside comes to a halt, and the best I can hope for is to get my butt out of this bush before Ron—or worse, his son—opens the door. If I thought I was going to be able to scoot out of here unnoticed, I was terribly mistaken.

I do a lightning-fast rundown to make sure nothing's broken and begin to hoist myself up, my fingers snagging between the branches. I've nearly regained my footing when I slip on a wet leaf, launching myself farther into the bushy pit, and I can't help but think this is some sort of karmic retribution for not refusing that damn bikini wax Rose tried to pawn off on me.

I'm going to die of embarrassment, trapped in the bushiest bush that ever dared to bush.

How poetic.

The lock clicks, sealing my fate. Instead of fighting it, I

allow myself to sink deeper into the shrubbery. Maybe if I'm very still, he won't notice I'm here.

"Myra Jean," Ron's voice calls. "Is that you?"

I pop my head up and nervous laughter spills out of me, as though the only thing that had been keeping it in was the unfortunate angle of my head.

"Oh, hi there," I say, popping my head up as though it's totally normal for me to be here. "Merry Christmas!"

"Are you okay?" he asks, rushing toward me. "Here, give me your hands."

I do as he says, and he holds on tight, pulling me until I'm right side up again.

"What are you doing out here?" he asks as I wipe dried-up leaves and seedlings from my backside. "You'll catch a cold."

"Well, you see, it's a funny story," I begin before remembering there's actually not one funny thing about it. "Okay, so it's not really ha-ha funny so much as it's—"

"Spit it out, why don't you?" he asks with a chuckle.

"I was on the way home after Christmas with the kids and Noah and Emily, but the day didn't feel complete without seeing you, and now, here I am." I sigh. "Ron, I like you. You've made me consider the possibility of a future I thought I lost when Henry died. I'm still trying to figure out what that even means and what it looks like. All I know is that I want to find out. I can't promise anything, but I think we have something here, and I want to see it through."

"What about tonight? Right now?" he asks. "Can you promise me that?"

I nod, the corners of my mouth tugging into a grin. "That I can do."

"Good," he says, reaching for my hand. "That's all I need."

"Thank you," I say, swallowing hard.

He slides his arm around my waist. "For what?"

"For being understanding. For being willing to meet me where I am."

He smiles and brushes my cheek with his thumb. "I'd meet you anywhere, Myra Jean. Haven't you figured that out yet?"

"I'm starting to."

I hold his gaze, my lips being drawn closer and closer to his.

"Dad?" A deep voice startles us apart. "Is everything okay?"

I look up to see a young man I recognize from the photographs on Ron's wall. He's holding a wriggling June Bug in the crook of his arm.

"Hudson, I have someone I'd like you to meet," Ron says, beaming up at his son. "This is Myra Jean."

A smile stretches across Hudson's face as he descends the stairs to shake my hand.

"It's nice to meet you," he says, shifting June Bug to his other arm. "I've heard a lot about you."

"Likewise," I say as June Bug practically leaps into my arms, covering my face in wet kisses. "And it's good to see you again, sweet girl."

Hudson nods toward the house. "You want to come in? My wife was just making some hot cocoa. We're about to watch *It's a Wonderful Life* before we head back to the hotel. Can you believe Liz still hasn't seen it?"

My breath catches in my throat. I haven't seen that movie in years. Not since…

A pretty redhead appears in the doorway.

"I *have* seen it," she insists, with a sniffle. "Well, most of it. Listen, it's a long movie."

Hudson's lips quirk as he bounds up the steps and curls his arm around her. "Myra Jean, this is my wife Liz, and she has a condition where she passes out ten minutes into any movie we watch."

June Bug yawns and settles into my arms. "Looks like this little stinker is getting a head start on movie naptime."

"Well, what do you say?" Ron asks, his wiry brows raised. "You want to come in and watch the movie with us? Or fall asleep to it, as the case may be."

"I'm not sure that one's going to let you leave," Hudson says, pointing at the sleepy pup I'm holding. "She looks pretty cozy."

"Yeah, she does," Ron agrees.

"I'd love to watch the movie with y'all," I say finally.

Hudson smiles. "Come on in."

"I'll pour you some hot chocolate," Liz offers, disappearing inside.

Ron places one hand on the small of my back and holds the other out in front of him. "After you, Myra Jean."

35

———

LINDSEY

I SET MY ALARM FOR EARLY THE NEXT MORNING, JUST BEFORE sunrise, but I'm already awake when it goes off. Catrick Swayze arches his back and straightens his legs, his claws digging into my comforter.

"Big stretch," I say, scratching the top of his head as I climb out of bed and slide my feet into my new fuzzy plaid slippers that the kids got me. I pull on a sweatshirt and pad into the kitchen to feed the cat and press the button on the coffee maker.

Ben brought me back to Mom's late last night, and despite how tired I was, I couldn't fall asleep. I lay there for hours, my mother's words swinging in my mind like a pendulum.

I'm a fan of watching the sunrise. The world makes a lot more sense there.

Maybe it's a little silly of me to do, but at this point, I'm willing to try anything. So, once the coffee's brewed, I pour myself a cup and carry it out to the back deck, curling up in the wicker love seat.

And I wait. I hold the mug between my hands, shivering.

It's quiet. *Too* quiet. But maybe that's the point.

The golden glow of the sun has started to rise, sending tendrils of light spreading out as though someone cracked an egg across the sky.

It's been a long time since I watched the sunrise. I've caught glimpses of it on my early days when I leave for work to prep for surgery, but I haven't stopped to take it in. Not since the morning after Dad died.

After we left the hospital, we gathered in our childhood home, unsure what to do or where to go. I alternated between crying and being so restless I couldn't sit still. I remember stepping outside on the front porch to call Daniel, but it went to voicemail. I didn't call him from the hospital or in the middle of one of my crying jags in the facility's parking garage. I didn't want to disturb him, and if that isn't a metaphor for our relationship, I don't know what is.

I asked Daniel to come to our family dinner a month later, our first without my father, but he declined because he had his weekly basketball game with his old college buddies. I asked if he could miss it just this once, but he told me those meetups were important to him because they helped him unwind. Feeling defeated, I asked if *I* was important to him, immediately regretting the words once they came out of my mouth.

I'm sorry I'd immediately said. *That wasn't a fair question.*

Of course, you're important to me he'd said, taking my hands into his. *Do we not have weekly date nights?*

Yes.

And I've come to your family dinners on occasion, haven't I?

In a little over a year, he'd come exactly twice. He chatted and joked around, but there was a shift in his demeanor when we were with my family, so subtle that it took a while for me to catch on, but once I did, I couldn't unsee it.

He opened his mouth to speak but shook his head instead. *Never mind.*

What? I asked. *What were you going to say?*

Daniel tilted his head and gave me a close-lipped, pitying smile. *Your family can be...a lot to handle. But especially right now. I know your mom is going to be all downtrodden and mopey, and I'm just...not comfortable, you know?*

Anger turned the edges of my vision black. *Imagine how we feel, Daniel. My dad* died. *My mother lost her husband.*

I know he said. *And I'm sorry that happened. Your father was a great guy. But sulking around isn't going to bring him back.*

I wilted like a rose in a vase without water. How could someone be so callous?

He sighed, raking his hand through his thick, dark hair. *Sometimes your emotions...*

I leaned my head back, extending the space between us. *My emotions what, Daniel?*

They can be a bit much. And the lying around when you get a "flare up." He curved his fingers as he spoke the words, his tone suggesting my fibromyalgia was about as real as Santa Claus. *It's just kind of a downer. All I'm saying is, I think if you put your mind to it, you could get past all of that.*

All of that. As though I could simply positively think my way out of my grief over my father's death and the subsequent fibro flare that followed.

Oh I'd said because I was too stunned to say anything else. What are you supposed to say when someone tells you that your darkest parts are too much?

I broke up with him the next day.

I don't know how I didn't see it before. We had a great time together as long as things were lighthearted and fun. But if I was ever frustrated after a tough day or if I broke down after losing a patient at work, I could feel him bristle, even if we weren't in the same room.

When I called him the morning after my father died, it was only fitting that I got his voicemail. He wasn't available then. At least not for anything *real*. Hindsight would serve to show me he never really was.

I was witnessing the dawn of a world where my dad no longer existed, and the person I should have been able to call wasn't there. So, instead, I watched it alone.

Back then, I was alone because I didn't have a choice.

Now, it's because I did, and I chose wrong.

I was so scared my rough edges would be too much for Oliver. So scared I'd lose him, whether by choice or by chance, that I decided to walk away first. Because nobody can leave you if you're already gone.

Mom told me that night Oliver was in the hospital that when it comes to love, there's always a cost and one way or another, someone will have to pay. I thought I could avoid it by not allowing myself to get close to Oliver or anyone else. But no matter how I look at it, I still lose in the end. Whether I let someone in or not, I still pay the price. At least if I open my heart to the possibility, I'll have something to show for it.

Oliver still hasn't replied to the text I sent him Christmas Eve, and I can't say I blame him after how quickly I walked away without so much as a real discussion. He didn't deserve that.

As much as I want to believe there's something special about my connection with Oliver, I have to accept that maybe Oliver came along to show me what was possible if I was willing to try.

And maybe I'll still be too much for the next person that comes along, but I'd rather live a life of too much than not enough.

The sun rises to kiss the horizon, blanketing everything it touches in a golden veil. The world and my mind are quiet except for the sound of my own breath.

"It's beautiful isn't it?" my mother asks. I was so deep in my own thoughts I didn't even hear her come outside.

I nod, taking a sip of my coffee.

"I see you listened to me," she says, taking a seat beside me, a steaming mug cradled in her hands.

"I do that more than you probably think I do," I say with a chuckle.

We sit quietly for a moment, gazing up at the sky.

"You asked me something yesterday, and I didn't answer you truthfully," she says, finally breaking the silence.

"Oh?"

"You asked if I thought you made a mistake ending things with Oliver." Her expression is serious as she faces me, placing her hand on my arm. "And the truth is, I do."

I open my mouth to say something, but she cuts me off.

"Lindsey, I need to say this," she says. "I told you that love always comes at a cost, but what I didn't tell you is everything else. I didn't tell you that even knowing how it would end, I'd choose loving your father every single time. Love *does* come at a cost, and I paid dearly for it. That's the truth. But what I gained is priceless. I got to experience the kind of love people dream about. The kind that makes you a better person and helps you get out of your own damn way."

"Mom—"

"I know it's scary, sweetheart. Letting someone in is a lot like feeling your way around in the dark. You can't tell if you're going to run into a wall or step into a bear trap. But just when you're certain you're going to trip and fall into a black hole, something amazing happens. Love turns the light on." Her eyes become misty, and she covers my hand with hers. "It'll show you colors you never knew existed and give you a chance to paint the rest of your life with them."

"I—"

"So, yes. I *do* think you made a mistake. I don't know what the future holds or if Oliver's even the right person for you, but what I *do* know is that you deserve to experience every beautiful, breathtaking, heartbreaking moment love has to offer. And you can't do that if you don't give it a chance. I know what happened with Daniel, and I don't want to see you go through that again."

"You don't," I cut in. "You don't know what happened. Not really."

She studies me, her face softening. "Tell me."

I blow out a breath. "I told you I broke up with Daniel because it was too much to deal with after Dad died and having to take over the business. What I didn't tell you is that it was only too much because he couldn't support me. Or wouldn't. He didn't understand why I couldn't keep going to his events or why I was in so much pain emotionally and physically that I couldn't get out of bed."

She covers her mouth. "I had no idea. Sweetheart, I'm so sorry. God, no wonder you broke up with him."

"It's okay. You couldn't have known because I didn't want you to. The last thing you needed to be worried about then was whatever drama was going on with me and Daniel," I say, raking my teeth over my lip. "But that's not even the worst of it."

Her eyes are glassy as she looks at me, but she doesn't speak. This time, she waits for me.

"I tried to get him back," I admit. "I convinced myself that what he did was okay somehow, and I tried to get him back three months later, only to find out he was with someone else. He was already *engaged*."

She gasps. "I can't believe it. That shithead."

"Honestly, I'm glad he turned me down. I understand now that I didn't want to get back with him because I actually loved him. I was just so desperate to feel something after being completely numb since we lost dad. But losing him and then feeling like there was something wrong with me, it made me scared to connect with anyone else," I say. "Until I met Oliver."

"You need to talk to him."

"It's too late."

She shakes her head. "I don't believe that. I saw the way he looked at you. Lindsey, he cares about you."

I drop my gaze, running my finger along the rim of my mug. "I sent him a text. On Christmas Eve. He didn't reply, and I doubt he's going to. What I did wasn't fair. I didn't treat him right."

"Tell him how you feel. He'll listen. I know he will."

"What if he doesn't?" I ask.

"Then at least you'll know you did everything you could."

I sigh, picking at a loose thread on my sweatshirt. "I wish there was a way I could show him how sorry I am. How much I care about him."

She taps a finger to her chin, a mischievous smile spreading across her lips.

"What?" I ask. "What's that look for?"

"I have an idea. I think I know of a way you can show Oliver what he means to you."

My eyebrows shoot up. "You do?"

She nods and takes a sip of her coffee, an evil genius masterminding her plan.

"I do," she says. "But we're going to need reinforcements."

"I CAN'T FEEL MY NOSE." KAYLA'S WORDS ARE SWALLOWED by her puffer coat where she's buried her face in the crook of her arm. She's waiting for Ben to put up another hook to hold the mistletoe in her waiting hands.

"I still think staging a fall would have been a better idea," Aunt Rose says with a huff, placing another luminary on the ground. "And far better for my back."

Ben shoots her an accusatory glance as he climbs down the stepladder. "Except for the fact that faking an emergency is wrong on so many levels and highly illegal."

Mom rolls her eyes. "Oh hush, Rose. You're moving faster than the rest of us combined."

"Seriously. You're almost finished." Lucy tilts her body from side to side, stretching her arms over her head. "Meanwhile, I need to take some Aleve."

"Maybe if you actually took one of my yoga classes once in a while, you wouldn't." Willow smirks from the top step.

We're putting the finishing touches on the surprise for Oliver. Willow, Ben, and Kayla are in charge of hanging twinkle lights and mistletoe from every available surface outside while Lucy, Aunt Rose, Mom, and I are artfully spelling out "NYE?" with luminaries across Oliver's yard.

Ellie rolls down the window of their van and pokes her head out. "Just giving a time update. It's ten till seven."

"And the rain?" I ask.

"Radar is still clear," she says, Noah and Emily's giggles floating outside. "Shouldn't be coming in for the next couple of hours."

"Oh my God, you guys. What if he says no?" I ask, scooping some sand into one of the white paper bags and placing the votive inside before lighting it. "What if he doesn't want to talk to me?"

"He will, Linds," Lucy insists. "Besides, didn't your friend who knows Oliver say he's been moping around ever since you two split?"

"Moping and being willing to hear me out are not the same thing," I say.

After my mother explained her plan that seemed only mildly crazy at the time, I called Tessa and told her what I wanted to do. She confided in me that Joe told her how sad Oliver was and that he missed me. It didn't take a lot of convincing to get Joe and the rest of the guys on the crew involved, and now, here I am, waiting to ask Oliver if he has plans for New Year's Eve by candlelight. More than that, I'm asking if he's still willing to take a chance with me.

The closer we've gotten to the time that Joe will be receiving a nonexistent call about a cat being stuck in a tree, the more nervous I've become. A sweeping grand gesture seemed like a good idea a few hours ago, but now I'm freaking out.

A cold drop of water hits me on the cheek, sending another wave of panic coursing through me, binding my stomach in knots.

"Was that a raindrop?" I ask. "Is this a sign?"

"Hey," Mom says, catching my attention. "You're doing the right thing, okay?"

"Yes. Right." I nod and shake out my shoulders.

We hurry to finish setting up, only seconds before we hear the sound of sirens in the distance. Joe said it isn't something they normally do when responding to a cat call, but for this, he'll make an exception to give me a heads-up that they're en route.

"That's our cue," Ben says. "I'm going to stash the ladder in the backyard."

Kayla squeals. "It's time!"

"I'm proud of you, kid." My mother reaches out and squeezes my arm. "And I know someone else who would be too."

Lucy throws her arms around me, rocking us back and forth. "We'll be up on the porch if you need us."

"Thank you," I say.

I blow out a breath and take one last look at our glimmering message before taking my spot at the front of the yard.

Mom's right. Even if Oliver rejects me in front of my family and half the fire department, it's *still* the right choice. I'd rather choose the possibility of love than a guarantee of nothing.

The moan of the sirens draws closer and the flashing lights on the truck are casting a red glow over the cloudy sky.

The wail grows louder as the engine comes into view. There's no backing out now. I can do this. I can—

A cold shiver collides with my skin, only this time, it's not from nerves.

It's a breeze.

Over my shoulder, my family is all smiles, and my mother flashes me a thumbs-up.

The truck rolls to a stop and cuts the siren, and seconds later, Oliver stands in front of me in his uniform. To my surprise, he's smiling.

"The last time I checked, I don't have a cat," he says with a low chuckle. "And though Ace is very agile, he can't climb trees."

I shake my head. "Nope."

His eyes shimmer as he takes in the soft glow of the sea of candles and twinkle lights.

"You did all this?" he asks. "For me?"

"I had a little help," I say, gesturing back toward my waiting family. "Oliver, I'm sorry I hurt you. What I did…It wasn't fair to you. I haven't been honest with you about my feelings or the fact that the real reason I slept through your birthday is because I have a chronic illness and it was flaring up. I should have told you the truth because you've done nothing but show me kindness and compassion. I've just been so in my head and scared, and the truth is, I think I was afraid because I already knew you were someone I didn't want to lose. So I panicked and ran."

"Lindsey—"

"Do you remember our first date?" I ask. "You were telling me what made you decide you wanted to be a firefighter. And you told me then that you'd rather be running toward something than running away, even if you're scared. I want to be brave like you. I want to run toward you, even though I'm completely terrified. And I want to know…what I'm asking is, will you still be there for me to run to?"

His Adam's apple bobs and his face falls, taking my heart shattering to the ground with it.

It's too late.

I drop my gaze and blink back the tears pooling in my eyes.

I nod. "I understand. I'm just—I'm really sorry."

"I can't be here for you to run to, Lindsey." He places his finger under my chin and lifts my gaze to his. "Because I'm going to be running beside you."

"Really? You forgive me?" I ask, tears escaping down my cheeks.

He wipes away the moisture with his thumb. "Just promise me something. It's okay to be scared. But I need you to talk to me, okay? Let's work through it together."

"I promise," I say, leaning closer to him. "So…do you have any plans for New Year's Eve?"

"I do now." He takes my head in his hands and places a tender kiss on my lips just as the breeze kicks up, stinging my skin, followed by the piercing shriek of my mother.

"Fire!" she yells, and I whip around to find the luminaries that made up the letter *N* scattering like flaming tumbleweeds in the wind.

I gasp as Oliver pulls me out of the literal line of fire.

"Uh-oh," Kayla says.

"This wasn't supposed to happen!" Lucy's shrill voice is shaky with panic as Joe and a couple of the other firefighters jump into action to extinguish the flying fireballs.

Willow presses her fingers into her temples. "I googled it. The sand was supposed to weigh it down and stop any potential fires."

"We were supposed to put sand in there?" Aunt Rose cries.

"It's like the cupcake incident all over again." My mother's shoulders are trembling from attempting to contain her laughter.

"Now, hold on a minute," Aunt Rose says. "Why is this my fault? It was Ellie's job to keep an eye on the weather."

Ellie's eyes are wide while Noah and Emily cling to her. "I did. The radar doesn't show *wind*, and even if it does, I don't know how to see it. I'm an interior designer, not a meteorologist."

"Should I help them?" Ben asks, scratching the side of his head.

"Everyone stay where you are, please," Joe barks. "Let us do our jobs."

I slide my hands down my cheeks and turn my eyes up to Oliver. "You sure you know what you're getting yourself into?"

"Not even a little bit," he says with a chuckle as he pulls me into his arms. "But I wouldn't have it any other way because I love you."

My breath catches in my throat as I gaze up at him, memorizing every detail of this perfect moment. The way he smells, the icy chill of the rain on my cheeks, and the exhilarating feeling that's taken root deep inside my chest.

I have a choice to make, and I want to make sure I get it right. I don't wilt or shy away at his words, and I don't hide, buried beneath the dirt. This time, I bloom.

"I love you too."

MJ

One year later

"GET A LOAD OF THAT VIEW, MYRA JEAN." RON PUTS HIS arm around me on the balcony of our Gatlinburg chalet, courtesy of the karaoke prize Oliver and I won at Mistletoe Fest last year. "Not a bad way to spend a holiday."

"Not bad at all," I say, kissing his cheek.

It's late afternoon, and the sun is shining, but it's just chilly enough to need a sweater.

Laughter floats outside by way of the open window. My children are finishing preparations for our Thanksgiving feast with the help of Oliver, Hudson, and Liz, while Rose keeps June Bug and the grandkids busy when they aren't playing sous-chef.

I'd be lying if I said my hands haven't been itching to jump in and take over—I'm only human, after all—but they insisted I spend the day relaxing. Rose and I watched the

345

Macy's Thanksgiving Day Parade together like we did as kids, while the scent of butter, cinnamon, and crisp apples made my mouth water. I'm not even allowed to know what's on the menu, but whatever's drifting onto the deck smells divine.

The autumn leaves are putting on a show for us, twirling and dancing as they drop to the earth. How do they know they'll be safe when they take the plunge? Or do they? Perhaps the destination isn't important to them. Maybe it's all about the fall.

"Sister," Rose says, poking her head out the back door. "It's time to eat."

"After you." Ron holds out one hand and places the other on my back.

"It smells good in here," I say, making my way to the formal dining room with Ron on my heels. June Bug bounds up to me for a scratch before heading off in search of food.

The sight of the dining table takes my breath away and makes me laugh, all at the same time. There's a golden-brown turkey at the center with a leafy green salad, dressing, mashed potatoes, green beans, cranberry sauce, creamed corn, turnip greens, roasted carrots with broccoli, and…pizza rolls.

"Noah and Emily made those especially for you, Mom," Ben says when he catches my eyes on them.

Noah bounds to his seat. "Yeah, because remember when we had those for breakfast last Christmas!"

"That was fun!" Emily grins.

"No holiday meal is complete without pizza rolls," I say as Ron pulls out a chair for me at the head of the table before sitting in the seat to my right.

Ellie chuckles. "You're definitely going to regret saying that."

"You've outdone yourselves, kids," Rose says, taking her place at my other side. "Everything looks delicious."

Once we're all seated, everyone chatters happily as they begin serving their plates and passing the food.

"I'm starving," Ellie says, patting her newly-showing baby belly.

"Here." Ben places two scoops of potatoes on her plate. "One for you and one for baby."

"Nobody slip June Bug any turkey. No matter how cute her puppy dog eyes are," Ron says. "It gives her the toots."

"MJ, you've got to try the dressing. Lucy made it." Willow beams with pride.

"You did?" I ask her.

"I'm a wife now," Lucy says, squeezing Willow's shoulder. "Figured it was about time I learn to cook. Otherwise, I'm going to be stuck eating kale for the rest of my life. I'll give you three guesses on who made the salad."

"Wait till you try the cranberry sauce Liz made." Lindsey passes the gorgeous dish to Rose. "It's to die for."

"And those brownies you made, Lindsey," Liz says.

Lindsey smiles over at me. "It's Mom's recipe. She got it from a cookbook at some estate sale when we were kids."

"Well, they're amazing." Hudson takes a sip of his wine. "I might have eaten one or three while we were cooking."

Liz pokes him in the arm. "Five. You ate five."

"Okay, brownie patrol," Hudson teases.

"Think we can sneak some of those into the Titans game Sunday?" Oliver asks.

"Now, there's an idea," Willow says.

"If I can't take food, I'm not going," Rose garbles around a roll.

Lucy snorts. "I'm pretty sure they don't allow food in your stadium-approved clear bag."

"Who said anything about putting it in my bag?" Rose asks. "What do you think bras are for?"

Lucy taps her finger to her mouth. "Aunt Rose, you might be a genius."

Rose arches her brow. "You're just now figuring that out?"

Joy overflows from the table like an uncorked bottle of champagne, and my heart aches. But it's nothing like the ache I felt this time last year—lost and sad. This is different. It's like how I felt when I started taking Willow's yoga class earlier this year. At first, my muscles burned and cried out in pain, but after a while, they stretched until it felt good to lean into the movements. Now, I can't imagine my life without my weekly yoga.

Just as I can't imagine my world without everyone in this room, though the possibility still lingers, lurking like a shadow in the dark. After losing Henry, it's impossible to turn it off completely. But when those thoughts start creeping in, I remember what I have. I remember what I've gained. And I love my people even harder.

Ron leans toward me and places his hand on mine. "You okay, Myra Jean?"

I nod and squeeze his fingers. Love may come at a cost, but it's the only thing in the world that can take everything from you and somehow leave you richer and better than you were before it came along.

"I'm wonderful," I say with a smile. "Just taking it all in."

And I do, every chance I get.

❄

"Merry Christmas, sweetheart," I say, kissing my fingers and touching them to Henry's headstone. I'm wrapped in the blanket I keep in my car, and it's shielding me from the cold grass I'm seated on. Shimmering beams of gold and orange stretch toward the sky while steam floats above the tumbler containing my coffee.

It's Christmas morning, and I slipped out of bed just before dawn, careful not to disturb Ron and June Bug as I dressed and bundled up so I could watch the sunrise with Henry.

I don't know if I'll come here every year, but for now, this feels good. I get to start and end my favorite holiday with the two loves of my life.

I've visited Henry a few times since last Christmas. I found that once I started living life again, I wanted to share it with him. We've had some long talks, Henry and I. Well, I suppose I've done a lot of talking and he's done a lot of listening.

At first, it seemed strange to tell Henry about my life with Ron, but at the same time, I couldn't imagine *not* telling him, so I did.

I came here when Ron moved in with me in the spring, and when Lucy and Willow got married in September, I brought him a peony from Lucy's bouquet. And when Ben and Ellie found out at the end of the summer that they were expecting, I came then too.

"I thought I might find you here."

Even though I know the voice like my own reflection, it still makes me startle.

"Lindsey," I say. "What on earth are you doing here?"

"Looking for you," she answers, tightening the scarf around her neck. "And I wanted to visit Dad."

"Come sit," I say, opening the blanket so she can nestle in beside me. "I didn't think anyone heard me leave."

"You're not as sneaky as you think you are," she teases. "Don't worry. Nobody's going to send out the search party because Oliver knows where we are."

"What are you doing up so early?" I ask.

"I wanted to talk to you before the day got away from us."

"Oh?"

"And actually, I was hoping to tell you and Dad at the same time. I want you to be the first to know."

She hooks her arm through mine, and there's something on her finger that wasn't there before. A sparkling oval engagement ring.

"Oliver asked me to marry him," she says. "And of course, I said yes."

Tears spring to my eyes. "Sweetheart, this is wonderful. I'm so thrilled. When did he ask you?"

"Last night." Her smile is radiant and warm.

"Congratulations, honey." I press a kiss to her cheek.

"Why don't you seem more surprised?" she asks with a laugh.

"Well, first of all, you two are crazy about each other," I say. "But also because Oliver told me over Thanksgiving when he asked for my permission. Which, of course, he did not need, but it was sweet that he included me."

"He's great like that."

I put my arm around her shoulders. "Are you happy?"

"I am." She releases a contented sigh and leans her head against mine. "What about you? Are you happy?"

I lift my eyes to meet the sky, and when I do, I see the sun has risen once again.

ACKNOWLEDGMENTS

I truly thought this book might never see the light of day. There will be people in your life, in your career, who will try to dull your sparkle, who will cause you to forget the magic that lives within you. None of us are immune. But if happens, I hope you'll remember that all it takes to start a fire is a single spark.

A million thanks and all my love go to my dear friends and fire starters, who are more like family. First and always to Jen Davis, my critique partner and friend, the grilled cheese to my tomato soup. On our own we are good, but together we are *great.* To Kate Oscarson, Reah Kelly, Kayla Kleffman, Sydney English, Tiffany Billingsly, and Abbey Ziemba, without whom I could never do this. Y'all are magic. And to Nicole Hazel, Kia Clay, Heather Weibye, Danielle Hoegy, and The Bridge Coven Book Club. You are all so dear to me.

Shout out to my editor Chris Wheary and cover designer Sam Pallincia with Ink and Laurel, marketing extraordinaire Brittney Wood, Jenny Bailey with Pen Pal PR, my former writing teacher Ms Ross, and Katie Garaby at Parnassus Books. So much gratitude goes out to Sarah Brown at Bound Booksellers in Franklin, TN and to Angela Redden and Thomas Wallace at Reading Rock Books in Dickson, TN, who have gone above and beyond to help this lil indie author soar. So much appreciation for Bryn Donovan and Julie Olivia who are two of the brightest stars in the business. My agent, the phenomenal Nikki Carrero, I am forever grateful for your belief in me. You're a steady hand in rough waters, and I'm so lucky to have you on my team. And of course, I could not do this without my street team, The Hostile Kitties, and all of the beautiful readers who have welcomed my stories into their hearts and lives.

Thank you to all of my furry writing partners, but especially June Bug, the puppy who is now a full grown dog (how?!?!) that came along and healed my broken heart. Thank you to my mom and dad and the original Myra Jean who is no longer earth side, but who is felt in every breath I take. And last, but never least, to my wonderful husband who never let me give up. I love you more than life.

MEET MELISSA GRACE

Melissa Grace is the author of the *Midnight in Dallas* romcom series, and *Marjorie & Me*. She resides just outside of Nashville, Tennessee with her husband and many fur children. When she's not writing, she can often be found reading or curled up in her bed with snacks like a trash panda, avoiding simple tasks because of her anxiety.

Find Melissa on social media @heymelissagrace on Instagram, Threads, Facebook, and TikTok.

www.ingramcontent.com/pod-product-compliance
Lightning Source LLC
Chambersburg PA
CBHW020231010826
48973CB00006B/1458